STROKE OF LUST

LILAH LANCE

TITAN SECURITY BOOK III

To the girl who felt unlovable
May you find a love that chooses you—every single time

AUTHORS NOTE

Welcome to the third installment of the *Titan Security* series.

Each book in the series has its own standalone HEA (Happily Ever After), but they're all connected by a larger mystery.

All the stories at Titan occur *simultaneously*, with Easter eggs and clues scattered throughout to help you uncover the full picture.

It is recommended starting with the earlier books to avoid **spoilers**, gather clues, and to gain a deeper understanding of the evolving mysteries within Titan.

～

This book is split into two timelines.

The first part happens during 'Stroke of Luck' Book I.

Selena and Kellan's journey continues in Part II, expanding beyond the events of *Stroke of Fate*, Book II.

MISSION BRIEFING

Welcome to Titan...

You are now a part of a team of security professionals working on saving face, saving lives, and sometimes saving their enemies.

This will be your third assignment with Titan.

Your objective, if you choose to accept it, is *gathering the facts.*

Your team consists of:

Agent Kellan Watts & Agent Selena Tavares

Together, you and your team will uncover secrets in the interconnected web of lies that Titan exists within.

This journey will be different from the others.

Don't get lost in lust with Kellan and Selena.

PROLOGUE

THE GIRL FROM HAVANA

SELENA

Your new handler is Gabriel Monroe.

I should've been excited to be in America. But this was no vacation for me.

No, this was me entering my new life. Selena Maria Tavares. Twenty-two. Fresh out of the shower, my hair wet against my robe, I was wringing my hands with my nerves waiting for my new handler to arrive.

Gabriel Monroe.

I looked out the window spanning the length of the hotel living room, for what felt like the hundredth time.

This place was big. Bigger than what I thought a hotel would be.

I had seen places like this on television but I had never stayed in a place that looked like this.

This nice. Pretty.

Just a few hours, I had been transported to Quantico—the military base—I was going to meet Gabriel here.

I wrapped my robe tighter around myself, ignoring how cold the room was, ignoring the ache in my stomach—and focusing on what I had to do next. Again.

I did not speak much English.

I didn't even know I could grasp the language, but I could do *anything* if I tried hard enough. I learned this from the CIA.

Mama was back in home, in Havana, and I had to do everything for her. She was the reason why I did anything. And I missed her right now.

Even though right now all I wanted was her hugs. And some food.

I felt my eyes sting as I shook with nerves.

I really hoped Gabriel was not a monster.

Or a bad man.

Or both.

But just to be safe, I made sure my face was perfect.

I was pretty. And I could only pray he thought the same. If Mama knew what kind of a woman I was?

She wouldn't be happy.

But sometimes in life we had to do things we didn't like to get where we needed to go.

But right now I wasn't sure where I wanted to go.

Maybe home.

Maybe somewhere warm. Take Mama with me. Get her out of Havana where I'd met the Agency guys who told me my eyes were gorgeous and captivating and that they could use a woman who looked like me. I needed a way out. I had gotten one.

And then the knock came at my door.

When I opened it the man on the other side was incredibly handsome. His wheat-colored hair gleaming under the lights, his smile light on me. He was the kind of striking that belonged in classic movies my Mama watched.

But it was his eyes that held a touch of unholy light.

Piercing pale blue eyes. Icy in their intensity as they watched me.

And the temperature around me dropped. From frigid to frozen.

This was Gabriel Monroe. And he towered over my much smaller frame in his tailored expensive grey suit. His broad shoulders, muscles and confidence obvious to me.

I was *terrified*. Nervously clutching the door handle, Gabriel took me with a gentle gaze that looked at odds for his face.

"Selena Tavares?" His voice was deeper than most and smooth, with an American accent I did not know where from.

I nodded, suddenly feeling even more self conscious than before. About my appearance. About my hair.

What if a man like him did not think I was pretty?

All the men in Havana had done was use me.

2

What if he did the same?

Gabriel Monroe might destroy me.

And despite the hunger and the weariness I felt, I straightened my posture. Met him in the eyes.

Determined to appear strong because I did not make it all the way here—to give up.

"No hablo ingles, pero…entiendo…" I told him. Hoping he might be patient with my limited English.

I don't speak English but I understand.

Those icy eyes of his crinkled, his lips tipping up a little. "Bueno porque mi español es malo."

Good, because my Spanish is bad.

Even if I wanted to smile, I knew what I had to do with him.

So when I let him in, I was more afraid of what *he* might do to *me*.

"My name's Gabriel," and he held out his hand to me politely. His hand was freezing cold. Gabriel. Like the archangel.

And I hoped he was a good man, but good men were few in this world. I didn't know why the more he stepped into the room the colder it got.

He was *really* big.

And I wasn't and the fear only increased as he walked in taking stock of my room. *To kill me? To take me somewhere?*

Nothing was going to calm me down.

Even if his cologne did smell good, the lights outside making him seem even more ominous. My thoughts were going wild.

What if he killed me in this country instead of opportunity?

What if I couldn't make sure Mama was safe?

My mind was going crazy.

But when he turned around, I had already closed the door.

I walked up to him, taking deep breath, my hands fluttering as I reached for my robe. And dropped it to the ground baring myself to him.

For a moment Gabriel's eyes met mine, stunned, but he didn't look at my body.

Those icy eyes held an unreadable expression but it didn't seem like anything I recognized in a man.

"What are you doing?" Gabriel was looking at the ceiling, taking a deep breath.

"¿Querías una mujer?"

3

You wanted a woman?

His hands moved towards his jacket, and a wave of panic washed over me—*Oh God, he's going to hurt me.*

I took a step back as he stepped forward, stripping out of his jacket and draping it over my shoulders.

I stood there a little stunned as his jacket fell mid-thigh and I got a better look at the expression on his face. His rigid shoulders. His tight jaw.

He looked ready for a fight.

He did not want me.

"Why did you do that?" He closed his eyes. "Why did you…did someone tell—teach you it was normal?"

When his eyes opened, they burned into me.

"Esto es lo que quieres, ¿no?"

This is what you wanted, no?

"No, it's not what I wanted." He turned back his eyes a little wild and wide.

"Who—the man in Havana—"

He's angry.

Something was in the room with us.

It was freezing.

Gabriel in broken Spanish with his accent looked at me. "Una pregunta." *One question.* "Mirame, el hombre de Havana—"

Look at me. The man from Havana.

"He touched you?"

He placed his hands flat on his body. Patted his chest twice with both hands and ran them down his body.

I knew what he was saying.

Yes.

Very slowly he said with his eyes closed. "The man in Havana. When he touched you, *you said yes?"*

What? Gabriel's eyes met mine head on.

"Mirame, Selena, *did you say yes to him?"*

Did I say yes to the man? No. I never said yes.

To *what* that man had done to me or how his hands made me feel when he did? Or to any of this?

I *didn't*. None of it. I didn't want any of this.

I just wanted to go home to Mama.

What was happening right now?

I was shaking in his suit jacket warmer than a blanket and still not warm enough. I understood what he was asking.

My heart raced as I answered him honestly. "No." I shook my head. "No, no dejé que me tocara…Cuando lo hizo, me dolió. Pensé que era normal"

I didn't let him touch me. When he did, it hurt. But I thought it was normal.

The temperature plummeted to the negatives. I was holding myself and felt my toes were frozen.

And then I told Gabriel in Spanish, I had to get out of my situation so I did what I was told.

I did not want to be that woman forever. I just knew I had to do it. I didn't think that yes had anything to do with it. He never asked. He touched me all the time. I thought it was normal and what I had to do for this job. This is not normal? Why do you look like that?

Ice cold, seeping into the room, chilling me to the bone. I watched as the lines of his throat worked, a sense of something washing over me that terrified me.

He looked around the room again, undoing his tie like he was ready to hit something.

"Do you have any food? Water?" And then he asked again in Spanish.

I didn't.

"I'm taking you with me tonight. *ahora.*"

Now? Tonight? Where? Panic gripped my chest, my mind reeling.

But I didn't own anything.

He got on the phone and began barking at someone named Reed. I caught brief flashes of his conversation. "*…Kill him, I don't give a shit—*"

Gabriel was cursing a lot.

Whatever this Reed man had said seemed to calm him down, but Gabriel spoke too fast.

His anger still in the room with us, beneath the surface, wild and sending the temperature in the room to ice.

And I saw him for what he was.

His suit was…a mirage. An illusion. This was who he was. Gabriel turned to face me, the phone in his hand, the ice-blue so vivid, that it felt as if he could see straight into me.

He kills people. Easily.

"Do you have any other clothes besides what you're wearing?"

I didn't understand. Sometimes when Gabriel spoke I heard one word instead of several.

Gabriel was struggling with me. "Tienes…blusa? *No, how the fuck do I say clothes Reed*? Ropa…limpia. *Limpia* means clean?"

Gabriel did not speak good Spanish. But he was asking me if I had clean clothes.

"Tienes limpia…ropa?"

It was not the right way to say it, but I understood him.

Do you have clean clothes?

He is trying. I shook my head. I didn't. I was just brought here with the clothes on my back and my passport.

No.

The thought of putting those same clothes back on made my skin crawl, the fabric still damp with sweat and clinging to my body in a way that felt suffocating.

"I need to get her clothes, Reed." He was back on the phone. "Yes, make sure Evie is eating something…"

My stomach was growling.

Behind him, the vast expanse of the night sky stretched out, visible through the windows of the massive hotel room I had been checked into and subsequently left alone in.

The darkness outside only seemed to create a bigger shadow around him.

The thought that echoed in my mind that first night when I saw him?

Was that Gabriel Monroe wasn't human. Not with his aura.

His energy so dark and violent, he looked ready to kill.

He couldn't be human.

"I'm going to step out of the room. When you're done changing, you come with me."

THE WOMAN WITH THE SUEDE BOOTS

SELENA

WE STEPPED INTO THE AMERICAN SHOPPING CENTER, THE OPEN SPACE filled with people and noises everywhere.

It was a *lot* to take in.

"I hate these places," Gabriel said quietly. "It's too fucking loud."

Too fucking loud. Loud. I mentally repeated it.

In the shopping mall Gabriel looked more human, but still he was at least six-foot five but the lights made him look bigger.

His hair wheat-colored and beautiful, his eyes bright pale blue—women noticed Gabriel.

I agreed. But for a man his size I noticed he knew how to be silent. I wore his jacket over my clothes now and it smelled like him which calmed me down.

Once I knew Gabriel wasn't going to hurt me and he didn't want to sleep with me? It helped me calm down, the constricting sensation in my gut and throat easing as I looked at the women, looking at him.

"This place closes in an hour, so let's get you some food and clothes."

I nodded slowly, while he translated it roughly. One woman stared so hard at him she almost hit a pole and he didn't notice her.

He ignored everyone who stopped and stared at him. *Madre de Dios, he's attractive.*

Breaking their necks—as Mama would say—to catch his eye.

But he must've had a lady...

7

There was no wedding ring on his finger, but a man that pretty and young would have a lady.

Maybe she's Latina and he's trained not to look.

One time, my Mama threw a spoon at my father when she thought he was looking at another woman. After that he learned.

Gabriel didn't look at *anyone*.

She is probably Latina.

Gabriel motioned for me to look at a store label that was arranged, and I resisted the urge to hold his hand like a little girl.

"Mas grande." Very big.

To my left Gabriel smirked. "Welcome to America."

We walked up to another floor before he said. "Pick a store. Anything. I need to go get you food."

So many choices.

I walked up to one where the displays looked like the girls in magazines I always liked. So many cute dresses. Pretty.

"Buy whatever you want," he was struggling to communicate with me in Spanish so it came out as—*purchase the store.*

I did not think he meant that. But he was trying.

And then he handed me a credit card that felt heavy and he left me there in the store to get food. Women in the store looked behind me at him with these big eyes like he was a movie star there by surprise.

I blinked down at the card in my hand and the unfamiliar sights and sounds took on a scarier scale. But I could do this.

I got this.

Gabriel is coming back to get you. Go find something pretty.

But just like the shopping center there were so many items. So many choices. After I had found things in all black, I saw them—the boots from the girls in the magazines.

I always told Mama I wanted to be one of the girls in the magazines. On TV.

But Mama always said that life was hard.

And now this was my life.

The boots were soft. And they went up to my thighs but I liked them.

Trying them on, the chatter of Americans all around me, I tried to mime them, understand them, but it was hard.

8

I settled on black being the practical choice. It was easier to hide anything and the boots?

They. Were. Perfect.

When I went to check out the lady at the front said something about a sale—a discount.

I didn't understand but I guess I could save some of Gabriel's money.

There were some perfume bottles next to her I saw as I handed her his card.

I probably smelled bad so I picked one up.

Pink pepper...and...lychee?

"How do you say this?" I said to her.

"Lychee," she pronounced and I mimicked it back as she looked down at Gabriel's card. I didn't understand. Was it because it was metal? And black? Why was she staring at it? "You came with the man in the suit?"

I was still wearing the top half of Gabriel's jacket.

I nodded. Her eyes went wide muttering something about 'sugar daddy' and I did not understand.

When Gabriel returned he didn't say anything about my appearance. I didn't even think he looked.

But I would never forget that night.

Sitting next to Gabriel with my brand new clothes on, the magazine girl boots, and the smell of his cologne, the greasy American food—it was perfect.

Outside was cold, so Gabriel turned on his heat, and I wanted to scream with how good I felt. I pointed to the drink he got me.

"Smoothie."

He shook his head patiently. "Milkshake. Same thing. But different names."

"It's chocolate."

"Mhm."

I took a sip. And a slow smile spread across my face. "Tan bueno."

It's good.

Gabriel ate quietly in the car and asked me questions in English that I responded to in Spanish. He understood me though.

You can say small things, only?

I don't understand some things like American's when they say break a leg. Why do I want to break my leg?

Idioms.

"*Idioms.*" I repeated.

A soft smile graced his lips, but a look crossed his eyes as we sat in silence eating again. Gabriel's eyes were far away.

"Who is she?" I asked in English slowly, curiosity getting the better of me. "*Tu mujer?*"

Your lady. Because I was not stupid. He had a woman. A man that good looking? Women would fight for him.

Maybe he was married to her.

His entire face shut down. Just as quick. She was *real*.

"I don't talk about her."

I recognized *that* look. But something happened to her.

It was the same one Mama wore after my father died, after Diego passed away. She was either missing or dead. Changing the subject, he asked me slowly. "What did you do before the man from Havana trained you?"

I told him in Spanish.

I had to support Mama so I worked different jobs. Sometimes for men. It was good money.

She didn't know.

The man from Havana said if I worked with him, one job, he would see if I did good.

He trained me. I can shoot and fight. I trained for a few weeks.

He said I'm good.

I was supposed to meet a team from America in Havana but they never showed up so I didn't have any purpose anymore.

Gabriel stopped eating, his attention solely focused on my words, though he didn't meet my gaze.

I told him about the team from America that was supposed to meet me here, their mission to hunt down someone named Marcus Hagen. But they had failed. They were either missing or dead.

And now, here I was, meeting Gabriel.

"Estoy en tu equipo?" *I am on your team?*

Gabriel tipped his head. "I came as fast as I could. I'm taking you to my home to meet everyone. Reed just got there a few weeks ago. He's rushing to get everything together for you."

Everyone?

"Dónde vives?" *Where do you live?*

"Connecticut."

"Connecticut." I repeated it slowly. I needed a phone to look up which state that was.

I didn't understand what lay ahead, but I trusted Gabriel. My toes wiggled in my new boots. I was warm. Full. The food was good.

I already felt better with him.

"We..." I started slowly. "Go on plane."

"Yeah. Si. Driving is a bitch in America. America is huge, we can't drive to Connecticut."

Huge.

"Mas grande."

Very big.

America was big.

"Finish your milkshake. After you're full we can go."

THE TITAN AT THE MANOR
SELENA

GABRIEL BROUGHT ME TO HIS HOME IN CONNECTICUT, TO A MANSION bigger than anything I had ever seen in Cuba.

Probably a little bigger than Cuba.

"Until you want to move out," Gabriel explained. "It's your home too."

"Esta es tu casa?" I motioned to the enormous manor and he nodded. *And he lives here alone?*

I chose a room called the Lions Den as my own, but found myself getting lost several times in the hallways until I met *Evie* Monroe.

Gabriel's little sister, Evie, was a tiny shy teenager who warmed up to me when she first met mine.

She looked nothing like Gabriel who towered over her tiny five-one —*maybe*.

Evie's hair was a blend of red and browns shimmering in the light.

Her eyes, bright and candy colored honey, Evie was brighter than anything in the manor surrounded by all the new lush green plants Gabriel got her all the time.

She was Gabriel's *princessa*, running into his arms when she saw him—she had that permission that nobody else had.

Gabriel would scoop her up and hug her to him all the time like she weighed nothing. But it was the first time I had seen him smile like that.

"Hey, shortcake."

"Did you see my new terrariums that came in?"

His smile grew wider than I had ever seen, her words tumbling out as he held her closer to him kissing her face. "You like 'em?"

"I love them!" She laughed, her hair all over him, as he cuddled her tight to him, brushing her hair back and it was the *most* human I'd ever seen him. He was like her father. "I missed you."

"Missed you too, shortcake. Have you met Selena? She'll be here with us from now on." He turned to me with her in his arms that smile in his usually icy eyes. "Selena, this is Evie my little sister."

Evie was snuggled into him like his child, not his sister, and despite her age of fifteen—to Gabriel she was not that. She was younger than that to him. And he *loved* her.

Evie was excited to meet me and I was charmed. "Hi, I'm Evie!"

"Hola...Soy nueva." *I was new.*

I introduced myself and where I was from feeling shy around his family.

Evie's eyes lit up as she spoke to me in Spanish. She was Mexican. Was Gabriel Mexican too? Half most likely.

Their dynamic taught me Gabriel wasn't just a murderer. I remembered my own father being like that with me when I was a little girl.

Gabriel carried her into the house with us not setting her down and using one hand to do everything.

I met his other friend here—*Reed* Whittaker.

The man from the phone call.

A man with steel eyes and enough tattoos to make me think he was in a gang. He towered over me and was similar to Gabriel's size.

Reed's smile was soft on me as he passed Evie and me food immediately. Evie sat down chatting with him while I felt out of place in the fancy home. A fancy kitchen. A new life.

"Everything here is yours as well," Gabriel said in Spanish as he moved around the kitchen passing Evie some vitamins and Reed a protein shake.

Reed was intense and handsome in a way that was a little scary, but he had been in the manor before me.

Standing a little shorter than Gabriel, he was built like a fighter, muscles and tattoos.

He wore a plain white shirt and had these grey eyes that always looked like a storm coming in. He was kind though.

The same Reed that was on the phone with Gabriel.

14

I didn't know if Reed knew what I had been through in Havana, but because he had been on the phone with Gabriel with orders to kill the men who did it to me?

I knew he knew *something.*

I knew Gabriel *knew* I was the result of a mission gone wrong.

A team that had failed their mission a few weeks ago in New York.

And when they didn't come get me—I had been stuck. It had all happened so fast.

And now I had a new team.

Because of Gabriel.

Which was nice.

He let me train under Reed, but when Reed saw how quickly I picked things up, he helped me brush up on my English. To speak with a tutor. With Evie mostly.

I got my drivers license because of him.

He'd almost had a heart attack when he learned how good my driving was. I didn't have *much* training but I was good.

"It's good, no?" I asked him as he looked like he was going to have a heart attack while gripping what he called the 'oh-shit' handles.

"Jesus fucking Christ," he swore. "Who the fuck taught you how to drive?"

"The Agency," I grinned at his expressions as he held his hand to his chest rubbing a little.

He spoke in broken bits of Spanish with me and he understood most of what I said.

I made friends with Evie too and we spent some time talking. I was surprised that Evie learned to speak Spanish but Gabriel didn't know. I just thought they had different mother's and Gabriel did not say a word about Evie being a half-sister.

I did not find it appropriate to ask her. Not when I was a guest in her home.

But there was still one thing that bothered me.

One thing.

I stood outside Gabriel's office upstairs in the manor.

It had taken me some time to get courage to come up to him but today was the day I was going to do it.

I was ready to take that step.

When he told me to come in, I ignored my nerves. Ignored the scents of leather and old books. Ignored the large office and towering book-shelves in there. The elegant furniture.

He was a king in his castle. And I was just…existing around him.

No, I focused on the man behind the desk himself. Fidgeting with the hem of the new clothes he bought for me with Reed helping me get them.

Reed and Gabriel had taken care of me like I was Evie.

With those pale eyes on his beautiful face, he looked otherworldly again, not human, not quite man—but something in between.

"Por qué me elegiste?"

Why did you choose me?

My voice sounded small, even to my own ears. He looked up from the black and white pages in his hand, his expression momentarily blank before clearing.

He almost didn't speak for a moment and when he did, my heart began pounding.

"No me conoces, pero me escogiste y ahora vivo en esta bonita casa con tu familia. ¿Por qué?"

You do not know me, but you picked me and now I stay in this nice house with your family?

Why?

"The team from New York who failed to get you, that was your ticket out of Havana. I picked you up because they failed."

"Pero ya no eres parte de la Agencia." *But you are not Agency anymore.*

He shook his head. *No.* Something came over his eyes as I said the words.

Something happened to him while he was Agency.

"And you are nice…to me," I was practicing my English.

He was no longer the intimidating figure I had met that night in the hotel in Quantico. No. He was a kind man. A little scary. But he and Reed treated me with so much good.

"Close the door. Cierra la puerta."

A sense of unease crept over me.

Had I made a mistake?

A nagging fear crept into my mind, wondering if I had somehow angered Gabriel.

I had witnessed the deep love he had for his sister, Evie, and the way both he and Reed treated me with respect and kindness.

Deep down, I knew he would not hurt me.

I was also *acutely* aware that I was in his house, wearing clothes purchased with his money. My nails dug half-moons into my palms and I clenched my fist so tight I felt like I heard my fingers creak.

Gabriel leaned against his desk, his jacket and vest discarded, and his sleeves rolled up.

He looked undeniably handsome, but I felt no romantic attraction towards him. I did not desire him in that way. Not really.

It was clear that he did not harbor those feelings for me either.

Because he loves his lady.

He didn't talk about *her* ever. But unlike Reed I had never seen him with anyone. Although I did not think Reed liked his ladies. Icy-blonde and a little mean. Which was funny because Reed was so nice. He did not date nice women though.

I got the feeling Gabriel's woman was...nice.

She must be for him to be nice and maybe he was learning Spanish for her...

"Can I hug you? *Puedo...abrazarte?* Sorry, I'm practicing and some of these silent letters get me."

No. I understood him.

"Por que?" *Why?*

He smiled slowly, looking like the pretty man he was, but still nothing for me.

"Quieres que me saque la ropa?" *Do you want me to take my clothes off?*

The words felt automatic, the words landed on the floor in front of me and I didn't know how to take them back.

I had already started to shake wondering if he was just getting me pretty for him—because there was no pride for me in being a whore.

A former whore.

"No. I'd like to just hug you, Selena. Just a hug."

Gabriel's eyes held infinite softness as his throat worked a little like he was holding back his emotions. Like he had muted down his supernatural presence.

"With your clothes on."

Like my father.

As I stepped closer to Gabriel, he moved forward, and in the next moment, I found myself wrapped in his arms, his cologne surrounding me as I inhaled great big waves of it into my lungs.

His scent was like nothing I had ever experienced before, a combination of the most wonderful things in the world.

Nobody smelled like that.

No one besides my family had ever held me like this. But in a way, maybe that's what Gabriel was becoming—*family*.

For a moment, all I could feel was his strength seeping into me, filling me with a sense of security and warmth.

Tears welled up in my eyes, and I did not understand why this man, out of every man I had ever encountered, had such an effect on me.

It was like when my mother would wake me up for school, shaking me out of the groggy sensation right before I realized I did in fact have to do something. I was coming out of the fog.

"Did you want this life? Querías esta vida?"

Gabriel was doing what Reed was doing, prefacing his English with his Spanish so I could learn faster.

"No."

I didn't want to be any of this. I wanted to be a normal woman. I told him in Spanish.

A normal wife.

A noise followed by a deep exhale left Gabriel's chest as he held me tighter, not uttering a single word.

And I loved this.

Gabriel's voice was quiet. "Your file said your father and brother were shot when you were a teenager? Drive by. Wrong place. Wrong time."

I remembered that day since it was the moment my life changed.

My father and Diego had been killed. It was not safe for them to be on the streets at that time and it was an accident. Mama had forgotten something and she needed it from the market. Papi had insisted on going out late. Diego had begged him to go with him because he was bored at home.

I remember yelling at Diego. I told him he was being lazy because he didn't want to help Mama.

We had fought for a little bit and he had left. I never saw Diego or Papi again.

But one night would forever be ingrained in me. *In Mama.*

She was never the same again. Or me.

Gabriel let out a breath bringing me back to the moment.

"I'm not your father or brother. Neither is Reed. But I was hoping we could be there for you." He said it slowly in Spanish telling me he had been practicing.

"I like your friend, Reed."

Gabriel smiled slowly. "He likes you too. Says your scary smart. English aside. I don't think you gotta worry about anything."

Reed was good.

He never made me feel uncomfortable like the men from Havana, and treated me as his equal despite me not speaking his language and him struggling through mine.

I didn't understand why he was with horrible women though. A man like Reed could do much better.

But Reed always made sure I had enough to eat, and clean clothes. We stayed in that embrace for what seemed like an eternity.

Gabriel was not attracted to me in a romantic sense. But I had never seen his lady and I didn't know how to ask him.

"You deserve some kindness after a lifetime of not having any," Gabriel murmured tucking a loose lock of my hair behind my ear. "I'm just trying to make sure you get taken care of."

"What…you want…from me?" My voice sounded small even to my own ears.

My heart was kicking in my chest wildly and it took Gabriel rubbing my back for it to calm down.

His voice was soft and his eyes even softer. "I was hoping I could be your friend."

"Men are not…friends. Men are not…good people." I motioned to my heart. I didn't mean him and Reed. I just meant the entire male population could go to hell. After Papi and Diego died? I lost faith in men.

He smirked then lightly. "Men are shit, Selena. But luckily, Reed and I won't ever take advantage of you. But I might ask you to work."

"I can work." I said with confidence eagerly.

He smiled wider. "I bet. But I'd like you to slowly let Reed in. Me. There's a first time for everything." He shrugged lightly looking

19

amused. "Besides, from now on if anyone hurts you, I'll just skin him alive."

I didn't understand.

"Like a chicken?"

Gabriel's grin was a wide flash on his handsome face. "Yes, Selena. Like a chicken." He looked like he was holding back laughter and a shy smile lit my lips.

I found myself nodding in agreement as he gently wiped away my tears. "Tan bueno."

He grinned.

"You..." I slowly struggled. "You kill people."

"Yeah."

Okay.

"But you were trained for that too." Gabriel leaned back looking like an angelic king in his throne. "Reed is a friend. So am I. We have someone else coming soon and even if he's an idiot, I hope you guys will get along. And Evie likes you too."

His entire demeanor changed speaking about his daughter.

It always did.

"I was hoping you might speak in Spanish with her and stay her friend," he murmured. "It's good for Evie."

I liked Evie. She talked to me about her plants Gabriel got her to distract her from her own thoughts. Her anxieties. Evie spent a lot of time curled up around Gabriel.

"Promise me something. Prométeme algo," he continued, his tone taking on a more serious note as he held my face in his larger hands. I blinked up into those icy eyes of his as he smiled a little. Reassuring. Kind.

A pillar of my own strength in another person. A man.

"*Anything*."

In that moment I knew—I would do *anything* for this man.

"If anyone hurts you? Anyone. At all. Ever. You come to me. You can go to Reed, but I'd like you to turn to me. If anything happens to you, you call me. Si algo te pasa, *llámame. Entiendes*?"

Without hesitation I answered him.

"*Entiendes*."

I knew without a doubt that I would go to him if I ever needed help. No matter what.

THE WOMAN WHO BECAME VENUS

SELENA

IT WAS A FEW MONTHS AFTER MY ARRIVAL AT GABRIEL'S MANOR WHEN I first laid eyes on Nathan Wyatt.

Tall, blonde, and annoying—nobody made me want to murder him like Nathan.

Reed had explained to me Nathan would be the final addition to the team he was building. A security company—Titan.

Private security and filled with former soldiers and agents. Operatives like me. But better. Without the bullshit and drama.

Gabriel and Reed wanted to start a company called Titan.

And Nathan was the last addition to this team.

He rode in on a motorcycle even Reed rolled his eyes at, in a leather jacket, and winked at me the moment he saw me.

I *hated* him on sight.

The fact that he was fluent in Spanish, just like me, did nothing to me.

The urge to strangle him was overwhelming. With stupid blonde hair and stupid beard and stupid Viking attitude.

He was six foot two and big and broad, like Gabriel.

But unlike like Gabriel, Nathan Wyatt made me want to murder him.

I shot Gabriel a *look*, but he seemed curious about the whole situation.

Reed had to intervene, separating us to prevent me from hissing at

Nate and attempting to stab him while he did this *stupid laugh chuckle thing.*

Evie, her eyes wide with wonder, hid behind Gabriel's body.

"*Why are you such a pendejo?*" I spat at Nathan in Spanish.

"*Tell you what, muñeca, you take me down, I'll back off. I win? I get you.*"

Rage coursed through my veins.

What do I get if I beat him?

I turned to Gabriel. He couldn't have been more different from Reed, who was dressed casually in a black jacket and a white shirt. Gabriel, on the other hand, was impeccably dressed in his sharp suit.

His pale eyes were amused as he looked at Reed who exchanged a glance with him, and then they *both* turned their attention to me.

"What do you want?" And just when I was thinking about the question for a moment—I felt Nathan *move.*

I caught it mid-air. "*That was cheap.*"

I turned back to Gabriel, ignoring Nathan's shocked expression. Reed's eyes were wide, and Evie emerged from behind Gabriel, her eyes as round as dinner plates.

A wide smile spread across Gabriel's lips as he watched me, his eyes gleaming like it was Christmas morning.

"I want a car."

Gabriel blinked slowly and tipped his head, his smile in place. "Kill him."

With pleasure.

In a smooth move, I took Nate *down,* using his entire body against his own weight, I stepped onto his thigh, wrapping my legs around his neck quicker than he could even figure out.

There was a loud groan from Nathan, followed by swearing.

Satisfaction.

Standing up with ease, I brushed my hair back, a sense of satisfaction washing over me. That was fun.

Nathan blinked a little wide eyed still laying there, and then he burst into a wide grin. "Holy shit, hot stuff, I like you more now."

Gabriel had burst into laughter. Reed's jaw was hanging open.

And Evie looked at me like I was some kind of superhero coming out from behind Gabriel who held her to him grinning wide.

Evie always asked me for my clothes and I gave them to her because she was Gabriel's heart and right now she wore one of my skirts. Gabriel had noticed and I did not think he liked it too much.

"I did good, no?" I waved to Nathan on the floor.

Gabriel's grin stayed in place as he tipped his head. "What kind of car do you want?" I told him without hesitation.

Reed didn't seem surprised at all.

A Challenger.

Later that evening, I turned to Reed who helped me on the internet to order her. "I want to call her *Paloma*."

And just like that, I had a brand new car. She was pretty, and cherry red, and I went places with her.

I got my own apartment and moved into the city, where I found salsa dancing clubs.

I hated driving everywhere in the city, but I loved *Paloma*.

Over the next few months, I focused on getting myself together, just like Reed had said. I worked on improving my English skills.

One afternoon while we were at the shooting range together, Nathan asked me questions.

"You the reason Reed had me in Havana?"

"*Que?*" *What?*

"I was supposed to start at the same time as you. Reed sent me down with a tasker for someone's head. Several someone's."

Nathan was a professional sniper. *Defense.*

For my offense. Reed had explained every two partners they paired were compatible and had sides to them.

Gabriel was Reed's.

As he talked to me, I realized Gabriel had been on the phone, issuing orders to Reed.

For Nathan.

Nathan had taken a detour to Havana where he spent weeks waiting and watching until his target was sighted.

"Reed would only issue an order like that for a few reasons." Nathan's hard navy eyes watched me. "I worked with Reed in the past. And you're a woman. You don't gotta say it. Judging by the look on your face I can guess."

I didn't say why, just turned away from him.

"By the way, what did you pick as your call sign?"

I answered easily. Reed had picked a planet so I picked one too.

"Venus. *Y tu*?" *And you?*

"Neptune." His eyes changed as he said it.

"Why?"

"I like the beach." Nathan kept a little seashell bracelet on his wrist the entire time I knew him. "A little too much."

It was lilac and pearl shades glistening off his hand in the shape of flowers. Tiny flowers and shells. Sometimes in the sunlight it shimmered. It looked more like it was for a woman.

"You like the beach or you like women at the beach?"

Nathan's grin was slow and lazy. "You volunteering to go to the beach with me, muñeca?"

"I will shoot you."

"I know, it's hot...you with that gun—*Ow*." I smacked him upside the head to his delight. "Jokes on you, muñeca. I like pain."

He clutched his head as we both walked out. I rolled my eyes realizing Nathan would flirt all the time with me. But he kept his bracelet close to him.

I noticed it and after a few days I knew—Nathan had a woman. He liked her. But he was single.

"Who is she?" I asked him one night. "Your woman."

I motioned to his bracelet after he had three beers in him. Reed had left to go back to K2, this building he purchased and Evie was asleep on the couch in Gabriel's arms while he listened to something on his phone.

I was interested in everyone's dating because it was fascinating. I had never dated anyone.

Reed only dated vicious women. Not very nice girls. Ice-queens.

Gabriel did not ever do anything but I suspected he did not have trouble finding a woman if he needed it.

Nathan was the one who threw himself at girls.

"Nobody."

I eyed him carefully. "You are lying."

He smirked, his too handsome lips turning up. Nathan was...attractive in a different way than Gabriel.

Nathan knew he was attractive, and he knew *women* knew he was attractive. And he used it to his advantage every single time. Or he tried.

With me.

"It's not working, Nathan. You are not cute to me."

He groaned looking away and I laughed lightly.

"One of these days, muñeca," he grumbled. "I might be your type."

"Only if you die."

"Ouch." He held his heart playfully. But I felt the air shifting between us. "Her name's Gemma. This is hers." He held up his seashell bracelet. "Stole it on the way out the door."

Knowing Nathan, he would only be upset over her for one thing.

"You slept with her?" I dared to ask.

Nathan tipped his head.

Which meant...

"And you broke her heart."

Nathan was quiet, his navy eyes held a faraway look. He didn't answer the question as he sat there like stone, only taking sips from his fourth beer bottle.

She broke his.

"You...talk to her?"

He shook his head. "Nah. Not anymore. It's over between me and Gemma." He smiled a little at me. "And that's all the answers I got in me tonight, muñeca."

I chewed my lip.

"How did she hurt you?"

His smile dipped. "Lena."

I was curious. "You know my past. In Havana. I know you killed those men. Who is Gemma?" Nathan never mentioned he knew what had happened to me, but the therapist I had let me know what it was. And it was not very nice.

He tipped his head back. "If I tell you, are you gonna tell anyone?"

"No."

He eyed me up and down making my heart leap out of my chest.

"Not even Gabriel."

Oh. "You are a bad man."

"True, but I don't like to kiss and tell, muñeca."

"What does that mean?"

"Means I don't fuck women and brag about it."

"I do not like this word."

25

"You don't like men."

Not true. I liked men. I did not like Nathan like that.

Navy eyes held mine. "Come on." He held out his enormous pinky.

I puffed out a breath. "Promise."

And so he spent the night telling me about Gemma.

And Nathan didn't try anything ever again.

SELENA

I worked with Nathan directly under Gabriel for years.

During that time, I grew *a lot.*

Nathan and I went on work missions all the time whenever Gabriel and Reed needed a team.

I was Nathan's partner, as Reed said—the offense to his defense.

The jobs we did together weren't pretty, even if I wore an evening gown, I still gathered intelligence while Nathan did recon, and we both killed people. No rules.

Just make sure we do not get caught.

Sometimes Reed worked with other governments. Sometimes he had me do it.

One assignment I'd almost fell off a forty story building in Dubai and Nathan had saved me. *"Jesus fucking Christ, try not to get killed."*

"Yes, I will be more considerate of the arms dealer."

I had rolled my eyes and he'd shot me a smirk as he hauled me up the side.

And somewhere in long hours, long assignments, and falling asleep on his shoulder, Nathan fixing my gear—we became friends. I didn't feel anything romantic for him.

When I needed help with *Paloma,* Nathan began volunteering to take care of her since I had never done oil or brake changes.

When I told Nathan about painting as a hobby to relax on my free time Nathan sent me a set of expensive paints from water color to deeper richer colors.

"Why did you send me so much?"

"Whatever you prefer, muñeca."

At work, Nathan was professional.

I began to understand that there was another kind of non-sexual relationship with a man.

Nathan reminded me of a brother, and only that.

There was nothing romantic for me there.

I could see in his eyes that his heart belonged to someone else.

Gemma.

It was the same look I had seen in Gabriel's eyes when Nathan talked about his Gemma. I hadn't seen her before but Nathan eventually showed me her pictures.

When we finished an assignment once, we had a few days of break, and Nate took me to an island called Capri. It was breathtaking, and it reminded me of Cuba.

Since I had been to America with Gabriel, I had not gone back.

No, instead he and Reed helped my Mama and she was now in Miami living her best life as Gabriel said, since he took care of her.

I didn't understand how Gabriel had so much money but I felt nothing but gratitude for him when he told me. Miami was a host to all things Cuba and in turn, Mama was doing great.

We talked sometimes but mostly I texted her and she sent me photos of her.

When Mama discovered Bingo?

The game with the numbers?

She was much happier.

Nathan took me to the coast of Italy. Where the warm sea and the scent of lemons were everywhere.

I'd never had lemons that wonderful. I wanted to wear that scent on my skin. The island's coastline was a masterpiece, with towering cliffs that plunged into the crystal-clear waters below.

I explored the island with Nathan, and he told me about *his* Gemma. Wandering through narrow, winding streets lined with whitewashed buildings adorned with vibrant blue shutters and colorful ceramic tiles—Nathan told me stories of who he had been before Reed had told him about Titan. His life. His world. His family.

Anyone could fall in love here. Nathan took me to the Blue Grotto, a sea cave illuminated by an ethereal blue light.

"Gemma brought me here when I told her about my parents and my Mama," he motioned to the cave, his blonde hair looking almost black, his eyes pitch black despite being navy outside of the cave. "I fell for her here."

Gemma *Marchand.*

A quick internet search showed me a stunning blonde woman of French descent, with a face cut from glass. Eyes like spun clouds and the sky. Hair fair like dolls. Gemma was *pretty.* A wealthy woman and model.

Not what I imagined as Nathan's type.

I saw Nathan's entire face change from the rugged Viking every woman lost their minds over.

A younger version of Nathan who was scared of loving a woman like her. Someone not so sure of himself. A young man who had been guarding a wealthy heiress.

"I was twenty something, with shit for brains. Young and dumb enough to think I could have her..." he looked a little lost as he said. "I couldn't."

He told me stories about her and that he had been younger when he fell in love with her as her guard. Something he shouldn't have done.

"Gemma was old money, you know what that means?"

"Old money?"

"Means, I was a nobody," he smirked but it was pained.

"You are not a nobody."

"I am to Gemma's family. The Marchand's are about as old money as you can get...former royalty..."

I had never heard Nathan talk about himself like this and it made a little bit of chest ache to think of someone who could make Nathan feel like that.

In my eyes he was larger than life, his smiles wider than anyone's.

He gave Evie piggy back rides.

Nathan was the only one who saw the worst of Reed's tempers and fought back. He was the only one who would take Gabriel in a fight which told me a thing or two about Nathan's skills.

He wasn't ugly either...I just preferred Gabriel's polished college/movie star guy looks to the rugged charm Nathan had.

"Her family didn't think so." He looked out at the horizon. "Thankfully, Reed got in touch with me at the same time."

"And now you work with us?"

He nodded while watching me carefully. "Do you ever think about getting married?"

I answered with zero hesitation. "Yes, I've always wanted that. A normal life."

A normal wife.

In another life, I would be like Mama. Stay home. Make food for my family and my husband. Be happy.

My conversations with Nathan ranged from deep and meaningful to casual like this.

Sometimes I wondered if I could go and be a normal girl. Instead of making choices I did not want to.

But Gabriel had made sure Mama was comfortable. He moved her to Miami Beach in Florida and Mama was having the time of her life.

"I was thinking…" He gazed out at the beach, his eyes fixed on the horizon. "When do you want to get married?"

"Thirty. Why?" I wanted many children but for a woman time was different. I did not want children now.

"I want to get married, but I realize our life doesn't allow for the same choices as a normal person. Eventually, I'd want kids, but you can think about it."

He continued, and I considered the idea of ever sleeping with Nathan.

"I want to be someone's husband. But not some psycho woman. You're the only one I can handle—"

I rolled my eyes, fighting the urge to punch him as I stopped feeling the breeze in the air.

Even I couldn't deny the offer was tempting. Something normal even when our lives weren't.

I have always wanted to be a mother…

"But I was thinking…"

And then he shocked me once more in my life.

He explained that he wanted to have children by a certain point, and since he already considered me his best friend, even if he didn't harbor romantic feelings for me.

Nathan said he would feel incomplete in this life if he didn't become a husband or a father.

I looked back at the water, the waves lapping at my feet as his words washed over me.

I had never heard or seen Nathan like this.

"Would you ever consider if neither one of us ended up with anyone by the time we were thirty, you'd want to be with me?" He turned to face me, his expression serious. "You don't have to say yes. Ever. And it's okay if you try and stab my balls with the knife in your beach bag."

I couldn't bring myself to laugh. "What do you mean, if I don't find a man to have kids with, you want me to have your babies? What about your Gemma?"

What if he wanted a life with her?

"Gemma isn't mine," he repeated to me gently. He said. "She'll never be. And they'd be our kids, not just mine."

"But you don't love me like you love Gemma."

And I did not want to sleep with Nathan. The words tumbled out of my mouth before I could stop them.

Not in the way I love Gabriel. I held my tongue.

I didn't want to have Gabriel's children. I just knew if Gabriel had babies, he would be a good father.

I thought about his relationship with Evie and all the memories of him with her as she showed him videos on her phone, and that smile on his face when he rubbed her hair when they watched movies. Evie was his baby.

Nathan was more like a brother.

"You and I are only just work partners."

"Don't they say best friends make the best partners?" his voice was filled with sincerity.

Having worked with Nathan long enough, I knew when he was telling the truth, his eyes deep blue as they watched me.

"I know you've been hurt, but—" He extended his hand towards me. "If you still want kids, and you don't have any, I'd like to have them too. A partnership in that sense. But you don't have to say yes right now. It's your choice."

Gabriel had told me in this new life of mine I had a choice to do all the right things.

I did not ask Nathan what would happen if we were with other people. Nathan did not do relationships. I had never met a man I truly wanted. It did not matter.

You have control now. You don't have to let anyone touch you anymore without your consent.

Do you know what consent is? No?

And he explained in detail. I learned.

Nathan was asking for consent.

It's your choice. I had control.

I had to give consent.

In that moment, I saw Nathan in a different light, his usual navy blue eyes unguarded and vulnerable.

"You want to have sex with me?" I didn't know how that was going to work. Nate did nothing for my lady parts.

"I won't sleep with you," he looked out to the sea, his hand out. "There are ways, clinics, and places to go to have kids."

Really?

"I'd be there for you through the whole way. I don't see myself ending up with anyone else. I just want to be a father."

What if I did, though?

Mama had that.

"Me too," I replied, my heart skipping a beat at the thought. I took his hand, and he kissed the spot right above my knuckles. *Sealed.*

A mischievous grin tugged at the corners of his mouth and he looked like some rugged God.

"You'd like to be a father?" he teased, his navy eyes sparkling with amusement, the wind blowing his dirty-blonde hair back.

This *pendejo*.

I reached into my beach bag, and his laughter ended.

As the years passed the idea of motherhood, once a dream, now felt like a longing. I found myself wondering if Nathan's proposal still stood if he truly meant what he had said that day.

I didn't want children without love. I wanted them in a happier home where their father would love me.

But I wanted them either way and Nathan proposal was practical for the two of us. I was growing older.

I didn't love anyone close to my love for Gabriel.

Not even Nathan compared.

I still *wanted* to love someone.

But maybe love was a luxury for a girl from Havana. A dream within a dream that I was only allowed to imagine. Not to have and hold in my hands. Not this Selena.

I took Nathan's offer because it was all I felt I deserved.

And then…I turned twenty-nine.

PART I | VENUS

PRESENT DAY

CHAPTER 1
SELENA

I CURSED UNDER MY BREATH, HATING NEW YORK CITY DRIVERS ALMOST as much as I hated airports.

"No, you hate people," Nathan said, a little breathless on the phone. "Watts just texted me. He's grabbing his baggage, and then he'll meet you outside. He's in his letterman jacket. You can't miss him."

Nathan was my friend, but that didn't mean sometimes I did not want to kill him.

He could not pick up Kellan Watts, the new hire, because he'd been *indisposed*, as he said.

Nathan *was indisposed* because he was with a woman.

Women. I knew Nathan; he had been with more women than I had ever thought possible. He groaned in the background.

I wanted to cover my eyes even though he *wasn't* there.

"*Are you having sex while you're on the phone with me?*"

"...Lena, don't ask if you don't wanna know."

He murmured something about 'deeper baby' to his woman in the background, and I rolled my eyes.

"I do not understand *why* women like you."

Women *all* over the world *loved* Nathan.

The tall, rough looking biker with his easy smiles and laughter whenever he flirted with them. And his dimples. And his abs.

I got it.

"I'm going to strangle you."

"Careful, muñeca, I might be into that sorta violence. Women don't like me, Lena," he muttered, sounding out of breath. "They like my big—"

"I got it."

He chuckled low as I heard a woman moaning in the background.

In the years I'd known him, I knew he wasn't shy about *anything*.

Carajo.

I would never sleep with Nathan.

If I did, I would rip his—No. ¡*Cálmate*! *Calm down.*

Exhaustion weighed on my shoulders as I navigated the crowded airport. I was so freaking tired.

How many hours of sleep did I get last night?

I pulled up in front of the mess of passengers at JFK in *Paloma*.

Nate was speaking low. "He got delayed three times coming in from Kuwait. Kid's got the patience of a fucking saint with the shit show he dealt with."

"Well, he better be ready to deal with me because I've gotten three hours of sleep." *Maybe.* "And you aren't here because you like blowjobs."

He groaned low, and the moaning in the background grew louder.

"Lena, every man likes his dick sucked. You can't blame me for spending the night with twins—"

Dios Mio. "Enough!"

He laughed. "Let me know when you're solid. Yeah?"

I cursed him out, hanging up to his laughter as I stepped out of the car. Someone honked and yelled at me. I shouted back in Spanish. I scanned the crowd for a letterman jacket. I heard some wolf whistles at my outfit.

Welcome to JFK. Hell on Earth.

I took long strides to the arrivals, hoping Mr. Letterman was waiting there. More cat calls. Nothing got me more infuriated than men feeling entitled to my body. I don't dress for men.

I dressed for Selena without clothes. The Selena Gabriel picked up at the hotel in Quantico.

The soft black material of my dress was *mini,* barely touching my thighs as I tugged it off the shoulder, adjusting the long sleeves. I looked *good.*

I looked *vampy*, as Nathan would say.

What did men think women wore?

If I could, I would walk around in lingerie; I would. Evie had already asked to borrow it for some convention she had gone to earlier this summer.

She loved it.

She liked all my clothes even if they looked different on her. Especially my dresses.

Since she was sweet and I was...not.

I could see Gabriel looking at me and her with frustration since he didn't know what to do with the woman child his *Princessa* was becoming.

But he never said anything.

I swung my long hair back with my bangs. I knew I was, as Nathan said, *straight fire. American idioms.*

What the hell was a Letterman jacket anyway?

Americans and their clothing names. A quick search on my phone revealed it was a sports jacket worn by those cute football players.

Not that it matters if he's cute. It's just a nice jacket...

Gabriel did not care who I did, so long as they did not hurt me. If he got a whiff of anyone treating me in any other way than respect—he'd shoot them and bury them in the backyard.

He called it his version of gardening.

But when I did sleep with a man, I did it far away from work.

Gabriel took a chance on me years ago when I thought I'd be kicked to the curb, and I never failed him.

Although I couldn't remember the last time I had sex.

Or the last time I *enjoyed* it. If not ever.

Besides, vibrators in America were insane. Sex toys? Got the job done better than men. But part of me longed for a man.

Just not...any of the men I had in my life. Maybe in a dream. In another life when I was not Selena Tavares.

Just...Lena.

I searched for Mr. Letterman, but he was nowhere to be seen.

Where was this pendejo?

I didn't even register the impact of people bumping into me; my patience was already getting thinner.

Did people not have the decency to watch where they were going anymore?

I knew I was being unfair, but it was hard to find the energy to care in my current state of mind.

Storming back to *Paloma*, I was so done with this place.

I was already on edge.

I looked at the photos and saw a flash of the same jacket.

That was him?

He was standing there, just past the double doors, with his backpack and a duffle bag at his feet.

Where did he come from?

"*Oye! ¿*qué estás haciendo? *Mr. Letterman!*"

CHAPTER 2
SELENA

WHAT ARE YOU DOING, MR. LETTERMAN?

The head of blonde hair turned to look over a broad shoulder, and his eyes widened. Clear, blue, like the ocean on the brightest day.

"Dios mio."

Neat wheat-colored hair and eyes that gleamed a little as he looked at me in his white shirt. Clean cut. Tall. *Handsome.* The same height as Nathan, six-two, but...*stronger.*

I could tell by the way the jacket hung off those shoulders.

Those biceps.

Without thinking twice, I strode towards him, confident in my steps, and I did not miss the way he blinked several times, his blue eyes, growing wide as I approached.

"Miss Selena Tavares?"

I felt his voice somewhere deep. Warm, sliding over my skin.

This was Kellan Watts? The new hire?

There was something about his eyes, his entire expression. A smile playing on his lips.

This baby.

The world was going to chew him up and spit him out.

I felt a surge of protectiveness for him.

Before I could respond, someone whistled at me and catcalled me, and I closed my eyes.

Snap out of it. He's hot. Not the end of the world.

Murder was not on the itinerary.

"Si. ¿Tienes tus cosas?" *You have your stuff?*

When I opened them, I paused at the expression on his face.

Those blues darkened, a protective gleam replacing the earlier playfulness.

"I do have my things, sorry about that, I got a little distracted by this car."

What was that accent?

I wanted him to talk to me like that while he was between my—*Not stopping.*

You just met the man!

Someone else whistled and shouted something vulgar that sounded like hot legs, and Kellan's expression went dark as he took a step closer to me.

"You want me to take care of them for you?"

I'd like you to take care of me.

In *Paloma*. At my apartment. *Everywhere.*

He was built like an athlete, with the cute jacket he wore.

I wanted to lean into him, to get lost in the sensation, but I quickly reminded myself that this was a job.

I couldn't afford to get caught up in the moment, no matter how tempting it was.

My hands went up against his stomach to stop him from coming too close, and he did his head dipped a little.

Now, I felt small compared to him.

He's like a rock underneath that shirt. I can feel his heat.

I blinked up at him, tipping my head back since he was so close to me. "What are you doing?"

"I don't like people disrespecting women." It was that accent. "Let me take care of it."

That's the accent that did me in.

My voice was surprisingly steady despite the butterflies in my stomach. They were going crazy. "I can take care of myself."

Reluctantly, I pulled away, putting a respectable distance between us. I saw a number of emotions going over his face.

He almost reminded me of when Reed was analyzing a problem, or Nathan was staring at a target or when Gabriel questioned Evie about her plans in the city.

It was as if he held a piece of information she didn't want to tell him. But he *knew*.

It was unsettling, and I did not like it one bit.

I thought he might push the matter further and make me reveal whatever it was that he seemed to have figured out.

But then, as quickly as it had appeared, the expression on his face shifted, smoothing back into that polite smile.

"Si estás listo, podemos irnos. Vamos."

If you are ready, we can go.

But when he didn't move and just watched me with that little smile on his face. And I was confused.

Why were we standing here? Did he not understand my accent?

"You understand me?"

Was Spanish not a requirement?

Softly he said, not looking away from me, that glint in his eyes. "Te entiendo."

Oh. He understood. And his accent was perfect.

Gabriel and I practiced words sometimes, but it usually ended with me feeling bad as he tried his best to teach me how to say things better.

He always had endless patience with me when I was first learning English with him.

I learned the basics and learned to imitate him phonetically.

In turn, I taught him better Spanish.

Over the years, I hadn't lost my accent, but Gabriel sounded like a native. Except Kellan didn't move, he blinked at me several times.

"Are you wearing contacts?"

Why wasn't he moving?

Someone's suitcase ran over the back of my heel, and I hissed, turning and swearing, reaching for my gun and remembering it was in *Paloma*.

Murder was not on the agenda.

I'm ready to shoot these people with three hours of sleep.

And just like that, Kellan was close again, his arm coming around me gently, and I gaped a little as he deftly brought me closer.

"Where'd you park?" I stared at the lady, ready to kill her, when he said. "*Selena*."

My head turned to him, unable to focus, until he dipped his head, his blues in my face.

Dios, he was so close.

"Let me, honey."

"I got it, Mr. College Football." Something appeared in his eyes as I said that, brushing out of his hold. Who was this man? And why did I want to rub myself against him like a cat in the sun? "I parked here."

I motioned as he picked up his duffle, and we walked to *Paloma*. My prized—

"That was *your* car?" What? His wide grin aimed at me. I wasn't paying attention.

"Do you not think women can drive nice cars?"

"No, not at all, I was just—" He put his stuff in the backseat and trunk and got in with an embarrassed smile.

Thankfully, he didn't say anything until I pulled out.

Paloma purred to life thanks to Nate. I huffed as I held her steering wheel while people were still catcalling.

"I didn't say that," he drawled. "It's just—*it's a really nice car.*" *He likes Paloma.*

And I like him. As I stopped at the next red light, I took a moment to adjust the GPS on my phone and put on some music.

The car purred beneath me, the smooth cream leather seats cradling my body as the engine's vibrations sent a gentle thrum through my bones.

A warm blush crept onto my cheeks at the thought of Nathan's care and attention to *Paloma*, knowing how much I loved her.

"Thanks." My voice was soft. Breathless. What was this man doing to me?

Losing myself in the bass of an old-school tune, I tapped my vampire red nails against the steering wheel.

It didn't take long for another car to pull up beside us, and I sighed heavily, closing my eyes.

Not *now*.

I rolled up my tinted windows, but not before I caught their yells.

Hey, mami, you can ride me any day.

Take a compliment, sexy.

Come on mama, let's see a smile.

With a sigh and an eye roll, I turned up the volume on my music, trying to drown out their voices. I didn't care to ask the passenger to my right, who I could feel the tension from.

Except, was every single song on this playlist about sex?

I turned it off. And it took him maybe two seconds to say something.

"What do you do when this kind of stuff happens to you?"

That had not been my first guess on what he would say.

The lack of proper sleep had taken its toll on me, leaving me feeling raw and exposed, like a live wire ready to spark.

"We don't have to speak. I am dropping you off. That's all this is."

Even as I said it, I ached. I didn't want to be mean, but nobody made me feel...I did not know.

I'm not getting enough rest.

Kellan was *really* gorgeous.

The kind of cute boy you wanted to kiss on the beach and just make out with for hours.

As much as I liked my vibrator, I couldn't deny this man made me feel things.

Things I couldn't quite grasp, like wisps of smoke slipping through my fingers, I wanted to understand it. But I also hadn't slept, and I didn't have the ability to process it.

"Just curious," he said, his voice softer than I imagined from a man his size. I felt my tongue dart out, licking my lips at the thought of that voice hitting somewhere low.

Come for me.

I clenched my thighs together. "What kind of accent is that?"

"Dallas." *Figures.* "You?"

"I don't have an accent."

It was the running joke in the team.

Pleasure coursed through me at the sound of his burst of laughter; I bit my lip, looking out my window where, thankfully, those idiots were gone.

I did not bother giving Kellan any more details.

The less he knows, the better.

I didn't want another Nathan.

And I felt so guilty for feeling like that. I don't know why I thought that. Once I dropped him off to the Manor, he was in the shark tank to prove himself. And one big shark—Gabriel—was waiting to sink his teeth into the new hires. One I missed and loved, even if that shark was driving everyone as insane as he was becoming.

"Cuban or Brazilian?"

47

"The one that does not matter to you."

I didn't care if I was rude. He was just another rookie who couldn't stack up to the team. And I would end up burned out like always.

I was working to the ground.

I handled international contracts for Reed when he was juggling everything else.

Sometimes, I took last-minute trips and overnight flights and moved around so much that the comfort of my apartment, in its pink glory, seemed so far away.

I couldn't remember anything about it sometimes. The constant motion, the never-ending demands, all of it blurred together into a haze of exhaustion and stress.

"Now why's that?" *Did he have to sound like that?*

I rolled my window back down, speeding up.

I did not want to do this. We had an hour-long drive ahead of us, and then I would have to train him. I needed to have my peace. And professionalism.

Even if his smile was one, I wanted to lick off his face.

I need to get laid, Nathan would say. *I'm just horny and I need to sleep with someone. Anyone. But him.*

Pretty sure the last time I slept with someone was a year ago, and I couldn't even remember what it felt like. Who was he?

Mr. Insufferable Hottie who wanted to speak to me.

Normally, if I'd met him at a bar, I would let him take me home.

Burn out a few orgasms with him and leave. Never call. Never text.

Never look his way again. But he was my *coworker.*

Why oh why?

It's also time for you and Nathan to get married.

Then there was Gabriel, and Kellan and the other newbies might not make it through the next day.

Another rookie.

At the next red light, I whipped my shades off and turned to him. *"Listen, Mr. College Football—"*

"Kellan," he corrected, his eyes bright with humor as he took me in, narrowing slightly as his gaze moved down my body to my thighs.

"Are you—" I shook my head in disbelief. *"Are you checking me out?"*

I turned away as the light turned green, swearing under my breath.

Looking down at my dress, I realized it had hiked up, leaving little to the imagination.

As I adjusted the hem, the top tugged lower, leaving my breasts indecently exposed as I swore in Spanish.

God would give me this man today.

From my right, I heard. "¿Qué día es hoy?" *What day is today?*

Madre de Dios.

Had I said that out loud?

I gaped at twinkling blue eyes, my heart skipping a beat at the sound of his voice.

Here I was, sleep-deprived and emotionally drained, stuck in a car with this *infuriatingly* attractive man who seemed to enjoy pushing my buttons.

His grin was wicked, and I saw the sharp sides of his teeth. Imagining them raking over my nipples.

"You sound like it's your first language." He didn't even have an accent.

"I'm full of surprises, honey."

"I am not your honey."

Through his devilish grin he said. "But you could be." And just like that my stomach flipped. And I felt myself involuntarily clench. I don't know why my reaction was to snap.

"*Listen.* We have a long drive ahead. I am already in a bad mood. So just sit there and twiddle your thumbs—"

I hated my accent right now.

"*—Try not to bother me.*"

"For *anything?*"

"*Yes, anything.*"

"What about the bathroom?"

"You'll live."

Was he laughing at me?

I caught it out of the corner of my eye. He *was.* That smile. His teeth were sharp on the side, and he looked like an adorable lion, the mischievous glint in his eyes present.

"What if I'm hungry?"

I swear to fucking—I stopped.

"*What?*"

I turned to look at him—*really* look at him—at the next light.

Why were there so many lights? His eyes were gleaming as he took me in, like he knew more than me.

"What if I'm hungry?" He said it slower.

Did they leave you any food, any clothes?

Disarmed. Reed would say, I was *disarmed.*

You have become the people who were awful to you. You can't be mean to him because you're afraid of him.

He's about to be your new partner. Just be nice to him.

Be Gabriel to him. No, not that version. Don't kill him. Be the version you love.

I took a deep breath, trying to calm the emotions raging through me. I had been so caught up in my own exhaustion and frustration that I had failed to see the man beside me as a person with his own needs and feelings.

He got delayed…

Kid's got the patience of a fucking saint with the shit show he dealt with. From *Kuwait.*

I had been left with nothing…

What had he been left with?

I closed my eyes, letting out a low breath. *This is not you.*

You are not this bitch.

It's not like they fed his six-foot-something body real food.

And all his *muscles…*

He must be starving.

You're being mean to him because you like him. Lena, that's not fair. Poor baby.

I was such a bitch. I shouldn't have been so mean to him. *Why?* Because he got under my skin?

Because he was hot? Breathe.

Reed's voice was in my head from training with him.

You can do this. Make the right choices.

It wouldn't *hurt* to take a detour.

I thought I was *human.*

I am not. I am an operative. I do not have emotions and cannot let them ever get the best of me.

I was not angry at Kellan.

There was *nothing* wrong with Kellan.

Something was wrong with *me.*

Shame on you, Lena. You know better.

I turned off the GPS. I knew this neighborhood. I turned the car to the right and changed plans. I would go somewhere good.

I don't even know how long he was in Kuwait.

He wouldn't be hungry for too long.

All the while, Gabriel's smile was in my head, his kindness in my heart. My first night in Quantico. My first night in his manor.

Purchase the store.

Reed dropping off plenty of snacks for me and Evie.

Nathan brought me burgers and milkshakes in different flavors every time he met me because he knew I liked trying new flavors.

I cannot do this to him.

You are not allowed to be mean.

Not anymore.

"Where are we going?" I barely heard him.

"To get you food, Mr. College Football."

This time, he didn't correct me.

I glanced at Kellan, taking in his chiseled features and how his eyes crinkled at the corners when he made that stupid, irresistible smile.

He was like one of those large golden dogs everyone loved. Including me.

He's the same age as Diego would've been.

And Gabriel would not be kind to him. Gabriel is going to eat him alive.

I had to remind myself to behave, even as I noticed his eyes taking in my body with a hunger I hadn't seen in a while.

One I returned for him.

CHAPTER 3
KELLAN

SHE WON'T SAY MY NAME.

She was out of her element.

I knew it from the moment she showed up.

Hands down, Selena was the most stunning woman I had ever seen in real life, tapping her ruby nails on the steering wheel of a fucking *Challenger*.

I had been staring at it, distracted waiting to see who drove it.

Long, beautiful brunette hair with wispy bangs, her face sculpted like a beauty queen, and a spitfire for a mouth?

No fucking way *this* was a Titan.

But it was those eyes, emerald green speckled with gold tints to it, it was like a starburst had gone off in those eyes, tip tilted and feline and almost exotic.

When she looked at me, it cut me to the quick. Just like that.

At *first* glance, Selena was a femme fatale.

The kind in movies that showed up to kick my ass. Or kill me. Or fuck me. Or both. I didn't care what Selena wanted to do to me.

As long as she did it.

She is so fucking gorgeous.

Nate Wyatt did not warn me. Nate, my point of contact after Reed, said he worked directly for Reed.

He explained Selena worked for the other boss I hadn't meet yet—Gabriel Monroe. Nate had explained everyone was split.

So, *I* was expecting a mousy lady. This was no mouse.

She is a lioness. She's going to kill me.

I'd had a little heart attack at the woman who approached me looking like a fucking Playboy bunny with dark brunette locks and eyes that could pierce through my fucking soul. The kind of pretty I had to hyperventilate around.

In that dress? If she bent over—*No. Don't do it. Focus on her.*

And then I watched her smile slip.

I couldn't stop my brain from analyzing her.

My parents were retired Federal Agents and my mom worked in the Behavioral Analysis Unit.

My sister, Becca had become a fucking lawyer and none of them were even aware I was working for Titan.

I had signed enough paperwork to know I couldn't talk about my work with anyone but the Titans.

Growing up with my parents?

Brandon and Kaia Watts were a super couple. They fucking loved each other, they were always all over each other. My mom juggled us —her hellion kids—and her career with my father as a stable, stay at home dad. Both of them worked, but his job let him stay at home more.

On the occasion my mom was home, she would often sit me down and talk to me, including me in on shit I had no business being a part of. But I loved it.

Analyze this with me. Tell me what you think.

I was grateful for was her ability to teach me to grow up.

Expose me.

To criminals, sure, but exposure was exposure.

I didn't discriminate.

Because over the years, my mom training my brain, led me to dissecting things.

Within seconds. And because everyone thought I was just some pretty boy, nobody was any wiser.

Selena's eyes widened when she saw, pupils dilated, her breathing hitched. My mouth salivated because she was into me. But *something* was off about her.

At a second glance, Selena was irritated by the fuckers who said the shit they did.

Irritated at the airport, which I was too. But no…it was deeper. It always is.

Those green eyes tipped up at the corners and bright, intelligent, drew me in. Her lips were pouty and pink.

And that fucking outfit—a black dress that left little to nothing to the imagination. Off the shoulder?

I could tear it off with my teeth. I'd spent a year in the desert with Garrett and a bunch of mercenaries.

But I got laid a lot, and it did shit for my mood.

Having bad sex was like eating cold food. *Constantly.* You were full but never satisfied. I didn't enjoy cold food or bad sex. I hadn't had good sex in forever. And even then, women just used me for what they needed—none of them striking me as anything worth having long term.

Plus, it made me want it more afterwards.

I always wanted more. I needed it. And I liked sex. I fucking loved it because just like everything else, when it was done right?

Fucking.

Perfect.

Selena Tavares was one of those women you saw, and you knew, you fucking knew, men dropped on the floor to let her walk on them. With those fucking designer heels on.

When I saw your mother, I knew that was not the kind of woman you let go.

That's how my father talked about my mother.

I saw her across the room, and it was just a flash, and I was like— what do I have to do to get her to talk to me?

Now I got him. *Completely.* I was *floored.*

She tugged her little dress down in those fucking heels. I wanted to fuck her with just those shoes on. I wanted to eat her. I could have Selena as my meal instead of food.

I had grown up in a house with a lot of love.

Becca and I got along. And she always joked about me being as whipped as Dad whenever I found a woman who knocked me on my ass.

I was into everything about Selena at that moment.

I knew what *she* saw.

Women looked at me and saw someone who looked like a six-foot-two football player.

Plus, with my looks and smile? I got around easily.

My mom always taught me that having manners with women would help me. Manners would not do me *shit* in front of Selena.

If we had met under circumstances other than New York's claustrophobic airport, I wondered if she'd be calmer.

But in New York? Everyone had a place to be at all times.

Even if that place was two steps to the left.

When I got closer to her and noticed how much shorter she was in heels, I wondered if she wore them to look taller.

Like Becca told me, she did. I texted my sister often.

Heels are not comfortable.

I saw a model in them at the airport.

I knew her toes were suffocating.

How do you know?

I'm a girl, idiot

Were Selena's toes in pain?

Maybe that's why she was irritable. If she was my girlfriend I'd tell her to take them off and I could massage her feet. She felt perfect against me, her curves molding to my hard planes.

I just got to New York, and I'm already dying for my co-worker.

When I saw the beautiful molten red Challenger.

Of course, she fucking drove that car.

She's like something out of a magazine.

She can't be real.

I wasn't sure if I irritated her with my question or *why* she was so irritated. But as she drove, I realized her irritation wasn't with me.

No, it was with…everything around her.

I got the feeling Selena didn't come out here often, and when she did, she hated driving. Did she prefer taking a cab?

Why hadn't she done that?

Didn't she have anyone to help her?

The flight had been a fucking nightmare for me. Delayed several times, cramped seats, and a flight attendant who couldn't take a hint.

She kept leaning over me, her perfume cloying and too sweet, suggesting we 'get to know each other better' once we landed.

I hadn't eaten much, just a stale sandwich and some lukewarm coffee.

And every single time I stood some lady kept brushing her hands on my pecs.

By accident.

Sure.

By the time we touched down at JFK, my stomach was growling, and my patience was wearing thin from the handsy ladies.

The airport was always a sensory overload for me.

The smell of jet fuel and fast food, the cacophony of voices and announcements over the loudspeaker, and the press of bodies as everyone rushed to their destinations.

I was tired, hungry, and just wanted to get the hell out of there.

And now? I sat next to a woman who couldn't stand me.

It was a day. For sure.

As she drove, I realized that besides being pretty fucking stunning, she had a hard exterior. Maybe to her, it was iron-clad armor.

I smelled bullshit.

I could tell in the way she adjusted the windows when those assholes hit on her, the way she adjusted her dress. Or how she squirmed when she caught me staring.

I kinda want to fuck with her a little.

She was pissed.

And I wanted to know what it was. Had I done something to her? She hadn't said my name either.

Instead, she looked at me like gum under her thousand-dollar shoes.

I fucking knew that label.

The kind of stuff princesses wore in the Middle East.

I decided it would be my fucking mission to get her to say my name.

Or the way she glared at anyone who glared back. Her dark movie star shades. Her lipstick.

She was checking me out at some point. So why didn't she say my name? Mr. College Football. Close.

High school.

Reed insisted I wear this stupid jacket, and now I kinda liked it because it made me look like I was in college.

I got treated differently and saw why he talked about deception from the jump.

Do I make her nervous?

That thought made me grin.

What if Selena wasn't a wildcat? But a kitten? I smiled at the thought of her having a mushy interior. And then I *kinda* wanted to find out...

Hmmm. "What if I'm hungry?"

Come on. Take the bait.

Someone pretending to be so cold wouldn't care. They'd tell me to shove it where it didn't shine.

Come on, honey.

I saw her go through something then. Her face broke the moment I said I was hungry.

Something was happening. I read and analyzed everyone around me, everything down to the *center*.

That's another reason why Reed had picked me.

Because I was *good*. I watched her.

And then she was turning the car around.

No way.

Where were we—I asked her.

"To get you food, Mr. College Football."

Atta girl. Not as bad as you pretend to be.

I couldn't take my eyes off her as she navigated the streets with ease.

She turned on her playlist, and I grinned at another song about having hot sex in a car.

This is going to be fun.

CHAPTER 4
KELLAN

I wasn't expecting her to park in an underground garage.

"It's a little bit of a walk, but it's good," Selena said as she led me through the unfamiliar streets of Queens.

Selena seemed to know the city like the back of her hand, navigating the quiet sidewalks with ease. But my mind was on something that happened earlier.

Something had changed when I asked her if I could eat.

"What is this place?" I asked. "This is my first time in New York. Not counting layovers."

"It's this Indian restaurant I know. It is owned by a man named Patel and his wife, Sashee? I can never say her name right." She looked at me with softer eyes. "But I do not think she minds."

As we crossed the street, Selena instinctively took my arm. She did this at three crosswalks, always walking on the side closest to the cars.

By the fourth time, I switched with her, liking how her eyes flashed like she was surprised, but she didn't do it again.

Hmmm.

"Why do you park so far away?"

"If I leave *Paloma* outside, they'll tear into her. *Destrucción completa.*"

Complete destruction.

Wait a second—

"Your car's name is *Paloma*?"

58

Definitely Cuban?

She stopped before a yellow restaurant entrance, spices wafting through the air. "We are here."

As we stepped inside, all eyes turned to us.

For a moment, I tensed, ready to reach for a weapon that I no longer had, but the only real threat was a group of elderly men and a family with a child.

Soft lighting cast a golden glow over the room. The smell of curry wafting to me with laughter and clinking sounds of the kitchen.

"Miss Selena!"

An Indian man came rushing out from behind the counter, his face lit up.

He wore a bright, multi-colored shirt and his eyes sparkled with warmth and affection as he approached us.

"Patel!"

I watched in awe as Selena's gorgeous face burst into a wide smile, her features softening and her eyes crinkling at the corners as she hugged him.

She is the most stunning woman I've ever seen.

A young boy ran up to Selena, hugging her leg. "You've gotten so big, Ravi!"

If I thought she was stunning before, seeing her interact with this child made her even more irresistible.

She comes here often. She cared about these people.

The more I watched her interact with them, the more I realized how wrong I'd been about her.

My mother's words came back to me; *first impressions, while good to note, most people are hiding.*

Find what they're hiding; you find the root of their character.

Selena was *not* a femme fatale. Patel noticed me and approached with a warm smile.

He shook my hand enthusiastically. "You are Miss Selena's husband."

"*No,*" Selena looked up from kneeling. "Just *friends.*" But Patel winked at me knowingly.

Friends, huh? Just a few moments ago, she couldn't even look at me. *Or say my name.*

"Miss Selena is a beautiful woman."

I smiled softly. "Very."

Understatement. He winked again as we were ushered to a table.

Selena seemed uncomfortable, trying to bring Ravi with her. This was not the setting I expected to find her in.

Maybe an upscale restaurant or a fancy tea room, but not a cozy, family-run restaurant with a kid coloring in the corner and doing his homework with dinosaur chicken nuggets.

"I need to say hi to Sashee. Just stay here, and you'll be fine." She looked me over. "Take off your jacket."

"Why?"

"Just take it off." She glanced around, then reached out and mussed my hair. "Trust me."

What was with this woman?

"All right, woman. If you wanted to get me naked, you could've just asked me." I'd gladly take off my clothes for her.

Thankfully, I had a long-sleeved shirt underneath. Layers were essential for plane travel. I looked up to say something to Selena, but she was already gone.

Why did she want me to take off the jacket?

Patel came over, surprised to find Selena gone. "Miss Selena?"

"Restroom." I got the feeling Patel's English wasn't the best, but I wasn't about to be a dick about it. "Miss Selena comes here all the time?"

Patel's face lit up, his eyes crinkling and his gold tooth glinting in the light.

I was used to the cultural shift as he explained to me, in his thick accent, how Selena had saved his restaurant when the city wanted to shut it down two years ago.

Selena gave Patel full ownership?

"Whatever you want, you can eat—" Patel broke off, his eyes widening as Selena approached the table. "Miss Selena!"

She was stunning. And with a heart of gold. As Selena sat down, a little out of breath, Patel took our order. I already knew what I wanted, and he seemed pleased that I was confident in my choices.

"I traveled a bit," I said to her surprise.

Plus, I spent enough time in the Middle East to meet people from all over the world. It was a hub for immigration and cultures, so I wanted to experience it.

"Miss Selena, your husband—"

"Friend," she corrected. I hid my smile behind the menu.

"He is most kind."

She smiled, appearing slightly uncomfortable, and I couldn't resist a low laugh at her discomfort.

It made her even more red. Patel rushed off to prepare our food. A delightful shade of pink crept onto Selena's cheeks.

"Are you going to stare at me the entire time?" She said it low while never looking up from the menu.

And if I do? I didn't look away.

Because deep down, Selena was a softie.

And she likes me.

By the end of the day, she was gonna say my name.

Just say my name, just once. Come on, honey.

Selena was deep in thought.

When the food came, she offered everything to me first, passing me everything she could.

I nodded as she asked me if I wanted more of something.

Selena made me a plate and asked for a mango lassi.

What the fuck happened to the lady in the car?

I didn't like the way her eyes looked. Something had happened in the car.

I didn't know what it was. But it was right after I told her I was hungry. Was that something she was sensitive about? Childhood trauma? Did she go hungry?

I wanted to know everything about Selena.

When she wasn't giving me attitude, her voice was musical, warm, and soft. And her accent?

It was fucking *adorable.*

"You're staring at me again, Mr. College Football," she said in that soft voice of hers, not even bothering to look at me.

I kept eating, savoring the flavors of the *best* Indian food I had ever had. *I understand why she saved the place.*

"Something you want to say?"

"Did I say something in the car to upset you?" Her eyes flickered up. I *had.* "What was it?"

She didn't speak as she chewed slowly, and she looked down at her chicken, running her tongue over her teeth.

I caught the movement low in my gut. I sipped the mango lassi I got. *I could drink this through an IV drip.*

"No, you did not do anything wrong." She shook her head. But that was a lie. I probably shouldn't tell her I knew when she did lie.

Her tells, her left shoulder shifting a little, her eyes flickering down, her entire body adjusting.

Better keep that to myself.

Switch it to something else.

"Why did you save Patel's business?" I asked after swallowing my last bite, genuinely curious. If she said it was because of the food, I would completely understand.

"How did you—*did he tell you?*"

I nodded in response.

"I did not save it," she mumbled, taking a bite of her samosa and covering her mouth. "I loaned him money."

That's a pretty big deal.

"Same difference," I countered, taking another bite, not understanding why she downplayed her efforts or acted like it wasn't a big deal. "I didn't take you for someone who liked down-to-earth places like this. I don't know how many people would do that—"

I broke off chewing slowly, as her eyes narrowed, and she set her food down, wiping her hands.

In an instant, her demeanor shifted, and I saw a glimpse of the operative within her.

Selena looked like a lioness waking up to danger.

"Don't move."

I turned to see two Latin men entering the restaurant, their oversized jeans and jerseys standing out.

Next to them were a few women, all part of the same group.

Before I could fully process what was happening, Selena ducked under her seat in a rush of air, the sudden movement catching my eye.

Where was she—I peeked under the table, only to find her appearing next to me.

With a fluid, graceful motion, she made her way to my side of the table, crowding into the seat beside me and pressing me further against the cool, smooth leather.

Gone was the soft, musical voice and the adorable accent. In its place was a focused, alert operative, ready to handle whatever threat had walked through the door.

She was reaching for my clothes again, messing with it, checking me over for something. "Don't let them see your jacket." *Why?*

I asked her.

"This is my fault. I'm sorry, I'm so tired. I did not think before I brought you here. You speak Spanish, and I forgot you are not Latino. But nothing will happen to you, *si?*"

I nodded back.

"In this neighborhood, they don't like people who look like you, if they come up to you, you are Latino, si?"

She turned, biting down on her lower lip, and she was trembling.

"I'm sorry," she repeated. "This is my fault."

I could feel the warmth radiating from her body, the faint scent of her perfume—

"What is that?" I inhaled her, closing my eyes. "That scent?"

"Pink pepper," she murmured before turning to the food on the table. "Don't turn your head to them. Get a little lower in your seat...good, now just eat. Or pretend."

"What does it—"

"My gun is in *Paloma*. I forgot it while I was talking to you. But the man on the right is armed. Don't look."

The image of her with a gun was hot as *sin...Damn.*

"Are we in gangland?"

"Not exactly," she shook her head, looking away. "They should've moved down south. This area should be safe. I don't know why they hang out here. I made sure they wouldn't." She stopped talking and I zero'd in on that.

"Made sure of what?" *What the fuck did she do?*

"Just eat, or try to. They'll be gone soon. If they come to us, don't interact with them. Entiendes?"

Understood?

"*Entiendes.*"

Her eyes flickered to me.

I speak Spanish too.

Her cheeks turned pink.

But I couldn't smile or eat, knowing she was in front of me.

She's putting herself as my shield.

63

I knew how to survive *anywhere*, but something as simple as this... she was familiar with it.

She either grew up in it, or she learned. Either way, she knew what she was doing. And I would let her take the lead until I got a feel for it.

I saw her shaking hands, and I couldn't stop myself. I reached for her. Sliding my bigger hand over them, covering them, squeezing one. She stopped shaking.

"I can fight."

"I'm trying to make sure we don't have to." Her throat worked. "My job is to make sure you are safe. And they don't fight like you do." I didn't know what to say to that.

"Remember when I said I was full of surprises?" I could fight dirty. Her lips parted as I took her hand. "Breathe, honey."

Her eyes darted up, then tracked movement like a lioness, just as a dark movement caught my eye.

One of the members of that group walked up to us after ordering food.

"Hola, Selena! ¿Quién es el gringo?"

Who's the white guy?

Straight to the point.

They did not like me. But Selena...

She's using herself as a fucking *shield.*

This fucking woman. Selena let out a laugh that was as fake as the plastic utensils as she playfully pretended to push me away while keeping her other hand on my thigh, holding me steady.

"¿*Gringo*? I translated what she had said. *White guy? You can't tell a white guy from a Latino? This is my boyfriend, Cristian.*

I saw his eyes take me in as I gave him a polite nod, popping bite of samosa in my mouth, refraining from smiling.

But I couldn't stop my brain from scanning.

Oh, he doesn't believe her.

I caught the fraction of movement in his body and his fist, and my scan caught every detail. *He's armed.* His eyes flickered to her, and Selena's fingers on my thigh squeezed. If she knew, she didn't show it.

Turning to Selena's own body, I didn't know what the fuck possessed me to haul her close on my lap, turning to me, to mark her, keep her tight to me if something did go off.

"Soy de Santa Clara." *I'm from Santa Clara.*

I was not. My mother was Brazilian, and she'd whipped Spanish into me and Becca from a young age. Her babies would speak her language. And so we did.

I told him I was visiting Selena.

I looked at her like she was the sexiest thing in the world, which was easy, and she let out one of those smiles that I knew held a bit of unease.

Adapt to her. Now.

I passed on an expression of annoyance like he'd interrupted my time with her.

"¿Cómo conoces a mi mujer?"

How do you know my woman?

Specifically? My wife.

Selena's breath caught as she looked at me, surprise flickering through them. Like she was wondering what game I was playing.

I let my tongue dart over my lower lip, loving the way her breathing hitched a little, watching it.

I turned to the man, letting Selena's nose brush my cheek as I did, looking annoyed. His eyes were wide. Relaxed shoulders, fists unclenched, jaw drop.

Sold.

One of the other slick looking guys covered in tattoos who had come up as though sensing trouble, looked surprised.

You put my mother in a restaurant, and a man stared at her ass?

My father, who was normally calm and collected, turned into someone neither I nor I recognized.

Now I did.

One of them said something, and I half heard Selena laugh that husky laugh of hers, and she talked to them almost embarrassed.

I could tell she was friendly with them.

Which means she knows them.

I didn't fucking know how, but I was going to find out.

Time to do my job as her man.

As she talked, I played up the jealous boyfriend act, not really being an act since I didn't want that smile of hers aimed at these fuckers.

I trailed my nose alongside her jawline and then lower. Finding her pulse, brushing my lips over it, and hauling her into my lap. When she gasped I knew I had her.

"*Gatita*, your body's perfect."

Kitten.

I don't know why it fell from my lips. But it did.

Why didn't I do this sooner?

She fit perfectly, her firm butt right on my dick which was currently very aware of her.

Now I was facing them while Selena was forced to turn.

That's *better.*

Selena said something to the guys, almost embarrassed, and it sounded like *we're just going back to eating.*

Selena let out a breathless laugh as she clutched my head to her neck.

The guy said something else I caught.

Damn Selena, I didn't know you was boo'd up. Lemme not interrupt you two. I see you. And he walked away.

"Clear," She breathed. "You can stop pretending to be my lover."

That word slid off her tongue.

Breathless. Heady.

But I *wasn't.* I wasn't pretending.

I was in her neck, hidden behind her hair.

I was so close to her pulse. If I wanted to—if I wanted to, I *could.*

Loving her shiver as I waited.

"I didn't know your accent was perfect."

A compliment?

"Is it?" And took the fucking chance, pressing my lips over that erratic flutter. "My mom's Brazilian, she speaks Portuguese and Spanish."

"What are you doing?"

"That was a thank you," I kept my voice low. "For protecting me this entire day. At the airport," I let out a shaky exhale.

"It's my job—"

"No, I don't want you to pull all the weight yourself," I didn't move, feeling her breath catch. "I thought I might help too. What is that scent?"

Distract her.

Selena squirmed as I moved my lips to the back of her neck.

"Pink pepper and lychee." I wanted this scent all over my skin.

"Thanks for picking me up, for getting me food, for when we crossed the streets, and now this," I stayed there. "I can move when they leave after they get their food. They didn't believe you. Make it believable. You look like I left you high and dry." She wasn't making a move to get off.

I felt my smile widen as she whispered. "How do you know that?"

"I'm full of surprises, honey," And then I opened my mouth on her pulse, and I heard that little fucking whimper. "Lean against me, there you go. I promise I won't let anyone hurt you either."

My hands stroked over her back and sucked until I was satisfied. She squirmed, and my cock, harder than steel, felt that.

In the booth like this nobody could see what I was doing unless they came over. I moved my jacket over her front, covering her so my hands could work.

"Can I taste you again?"

That little nod as she closed her eyes told me everything. I fucking knew it. I opened my mouth again, working my tongue alongside her neck, under her ear, tugging on her earlobe. Selena let out a tiny little moan.

Good girl.

She is so lovely.

Bringing her on my lap was a no-brainer, even if my dick was currently so fucking hard I was tempted to take her back to her car and work one out in her.

For *hours*.

My hands moved of their own accord; if she wanted a show, I could give people one.

Go for it. She's into you.

I cupped one of her breasts, sucking hard on her neck while massaging that soft skin through her dress.

"*Kellan*."

Now we're talking, honey.

CHAPTER 5
SELENA

SOMETHING IN ME SNAPPED IN THAT MOMENT AS HE MASSAGED MY breasts through that flimsy dress I wore.

Take me back to *Paloma*.

Take me in Paloma.

Nobody could see us since he'd taken the booth in the back, and his jacket on me was enormous, swallowing my shoulders whole reminding me how huge he was.

I gripped his head closer, my head tipping to the side to let him, as my hips moved back onto his lap, feeling the hard ridge of his cock.

"Kellan," I gasped at the sight of him, mouth hungrily moving over the tops of my dress, I tugged at his hair.

The playful, goofy man had melted away, revealing a man I did not recognize. His eyes burned with an intensity that was a little scary.

I bit down on my bottom lip. My nipples achingly hard as pebbles as his lips hovered over mine.

I did not know who I was trying to fool.

Take me. *Now.*

He whispered, his mouth dropped lower to my chest. He licked his lips and I knew, I knew this man was wild because he was going to—

"Not here."

I was turning pink already. And then he pulled back. Just an inch. Blue met my eyes. "Then where?"

Dios.

I thought I could bring him here because—*why would a gang show up at a random time during the day?*

Now, my appetite was ruined in case they came back. It was going to be hard protecting Kellan and also being on his lap. I had to make sure he was safe. It was my fault he was in this situation.

"*Kellan.*"

"*Selena.*" I heard his light laughter with the way he said my name and I ducked my head unsure of myself.

Why did this man make me feel like this? What was it about him?

I forced myself to speak. "You have to eat, you said you were hungry."

"I'm hungry for something else now."

Dios.

Right here? Who raised this man?

I covered his mouth with my hand, feeling that glimmer in his eyes somewhere deep and low as he watched me.

"Not here."

His expression changed and all the lust left his eyes, the traces of it lingering but he was...focused now. He nodded as my hand dropped from his lips.

"They're still here. Are you all right?" His question caught me off guard. "You're shaking."

How did he know they were still here? He had not even looked.

Who was this man?

I had not even noticed, but he was right. I could not stop trembling, my body betraying the intensity of the moment we had just shared.

"Was that a lot for you, *Gatita*?" He slid his letterman jacket up my shoulders. "Did you need me?"

I tried not to clench internally and failed. Shamelessly.

Our moment was interrupted by Patel. "Very sorry, Miss Selena. Sometimes, they still come for food only. No problems."

I managed a smile, attempting to extract myself from Kellan's lap, but his arms held me fast like iron bands refusing to let go.

Embarrassment washed over me, and I wanted nothing more than to hide my face.

"Patel, can you get my wife a glass of water?"

Before I could muster a protest, Patel had already disappeared to fulfill the request. Turning to Kellan, I managed to find my voice.

"You can stop pretending, I think they got it." It ached that he did it so well. His eyes went low as he watched me.

"You're sitting on my dick right now. Does it feel like I'm pretending?"

I closed my eyes at the sound of his voice caressing my skin. Molten heat rushed to my womb at the mention of him.

"*Kellan.*"

I wanted to feel him and that hard ridge of him inside of me. I looked around us and noticed people were not paying us any mind.

Kellan's lips brushed my shoulder, a deep, smooth timbre that sank low. "I love the way you say my name."

Why was he so...sexy?

I met his eyes, and his *smile.*

I had been avoiding this all day, the well of emotions bubbling up inside of me—frustration, irritation, desire—all of it wanted him.

I just want to kiss that stupid smile off his face.

So I did.

The moment my lips made contact, his warmth with mine, my entire body sighed.

A moan left me when he brushed his tongue across mine. I sucked on it, moaning louder around him.

What was happening to me? Gasping, I pulled back, and his hands went to my cheek, his eyes wide in awe.

"*Nonono*, don't freak out." Was I breathing hard? He drew closer. "Come here, honey."

I melted into him as his lips touched mine again. My hips moved a little to get comfortable on him as our tongues tangled and I heard him sigh into me. When he kissed me my brain went blank. Completely silent. All of my thoughts muted and underwater. And I felt nothing but his tongue consoling me.

"Here's what I want from you. You sit here. For a few minutes, let someone else take care of you. I asked Patel for water because I think you've got nerves of steel, but even you look like that shit had you worried."

I tried to look away, and he grabbed my face, turning my head to him, his hand warm against my cheek, and kept it there. He was intense.

"No, don't do that. I know why you're stressed out. I got it. I'm trying to take it off your shoulders right now."

70

"Why do you keep kissing me?"

"You're pretending to be my girlfriend. I like to kiss my girlfriend."

And then he leaned back into my neck and he kept his voice low but it felt like it was sinking into parts of me I didn't know I could feel it in.

"I was planning on having this conversation in the car, so let me just have it right here."

Was I breathing that hard?

His fingers tangled in my hair and began massaging my scalp.

I let my eyes flutter shut as he began to speak.

"And since you're pretending to be my girlfriend, let me make a few things clear if you were. I know today was tough on you, *Gatita*. I wish I could go back and break that guy's face in the car next to us. Nobody disrespects my girl like that. Especially not around me."

Oh God, what was he? Some sort of Lena whisperer.

I couldn't pull away because it was like listening to someone who read my mind and he was giving it to me straight.

But then he kept going.

"You brought me here to eat, not put on a show for delinquents. Which reminds me, what deal did you make?"

I didn't want to get into that.

Truth serum. That's what was in his lips.

"I danced at a club."

Kellan stiffened under me His eyes met mine, pupils dilated and pulse racing beneath my fingertips.

"What kind of club? Alone?"

Why did I like the feeling of him getting angry about me?

I told him in Spanish.

"I should've fucking known you could strip," his voice dangerously low, shaking his head like he wanted to do more than that. "You danced and left? That isn't the whole story, is it?"

His eyes narrowed. And I got even hotter. *No.*

I caught a glimpse of someone underneath that golden boy.

There had been an entire riot, and I'd had to shoot someone in my bedazzled underwear wearing a pair of wings.

I had called Reed, who called Gabriel and Nate, and they had arrived not only to rescue me but with the police.

Gabriel had banned me from ever going to clubs like that. And Evie.

And since several of the people who would've been in this neighborhood had gotten arrested?

Patel's family had no issues. I didn't do much.

And since then Lt. Cameron Giroux had tried to ask me out.

Something told me if I told Kellan, he'd be more than pissed. He'd throw me down right here and probably fuck me in his anger.

And suddenly, I wondered what hate sex would feel like with him. I wanted that.

No. He's your coworker.

That sobered me up.

"Listen, Mr College Football, you can—" I gasped as his knuckles brushed my nipple. "*Kellan.*"

"*That's better,*" his voice was dark.

He let go just as fast.

I didn't even see when Patel brought the water over then, and I was aware of how it looked.

I flushed, covering my face as Patel winked at Kellan.

"You need anything else? Let me know."

God bless that man.

I turned to get off his lap, to do anything other than sit here on this man's lap. And he captured my mouth.

How many times had he kissed me now?

Had I kissed him?

I lost count.

His tongue brushed mine, and I leaned into it. Over and over.

When was the last time I had been kissed?

His mouth over mine, softly, exploring, I felt a soft moan leave my lips.

Using that leverage he slid his tongue in and I did not think, I sucked over and over. My fingers threaded with his without thinking.

He pulled away almost instantly, his hand coming to cup my face as he stared at me in wonder.

"Damn." I felt like I was under a spell looking at those true blues. "*There* you are, my good girl."

Why did parts of me squeeze when he said that?

I did not know who reached first.

But my mouth was all over his again.

Slowly, steadily taking his tongue, gasping, and grabbing his hair. I felt electrified all over.

I wanted this man.

He got under my skin.

I wanted him under my dress, *everywhere* but here.

He did more for me with a single kiss than any man ever had.

I can't stop.

I didn't know how long I kissed him. It felt endless.

This was—this was *something*.

His heartbeat under my palm felt comforting, and I felt myself loosening up, and my muscles calmed down.

I couldn't stop as he tangled his tongue with mine, and I couldn't stop.

But he pulled back, his hands running over my hair, pushing it back.

"You said no." *What?* "I just want to kiss you. I didn't want to do anything else."

I didn't know what he was even saying.

"I won't do that to you. Distract me. Say something. Tell me why you saved the restaurant."

All of my emotions were too complicated. I did not understand the first ones that bubbled up.

Not here.

You said no. I just want to kiss you.

On Kellan's lap, his arms wrapped around me, I felt a sense of unfamiliar warmth that was both familiar and foreign.

I had experienced feeling safe with Gabriel and Nathan, but this— *Kellan*—was different.

It was as if every nerve ending in my body was intensely aware of his presence, magnifying the comfort and security I felt in his embrace.

The words came out of me like a steady flow of truth. Truth serum.

That's what was in his lips.

I shared my memories about Patel and his family. Surprise flickered in his eyes as he listened intently.

It's just them in America. Just their little family.

Someone has to protect them.

He looked at me the same way Reed looked at his crush, Alisha, completely captivated by her presence. *I don't think he's pretending.*

When my vision blurred a little, he pressed his lips to my face where my tears tracked, and I closed my eyes for a moment, wondering if I was dreaming.

And I did not know what to do about my emotional response to this man I've only just met.

It was different from how I feel around Gabriel, and the intensity of it caught me off guard.

I blamed it on not getting a real break and working myself to the ground.

But I couldn't leave Gabriel. I had to stay for the team. For Gabriel. I was his Selena.

A Titan.

Kellan's eyes softened with compassion as he asked. "Did they remind you of your family?"

To my surprise, I nodded, feeling like I was in a fog.

"Mi familia era como la de ellos. Un día todo se fue."

My family was like theirs. One day, everything went away.

I told him that Patel's family was on that path when I found his place; he was putting up signs closing it.

He'd been sad. "He is not sad anymore."

As I said it, Kellan's eyes softened on me. "No, he isn't."

I didn't tell Kellan the ache in my chest grew at the thought of, the missed meals, and the gnawing hunger.

But then, a sliver of hope came as I remembered the opportunity that was offered to me, a chance to become someone better, someone different than the hungry girl from Havana.

"You see what could have been," he says, his voice gentle and understanding. I felt shy around him and I didn't know why.

"Maybe you think it is stupid—"

"I don't." When his soft blue eyes met mine again, his voice was low. "I don't think it's stupid at all. Stop biting, baby. It's going to bruise."

The sounds of the restaurant seemed to rush back in, but I was still lost in the depths of his eyes, feeling a connection that I couldn't explain.

"I'm going to kiss you again."

"Why?"

"Because you're sitting here with your bleeding heart on my lap

74

after you kept protecting me all day. Let me take care of you for just a second—"

"But I can take care of myself."

"I know, honey. I'm asking you to let me…for just a second. Do you think you can do that?" His lips stretched into a wide grin, flashing the sides of his sharper teeth—the adorable lion was back as I was thinking about it.

Kellan's grin was wide on me. "Is it alright with you if I kiss you without people watching anymore?"

They were gone? But how had he seen?

He hadn't even looked away.

My head turned to look, and I glanced back at him.

He isn't pretending…

"But they are gone," I whispered, my eyes unable to stop looking at his lips, now rosier from my kisses. "I am not your girlfriend anymore."

Or his honey.

Kellan leaned in then, his lips over mine as he whispered. "But you could be."

Is it alright with you if I kiss you…

"Yes."

CHAPTER 6
KELLAN

My new and old boss, Reed Whittaker stood at an imposing six-four looking like a Greek god who had accidentally crash landed on Earth and decided to live there.

Like he was trying to blend in among people, but he was failing. Nobody carried themselves like Reed did.

His broad shoulders stretched a black long-sleeve shirt rolled up to his forearms, one arm revealing the tattoos he'd gotten more of since I knew him.

He'd been working on that sleeve since he got into the military.

I had known a younger Reed when he'd been my superior. And he was still enormous and scary as fuck.

Those stormy gray eyes were roving over his laptop screen as Garrett and I sat with him just about finishing up our pseudo orientation.

It had taken him a few days since he'd been busy in Midtown and around the city.

In the meantime, I had settled in this mansion.

Reed looked a little out of place among the old-world mansion interior.

Because this is Gabriel's home.

Reed looked like a man who had the potential to wreak havoc and chose not to, his presence filling the room with a sense of something restrained. As always. Restrained violence.

I tried to ignore the hickies on his neck that hadn't been there when he was at the manor when Selena dropped me off, but they were still dark, and something told me nobody here gave a shit about it.

Which was a fucking relief.

Judging by the coffee he was chugging, the dark circles under his eyes, and the way he kept glancing at the wallpaper on his phone screen of a woman tangled in sheets?

He had a girl. And Reed missed her.

Good for him.

I was trying to make Selena mine.

"Watt's, you'll be working with Selena. You already met her at the airport last week instead of Nate."

Oh, I met her.

I heard a sigh as Reed said Nate's name, but Selena was front and center in my head.

Memories of kissing and cuddling Selena at the restaurant flooded my mind, the softness of her skin and the noises she made against my shoulder still vivid in my senses.

After switching positions with her so she'd be against the wall and I could be her shield, she slowly relaxed.

I haven't slept well.

Why's that, honey?

We sat there for an eternity.

The seconds stretching into minutes as I listened to her slowly open up, her words tumbling out in a tired, vulnerable stream.

She was overworked, pushed to her limits, and desperately in need of support. *She needs a break.*

Someone to lean on.

Someone, not Nate.

Whenever her attitude flared up, a spark of defiance in her eyes—I leaned in and kissed her until she melted against me. Until I felt the tension drain out of her.

I could kiss this woman for hours.

If she let me in, I would.

I am sorry for being mean to you. That's not fair to you.

You can be mean to me any day, honey.

As long as I got to fuck that attitude out of her when the night was over, and tuck her into bed with me? I didn't give a shit. Selena all but curled into my side, quietly eating her food at the restaurant.

I pressed my lips together to not grin my 'stupid' smile as she called it.

She had been running on a few hours of sleep when she'd come to pick me up.

Selena mentioned Nathan Wyatt had been with a woman. But not there for Selena? Rage boiled in my veins.

I was here *now*, and I vowed to promise that I'd never let her go, never let her down. If I ever laid eyes on Nate fucking Wyatt, I wasn't sure I could contain the growl that threatened to tear from my throat.

Reed had mentioned finding a replacement for Nate initially and now his line of questioning me made sense, and I knew *without a doubt* that I was the one for Selena. Her partner. Her team.

I could work with her.

Take her home. Fuck her until we both fell asleep. I could do both.

Part of me wondered if she had a romantic relationship with Wyatt, and that's why she couldn't commit to me. But then I realized if she had been?

He wouldn't be getting laid with other women.

Nah, Selena and Nate had nothing between them.

After our lunch that day, Selena snuck a few hundred dollar bills to Ravi, and I ended up carrying Selena in my arms the entire way back to the garage, her heels in one hand.

I spent my time distracting her with questions that made her laugh lightly into my neck.

I can walk.

I know.

So then why are you carrying me?

I'm your partner. Tell me your favorite color.

Pink. Why do you look surprised?

Never took you for a pink kinda girl. Favorite movie.

Dirty Dancing, Havana Nights.

Is it the dancing or is it—

Definitely the actor. His name is Diego like my baby brother.

I peppered her with enough questions to fill in my knowledge about her. And what do you know, once I got her cornered with kisses? Selena. *Melted*.

Nobody takes care of this girl.

I thought I'd flirt with her some more, but by the time I set her down at the garage, I realized the walk, the food, and the time difference had slammed into me. I felt more exhausted than I had when I got off the plane.

On the car ride home, I fell asleep.

I woke up to her gently shaking me. I saw my jacket was under my head, but I didn't remember putting it there.

Kellan, wake up. We are here.

I'm coming, honey.

She'd walked me to the manor , and I had a moment to gap at what the fuck I was staring at.

We work in a mansion?

You'll get used to it.

Reed looked up at me, and I realized he'd asked me a question, the full force of those eyes hitting me.

"Yes, sir."

He nodded as he looked back at his laptop. I had respected Reed when he'd been in the military.

Now, outside of it, I worked for him again. But I understood it was in a different capacity. When I took the job, I knew it meant different things to work for Titan.

For one thing, this wasn't a typical job.

Rules were just a bunch of words cut together. I had signed enough paperwork to know that. I was under no illusion that Reed was a rule follower. He'd skirt the lines if it meant getting what he wanted.

When I say jump, you jump. You don't ask how high.

The other two folks, Garrett, was a six-foot-six Goliath with buzzed blonde hair and hard green eyes.

The third addition to our team wasn't going to need to meet us since Reed had handled all of his stuff personally—*Liam Sullivan.* I knew nothing about Sullivan.

"Garrett, I want you to stick to Mr. Monroe. I'm apologizing in advance for him. Don't let him win when he fights you. And Kellan? You're Selena's. You're the most proficient in Spanish. You'll be good at working with her."

You're Selena's in one way.

Reed paused, giving me a meaningful look. "I expect you to watch her back and follow her lead. She's in charge when I'm not here. Is that clear?" *Crystal.*

"Yes, sir."

"And for fuck's sake, if you see Gabriel, don't provoke him."

Got it. Gabriel was not friendly.

But he was Reed's boss in a way, too. I got that he deferred to him, which was odd, considering Reed owned the company.

And I was living in Gabriel's house.

We worked out of a fucking *mansion* that spanned thousands of feet of land. Every single room dwarfed any house I'd ever lived in growing up. I'd taken some time to process that this was my new…workplace.

I hadn't even met my other boss, Gabriel. Yet.

That's what Reed referred to him. I'd been dropped off and shown the gym and the kitchen and told to help myself. Like a hotel. Only enormous.

I caught a flash of shimmering fabric, black and stunning, at the door.

"Selena—" Reed called out. "Sneaking in?"

He sounds like my Dad.

I sat up straighter as Selena walked into the room.

What the fuck was she—

"How was salsa dancing?" Reed didn't look up from his phone. But I did. I fucking saw Selena Tavares walk in and gut me with that dress she wore.

That wasn't a *dress.* All thoughts left my brain. Rational ones anyway. The ones that involved tearing into her? They stayed.

It was some slinky, sparkly fabric held together by two measly straps. *Straps* that I could snap before using that fabric to hold her steady while I—*Reed is right there.*

She stopped next to Reed, who was standing next to him and peering at his phone.

"It was good," her lips curled into a knowing smile at the screen and then at Reed.

She knows that woman Reed's with. The one he can't take his eyes off.

She took in Garrett with a polite survey. Garett's brow rose slightly, a hint of admiration in his expression. *Don't look at her.*

She seemed to assess everything. *But me.*

80

I resisted the urge to growl. And if she could tell I was getting frustrated, those green eyes finally landed on me. Nervous. Unsure.

You were moaning my name last week.

This week you don't want to know me?

She nodded politely in my direction after a moment. "This city does not sleep."

Neither did she, apparently.

Question was, who did she sleep with when she did?

Reed muttered a small *thank God* under his breath, rubbing the back of his neck. He gave me a look.

"None of us here keep a normal schedule."

"What do you need?" I closed my eyes at her musical voice. I could listen to Selena all day.

If she moved a specific way, I could see the swells of the side of her breasts, her nipples almost flashing. I swallowed, noticing Garrett's eyes on me, and I looked at Reed.

Who looked down at his phone. "Watts got settled last week. Whenever you are ready, you can take him."

Take me, please.

"Mr. College Football," she nodded with an impish grin at my letterman jacket. Or she tried to.

I caught the flash of heat in those green eyes. Reed wanted me to play up the dumb blonde act in this jacket.

Not Kellan anymore? *Hmmm.*

"Miss Selena." Did she just shiver?

It was so subtle. But I caught that.

Hmmm.

I couldn't resist needling her.

I was past *needling* in that dress, though.

Selena looked like suddenly she'd rather run.

Can't be alone with me can you, Gatita? I didn't miss the way Garrett looked at her and then me, his face impassive.

I'd worked with Garrett in Kuwait enough to know he was silent and steady. Always watching my six.

I didn't know shit about him.

I didn't need to. He was always there with support, and on long shifts, he was the one you wanted on your back.

If I got hammered, he brought me back to our trailers.

Solid man.

"Which room did you pick?"

"The Lions Den." It seemed apt. Reed had shown Garrett and me the spare rooms downstairs. Upstairs was Gabriels, and under no circumstance could we venture there. "Where are we going?"

"I need to get changed, and then we can head to the gym. Did you already see the entire manor and meet with Gabriel?"

I had yet to meet Gabriel Monroe in person, but it was clear he spared no expense.

The man undoubtedly had the means.

But something about this house was strange.

There were touches of a lady all around, the flowers and plants, the soft lighting along the ground, and everywhere else.

No fucking way he picked out chandeliers and sconces.

And I swore Selena was nervous next to me being here. Besides, I had seen way too much of her lush tits this morning.

"Are you familiar with the Lion's Den?" She worked here. She had to be. Was it her boots in the closet?

"No," she replied a little too quickly. She is. "Listen, Mr. College Football—"

As she turned to look at me over her shoulder—I *snapped*—I had her in my arms a moment later, crowding her space in against the wall.

My hand instantly going to protect the back of her head as I cornered her.

"Where did you go, *Gatita*?" I kept my voice low. "In that *dress*? Because it wasn't dancing."

I loved the way her mouth parted in a gasp, taking me in.

"Did I leave you so hot and bothered the last few days you had to get relief?" I kept my voice deceptively low. *"From another man?"*

This woman pushed *all* my buttons.

I blamed it on the city that never slept and a green eyed Cuban with enough sass to keep my dick hard forever.

Her breathing hitched as her tip-tilted eyes widened at me. Speechless.

Good.

I took her words.

She took my sanity.

"Is that why you were out all night? I don't blame you, honey. You had me wishing I asked you for your number after you spent that day moaning my name. You asked me what room I'm in. Now you know where to get some relief."

I lifted her into my arms, loving the way she gasped, her legs wrapping around my waist, my cock instantly against her heat.

She feels so good.

"Go on, *Gatita.* I asked you a question. *Tell me why you're dressed to get fucked.*"

CHAPTER 7

SELENA

THIS MAN IS A SAVAGE.

With this *hunger* I couldn't even describe, I wanted Kellan.

He was so cute and there was something about the way he moved around me that got underneath my skin. Or how he carried me to my car. Or the way he spoke to me in general.

I *liked* this man.

I wanted to taste his skin while he moved over me. Inside me, never stopping, and in turn, I would let him have me however he liked. Whenever he wanted. All the time.

I saw nothing but his blue eyes, golden hair, his teeth all over my skin. And. I. *Wanted*. Kellan. Watts.

Hot and feverish, I couldn't make myself calm down like I usually did. *Never*—I had *never* felt this way about a man. And I knew men. My panties were *soaked*.

I was also slightly delirious from dancing all night so maybe it was that. I needed *release* since multiple orgasms at my own hands, did nothing for the hunger Kellan had put into me when I left him last week at the manor.

I wanted nothing more than him to sink into me right then. Take me like an animal. I felt his cock, hard and hot, against my panties, and I panted, fingers gripping his back, looping around his neck.

I wanted to ride this man until my body was sore. Make him, make *me* come, for all the damn frustrations he made me feel.

How dare he?

He ground into me, his lips against my jaw, my neck. I had met him a few days prior, and he'd gotten under my skin.

"What are you doing to me?" The question left before I could stop it.

"Who did you take?" He growled against my throat nipping the sensitive skin there making me shiver. "Until you realized nobody could satisfy you the way I can? Did it drive you crazy like it drove me?"

Yes. It did.

His voice was so low and soft it didn't even sound upset or like he'd judge me if I gave him a number and lied. And he'd probably still croon to me in soft words telling me I'd been a bad girl for taking so many cocks in me.

"Why do you care?" My head was spinning. "*I'm not yours.*"

I'm not your honey.

But you could be.

I imagined that accent in my ear while he worked inside of me. I had imagined it all weekend and then before I *finally* left for salsa dancing.

I needed an *activity*.

One that did not involve me and Kellan naked in my bed. All the time. Heat spread through my body.

His eyes flashed *dark*, and I felt warmth rush into my center.

"You did?"

I wanted to lie. I wanted to protect myself. From him. He terrified and excited me in the best ways and it was even worse to let him know, I had not slept with anyone.

"And if I did?" I hissed back. "Why does it matter?" He doesn't know me.

He just pushes all my buttons.

He growled. "Is that why you showed up dressed like that, knowing you'd see me?"

He ground his body into mine, the sensation electric. I was ashamed of the noise that left my lips against his lips.

"There it is, that fucking sound. I know he didn't fuck like me, *Gatita*. You can bullshit me all you want. You wouldn't be panting on my fucking cock, if he satisfied you."

My lips parted against his.

Dios Mio. Who was this man?

This man was a far cry from the laid back, golden boy grins he wore, and then he did something with his hips.

Stroking me with his cock, like he was fucking me with his clothes on, I gasped against his mouth, as he locked eyes with me.

"I can feel your heat from here. I bet I could slide right in there if I wanted to. And you'd let me, *wouldn't* you, honey?"

Lightheaded off this moment and everything else, I couldn't think straight. I was more than a little delirious right now.

I moaned into his cheek the moment he slid over my clit. He smiled dangerously, working me on his cock, just like that. Every graze of his jeans was heaven.

I moved with him, stamping my lips over his mouth, feeling a rush going through me, sizzling through my senses. My legs shook around him.

"That's good, isn't it?" He dropped his voice. "Now imagine me inside of you."

I was. I already *had*. All weekend and the days leading up to seeing him.

Based on how smoothly he rolled his hips, I knew. I knew this man was a savage in bed. He'd drive me insane. He already did.

I moaned into his mouth, capturing his lips again, unable to think straight, working my hips against that hard ridge until my clit rubbed into it. *Dios*. That was so good. *So good.*

I couldn't remember the last time I had sex, maybe over a year ago. I was already close.

And I could kiss him for hours.

Kellan's mouth drifted down my neck as he groaned. *"Say my fucking name."*

Right here. In the halls. *Anybody* could see us. And that made it hotter. His lips trailed down my neck, down his hands molding to my breasts pressing, and it was electric. I was close. *"Kellan."*

Dragging his head up by his hair, feeling myself get closer. Yes. Yes. *Yes.*

"Kellan, I *need*—" I whimpered into his mouth.

"You need to come, honey?"

"Yes."

I nodded frantically, my lips open in a gasp against his lips.

"Just for *me*. Or was it the same with him?"

It was like a bolt of electricity shot into my body, my eyes going wide in horror.

My arousal vanished, and horror replaced running through my body. I saw his expression instantly change at mine. I closed my mouth, shaking my head out of the fog he put me in.

I did not even recognize him.

Or myself.

I felt the blood rush out of my face, and I began to shake as I processed what he said.

His face fell as he watched me. "Honey, I'm sorry—"

I pushed at him, and he quickly let me down. I was shaking as I adjusted my dress. I looked away as he reached for me. I brushed away.

This is what he thinks of you.

I mean, I let him. But it still *stung.*

I was not his honey.

And I did not do things like this.

A swift wave of embarrassment went through.

Memories of being a woman used by men came back to me. I swiped at my eyes suddenly, and I did not know what this feeling was, but it was agonizing.

I covered my mouth with my hand to keep from making noise. Grateful for my bangs, for my hair hiding my face as I moved back away from him. "*Selena—*"

"*Did you make your point?*"

"*You threw someone else in my face.*"

"*There was no one else!*" I didn't lose my temper all the time. But I saw his expression fade, all the jealousy draining from him. "I went salsa dancing, *pendejo!*"

"Then *why* did you push my buttons?" His throat worked then. Kellan's entire expression was one of confusion, blonde hair messy, and he looked so devastatingly handsome I wanted to scream at him.

Because you push mine. All of them. Who told you, you could come here and be cute? And handsome? Who!

Except I was too much of a coward to say it.

I shoved him back, feeling terrified and embarrassed as I shakily walked away from him or tried to as he hauled me back to him.

"*Wait—*"

"No, you wait!" I turned on him, shoving him back. *"¿Por qué eres tan salvaje? Mr. College Football?"*

Why are you a savage?

I did not even know what I was saying.

Savage.

Since I met him. He was a savage.

"A savage?" He was in my face, blue eyes flashing. *"Why did you let me think you were with someone else?"*

"I don't know!" I was so confused. *"Everything about you is confusing!"*

"I'm confusing?"

"No me toca!" Don't touch me.

It echoed in the hall we were in. I did not care that he reached for me, but I stopped moving the moment the temperature sank around me. It ran down my spine.

A chill skating lower.

Oh.

No.

I knew *that* shift. Everyone did.

"What's wrong?"

I knew when *he* was in any room.

Gabriel.

"Selena—"

I did not hear Kellan. Or feel his hands pulling me to him. His soft words against my skin, my shoulders.

Nothing went through me but the chill in the air.

Gabriel is here.

Hot tears formed in my eyes that hadn't come with Kellan as I caught the familiar back of a designer gray suit at the end of the long hall. He was leaning his shoulder against one of the columns, but I knew that outline. Knew him like the back of my hand.

Gabriel saw me.

"Honey—"

I held up a hand as I watched Gabriel tip his head back.

He knows.

He is going to kill Kellan.

I wanted to tell Kellan to leave me alone. Or fuck me.

One or the other. I didn't know which one.

Except he *couldn't*. He was my new partner.

And he had to stick to me. But this was not how I wanted to meet Gabriel today. Not feeling like this, or even remotely, with Kellan fucking me into the wall.

Even if his body heat felt like heaven at my back. I was staring at Gabriel's back.

How long had Gabriel—No. I knew him. He knew. If not everything, he knows *enough*. I bowed my head for a moment, my back against Kellan's chest, to gather myself.

"I am not your honey—"

"I didn't know—"

"You *assumed*—" I couldn't even say it because I did not know what *it* was.

I saw his head tip over my shoulder. His eyes were soft, those lips turned down a little. "I don't *want* anyone else but you."

This baby.

Jealous and sweet.

But I couldn't continue this conversation.

Our voices carry, and that is my boss.

"I cannot do this right now. I need to change. I can meet you at the Lion's Den after." Big blue eyes met mine, sad as I said that.

"Honey—"

"Por favor. I'm trying—"

I broke off, pushing off him, feeling my heart clench as I strode away from where Gabriel had been standing.

He was out of sight, but I knew he was *there*.

When I walked to the end, I saw him hanging back in the shadows. I followed him into them like always.

Evie always said he resembled a portrait of an archangel named after two. *Gabriel Raphael Monroe.*

If Reed was a force of nature restrained, Gabriel was not.

I knew that much.

His pale blue eyes looked at me curiously.

"Mr. College Football?" He said in that smooth, deep voice. "And here I started calling him Quarterback."

My throat worked as my fingers shook.

The temperature around us was arctic, and I shivered.

I was about to say something when he began undoing his jacket. He handed it to me and waited until I slipped into it.

Without another word, he began walking down the hall, and I followed.

I didn't need to look to see if Kellan knew his boss had witnessed what we'd done.

Because Gabriel had.

And now he had his eyes on Kellan.

CHAPTER 8
SELENA

"I HEARD THE TAIL END OF THAT WHILE I WAS WALKING BY. I WAS GOING to shoot him, but I figured I'd get the whole story from you before I did."

To see how far he had to go.

That was how Gabriel measured his kills.

Thank God he hadn't. I did not ever want to see Gabriel digging another grave. The last man who'd broken into the compound had not left alive.

They never did.

"It's okay, I'm okay."

Gabriel looked skeptical. "Right."

"I am, he was just talking to me."

"With his tongue down your throat."

I turned bright red at the casual way Gabriel spoke. Sure, I heard worse things, and sure, I heard him say things to Reed that made my ears turn red. But I had never been the subject of it like this.

And even if Gabriel had seen me naked once? If not multiple times since then? He never took advantage of me or joked around with me about sexual things.

Not like now.

But I knew even now, he was not teasing.

"It is a longer story."

"Good thing I got time."

I walked with him to one of the spare rooms we had down the hallway.

But the moment he closed the door, I felt my heart rate escalate.

The moment Gabriel walked over to me and I was in his arms? His scent filled my lungs and the tension seeped out of me. Nobody smelled like Gabriel. After that entire moment with Kellan, I felt out of it. Shaken up. Like a margarita in a blender.

Gabriel's large hand cradled the back of my head, his fingers rubbing my hair.

The jacket he'd wrapped around my shoulders swallowed my frame, his cologne all over me.

Over the years, Gabriel's strong arms had been my safety. But right now? *I need a break.*

Gabriel was the only reason I didn't take one. Partially because I knew with Nathan gone, Reed was stretched thin, and the new hires needed someone.

And I was that someone.

I loved Evie, but she was with Liam for a reason.

They are not field operatives.

Nobody had met Liam besides Reed, and that was another thing I hadn't figured out.

But Reed and Gabriel kept their secrets for a reason.

"You went to go get him from the airport?" Gabriel's voice was deeper, smoother. "And now he's making out with you in my house."

Ay. Dios. Cuál es mi suerte?

What luck did I have?

"And when he touched you, you said yes?" Gabriel's voice was a dark rumble. One that promised death. I knew what he was asking.

That single word.

"Si," was all he needed to confirm what he already suspected.

"Si."

Gabriel made a curious noise. For years, I was comforted by him.

"He and I…" I was struggling. "Yo sí dije que sí." *I did say yes.*

"Why? Did he force you?"

Gabriel did not trust Kellan. I could already tell now.

"No," in a sort of ramble I began slowly telling Gabriel in Spanish about Kellan. The airport. Nathan. The drive. The Indian food place. And it all came out. I could not lie to the man.

His eyes saw everything. When I got to today Gabriel made a noise.

"Hm, he's jealous."

I looked up at Gabriel's face now daring a glance, and his eyes were contemplative and cold. They were pale beams in his tanned face.

Many years ago I first thought Gabriel was too pretty to be real. Sculpted lines of his face and those eyes? *Peligrosa. Dangerous.*

Kellan held some weight to him now looking at Gabriel.

Although I didn't see what other women saw lusting after him.

I just saw a man who wore his heart on his sleeve unlike Reed who kept his heart locked in a box far away from the world.

My two commanding officers were polar opposites and the same at the same time.

Gabriel had been the one to save my life.

Reed had been the one to help me build it.

The car, the apartment, the clothes—Gabriel and Reed had both given me a life I could never have dreamed of.

But more than that, they gave me a sense of belonging, a family.

I saw his exhaustion on his face.

The past few months had been hard on all of us. Nathan and I were stretched thin, but Nathan was burning out faster.

As my partner, Nathan was a muscle that I was not. I could fight and shoot and stab, but Nathan was one of the few people who could fight Gabriel.

Which meant he could fight *anyone.*

Reed and Gabriel had been at each other's throats about the team. Never fighting too much in front of us but when it slipped, it did.

And we all knew.

Nathan more than anyone since he broke them up yelling about them being bickering parents or a married couple.

It was always about the team. Gabriel, protective of his family. Us.

Reed was aware we weren't just a family but a team. A unit. And we needed competent replacements to help us breathe.

To Gabriel, we were something to be protected.

But to Reed? He operated the company side of the house. And now, with new members joining our already strained family, I could feel Gabriel's tension radiating off him in waves.

Gabriel looked down at me then.

"When he hurts you, call me. Entiendes?"

And I met his eyes seeing the ice in them. I knew he meant it. Talking to Gabriel was like playing a game of chess.

Every word was chosen carefully.

Everything had a hidden meaning. And by the end of it, he knew more about me than I did about him.

Always three steps ahead. Always dissection.

It was a trap. If I questioned him, it would confirm my desire for Kellan. And if I didn't say anything? I'd be left in this agonizing wait.

He's already seen you.

Gabriel knew exactly what he was doing.

I studied his face as he observed me, gathering data.

Evie often referred to him as an angel, but to me, Gabriel was simply an extremely sharp weapon.Shiny and lethal when he could be.

But one of the greatest operatives I'd worked with.

"When he hurts you, *you* call *me*." His eyes were ice as he repeated what he said to me in Spanish. "*Do you copy, Selena?*"

I realized I had been so lost in thought, I'd neglected to answer his question.

When he hurts you, you call me.

When. Not if.

"*Entiendes,*" I managed to say. I *understand*.

Gabriel had set a trap.

I walked into that one. And he had gotten whatever information he needed out of me from that one moment.

Gabriel pulled me back into his embrace, my head resting against his chest.

My tears had soaked through his shirt, the fabric slightly transparent now.

That's when I saw it—a tattoo I never knew Gabriel had. An elegantly scripted design on his left pec, though I couldn't quite make out the words. Over his heart.

"Never thought I'd see the day a man left you speechless."

Neither did I. I tightened my arms around him.

"I don't know what to feel," I confessed to Gabriel, opening up about Kellan while omitting the more intimate details.

"I just met him, and already my heart is going like a bee, like buzz buzz," I made the buzzing noise, looking up at Gabriel.

His smile got bigger as he looked down at me. His hands rubbing my hair back didn't stop.

"That's not a bad thing," he said gently, his eyes shining warm down at me. Everyone thought Gabriel was made of ice. *Sometimes.*

Sometimes he was this. I liked this part of him best.

He held me closer. "Sometimes that's how it starts."

I turned a little pink, listening to him sound wistful.

"You like Quarterback."

I did.

What about Nathan?

I never told Gabriel my pact with Nathan. He might be angry with Nathan. He was always angry with Nathan.

I just knew I never liked Nathan this way.

Kellan was different.

Sometimes I liked Kellan so much that in the last few encounters I had with him my heart did not know how to function. I just met him.

This was not normal.

Maybe I just wanted him but I certainly did not love Kellan.

Not like I loved Gabriel.

I told Gabriel about the restaurant and how he had become my partner.

"...after he carried me to *Paloma...*" I trailed off. "With my shoes in his hand." I did not even want to look at Gabriel's face as I said the words.

Gabriel's voice was low. "You have complete control over your situation."

He smiled dangerously his eyes so cold I felt a shiver run down my spine imagining all the ways Gabriel would torture Kellan.

"If he knows what's good for him, he'll remember that too."

Sometimes it felt like I had no control at all around him.

When I told Gabriel that, the smile never left his lips. "Maybe he'll prove me wrong."

Which usually never happened.

If Kellan proved Gabriel right, he would end up in the backyard with the rest of the people Gabriel did not hesitate to take out.

I doubted even Evie fully grasped the extent of her brother's capabilities.

Or what any of them were capable of, for that matter.

Just two mornings ago, Nathan had informed me that when Reed went to Midtown, he was tearing into someone for touching his *mujer*, Alisha—his longtime crush on his phone today.

Evie had texted me, mentioning that she was preparing a slideshow for Reed's Alisha, and Nathan was planning to come by later after completing some tasks Reed had assigned him in the city.

Including Nathan cleaning up Reed's bloody messes.

All of them.

I had seen Reed lose control a few times. He was just more controlled than Gabriel.

We never judged him for it since we all killed people.

And because he was second in command to Gabriel, most of Reed's choices were Gabriel's.

Reed took on more than anyone.

Because they were like brothers even though they weren't related. Gabriel and Reed had no qualms about killing in the right moments. Reed just hid it better.

And everyone in Titan had been snapping lately.

Gabriel pushing everyone away. Evie escaping with her life and nobody could blame her. Reed was fighting his demons and they were winning. Nathan sleeping with every woman in New York that landed him in trouble, and me?

I was…crashing. Burning. Tired.

I didn't feel the same anymore.

The team is crashing.

I could feel it. I could do nothing to stop it.

Reed was trying so hard I had seen the dark circles under his eyes, the constant coffee in his hand, and now he was with a woman? He was *trying*.

We all were. I did not want to blame Gabriel. I understood why good enough got your team killed. I knew if we let in the wrong people, we would be dead.

And then Gabriel would come back from the dead to re-murder Reed for letting it happen.

But me? I did not have the ability to tell Gabriel what I needed.

He issued orders. I took them. I was his.

And in return, Gabriel never complained. Not once.

He never took a break. Never stopped.

The haunted look in his eyes as he worked long hours. Some days, I did not know if he took breaks.

In return, I did the same, wanting to honor him.

I had been up odd hours all weekend.

Downtown, I spoke to a few girls involved with the local gangs that told me one of their girls had gone missing at her college.

I needed to go and look into it.

And stop by the Brooklyn Bridge to clear my head.

The stretch of water calmed me down and as much as I enjoyed the city, that was my favorite part.

In the Lower East Side, I got to feel just a little bit better.

The cops would not help the girls in that community. Someone had to. And now Kellan was my partner.

Something told me he would want to be a part of that, unlike Nathan, who let me do my own thing.

Kellan wants to be a part of you. *And I wanted that, too.*

Gabriel's phone buzzed, but he remained motionless. Slowly, I unwrapped myself from him.

"I need to go meet Kellan," I said softly, long moments later, and I caught my slip-up. *Kellan.*

Not Watts.

Fortunately, Gabriel seemed too preoccupied with his phone to notice.

I caught a glimpse of his wallpaper—a woman with dark hair in a red dress laughing—before he shut it off.

He never talked about her, but she was…*she's pretty.*

He nodded, saying. "I need to go."

As I went to return his jacket, he stopped me.

"Keep it. That dress…" he trailed off, a flash of amusement in his icy blue eyes. "…Quarterback is going to lose his mind."

CHAPTER 9
SELENA

I was losing it, too.

I stumbled through the halls, making my way to the Lion's Den while leaving Gabriel's jacket behind in Reed's office.

The thought of walking in there wearing another man's jacket, especially after seeing Kellan's reaction to my dress, made me think he'd completely lose it.

If you saw him with another woman, kissing his smile, you'd feel the same way.

Deep down, I knew I would. I wanted to kiss that stupid smile of his. Again. And again.

Kellan was waiting for me in the Lion's Den.

I had been up all night, and now I could feel the crash coming.

When multiple orgasms at my own hands this weekend hadn't worked, I'd gone to Club Havana, a low-key salsa dancing club run by locals who just wanted a good time.

No guns allowed.

They had just opened at midnight.

You need sleep.

You need release.

You need Kellan.

He could do all that for me.

As I walked, my head spun a little, but I kept going, moving on autopilot.

The manor I had grown familiar with now stretched out infinitely before me.

Gabriel never skimped on any part of the manor. I had no idea how a man in his position had this much money, but over the years, I had made money, and I no longer questioned it.

I knocked on the door, barely able to make out the name.

When Kellan opened the door, the sunlight washed over him, making him appear brighter and broader.

The room was smaller than some of the others, still with a tall ceiling, but it was my favorite. It was cozy.

The light from the wide arched windows flooded in, illuminating his golden hair and drawing me into his bright blue eyes.

He wore a t-shirt that exposed his biceps and forearms. Since when do I notice forearms? And his eyes, that color, reminded me of the beach.

The sky right after the sun came up.

He is so beautiful.

"Miss Selena."

"Miss?"

Why was he—Gabriel.

"I'm sorry," he said, catching me off guard. "I didn't mean to imply...or that you were...I saw you looking pretty in that dress, and I lost my shit. I thought you might've been with someone else. And I guess—"

This baby.

"I'm sorry. I know you're not mine, but I can't stop thinking about you since you dropped me off." He blinked at me, his eyes filled with a mix of softness and something deeper—something that made my heart race. "Did you think about me?"

Madre de Dios.

Who raised this man?

I didn't know how to respond, didn't know how to put into words the way he made my heart buzz with every look, every touch.

I think about you all the time.

All the time.

You were in my thoughts all weekend.

As he watched me, his gaze intense and unwavering, my heart ached at the sweetness in his expression.

It reminded me of Evie when she stared at me, silently pleading to borrow my clothes.

As if she had to ask.

The answer was always obvious to me. I couldn't say no.

Standing there, my lips parted, struggling to find the words to express the emotions swirling within me.

I didn't know what to do with him.

"I figured, seeing as you kiss me the way you do and that you're single and you want me."

I couldn't stop thinking about him, I had not been able to escape the pull of his presence, the way he made me feel alive in a way I never had before.

I told myself it was because I needed orgasms or to get laid. It was just stupid lust. I did not want this younger man who just showed up to Titan with his stupid smile and his stupid abs. It was just lust. That was it.

And I knew I didn't believe myself.

My vibrator had died several times with no satisfaction compared to the feel of him.

I want him so much.

"You're shaking, honey."

Was I?

He stepped closer into my space once more, and I found myself captivated by the piercing blue of his eyes as they watched me, taking me in.

I couldn't move, frozen in place as he crowded me.

"You were up all night?"

I managed a nod, not trusting myself to speak. "Let's just move on, fr—"

"I don't think so," he interrupted, his voice firm as he drew even closer. "When was the last time you got any rest?"

My gaze drifted to the bed, then to my left, where sunlight illuminated rumpled sheets. My previous room.

His jacket was thrown on the end of it, and I bit my lip, imagining him there naked, tossing and turning, and then me with...

Dios. Here I go again.

"I have to show you around."

"Selena."

My head swam, the room spinning around me as I rubbed my eyes. I didn't know how to process any of my emotions.

But I no longer wanted to snap at him or fight him.

I did not want to fight him at all.

Heat circled me as his arms came around me, and I found myself against his chest, my head dropping as a wave of lightheadedness washed over me. Mumbling something, my words slurred together no longer able to keep my head up.

I murmured, my head feeling heavy. "Can take care of…"

Myself. I could take care of myself.

But even as the thought crossed my mind, I felt the darkness I had been fighting all morning finally creeping in, the exhaustion seeping into my bones and the scent of clean linen all over me as I was floating.

I was sinking, my body molding to his as if it had always belonged there.

I felt his arms tighten around me, his strength supporting my weight as my own legs gave out.

"I've got you, honey."

The last thing I felt before the darkness claimed me was floating.

A HAND GENTLY BRUSHED THE HAIR BACK FROM MY FACE, FINGERS running through my scalp, massaging it, deeply. I sighed.

I was cozy.

Nuzzling my face against a firm, warm chest, I was breathing in the scent of soap and a masculine scent. A contented sigh escaped my lips.

"You're all right, honey." His voice was like warm honey drizzling all over my senses. As my eyes fluttered open, I was staring at a white shirt Kellan had been wearing earlier, now creased from my weight.

I mumbled something about having to go somewhere, a vague sense of urgency tugging at the edges of my consciousness.

There was always somewhere important to be…

"We don't have to go anywhere, honey."

He was almost curled around me.

Just a second. That's all.

He made a soft noise in agreement. "We can just be here for a second. Just a second…I promise…"

I felt his breath over my temples.

"A break," I mumbled.

"We can take a break…yeah, that sounds good, doesn't it?"

A break sounded good.

I mumbled something incoherently.

I was so delirious and out of it. Any kind of rest felt great. Especially inhaling his scent.

I felt his smile against my cheek as I snuggled closer. "Go back to sleep, I'm right here."

He moved something over me and held me tight to him and I lost myself.

Tension melted from my limbs, as I let my eyes drift shut once more despite my heart buzzing around letting me know I was in bed with this man.

And he did not move, he kept his arms wrapped around me, his lips brushing my hair pressing kisses into it.

Sometimes that's how it starts.

And I fell back asleep on Kellan Watts.

When I woke up, I was alone in bed.

My eyes fluttered open, and I instinctively reached out my fingers to feel the space next to me, moving some of the blankets off me.

The sheets were cool to the touch, and the indentation where Kellan had been.

I caught a pair of my boots in the open door of the closet in front of me.

So that is how he had known.

He just let me sleep? Next to him? In his arms?

And now I want it…

I wanted that again. Slowly, I sat up, my eyes searching for my phone.

When I found it and saw that it was already afternoon, a pang of disappointment hit me. I knew I had to get up to face the day and whatever responsibilities lay ahead, but a part of me wished I could stay.

As I swung my legs over the edge of the bed, my gym clothes still intact, a sudden thought struck me—

Where had Kellan gone?

Why had he left me alone?

As I splashed cool water on my face, I tried to shake off the lingering sense of unease and the questions that swirled in my mind.

I needed to go find Reed today at some point since he had said he wanted to finally speak to me and Nathan with Evie. I needed to change.

Somewhere to go…always…

The idea of seeing Nathan, his promise, my words still in my head after all these years—now that I had met Kellan…and the way I felt?

I did not know why I was not looking forward to it.

Because I don't want Nathan. I never have.

THE SUN HUNG LOW IN THE SKY AS NATHAN, AND I SAT ON THE tailgate of his truck, the metal still warm from the afternoon heat while I slurped on my milkshake.

Reed had left earlier, leaving Evie to meet with Liam Sullivan. I had stepped out with Nathan, who looked like he was going to be sick.

I had devoured half of mine, my hunger getting the best of me after a long day.

Nathan, on the other hand, held his cup with a distant look in his eyes as if his thoughts were miles away. "Gemma's back."

Reed had tasked him today.

And Nathan was leaving to go be a bodyguard to Gemma Marchand. His *Gemma.*

I watched him closely, remembering the stories he had shared about Gemma and her family.

"She's different now," I said softly, trying to catch his gaze. "You said it yourself, she left her family. Maybe this is a chance for…"

Nathan shook his head, his jaw clenching. "She made it clear she didn't want to see me. Not after everything that happened." He let out a bitter laugh.

The headlines had followed Gemma Marchand's exit from her family. For some reason, people cared about her because her family was one with money.

I did not know if Gemma had money from them, but getting Nathan to work for her was not cheap. She needed someone who could protect her in public without getting into trouble.

I did not think Nathan was the right person, but we did not argue with Reed's choices since I did not know if Reed knew about them.

I read the email Reed had sent Nathan.

Gemma needed a bodyguard to escort her to work events and meetings, and when she left her townhouse, which was gated property,

"You are not the same person you were back then. You've made something big for yourself."

Nathan had businesses in cars, alcohol, and everything I could think of. He had money.

But this was his first time seeing her after being young and humiliated by them. And now she had left them.

"I can't say no to Reed. He already asked me for a few favors and I got in touch with his jewel thief so you know he needs shit done," he said. "What am I going to do?"

Reed's jewel thief was Lucy Devereaux, a woman he had privately hired that nobody talked about out loud. I only knew in passing since she was one of Nate's many partners whenever she was back in town.

What Reed was doing with a jewel thief was beyond me—half the time I did not understand *everything*.

My throat felt like I swallowed nails.

Just go for it.

But if he does, then you lose Nathan, any prospect of babies, and a potential future.

But you don't love Nathan. You like Kellan.

"You can just be her bodyguard," I said softly. "You do not have to do anything else for her."

The good part was our boundaries as security professionals only blurred if we wanted them to.

If we didn't? It didn't have to.

Minus all the women who tried to get Nathan into bed?

Most was his choice.

And then he opened his mouth and asked. "This doesn't change our deal, does it?"

Kellan's smile flashing in my mind.

"No," I managed, forcing a smile with something bitter on my tongue. The sun was setting over his frame, but he was still in the shadows.

Nathan would be thirty in a few weeks.

I had just turned twenty-nine.

And he'd wait for me. But even as I said it, I knew it was a lie.

My feelings for Kellan were there, but no matter how much I tried to ignore them? I just couldn't throw it all away for the big picture. Kellan did not know me. Not all of me.

Nathan knew enough. And he had wanted me. Kellan might not want me the same way if he knew.

Even if I didn't love Nathan.

And he didn't love me. It didn't matter.

Love never mattered for us.

That was asking for a sandwich in the middle of a desert when you needed water first.

I did not have that luxury.

Nathan studied me for a moment, then nodded.

We ate in silence for a while; the only sound was the crinkle of the fast food wrappers and me chewing my burger.

This was still really good.

"This was my first meal in America. It was the only place still open at the shopping mall," I said. "Milkshake."

His expression softened. "I'm going to miss you, *muñeca.*"

Would I miss him?

Over the last few years something was happening to the team. There was this…tension, something coiled, ready to snap.

I needed a break. From everyone.

Everyone was riding on this *edge* and had been pushed to their limits, and we all broke in some ways. I felt far away from the Selena from years ago.

She was somewhere underneath it all.

And she likes Kellan.

I did not even blame Nathan for being exhausted, but I did blame him for dumping things on people. I didn't understand what he was going through. Or Gabriel.

They did not reach out to people. But I remembered Nathan had wanted to settle down and be married and have a family once.

Kellan was good for you.

At the restaurant. Nathan never did that.

Nathan and I would throw ourselves into a fight because it was fun. And then, after, he would get drinks and flirt with me until I threatened to shoot him. Because with Nathan, it wasn't real.

Kellan was real.

He was adaptable and intelligent.

Sometimes, that's how it starts.

Reed would call what Kellan did diffusing a situation.

Reed had hired Kellan to make sure I did not have to push so hard anymore. I knew that.

I also knew he was moving Nathan for many reasons.

He was splitting up Nathan and me to give us a new direction. Nathan went off to his Gemma.

Maybe Reed knew something because he had done his intake interview with Gemma personally, not me, and it had been *long*.

"I'll miss you too," I lied, the words struggling to escape my lips. "I'm just exhausted."

And I like Kellan Watts.

Too much.

"You need a break," he murmured, his deep voice rumbling in the twilight. "You're not Reed or Gabriel. You can't push like this."

But I could take care of myself.

"What about you?" I asked his fingers instinctively tangling with mine. "Are you sure you're going to be good for this?"

"Guarding an heiress who has lunch with prime ministers? It'll be a vacation compared to the last few months."

"Gemma is not an heiress anymore." I was not sure what she was. But she did not look bad like her family. "She is not her family."

"She's not you," he breathed, his words barely audible above the pounding of my heart. "And you're still my wife."

I'm not your honey.

But you could be.

Nathan isn't love.

But does a woman like you get love?

Maybe not.

"She may not be the same girl you remember. Not the same Gemma. You are not the same, Nathan."

"Maybe not," he said, the words melting into the space between us. "But I guess I'll find out."

CHAPTER 10
KELLAN

I'M NOT YOUR GIRLFRIEND.

But you could be.

Selena was gone when I brought her some food.

I got lost twice on the way to the kitchen and finally found it.

Reed had been there chugging some pre-workout, looking like he would rather sleep than go to the gym, but I didn't say a word.

Instead, I ate in the room, wondering why she'd left. If she had work. If she ran. She was someone who needed a firm hand to take care of her.

Someone not Nate fucking Wyatt.

I didn't even know where it came from inside of me, but I couldn't linger on it. Despite wanting to lay next to Selena the entire time I had, I had to eat and take off to meet Monroe.

My other boss.

But when I did, I wasn't expecting a tiny little lady named Evie who introduced us as his sister.

She'd been in these baby blue cloud pajamas, for fucks sake, and speaking technical jargon neither Garrett nor I understood in all the languages we spoke. I thought Monroe was Gabriel.

Who was that man in the suit then that Selena had walked in the direction of? *Was that Gabriel?*

He looked nothing like Evie.

Maybe Nate Wyatt?

But somehow, I didn't imagine the gruff man I'd spoken to on the phone wearing a gray suit.

She was a sweet looking kid with this deep auburn hair, waving down her back answering all of Garrett's questions patiently.

Gabriel Monroe, had his sister working as a killer?

Sensing our unease, Evie's demeanor shifted, her tone becoming more reassuring.

"I'm just here for all your cyber needs," she explained, her voice soft and soothing. "But please, if you ever need anything on that front, don't hesitate to come to me. I am here to help."

"You're Mr. Monroe's little sister?" I had to ask.

She smiled and nodded. "He's around somewhere. Have you met him?"

I think so.

"Grey suit? Blonde? Seven feet tall?"

"He's six-five," Evie whispered.

Oh. Shit.

I fucking had. And he saw me totally nailing my fucking partner to the wall. I hadn't seen anyone who looked similar to Evie so I didn't think I met anyone related to her.

"You've seen him?" Evie asked. *Why did she look nervous?*

"No, Reed mentioned it," I lied smoothly. "Just curious."

She breathed a sigh of relief, the soft sound mingling with the gentle rustling of leaves in the breeze.

Garrett broke off into a conversation about plants and gardening as a hobby, Evie's voice was sweet as she responded. I hadn't even felt him. That's why Selena had looked that way, not *just because of me.*

Gabriel fucking Monroe saw you trying to fuck his operative.

As I was walking out, I saw Selena, her dark hair cascading down her back, her steps purposeful in her thigh-high boots; the bottoms were that designer label.

However, it was the man beside her that made my blood run cold.

Grey suit was Gabriel.

This was Nate. Fucking. Wyatt.

She didn't see me.

The moment I laid eyes on his douchebag leather jacket like some wannabe biker, and his fucking beard, I knew it was him.

This fucking asshole was Selena's old partner?

The reason she was burning to the ground.

I eyed him up and down, my gaze cold and assessing. *I can take him.*

Nate turned his head and caught my eyes as I stared, our gazes locked and he tipped his head walking out with Selena who hadn't turned back to see me.

I couldn't shake the image of Nate's smug expression, the way he walked with an air of laid-back entitlement.

And the third and final fuck you came as I walked back to the Lion's Den.

Gabriel Monroe was walking down the hallway coming up from somewhere, his shirt torn a little, so I could see ink on his left pec.

A name I couldn't make out in a neat script.

In his grey suit looking like a shark with a cut lip, his appearance screaming that he had just gotten out of a fight and was itching for another.

One hell of a way to meet Selena's boss.

His suit jacket was in his hand as he wiped the blood off his mouth, his eyes taking me in. The moment he drew closer, the room dipped several more degrees.

He's fucking enormous.

His eyes, an eerie and unsettlingly pale blue, locked onto mine, and I felt the weight of his gaze as he sized me up.

"Mr. Monroe," I greeted him with a nod.

A glint flashed in his eyes, his lips tipping in a dark smirk. "Mr. College Football."

Oh. Shit.

He knows.

I TRAINED WITH SELENA FOR MAYBE A FEW DAYS.

After I was introduced to the men in Selena's life, I found out Reed's girlfriend had gotten a threatening note at her apartment, and Reed was burning out too fast to track it all without help.

He requested me.

And so I got pulled away from Selena.

I was on Reed's girl so he could do his job because he wouldn't trust just any operative. He wanted someone familiar but competent.

Swiping through Alisha Malhotra's social media, I saw she was insanely popular and beautiful, but that stuff was easy to fake.

But *then* I met her in person. Alisha was *one hundred percent real* as she led me into her vibrant, colorful apartment in a tiny black robe that made her look stunning.

With all her raven hair tumbling all around her, and this luminous doe-eyed hazel looks to her, glowing, making her look unearthly.

Her body dipped and curved despite being petite, maybe at five-three. I ignored the hickies on her neck. She smiled up at me, and I saw *why* Reed liked her.

Not what I expected from Reed, considering he had always struck me as a private person with *don't fuck with me* vibes.

This lady's sweet as fuck.

Did I like leaving my Selena? No.

But Nate fucking Wyatt was guarding some woman named Gemma, so I had nothing to stress about since Selena was holding down the fort at Titan.

And Alisha, who seemed curious about us.

She doesn't know what Reed does.

I could see it in her eyes.

Normally, I'd ask if she was good, but Alisha looked at Reed like she couldn't get enough.

Even in work mode in her apartment, bursting with *this* color and *that* odd-shaped pillow and books everywhere, he would steal glances at her.

That's why he had her on his phone. Alisha would steal glances back and the two of them smiled all goofy at each other.

Growing up with two parents that were in love, I knew they were solid. Here, in *her* space, Reed was in love with her.

Meanwhile, I didn't know what I felt for Selena.

In the week I had been with Selena I learned a lot.

I got to see the entire manor and parts she told me were strictly Gabriels, and I should not under any circumstance go into them.

Especially not upstairs, which was where he lived.

It was a little weird living with your boss, who you never saw, but I was always with Selena and in turn she kept me close to her. And I never saw him.

She did everything with me, and I became her shadow, trailing with her everywhere she went.

In turn, I learned Selena was *sharp*.

She worked out of the kitchen island or breakfast nook, and I snacked often while we did.

I caught Evie in and out making matcha lattes in her pajamas, and the few times I did see Gabriel, he was too absorbed in something.

I saw why Reed had apologized for him.

The few times I'd seen Gabriel tearing into Garrett, Garrett had taken Reed's advice and given it back to him.

Selena and I winced at the way they tore into each other as we passed the gym one day.

And when they weren't off, Evie was on him or in her sunroom, which was a green wonderland.

It threw me off a bit, knowing Gabriel was a different person around her.

Smiling easily at her when she followed him around the manor.

"Evie is Gabriel's heart." Selena had explained to me Evie lived in the side of the house with the sunroom, so we didn't see much of her.

The place was pretty big, and I was pretty sure some parts of it were haunted by how chilly they were.

Selena didn't seem to mind. She walked around comfortably. And in turn?

I gently suggested we should have lunch at work.

"You think we could grab some food," I mentioned lazily. Selena looked up from the tablet she was on and nodded.

Or dinner.

Or breakfast sometimes. And I definitely slid in if she stayed late with me, she could sleep at the manor.

Maybe I kept her late some days to make sure she did.

She did, just not in the Lion's Den, but she was *close* by.

I was determined to keep her on a schedule. I found out that if I told Selena I was hungry, she would drop everything. All the time.

After she slept in my arms that day, neither one of us brought it up.

You are confusing.

I was confusing her? Or was she confused about my *intentions*?

Not that I wanted to know her dating experience, I wanted to at least understand her.

Through Selena, I learned how Reed and Gabriel led and what they wanted.

She motioned to the letterman jacket with a soft look that Reed wanted me to be a chameleon.

But Gabriel would want something else from me should I ever work for him. She didn't know what that would entail from me.

Reed let me take a private car from Titan to the city to get me squared away. I didn't tell Selena I met her old partner. I didn't want to mention Nate fucking Wyatt.

She was fighting me, and I didn't know why.

Unlike Alisha, who I was tasked on guarding, who did not fight Reed for shit.

No, Alisha melted into his arms, and I didn't know he had done it.

I didn't even want to ask him.

One day, Reed wore a suit, and even I had to admit he looked like a smooth motherfucker with his tattoos peeking out, his usually tousled hair smoothed back, and clean-shaven.

Alisha had sputtered as she walked out of her room, and it looked like she hit a wall.

And I knew *that look.*

The electricity between them had me grinning. *Better get out of here before Reed tears her up.*

I beat feet at Reed, waving his hand at me, never taking his eyes off her, and saying something about the sun being out today. I grinned wide at the clouds outside.

I hadn't even left the room when I heard the sound of things crashing.

Maybe if I put on a suit, Selena would be all over me.

Alisha and I spent days together.

She let me raid her fridge, which was well-stocked thanks to Reed's grocery deliveries. "Make yourself at home, Kellan." And from Alisha? That shit was genuine.

For a social media model and actress, she was pretty fucking down to Earth. So I did.

In turn, I switched out with Reed and went home to the manor , where Selena didn't stay, leaving me alone to fall into exhaustion, my thoughts consumed by her presence.

Some mornings, I found myself at Alisha's, trading shifts with Reed, noticing how, despite his tired appearance, he seemed calmer, her scent all around him.

Don't let anything touch my girl. Do I make myself clear? Don't leave her side.

Yes, sir.

During my time with Alisha, I chilled, watched old TV shows, and ate all her food. Alisha was my age but in a different area of life. Alisha was *all* over social media.

My sister would love her *and* her skincare routines, which left Alisha glowing and unearthly.

Instead of being a snob, Alisha had a younger sister she loved and took care of, Avani, something I related to.

We talked about our siblings, what we liked, and everything under the sun.

Alisha treated me like I was her family.

In turn, I treated her like Becca.

I held off on asking Alisha about her relationship with Reed, but seeing the hickies and bruises on her? How Reed looked at her some days, and how close he worked?

I knew I could try and ask her as a woman in a relationship.

But he was my boss.

So I waited until she asked me.

I told her the truth about being at Titan as professionally as I could. And then I talked to her about Selena.

"Mr. Whittaker's good," I said eating cereal on her couch. "He's been nothing but helpful. Everyone there is. I suppose Mr. Monroe can be a little scary, but everything has balance."

I stopped talking when a video of a brunette dancing began to play reminding me of Selena.

"Miss Alisha—"

"*Alisha.*" She smiled at me.

"Can I ask you a question? Would you like Mr. Whittaker if he were younger than you?"

"I would. I like him for who he is. His age wouldn't matter." She paused eyeing me discreetly. "Is there…someone you like who might be older?"

I didn't know if I should admit it so I took another mouthful of cereal. "What did you like about him, if not his age?"

She turned to me brushing her hair back. "Kellan, why don't you just ask her out?"

"I did." Several times.

Alisha's eyes were big on me. "Are you asking me why she said no, or what you can do to convince her to say yes?"

I shrugged lightly unsure of myself. "Both."

"How old is she?"

"Twenty-nine."

And then Alisha stumped me. "Does she want to get married and have kids?"

I blinked as Alisha chuckled.

"She's twenty-nine, which means for many women, it's a time when those without kids feel this pressure. Maybe she thinks that if she doesn't have children with you, there's no point. Or the promise of something more. You're twenty-five, but to a woman who wants children...she might not just want to have a fling, but something serious..."

What? At my expression Alisha quickly explained.

"I'm not saying she doesn't like you. You seem like a really nice man, but you should make your intentions clear. I also think that instead of trying to convince her, it might make your case stronger if you're simply there for her. It's like she's a scared cat—the nicer you are to her, the more suspicious she'll become. But if you happen to leave food out on your porch and walk away..."

She would take the bait.

"*Gatita...*"

"I beg your pardon."

"She'll say yes!"

Alisha laughed, her eyes sparkling a little at me. "She may consider it, yes."

"Miss Alisha—"

"*Alisha*—" Alisha's grin was infectious.

"Thank you."

I ate quietly after that letting Alisha scroll on her Instagram while I watched her edit and post content she had on backlog since she didn't want to do much recently.

My first suspicion about Selena's holdup with me—I thought came down to the fact that she was older than me.

I didn't care.

The only one Titan I wanted was her. *Venus.*

I was twenty-five, and Selena knew that. I didn't know her real hold up, but I thought maybe *that* was it.

Selena never said it, but I saw the way she looked at Reed; he was her equal. I didn't know how to do that if she wouldn't even give me a chance.

Did Selena not think I wanted something serious?

Did I want something serious?

I knew I physically wanted her.

Did I want kids with Selena? I just met her. I knew I wanted kids. A wife.

I hadn't taken the time out to dissect my own emotions.

And I got along professionally with Selena, ignoring the fact we both wanted each other like nothing I had ever experienced before.

I was fine with my situation-ship.

Until I was shot at it.

CHAPTER 11

KELLAN

IT WAS ONE THING TO GET SHOT AT.

It was another thing to get shot at while protecting the woman that mattered the most to your boss.

Reed's going to kill me if something happens to her.

Alisha looked like she'd been through a fight when I got her home.

I scraped my arm and sides raw, and my face was cut up.

But Alisha was alive, and she'd checked in on me several times before I told her to go lay down or else Reed would have my head.

After getting her home safely, I made two calls—one to Reed, bracing myself for the storm, and another to Selena.

I had no idea if she was in the vicinity, but when she showed up before Reed, she was breathless, looking like she ran to me.

Selena had a first-aid kit ready, and I didn't even attempt to resist as she tended to me, helping her remove my shirt to assess the cuts on my body.

I didn't even know how I got cut up on my side.

Gravel was not anyone's friend.

I watched her quietly as Selena took out bandages and cleaned me up, not feeling the sting of the alcohol over her hands burning a trail down to my navel.

Her palm was flat against my stomach, her head bent over me. I watched her blink furiously as she did.

Push you too hard, and you'll run.

Don't push enough, and I'll lose you.

As I was about to speak, Reed burst in, demanding to know where his girl was. I saw his eyes and knew he was in a killing mood. Selena responded by tipping her head, and he moved through the apartment, not sparing us a glance. I watched her, realizing she was biting her lower lip. Hard enough to bruise.

The way she angled her body towards me let me know she was being my shield again.

From Reed?

Alisha had gotten a note before, but I didn't know what it had to do with the shooting. But Reed clearly did.

And I needed to find out.

For Alisha's sake, at the minimum.

I liked her a lot. She reminded me of my mother in a lot of ways. And she was good for Reed.

Just like Selena was good for me. I could tell. She was close enough for me to see her eyes water a little. *Maybe she thinks that if she doesn't have children with you, there's no point...*

"Do you want kids?"

I never factored that into the whole femme fatale image she had.

No, it brought up an entirely different image of Selena. With her bangs out of her eyes, bright as she watched me, her body was different.

Soft. I don't know why, but I could see it. I knew she was in there, underneath the razor-sharp-heeled boots, and her dark energy around her. The real Selena was in there. I wanted to pull her out.

Selena's body stiffened, her eyes growing wide. Like she knew I knew something. *She does want children.*

"I want kids one day. Not right now. But I know you—"

She clapped her hand over my mouth, giving me a haunted look. She closed her eyes as if I had said something painful.

"We can't do this."

"Why is that?" I gently removed her hand from my mouth, refusing to release her from my grasp. "You have feelings for me. I can see it in the way you look at me. *Why are you fighting it—*"

"We are just work partners—"

"Bullshit."

"This is nothing—"

"You don't taste like nothing, Gatita—"

She put her hand over my mouth once more.

Green eyes met mine as I held her steady at her hips. I gently moved her hand down.

"You don't react with everyone else the way you do with me. I'm with you, I watch you, I know what I'm talking about."

And then I lowered my lips, moving over hers.

"I know they haven't tasted you."

When I got inside of her?

Nobody else would matter.

I would be with her for hours, making my point.

Marking her with me. Her fingers flexed in my grip, her eyes looking everywhere but me. *She's nervous.*

She's scared of me.

Why?

"Your hands are all over me. You keep trying to take off my clothes all the time. Now you finally get me shirtless. And you won't look at me?"

I resisted the urge to smile again.

I got the feeling it might scare her.

"I almost got shot today. And the only thought in my head the entire time was that I didn't get to kiss you before something worse happened. I had to protect Alisha, and I did. But the entire time? I just wanted to come home to you."

That I didn't get to have her. Taste her. Her eyes welled a little at that, and I saw her biting down on her lip and her mouth turning down. *Just a little more.*

"What if we just tried it out? It wouldn't hurt nobody, would it?" I wouldn't let it.

Her exhale was a shuddering breath.

"How do you know that?" It was a tremulous whisper, but I had her. I had her right *fucking* there.

Just her and me.

I watched her take in my bare chest, my arm, my face. She was checking me out, but in a way that was out of concern.

Wherever her fingers trailed fire on my skin.

I want this woman.

"We just go with it…" I trailed off. *"Give me a chance, Gatita."*

"Why do you call me that?"

119

My lips tipped up. "I can tell you over dinner."

She turned a little pink as I said the words, and I had her. *Come on, honey.*

Her eyes darted to me. "Just..." I nodded. I didn't know what else I wanted right now, but I wanted her. And she wanted me. "Just you and me?" She can't say it?

Wait...

"Unless you want more than me?" I never took her for the type as she flushed pretty. But I did have a problem sharing.

"No," She turned so pink, I did not see that coming. "Just you."

Just me would have to do.

Her pretty fingers shook as she touched my chest, right over my heart.

Her eyes closed as she pressed her palm flat to that spot. I wasn't opposed to playing dirty for Selena's heart.

I wanted this woman so fucking badly. I could see her thinking about it. Her mind was running through it.

She's considering it.

Now, tip the scale.

"It wouldn't get in the way of work," I said, coaxing. "I'd be professional. Obey you at work. It's perfect."

You obey me in bed.

I would make sure I had my shit together.

And then her shy eyes met mine, looking so far away from Selena Tavares that was a man-eater. *Come here, kitten.*

Her eyes went a little bit hazy. "You are asking me?"

Don't freak her out.

"I am asking you. What do you say?"

She's right fucking there.

The wheels were turning in her head. I nodded slowly.

Her lips parted slowly. "Yes."

What?

At my expression, she smiled shyly. "Yes."

Yes!

And just like that, I had her mouth on mine. Her tongue moved with mine, hungry and desperate, just like me.

Don't run from me, Gatita.

I got you.

I pressed my forehead to hers, holding her steady, crowding her into the counter, keeping her close to me.

Not gonna let you go.

The spell was broken when Reed burst into the room, bombarding me with questions about the shootout. He immediately noticed us.

Great, now my other boss knows I kissed Selena.

But Reed wasn't Gabriel. From what I knew from Alisha, Reed didn't give two shits about who fucked who so long as it didn't get in the way of work. And Alisha. My man had eyes for one woman and she was it for him.

I didn't mind answering, but what I did mind was the way Selena averted her gaze, busying herself with gathering the discarded alcohol pads and bandage wrappers.

Reed asked Selena to go visit some cop and I didn't know why he didn't ask me.

I also realized there were relationships already established among the Titans and this was Selena's job. Not mine.

I didn't have my place yet and right now it was as Alisha's guard. Which Reed entrusted me with.

I watched her leave with Reed's eyes on us.

She said yes.

But neither Reed nor Gabriel hadn't fucked with me yet, not like how Gabriel fucked with Garrett.

But it was his eyes.

Gabriel's eyes held the look of someone who had seen too much and had been through enough to hurt everyone else around him.

Reed dismissed me to go home. To the manor.

And I stayed calm despite wanting to grin like an idiot.

I walked out of Alisha's apartment, knowing full well that Reed was about to tear into Alisha by the look in his eyes.

That made one of us.

CHAPTER 12
SELENA

Lᴛ Cᴀᴍᴇʀᴏɴ Gɪʀᴏᴜx ᴡᴀs ᴇxᴘᴇᴄᴛɪɴɢ ᴍᴇ ғʀᴏᴍ Rᴇᴇᴅ.

And I guess, he was attractive if you were into clean cut sexy cops with hard navy eyes. He usually stole glances at me even when I brought someone with me.

All it took was a rhinestone bra and panties and a pair of large wings Nathan had stared at, impressed.

Men.

Giroux was Gabriel's in, a connection to the NYPD since they had served in the military together.

Reed and Gabriel often went to him for petty things like this.

And in return, Giroux liked to be of service to Gabriel, who had saved his life countless times.

Gabriel had done incredible things in his career, which Reed sometimes mentioned. I just didn't know why he had left it all behind.

Sometimes, when Gabriel talked to Giroux, I got a glimpse of him as a younger man with his teammate.

Today, I was alone, my thoughts swirling with Kellan.

His offer and how I had said *yes* to the want running through me. I needed him. I did.

Nathan be damned. Kellan had been shot at.

And my *entire* body reacted to that.

I wanted him so badly at that moment. I wanted to climb him in Alisha's kitchen and just let him take me.

Take him.

I had been so worried, I was in the neighborhood telling myself it was just to be in the city, but I ran so fast.

I took *Paloma* and drove like *el diablo* was on Kellan's back.

When I saw him alive and safe, I couldn't hold it back. *Haven't even gotten a chance at you.* Wanted to kiss his sweet smile off his face. I held back this entire time.

Because of that promise to Nathan, I did not want to.

I didn't understand why he scared me, but he did.

He terrified me today when he gave me an offer, and I don't even know how or why I said yes.

The fire in me was gone when I realized I couldn't be mean to him.

And everything after that was, as Nathan would say, *a slippery slope.*

I am losing my mind.

I had to focus on the Lt since he had stopped what he was doing to take me as a caller.

"Miss Tavares," he took my hand. I politely shook it, not missing the way he checked me out. He was not my type.

No, I only wanted one man who smiled like I had said something funny all the time. And his sharp canines. I shook Kellan's beautiful face out of my head.

"I need you to drop the shooting…"

And I cut to the chase, not missing the way he snapped into business mode.

His blue eyes so different from Kellan's not missing anything I said. He frowned.

"Reed wants that?" He looked down. "I can give you the bullets our guys found, but I don't understand what the random shooting has to do with anything you guys are doing."

We did not either but it did not matter.

Reed asked. I moved.

Either way if Giroux did not do what we said, Gabriel would come down here.

I did not tell Giroux about the note until it turned out to be something more.

And something was bothering me in my gut to know two things like this had now happened to Alisha.

When he tried to ask me out I politely declined. I was not a bitch to Giroux because deep down I think he had good intentions.

But he never made me feel like Kellan.

I would find out what I needed to know by asking around. I knew where to look for any shifts in the city like today.

Especially since I told some of the girls, I would check out their claims downtown of a missing girl.

Reed went to the police.

I went to the streets.

When I first started at Titan, Gabriel had told me that every single person he hired had their own strengths.

His and Reed's were opposites, so they worked well together because they balanced each other.

Nate and you balance each other in your own strengths. Don't try to change and be anybody but you.

Gabriel understood that people, when they focused on their best and their strengths, made a team, rather than one person trying to be everything. He didn't do it, and he didn't expect us to.

I pushed Kellan's offer and his smile out of my mind when I went down to the Lower East Side, to a part of the city where I knew I couldn't dress like Gabriel's Selena.

I had changed.

I had traded my shoes for a tank top dress and low boots, topped with an oversized jacket and a ball cap to blend in seamlessly with the locals.

Making my way through the streets, I found myself drawn to the group of teenage girls I had befriended.

They hung out near the private college nearby. Vibrant murals decorating the brick walls caught my eye.

It was an old-school Latin neighborhood, and it reminded me of my own.

The artwork depicted scenes of Puerto Rican art, flags of all over Latin America everywhere, portraits with bold colors and intricate designs.

It reminded me of the houses in Havana.

The sidewalks lined with street vendors. Carts overflowing with fruits or jewelry. Sometimes, when I worked around the Titans, I felt like I was losing myself. I would never bring anyone here.

This was my *slice of life,* as Nathan would say.

But I had not even brought Nathan here.

Distantly, I could hear the screaming children playing in the local park, the loud and lively conversations in Spanish spilling out from open windows, and the distant sound of a band practicing in a nearby park all blended together.

Where Gabriel lived, the street was silent. He said it helped him think.

Sometimes, it drove me crazy.

I loved this. Every now and then, a passing car would blast reggaeton, its bass thumping, and I knew I was not in Greenwich anymore.

Not a Titan anymore. *Just Lena.*

And I liked this sometimes.

I pretended to be one of the girls in the private college nearby and started chatting with them to see if I could pick up if anything was happening in the streets.

I had never been to college, but it was fun pretending.

All I did was pretend.

And the girls talked to a Latina. *Use your strengths.* Gabriel's eyes flashed in my mind.

Don't try to be anyone else on the team.

Just be you, Lena.

When I got there today, there were two girls on the curb.

High school students and seniors, one with curly hair and glasses, the other dark haired long and straight like mine to her back. Both of them were Puerto Rican.

The curly-haired one, Valeria, turned to me with an easy smile.

"Oye, Lena."

As I smiled talking to them, I was reminded of times like these in Havana.

With women who looked like me and talked like me. Sometimes like this…when I was with these girls, I felt normal.

I was *Lena.*

Nothing special. And my heart liked that.

We just bullshit and talk about silly things on the block. And it felt more familiar some days than being a Titan.

Did you want this life?

No.

But now, it was all I knew.

I asked them to tell me about the missing girl.

Diana.

I mentally took notes on how they said Diana hadn't been seen in two weeks.

She went to the college Downtown I was supposed to be attending. Astor University. Private school. *Fancy.*

Clara mentioned. "*...there are shitty cops who come around sometimes, but that's nothing new.*"

As she said in Spanish, she told me about how the girls around here didn't like the cops. I could talk to Giroux about this.

I didn't know what the shooter had to do with Alisha, but Reed admitted someone was after Alisha because of him.

There were plenty of shitty cops all over the city, and that kind of information wasn't particularly useful to me.

I needed something substantial, something that could actually help me with my investigation.

I told them if they heard anything to give me a call. No matter what it was. *Someone has to protect them.*

Just like Gabriel protected me.

When I looked down at my phone, I was surprised by the text.

Kellan

> Reed sent me back to the manor tonight.
>
> Just thought I'd let you know I was safe and sound in my room.
>
> Nothing to worry about.

I read the message. Re-read it. And re-read it three more times. He was at Greenwich...I mean...I was planning on going back to Titan either way. It would not hurt...

I could always check on him and get some work done after making sure he was safe. I told myself it was just that. And not his voice in my head. *Not even Nathan.* With Nathan gone? He never even crossed my mind.

It also allowed me to be with Kellan without Nathan crowding into it. If he had been around?

126

I didn't even want to think about it.

Just go with it.

I'm asking you.

Give me a chance, Gatita.

*I know you want this too. I almost got shot today...*And I had *wanted* him.

I had wanted nothing more than to skip going to Giroux and pounce and tear into Kellan.

Kiss his smile.

And so, somehow, I found myself going back to the manor. Somehow, I was walking up the garage. Somehow to the Lion's Den.

I did not even remember the drive here; it was just Kellan's smile in my mind.

I saw Evie's car gone.

She'd been gone every so often now. And I was happy for her getting out. Even if she was hiding her hickies in hoodies.

With a man. I only hoped Gabriel did not catch on. But he had been preoccupied lately, too.

I walked up mindlessly somewhere, anywhere but my thoughts. And his smile. A smile I did not know if I would see again. And I just *moved.* The house layout just a memory I followed.

And then, I was in front of the Lion's Den, my fist raised and knocking. My hands shook.

What if he didn't want me here? What if he didn't want this the way I did?

The door swung open a moment later, revealing him in all his towel-clad glory, fresh out of the shower.

The sight of him all golden-skinned, blonde hair, those blue eyes on me made my throat work.

He is beautiful.

At that moment, *nobody* else mattered; I lost all sense of what I was doing, my body moving of its own accord. Nathan did not matter. I did not want Nathan like this man.

There was no other thought than him.

Kellan.

Before I could even process my actions, I had already closed the distance between us, my lips crashing against his.

He almost got shot today.
He could've died.
Did anyone else matter?
No.
Nothing else matters.

CHAPTER 13
KELLAN

SELENA IS KISSING ME.

She was in my arms. And she looked *edible* in that little dress.

I was inhaling pink pepper and lychee into my body as I let go, giving myself over to this woman.

This fucking lady who took my breath away.

Every. Single. Fucking. Time.

I slammed the door shut, locking the damn thing to make sure we didn't get visitors. Blood rushed down to my cock, as I just absorbed her. Soft. Supple. Toned in some places. And just fucking perfect.

My hands ran down her body, her waist, her hips to the taut globes of her ass, bringing her close to me.

Dropping my towel, I walked her backwards, never leaving her mouth. Eating at her like a starving man. I was still dripping from the shower, and I didn't give a shit. I didn't care about anything but her.

Selena.

My cock lengthened and thickened with every step.

Without her heels, she was *probably* five-five and fucking adorable the way she fit against my frame. I towered over her now without her heels.

I love kissing this woman.

And she fucking loves kissing me.

She kissed me like her life depended on it. I tucked her body, feeling all her soft curves molding into me, melting, and calming me down.

All my nerves were fried after holding Alisha down to make sure she didn't take a hit.

I felt like I was gonna get hit for a second.

And if I had? Alisha would've been vulnerable. I didn't want that.

But I think Selena felt the same, judging by the desperation.

The heat in her kiss escalated the more our tongues tangled.

The intensity coasting over, and I found myself responding with equal fervor, knowing that if I didn't reciprocate, she might stop existing.

And if she were to stop? I didn't even want to think about that.

I had come back and changed, and after my shower, I heard the fucking knock at my door.

Did I guess it might be her?

I fucking hoped. I did.

And she'd launched herself at me. I couldn't think anymore.

Come to Daddy, honey.

When her knees hit the bed, I was about to move us when she pulled back. Her eyes were dark and low-lidded as her hands moved to her dress.

My eyes went wide, pulling back.

"*Gatita*—" I stopped as she whipped the dress over her head, leaving her with nothing. *Nothing.*

My brain stopped working as I held a naked Selena in my arms. "You sure?"

My eyes raked down that stunning figure of hers, her rounded breasts, tipped in peach, her waist dipping, hips fanning out, and that little—I groaned, not even surprised she had tan lines.

Summer just ended. I was going to lick every bit of her.

My cock was painfully hard, and I know she felt that.

Those eyes met mine with complete surrender, and she swallowed. *Why was she shaking so hard?* "Kiss me."

That's not the same.

With one hand, I gripped a handful of her long hair back, dipping my head to look at her, feeling her nipples against my chest.

Loving the way her eyes closed for a second as I tugged gently.

Oh, honey, you're going to love me.

"*Gatita*, answer me."

Her eyes fluttered open. "*Yes.*"

130

I slammed my mouth into her, hauling her onto the bed, grappling until I ended up over her. My hands were all over her.

There was a desperation that I know I felt today at the prospect of not tasting Selena.

Not ever having her.

Being inside of her.

I *knew* she felt the same thing.

She wanted to jump my bones. Since day one. And I couldn't put my finger on why she hesitated with me.

Because she was scared? Even if I saw in the glances she stole. I texted her because I wanted her to find me.

Come and be with me, honey.

Up until Selena, I never imagined that making out with someone could feel all-consuming.

It was as if the world around us had faded away, leaving only the two of us lost in the depths—and I drowned in her for long moments.

Desperation fueling half of it, but the attraction from the first day.

She was gasping. "*I never kiss anyone like—*"

"*Me either—*"

I went back to her hungrily, not even touching her, just absorbing having her under me. I trailed my mouth down her throat, loving how she moaned as I sucked, licking a path to her nipples.

Taking one in my mouth, I massaged the other, groaning.

She let out these fucking whimpers as her hands tangled in my hair, tugging gently enough. I sucked harder. My fingers worked lower, finding her clit.

Her response was electric. I bit around her nipple. "You're soaked." My fingers circled her clit, sucking at the same time focused on making her feel good. Making her feel me.

"*Kellan.*"

'That's right, honey." I heard her moans, her whimpers, my *name.* "Say my fucking name."

I kept going, switching and giving the other one the same treatment, my dick harder than steel, grinding down automatically on her thigh as I worked.

With a groan, I pulled away. Loving the way she moaned and gripped my hair like she was tugging me back down.

I'm not done with you.

She panted, and didn't she look fucking beautiful like that, and I kissed down her body, her stomach, her hips, lower until—

"*Wait.*"

I stopped, pressing my chin gently to her lower belly, looking at her, watching the flush from her body coast all over.

"What's wrong?"

Her eyes were closed as I felt her shake all over.

"I never—"

What? Had sex? No way.

I mean, no judgment, but I knew my eyes were wide. She wielded her sexuality like a weapon. Even if I knew it was just an act, her armor?

This woman in my arms, in my bed, was the real Selena.

I was patient.

Pressing my lips to her stomach, I loved the way it quivered. My dick could wait. I never thought I'd imagine Selena shy, but she was.

I guess I could see Selena as a virgin trained to be a spy. I mean, I would still be good to her no matter what she was.

Why was she—Her hand moved over her pussy. Batting me away. Trying to push at my head.

She shook her head, looking adorably shy.

Then it *clicked.* I could feel the dark parts of me rising and coiling, settling into the way she squirmed, her thighs shaking even harder.

"Nobody's ever gone down on you before?"

Oh. Shit. I felt the slow grin spreading on my lips. The one that made her blush and turn ten shades of tomato red.

No. Fucking. Way.

She nodded, blushing ten shades of red, unable to look at me.

A soft noise of appreciation left me. It was like my fucking *birthday*.

I privately tucked away that Selena had only ever been with idiot fuckbags.

And I'm determined to not be one.

I grinned into her belly, loving the way she shook, resisting all my darker urges to tongue fuck her wildly for her confession.

Later on, I would take a minute to dissect why no idiot had ever gone down on her before, but it didn't even surprise me that the men she'd been with were scumbags who used her.

That's why she was so fucking afraid of me.

I was nothing but kind to her for that exact reason.

Selena's never had anyone eat her out?
I could sigh with happiness.
Today was *my* fucking day.
And all it took was getting shot at?
Bet. I could barely talk around how I felt right then.
"Can I taste you?"

CHAPTER 14

SELENA

I CANNOT BELIEVE I'M TWENTY-NINE, AND NO MAN HAS EVER DONE THIS to me.

But most men did not sleep with me for anything other than my body.

Just to use me like an object for their pleasure.

I did not realize until recently I had avoided sleeping with men when I realized my pleasure would never be catered to until now.

I couldn't even look at Kellan right now.

"Do you want to try it with me?"

Who is this man?

I was shaking with the need in my body. Why did he not just get inside of me and get it over with?

That's what everyone else did.

Kellan is different. He is kind. He may like you.

But that is scary.

Because if Kellan likes me, there's a possibility of him not liking me. If he doesn't like what he finds.

"I don't think you should," I mumbled.

"I think I should—"

"Maybe not—"

"Maybe I could—"

A soft noise left him. I did not know what that meant.

Kellan's hands were warm against my thighs, his touch sending shivers through my body.

I swallowed hard, my heart racing in my chest. His tongue traced delicate patterns on my belly. The wet sensations delightful to my senses. Electric. Igniting a fire within me that threatened to consume me entirely. But I was nervous.

Shaking.

Unable to stop trembling. Men were not known for being nice. I learned the hard way that besides Reed and Gabriel and the Titan men, most men in the world wanted nice things so that they could break them. And then they would find a new toy to break.

But not Kellan.

He would…like me? Maybe.

How would that feel?

"What if you like it?" His voice was wicked and low over my stomach, the heat of his breath making me shake.

"What if you don't?"

"What if I do?"

His chin rested gently on my stomach, his eyes wide and filled with an adoration that stole my breath. Kellan's eyes held the same glint from the airport.

"Are you laughing at me?" *What was I even doing?*

I tried to shift away, but Kellan remained, his hands tightening on my thighs.

"No, I just think you're adorable."

Squeezing my eyes shut, I pressed my hands against my face, trying desperately to hold back the emotions I felt. The tears I felt slowly seeping into my eyes. I did not feel confident.

I had been so confident earlier.

What happened to her?

Why had I said yes to this?

I felt so out of my depth, like a fraud playing at being the confident, self-assured woman I pretended to be in the glossy pages of magazines.

I was stripped off all things that made me—*me*. And I felt nothing but anxiety.

Kellan made a soft noise, pressing his lips to my thighs, and spreading my legs gently.

All I had wanted was to come here and lose myself in his kiss, to let the world fade away until nothing existed but the two of us, just like I had longed to do back at Alisha's apartment.

I'm in over my head.

"Kellan, I think you should—" I gasped at the sensation of his tongue against the most intimate part of me.

That feels so good.

He did it once, twice, licking at it, and then with a groan, he spread my shaking thighs wider, and the moment his tongue speared into me, into my body for long seconds, I felt a wild noise leave me.

I was shaking now for a different reason, my heels digging into the bed hard.

"You were saying?" A whimper left me. "Sorry, I got distracted by the fact that you have tan lines here but not your nipples."

What? And then he kept going, his tongue a different sensation that felt so sweet I moaned.

I hate all men. All men except for him.

I gasped, my hands tangling in his hair as he growled. "Just want to figure out where you're walking around topless. Who gets to see my girl's beautiful tits like I do."

I fell asleep for a little longer in the sun at the beach on a trip to Spain. I couldn't think straight as he went back with his tongue.

I moaned his name as he chuckled low. "Selena, I don't think you realize who you're in bed with."

No, I did not know this man at all.

And then he sucked my clit into his mouth, and I screamed a little.

"*Kellan.*"

He was relentless as it built low in my womb. Something that I only have to do with myself. I never had an orgasm with a man.

None of them cared, and most of the time, I faked it because the experience was painful.

This was new for me.

His tongue thrust into my body and a relentless current of bliss coursed through my veins. I couldn't stop the noises I was making. Gasps, moans, and embarrassing squeals as he worked me like a savage.

"Should I stop?"

No, never. Don't ever stop.

"*No.*"

I clutched at his blonde hair, meeting his eyes a little wilder now, dark blue and even darker with desire. His mouth pressed to my inner thigh as he watched me, more animal than man.

Untamed. *Savage.*

And I loved him like this.

"Don't stop."

I caught his smile as he went back to it, and I moaned, clenching my fingers into his shoulders, his hair, anywhere I could reach. His tongue was taking from me like he couldn't get enough of me.

I had never—*never*—*I had no idea it could be like this.*

For long moments, he just did that. And I couldn't stop crying out in pleasure as it coursed through me. It had *never* been like this.

And then I felt the press of his fingers, gentle, firm, and sliding into me. A noise left me at the sensation of him, stretching me just from *that.*

"It's okay, honey. I'll take care of you."

His fingers took up space. I felt him against my stomach, my thigh, earlier, and he'd been huge.

I felt them curl into some part of me as he sucked.

Somewhere sweet and sensitive, only I got to.

My stomach was trembling, and my thighs even harder.

Nearly threatening to close as he growled over my skin, sucking and working his fingers in a way that made my hips work shamelessly against his tongue.

Relentlessly.

I sobbed his name into the pillows.

As the pressure built to a crest, I clung to the sheets. I was right there, just *there*—about to tip over as his fingers hit that spot over and over and *over.*

"That's my girl, let me fucking have it."

And I came from that, crying out. Ripples of pleasure pulsed through my being as I screamed into the pillows unable to hold back as my hips bucked into his mouth.

"Kellan."

Don't stop. Don't ever stop.

"I'm not going to fuck you tonight. I just want this." He didn't stop as he used his tongue to lick every part of me.

Noises left me that I knew were embarrassing. I pushed at his head a little. Electric streams of pleasure raced through me at the touch of his tongue.

"Sensitive?"

Yes.

A little yelp left me as he sucked harder, his tongue flicking my clit with a pressure I didn't imagine would make me scream. Pleading with him to *please come up here.*

My legs had never shaken so much. A noise left me as I gripped his head, trying to push him off.

Instead, he slipped his fingers out, and both of his arms banded around my waist, keeping me still.

That felt *incredible.* His sheer strength holding me down felt like heaven as he ate at me.

I could not dislodge Kellan as he followed my hips, growling and holding me down as I sobbed through the sensations. *Kellan.*

This is intense.

My back was arched as I gripped the sheets, my entire being pulsed in his mouth as I shook noises leaving me wildly. "*Kellan!*"

It was endless, and I lost it.

I let out a longer scream as I came again on the heels of my previous orgasm, my abdomen clenching and my hips working in his mouth, and he made a noise of appreciation, taking me in.

I felt that against my clit as I came harder this time. Even harder than my first orgasm and it was relentless.

It went on and on as he growled against my clit.

I felt *everything.*

This man is a savage.

I was a throbbing mess, my entire body shaking with the pressure, when he *finally* let me go.

Tears flowed down my cheeks as he trailed his tongue slowly across my trembling thighs.

My stomach was quaking as he worked his way up. The feeling of his weight sinking onto my body was a relief.

The first flick of that tongue to my nipples, an animal noise, left me as he settled like a hungry lion over my body sucking.

"*Kellan.*"

I was going to die. I sobbed as he didn't stop. It was—

"*No.*"

I felt him wiping my eyes as he dropped his lips over mine. And he kissed me hungrily, shaking as he settled his body over mine, hot heat against me.

"How's that for your first time?"

I felt my cheeks heat at the implication. I couldn't even speak as I kissed him. I was ruined.

Once I had him, I couldn't stop.

CHAPTER 15

KELLAN

THAT WEEK, I TOOK SELENA OUT TO A COZY CUBAN RESTAURANT THAT Alisha had recommended.

Alisha had a lot of options and choices for me but she suggested this one since it was cozier and she liked smaller businesses instead of fancy shops.

Despite being a multi-millionaire in her own right, Alisha was down to Earth from her upbringing and had stayed that way.

I hadn't told her about Selena. I just wanted some pointers.

The moment I took Selena though and we stepped inside, I was taken by the colors *everywhere*. I could see why Alisha liked it so much.

Selena's eyes lit up as she took in the décor and the family photos adorning the walls. The warm glowing lights, the decorative pieces all around us.

Thanks, Alisha.

"What's your favorite Cuban dish?" I asked her after we sat down in a cozy nook.

Selena mused, her emerald eyes alien bright on her face. *Oh fuck, she's beautiful.*

"I can't decide between the picadillo because this is my Mama's favorite—"

So the stewed dish with meat and potatoes.

"—Or the tostones. Because the tostones here are delicious and they fry them nicely and salt them after and I like the taste of that."

She picked one of the fried plantains up, popping it into her mouth and nodded. I bit my cheek to not laugh like a fucking *loser*. But I was absolutely fucking smitten with this girl.

She's so adorable. My heart was gonna give out because I just wanted to cuddle her right then and there to me.

"Your family lives in America still?" She asked, her eyes meeting mine with genuine curiosity. "Your sister and mama?"

"My dad too. My parents moved us from Dallas to Virginia for work when I was a teenager. But I was in the military for a bit…"

I talked to her about my parents, telling her about my middle-class upbringing, before making my way overseas to jobs that paid a lot more money for muscle.

I did in fact play football, but in high school. And something about growing up with two parents with a penchant for trouble and solving crime and led me into this life.

"Your parents are together?" Selena inquired, her head tilting slightly. "And your sister is with them?"

"They are. They work in the BAU, the behavioral analysis unit of the FBI," I told her about Becca being an immigration lawyer, and her eyes lit up. "What about yours?"

"No. My mother is in Miami. But that is all." She told me it was just her mom. She told me in the Indian restaurant a long time ago her family had been…a family. And then one day it was all gone.

There's more.

"You don't gotta tell me, honey." I got that it was painful for her. And for Selena it meant a lot to guard her heart. That's all she did.

"My father, he was with Diego. It was evening, and they were coming home with some groceries. I think Mama was missing something from her recipe. Papi said he would go and get it and Diego begged to go with him…" she broke off blinking.

And they'd died. She didn't need to say anything else. I saw that look on a lot of people's faces.

She stared down at her *tostones*, her tongue playing on her teeth as she blinked. "I did not have anyone but my mother."

Selena told me she had grown up without a father or a male figure in her life, a fact that didn't surprise me, given her fiercely independent nature and her need for taking care of others.

Her brother was younger than her, and he was killed.

141

She probably raised him based on his age. Loved him. Lost him. Her father. Selena wasn't going to let just any man in.

If anything happened to Becca, I would murder someone.

What had Selena done?

"What did you do to take care of yourself and your mother?" I asked gently, my heart aching for the girl she was. I want to hold her now. "That couldn't have been easy."

Not many opportunities for a girl her age in that state of living.

Selena paused, taking a sip of water as if to gather her thoughts. Something passed through her eyes.

"Everything," she said simply, a small shrug accompanying her words. "Anything." Her smile didn't touch her eyes. "I do not want to talk about sad things. I don't like to."

And in that moment, I understood a few things about the weight of her confession. Saw it in her eyes.

Little girl from nowhere scrambling to make ends meet. So, a hard knock life. And that girl became this woman. Split into two.

One the world got. And one I got. Selena had been CIA before me. So she was good at her job. Scary good.

"I don't care," I said it low. Her eyes flickered to me. Soft green. Light. "I don't care *what* you did, it doesn't change how I see you."

The words seemed to be suspended in the air between us.

I meant it.

I was a former contractor, I wasn't a stranger to what Agency spies did. Or what a body like Selena's and a face with eyes like that got. Not easy jobs. No. She was an asset. Every part of her a weapon. And she knew it. I didn't think anything less of what she had done to put food on her table. I never would.

She needed to know that.

"How?" She said softly to me. "How do you see me?"

Effervescent. Beautiful. Lush.

Mine.

I hadn't known her for long. But I trusted my instincts and my gut. I was damn good at reading people. From the day I met her, she'd been nothing but a good partner. In more ways than one.

Selena adapted to me and I moved with her. Partners.

A team.

It was as simple as two puzzle pieces fitting together after being thrown apart in a set of a thousand. I would recognize her as my other half in the pile. Every. Single. Time.

Nothing would stop us from finding each other eventually. I knew that. I wasn't a dumb blonde.

But the words words caught in my throat. My lips parted as I watched her take me in, her eyes growing wide like she could see it in my face.

I caught every bit of it as she adjusted in her tiny black dress and those suede thigh-high boots in the warm restaurant conversation bubbling around us.

I began coming back to Selena in the manor in my bed or waking up at night to feel her sliding across my body, cuddling deep into me. By *herself.*

Curling into me like a curious kitten. I smiled at the thought. I relished those moments because she was slowly trusting me.

She was beginning to let me in. I held her to me all night, inhaling her scent all over, her hair on the pillows, and her face buried in my chest.

Both of us too fucking exhausted to do anything but sleep together like sun-warmed lions.

And after that night, I didn't want to push her, telling my dick to behave and to calm the fuck down and not freak her out anymore.

This was our first date. Life had settled a little for Alisha and me, so I had time to date my girl.

While out, she caught the eyes of men staring at her, and I didn't give a shit because she was mine.

I was only jealous when she wasn't.

Now? She was my honey.

I didn't give a shit about anyone else.

She chose me.

Halfway through the night when a group of guys had come in, I asked her gently to move into my arms and when she did she willingly nestled close.

Her body molded perfectly against mine, her biting that lower lip of hers casting wide eyes at me.

"You wanna know how I see you?" I whispered to her.

She nodded slowly. Unsure.

Damn, she's cute.

Pride swelled within me. I fed her guava ice cream that I wanted to taste on her, in her. I whispered that to her loving the way she turned pink, kissing me quietly.

"Like someone I want to love," I murmured in her ear, against that spot of her neck I knew made her shiver. "Like someone I want to keep."

In response, Selena snuggled even closer, and I saw her walls slowly shift. "Can I keep you, honey?"

Her eyes met mine, wide and vulnerable then. I held up the spoonful of guava ice-cream.

"I can do that." She motioned to the ice cream and me feeding her.

I felt my lips curve. "I know you can, but let me, just for a second."

Let me take care of you.

She bit her lip and nodded. Unsure emotions written all over them I intended to change. I intended to be there for her starting now.

I didn't miss the way men watched her. In my arms. And they could stare all they wanted because she was mine.

I wouldn't let her down. I didn't want to hurt this girl. I just wanted to love her.

Tonight, I had foregone my usual letterman costume, opting instead for one of those designer sweaters in my closet I got from Reed. Something casual since Selena liked that from me. Reed spared no expense for his Alisha.

Once I had settled into my role, I ended up with an Aston Martin and a closet filled with labels at the Lions Den.

I just opened the closet, and it was there. I never asked outright who I had to kill.

But now I got it. Complete obedience.

I could do that. When your boss was someone like Reed, you followed orders without question.

That's how it worked.

When he says jump, you jump.

You don't ask how high.

The sheer scale of the world I had entered with Titan's financial power was beyond my comprehension. I couldn't even wrap my mind around the manor. Now I had a car, a closet, a girl, and a life that I didn't know how to process.

Life at Titan was fast.

And I was enjoying the ride.

As Selena cuddled close to me, her voice was soft and uncertain.

"You are nice to me."

"What else would I be?"

"I don't know, but you are different."

"Different can be good, honey."

"I am your honey, now?"

I hardly recognized the woman in my arms. So different from the fierce and confident persona she usually projected.

In this moment, she had transformed into someone entirely new.

"Yeah, you are."

And as I said it—I swore I didn't think she felt it—Selena fucking melted into my side. Melted. Like ice-cream. Softer. Sensual.

There you are.

The look in her eyes there, just beneath the surface, she was almost there. I could see her. My heart swelled with affection and longing. It was beating wildly.

Her shoulder shrugged a little as she bit her lip. My thumb instantly brushed over it as she stopped.

"You deserve kindness."

After a lifetime of not having it.

Her eyes widened a little taking me in and she turned a lovely shade of pink.

"I think you carry a lot on your shoulders. I'd like to take some of that weight off you."

Carry it myself.

"We'll go home together from now on?" she asked, her words laced with a vulnerability that tugged at my heartstrings.

Those eyes big and bright as she looked at me with complete openness.

It's like she's a scared cat... This fucking woman was *starving* underneath for something. For love. I would do anything to protect this girl.

And even if I was sleeping in the same bed as Selena, I wasn't ready to have sex with her just yet. I wasn't a tool. I wasn't going to hurt her.

I didn't want to fuck up what I was working so hard to build.

"Yeah, honey," I kept my voice low as a whisper, rubbing that spot behind her neck, and she softened over. "I'll take you home with me."

For weeks, Reed and I had established a routine, and he made an effort to adhere to it for my sake.

In an attempt to spend more time with his girl, he often arrived earlier in the day to relieve me.

Although our primary objective was to protect Alisha, we both shared another goal: to return to *our* girls.

The way Alisha and Reed navigated their lives together reminded me of my own parents' relationship.

I'd already accepted that things at Titan weren't going to be normal.

Everyone did their thing at their own times on their own schedule.

Freedom was liberating and absolute shit at times. It was tough. It wasn't a twelve-hour shift. No, some days I got to do nothing with Alisha and I napped, while she took photos and had time to surf her social media.

On the rare occasions when I encountered Nate fucking Wyatt, he was with his charge, Gemma Marchand, a leggy elegant blonde who seemed to tolerate him during meetings at Alisha's charity, Poppy.

Gemma, who looked the part of a former heiress, was more commanding than I took her for.

She, for the most part, paid little attention to him when wandering around the place in one of her many ankle-length dresses that made her look like a princess.

Nate looked out of place next to her, looking more miserable than I'd seen him. No more smirking.

I took great pleasure in witnessing Nate fucking Wyatt sitting in the back of the room, looking sullen in the suit and tie that Gemma likely insisted he wear.

Meanwhile, Alisha allowed me to wear whatever the fuck I wanted, made sure I was good several times during the day and tossed me smiles over her shoulder.

In return, I would have no qualms about breaking any man who dared to make a move on her. Reed's orders.

During all of Alisha's meetings, she had me sit beside her, treating me as an equal.

In turn, I witnessed how Alisha was deeply committed to helping others.

She had established the charity in memory of her mother, who had passed away years earlier.

As part of her work, Alisha organized community outreach programs, and she always invited me to participate in every activity she undertook.

Some occasions spending it with Avani, who was seventeen and volunteered when she could.

Avani's soft cinnamon-colored hair and darker eyes than Alisha's were the only real difference. She was sweeter than Alisha, which I didn't know was possible.

She blushed whenever I talked to her, which I took as her not having many men in her life growing up.

But she reminded me of my sister, so I talked to her like Alisha. In turn, Avani slowly opened up.

We talked occasionally, and I got that I made her a little worried due to my position, only because she loved her sister. They were all they had. With Reed now.

On other days, I found myself busy, and I came to realize that even for a social media influencer, no two days were alike for her. In a way, it was like Titan.

Alisha was in charge of her own schedule, and more often than not, she dictated mine as well. I loved the days when she would text Reed, asking him to come home.

Because when she did, he *ran*.

And I got to be with Selena.

Alisha had no idea I was crushing hard on Selena, and I had no intention of sharing it with anyone. That little moment Reed caught us or Gabriel was all they'd get.

Selena didn't run from me which had taken me by surprise, but I learned if I just left out my heart and walked?

She came back. In spades. Asking me for more.

More nudges into my chest, more kisses, more snuggles.

And I gave it to her, cuddling her every night in my bed. In turn, I got texts.

I'm going to work out of Midtown more often

Did you want something different for dinner?

And I fucking *loved* it.
She cared by hovering around me.

We had come back from Teasers, a burlesque club owned by Lara Ford, one of Alisha's other best friends. Lara was a gorgeous Mexican girl who stood at maybe five-feet even. Long, lush dark hair and darker doe-eyes on a stunning face.

It was *wicked* as much as it was beautiful. Decorated in a 1920s style, it was elegant and lavish while being calming at the same time.

There were trees inside the place over the mezzanine and a waterfall on one wall surrounded by lush greenery and plants popping up here and there.

I stepped into another world at Teasers.

And I had never seen so many half-naked women walking around with all the wings and feathers.

At Teasers, I bumped into the third new hire, Liam Sullivan, and got intimately acquainted with Lara.

It was my first time seeing him in person, but he'd introduced himself as the cyber security liaison for Titan, and I knew.

His dark green eyes had been sharp as he took me in. He didn't offer his hand, but I noticed his cane. And the look in his eyes.

Gabriel had the same look in his eyes.

Like they'd seen some shit.

And *that* explained his position.

I knew he had something with Lara the moment I took in how he looked at her.

I didn't focus for too long on them when I saw an enormous wall of sex toys behind Lara's violet-purple desk.

I had gotten some to try from Lara, the pint-sized Latina who had an entire collection.

I let her and Alisha talk amongst themselves.

Reed got off his phone as I headed out, his dark chocolate hair mussed and cheeks a little red. "How's our girl doing?"

"Pretty good. We went to visit Lara today."

I didn't say anything to Reed about anyone else. It wasn't my business what anyone else did. *Who they did.*

I didn't know Liam Sullivan. But I wanted to respect his privacy and since he was new to the team? I didn't want anyone's first impression of him to be Lara's boyfriend.

As Reed unzipped his jacket, he caught me by surprise with his next words.

"I wasn't talking about Alisha."

I paused in putting my shoes on.

Alisha had gotten me these fluffy gold house slippers she thought would be cute. Reed had seen a little bit of me and Selena.

But it didn't mean I had to say anything. I didn't kiss and tell.

"Lara's good too."

Reed's eyes met mine with quiet respect as his lips tipped up.

He shook his head, walking into the apartment, stripping off his shirt. I caught a glimpse of the mean-looking gash on his back I knew he had gotten before his life in the military, along with his tattoos stretching out to his shoulder as I left for my girl.

Reed never talked about it, and I never pried. And I knew exactly what he was planning with Alisha. Those two couldn't keep their hands off each other.

I felt the same about Selena. But unlike Alisha who was the most willing little submissive in the world—I wasn't dating that kind of girl.

Selena was...a lioness. My lioness. And I needed to match her head-on. I couldn't just throw her around and fuck her on every surface.

Unless...she asked. Right?

I shook myself out of those thoughts.

When I met Selena for dinner that night, I talked to her about our job, and she responded in like. She said when she was twenty-two, she had been recruited by Gabriel.

"Did you want this life?" Because I did, but I had no clue what to do with it now that I had it.

Selena nodded her head, shifting in her seat, her left shoulder moving a little.

I didn't tell Selena. I knew her tells when she was lying.

She didn't want this life.

So why did she do it?

149

Reed was only four years older than me, and I had worked with him before.

Reed had started Titan younger than me with Gabriel.

They'd accomplished a fuck ton, and I had no fucking clue how to wrap my head around the level of power those two had.

Selena shared with me the story of how she first arrived at Titan and how Gabriel had taken care of everything from start to finish.

Everyone at Titan was well-compensated, and Reed and Gabriel always looked after their people.

"They've been through a lot," she said, her voice low and somber. "Both of them. Reed is the one who handles operations."

"And Gabriel?" She looked down at the table, and I knew there was more; it didn't look like she had anything romantic with him. "You're close to Gabriel, aren't you?"

She nodded, the fine lines of her throat working. "He knows."

She motioned between us. I was sleeping in the same room as Selena, and there was no way they knew her car was parked outside.

Right next to my car?

I just hadn't fucked Selena.

I just did everything else, and on the occasions we were both at Titan, I made out with her everywhere.

It killed me a little, but I would rather gouge my eyes out than hurt Selena like every other scumbag in her life.

Initially, when I met her? I wanted her with a viciousness that scared me. *And now?*

Now, I calmed down the closer she got to me.

And a part of me knew Selena had been with fucking shit stick dumbasses. Politely.

They didn't love her.

But I can.

I was determined to be different. I was processing data from her all the time. Every single night, she was in my bed.

Some nights, I'd just sleep next to her.

And other nights, I'd eat that pussy like a motherfucker.

Until she did that thing where she shook so hard I had to hold her down while I finished her again and again.

Loving the way she screamed my name and bit down into the pillows. I growled and went harder on her.

My Selena.

And then Selena started rolling me over and taking me in her mouth, her lips all over me, her tongue stroking my dick and her throat—*Fuck.*

Those nights and mornings were the hardest.

But despite how hectic it was, I rarely saw anyone else, and even Evie was out a lot of the time.

I just came home, grabbed food, and crashed in my room until Selena came.

She also told me there was no pressure for me to move out, and Evie liked having people around.

It was better than her being alone sometimes.

I didn't even know where I wanted to stay. I just knew I didn't want to leave my girl. Selena told me just to go with everything.

The less I fought things, the more I would mesh.

"Just don't provoke him," she'd told me about Gabriel. "He's been upset about something."

I didn't know what the fuck he was pissed off about, but he rarely showed up around me.

"He doesn't come near me."

"That's for the best."

CHAPTER 16
SELENA

GABRIEL *HATED* MIDTOWN.

He got edgier when he was down in the city. Even I noticed it on his expressions.

However, lately, Gabriel had been making more appearances there.

Reed's tower of technology stood in contrast to Gabriel's elegant and upscale manor.

It was a more technical space, filled with monitors, servers, and a dedicated area for his various devices, all spread out on his desk.

Sometimes Reed had to spend time here and so there was a space in the back for him to sleep even temporarily.

The environment was darker than Gabriel's, with sleek black and navy tones everywhere.

If anyone looked at this, they would think it was beautiful. But I knew the things Reed did here.

This is where he came to hide the blood he did spill.

Anyone coming here was not coming for anything good.

Titan Midtown was where Reed kept all his secrets.

Gabriel sat at Reed's desk today, and adjacent to it was another setup, far more advanced than Reed's. A lot of monitors and space.

A silver nameplate in the front, had the name "Sullivan."

The desk had no personal items, with only electronics.

Kellan had mentioned that the third new hire, Liam Sullivan, walked with a cane. He had an injury.

Reed had strict orders for Liam and the rest of us regarding him. And it seemed like right now, Liam was much more of a pro than Reed.

Liam is not here today.

Gabriel had never even mentioned Liam. I doubted they had even met yet.

"I don't know what Giroux knows about her," I brought it to Gabriel about Diana, the missing college student going to Astor University.

Diana Martinez, nineteen, five foot six, beautiful girl, Mexicana.

"She goes missing, and I checked; there's another Latina missing in this private college, with the same description but shorter. How come no one is looking for them?"

Because she is not important enough.

"Giroux's guys don't have any patterns for this?" I shook my head. He took the file from me as he flipped through it, his eyes scanning.

Gabriel's eyes shifted as he read the two girls. "Ask him to take the case out of some idiot's hands." I nodded.

"Do you know why Reed is looking into the shooting Alisha was in?"

Gabriel's face went blank at the mention of Alisha.

"No," he replied, his eyes steady. "Talk to Giroux, and I'll work with you from there."

They were keeping something from us. I could feel it.

I just didn't know why.

I nodded, unsure of why he had suddenly shut down.

Was he not happy for Reed? Alisha was *beautiful*. And from how Kellan described a nice lady.

I didn't know her, and after Reed's last relationship, I didn't know if I wanted to.

"Let Quarterback in on this stuff. He needs to track this for his sake with his charge," Gabriel added, his face framed by the shadows of Reed's office.

It was always strange seeing him outside of Titan.

He seemed less human. I understood when I began working for him —Gabriel was Reed's shadow. The darkness within Titan was him. But he was my friend. My boss. But right now?

I knew something was bothering him.

I wondered if he was in town to tear into someone. Kill someone. Something. Hence, he was at Titan Midtown.

Gabriel's movements were always in shadow.

I did not know his next move and he liked it that way.

"He isn't Nate, is he?"

I knew both Gabriel and Nathan tolerated each other because of Reed. They couldn't be more different—Nathan was easygoing and a flirt, while Gabriel was closed up tighter than a locked box.

I got the feeling Gabriel did not approve of Nathan's promiscuous behavior. Reed didn't care about anyone's personal life so long as it never interfered with the mission.

Gabriel disliked people who were so blatant. I had been a whore with no choice.

It was an odd sensation, even for me, to watch Nathan.

Both Gabriel and Reed were private people. Gabriel had never even brought a woman around us.

Kellan was not Nathan. And it felt like a relief.

I had never told Gabriel about the promise, and I never would. But it was burning at me to be with Kellan, who didn't know either.

Nathan was turning thirty.

"He is not Nathan," I said, realizing Gabriel was staring at me as I drifted in thought. He nodded. I took a breath. "I'll go to Giroux."

I had a few other things to do around the city. As I walked out, Gabriel's eyes drifted back to Liam's desk. I wondered if he was waiting for Liam, considering they had not met yet.

But from what I knew, Reed had Liam work alone or with Evie.

As I walked out of the office into the bustling streets of New York, my mind was racing with thoughts of Kellan.

When I said yes to him, I had no idea what I was getting myself into, but I didn't fight it. I simply let myself be.

Just go with it.

Kellan explored every part of me, tangling me in the sheets, only for him to pull back at the last moment.

Every single time. It left me confused, unsure of what he truly wanted. Kellan never pried into my history.

And while I grappled with these thoughts, I found myself avoiding Nathan, not because I felt like a coward, but in an attempt to figure out Kellan.

Could I just throw certainty away for a chance with Kellan?

Nathan was right there. Holding his hand out to me.

I'm not your girlfriend.

But you could be.

And then I saw Kellan's smile in my mind at the thought of Nathan. And I didn't know what to do with myself. *Or who I was becoming.*

The team was shifting again. Reed's newcomers were adjusting for once.

Gabriel was behaving better, or as *better* as he could.

Gabriel had taken Garrett under his wing, and the man was quickly becoming his right-hand man.

Garrett followed Gabriel's every command, and he was one of the few who could match Gabriel's strength.

Despite Gabriel's respect for me and his distance from Kellan, I knew it was only a matter of time before he found a way to sink his teeth into my partner.

Gabriel had a way of molding people in his image, and over the years, I had become a product of that training.

Not Kellan.

Not his smile.

As I walked, I received a message from Valeria from downtown that another girl had been missing for two days with the cops not looking into it.

Another girl?

This is a man. A man is doing this.

After my trip to Giroux, where I provided him with three names to look into, I left the precinct with a prickling sensation on the back of my neck.

I texted Gabriel from the area. I let him know everything.

But as I glanced around, I realized it was just the usual array of cops.

But even then, I felt watched.

CHAPTER 17
SELENA

Kellan texted me, saying he was off earlier than usual that day.

Without hesitation, I invited him over for an indoor picnic.

Evie used to want to have those whenever we were all in the manor.

As I entered my apartment, memories of those gatherings flooded my mind from the beginning.

The five of us huddled together, with Evie sandwiched between Reed and Gabriel, playing a board game with them.

I would watch Reed playing his cards as Evie struggled over the island to reach for more.

Gabriel would always bring her closer to him until she was perched on his leg, and he would adjust his bar stool, moving things closer to her.

Every so often I saw Gabriel peek over at Evie's cards and adjust them for the best play—with Reed pretending not to notice.

Gabriel was a good father to his *princessa*.

I would listen to Nathan's laughter echoing in my ears as he argued with them about a bad play, only to be silenced by a well-aimed spoon thrown by Gabriel.

Reed, and Evie's laughter bouncing off the walls.

I wanted to share my version of those rainy-day indoor picnics with Kellan.

Which was how I found myself in the kitchen finishing up dinner. *Like a normal girl.* Cooking for her man.

I wanted to scream because it felt so good. Kellan always took me out to somewhere nice. I wanted to do something for him.

The bell went off, and since I was only expecting him, I shouted. *"It's open!"*

I saw his smile before I saw him holding an enormous array of pink roses as he took me in. *He looks beautiful.*

All golden haired and blue eyes with his jacket on. He looked like something out of a dream. He grinned wider at me. "Hey, honey."

"You got me flowers?"

My cheeks are going to hurt from smiling so much.

I could feel his gaze traveling down my body, taking in the silk black nightie that hugged my curves. His lingering gaze sent warmth sweeping over me. Everywhere his eyes touched, I felt burning.

"You cooked?" Kellan stepped into my apartment, his eyes widening.

In one sweep he took in the blush walls, the hot pink peonies my housekeeper kept refreshed, and the flamingo-printed umbrella holder I loved.

I peered at him from the lights, shaped like large multi-colored flowers descending from the ceiling, casting a soft glow over the space. He was looking at my home.

"This place is *unreal*, honey."

"Thank you. Comfy?"

His eyes widened as he nodded, his attention drawn to the 3D flower sculptures covering an entire wall in shades of pink. Some with hot pink butterflies. "Are those real?"

"No, just art. I wanted some when I was younger, so I got myself some now." As an adult.

If Mama could see me now.

"When I was little, I wanted to be an artist. And I made things like this. In New York, I purchased them from a street market and thought they'd be pretty."

"They're beautiful, *Gatita*."

But now I didn't know what I wanted sometimes anymore.

I turned off the sink and dried my hands. I could hear Kellan moving around the island, his presence sending butterflies through my stomach. I can feel him changing the energy of my place.

"I thought maybe we could stay in tonight—"

Kellan turned me to face him, his hands gently taking the dishcloth from my grasp and setting it down behind me.

"It looks great," he murmured, his lips brushing against mine. "Thank you, honey."

"I found a few recipes, but I thought you would like something from your culture."

His eyes took me in then with a soft look as he nodded at me before kissing me softly.

"I was thinking I could put on a movie for us. Do you want to watch something?"

That smile was back. "I would love whatever you put on."

As Kellan's gaze swept across the room, it lingered on the vibrant hot pink accents I had carefully woven throughout the space.

"Can I help with anything?" His eyes drifted to the flower lights, one hand reaching for one, brushing over it with a smile on his face.

I glanced over my shoulder to find him standing in my kitchen, bathed in the warm glow of the lights.

His hair fell slightly over his eyes, and with his jacket off, his muscles were on full display—he looked young and adorable even if I knew he was a little dangerous on the inside.

I swallowed, momentarily distracted by his looks, before handing him the guava juice.

"Are you making the drink from that restaurant we went to?"

"I am. Want to help?"

"I do. Just tell me what to do, honey."

Together, Kellan and I moved around the kitchen, our hands brushing as we combined the ingredients. And it was nice. It felt like a home.

Only this time, with him it didn't feel like he was disrupting my peace.

No, he felt like my peace.

Amarte es paz.

Loving you is peace.

The thought drifted over me quicker than I could take it back, like wisps of smoke through my fingers. And I quickly shook it off.

I did not love Kellan.

Not like that. Not right now. I just met him. This wasn't love the same way as—

How would you know? Nobody has ever loved you. Not like this.

I motioned with a spoon to the food on the table to distract myself. "What do you want so I can make your plate?"

His eyes blinked as a slow smile spread across his lips.

This man would smile at everything.

We took our food into the living room, where I just wanted to watch a movie and relax. It was a good date.

"Reed and Evie are in love with this murder mystery series. It's a comedy with these two actors…" I started telling him about the movie Evie had convinced me to watch.

I'd seen the first one with her and Reed. "I've been wanting to watch the second one."

"No way," he grinned, his eyes sparkling. "Reed was just telling me that the fourth part is out in theaters right now. He wants to take Alisha at some point."

When he wasn't running a company?

"Reed loves murder mysteries." I realized I had forgotten utensils. "I'll go and get—"

"Let me just—"

"*No*, I can do it." I didn't bother trying to decipher his smile as I went to grab them.

"I know you can," he looked at me softly. "But I'm asking you to let me."

I blinked unsure of what to say. All I could say was.

"We should sit on the floor with the cushions," I motioned to the pillows. "Trying to eat on the couch is going to be tough."

We settled on the floor, using the cushions as makeshift chairs, leaning back against the couch. It was comfortable.

With my legs stretched out in front of me, I ate quietly, watching part two of the murder mystery movie series Reed liked, having dinner with Kellan.

The sensation went through me of this being something I only did with the family I had here. But this was different.

This is Kellan.

"I know I haven't seen part one," Kellan mused, sipping his guava drink. "But is it just me, or can you not figure out who the killer is?"

"*This* is why Reed loves these movies. He says he can never guess who the killer is." And he absolutely loved that. He saw it as a personal challenge.

It was surprising to everyone that Reed was in a relationship with Alisha.

Nathan talked about Reed's long—standing crush on her for years. Especially when he was as busy as he was.

Everyone knew Reed was in love with Alisha, always looking at her social media as the background of his work.

But nobody ever thought he would go for it, given our jobs.

I discovered that Alisha was best friends with Gemma Marchand from one of the photos Evie had been looking at on Alisha's social media.

And I knew that was why Reed met her and assigned Nathan to her.

Because at the end of the day, Nathan would die on the job rather than let anything happen to his Gemma.

Nathan's Gemma.

Who he basically lives with. Reed had initially said she wanted Nathan for work events, but something had changed.

Now, Nathan was with her all the time.

And I was with Kellan.

I didn't know *where* it was going, but…sometimes, in my heart, it did not matter. I did not see us getting married or having children and for me? It felt good either way.

It was a scary thought because Kellan *challenged* a lot of my thoughts.

All the time. For everything.

Without disrespect. Just making me ask myself if that was what I wanted. In all ways.

And Nathan? Nathan was…not like that.

Gemma was this gorgeous blonde French heiress who was a former model and Alisha? Was also a model and an actress. I had seen Evie's slideshow.

They made a striking pair, grinning into a throwback photo from a trip they'd taken together, wearing beautiful dresses with towering rocks on a beach behind them.

I recognized that beach.

It was the same beach where Nathan had asked me to be his *wife*. When I was thirty. Just like that, my appetite vanished.

*Nathan...*I'd been avoiding him, barely responding to his texts, claiming I was too busy. I was just enjoying what I had. With Kellan.

Who had no idea about my arrangement with Nathan. *You are living a lie. This isn't fair to either one of them.*

"Where did you go, *Gatita*?" I looked over and saw he was watching me instead of the movie, concern etched on his face.

The sounds of the movie came rushing back in, and I saw Kellan grabbing the remote to mute the TV.

His blue eyes seemed to see through me.

But I didn't know how to tell him about Nathan.

My promise. Nothing came out of my mouth.

The thought of hurting Kellan, of seeing disappointment or betrayal in those eyes? It made my stomach ache.

The food not sitting well with me at all.

He doesn't know you used to be a whore.

He will never know the ugly things.

Trying to push those thoughts aside, I shook my head and shifted on my cushion, looking down at the food.

"Would you like more?" He nodded slowly. "Should I make you another plate? I can—"

"I can do it," he interjected. Before I could say a word, he continued. "I know you can, but I'm saying you don't always have to. You can let me help."

His words caught me off guard, and I blinked in surprise. *Tell Watts.*

I still needed to fill him in on Giroux and the case, but now was not the right time. There is always so much to do.

Nodding, I moved back and noticed the look in his eyes.

Sometimes that's how it starts.

"What were you thinking about, honey?"

Taking a deep breath, I decided to share some of my thoughts with him.

I told him about Reed's ex, avoiding the term "girlfriend" since Reed hated calling them that in the past. Reed's choices in women were about as friendly as ice cubes.

Until Alisha.

Kellan blinked, a little surprise written on his face. "I didn't know that about Reed. Alisha's nothing like that. I think Reed likes her because of that. Because she's different from everything around us. You should see his face when he's around her. I barely recognize him. I think you'd like her a lot."

I trusted his judgment, finding it easier than trusting Nathan's.

If I had told Nathan about this, he would have dismissed it, saying it did not matter because Alisha wouldn't last long in Reed's life anyway. Just like the others.

He is such a sweet man. I never want to see him hurt.

Kellan and Nathan shared some similarities but were so different that I felt I did not know what to do with them.

Kellan seemed better for me, and even my mind and body recognized it.

"You are a good partner," I admitted softly. "Better than Nathan."

The words slipped out before I could stop them.

His reaction made my heart explode a little. Lips stretching into a grin, canines flashing, and his eyes sparkled with delight. *That smile.*

This baby.

"Hmmm," he hummed. A sound I'd never heard him make before.

Laughter bubbled up from my chest, the butterflies freeing themselves from my belly. I felt the buzzing sensation all over my skin. I was delighted by his response.

He makes me feel like it's my birthday. Every day.

Sometimes that's how it starts.

"What was that noise?" I asked, kissing his silly smile, his nose, which only seemed to make him grin even wider. "Why are you so cute?"

"You think I'm cute, honey," he said, licking his lips before capturing my mouth in another kiss, his grin never leaving.

"I think you are very cute."

I melted into him, tasting guava and Kellan as his arms wrapped around me, pulling me closer.

"Thank you for dinner," he murmured against my lips.

I had been wanting, aching for his touch since the moment he walked through the door, my body responded to his presence in the most savage way. But I tried to maintain my composure, not wanting to rush things. *Don't pounce.*

Aware my body had been soaking and ready since he walked in, but I controlled myself.

Right now, the longer I kissed him, the more I lost myself in it.

The less control I had, as I climbed into his lap, making out like we were teenagers, the movie playing forgotten in the background.

Awareness went through me that he was still in his jeans and shirt while I wore nothing but panties and a nightie that he could tear into any moment.

Warmth curled around my body from his touch alone.

It had changed between us since we started dating. *Sometimes that's how it starts.*

He had almost calmed down around me, and I did not know what that meant or why, but he'd been respectful since he stepped into my home.

Not once did he touch me anywhere and just kissing me softly. *He is different.*

But now?

All of that was gone as I felt him against my core, and I ground down on him, gasping. "You will make love to me?"

That smile was slowly back as he whispered it over my lips. "Yes."

CHAPTER 18
KELLAN

I WAS NOT ABOUT TO FUCK HER ON THE FLOOR.

I made out with her stripping out of my clothes.

Lifting her into my arms, making out with her stumbling into the hallway and us breaking off into easy laughs as she pointed the way to her bedroom.

I'd long since realized I couldn't *fuck* Selena.

I mean...I *could*.

But not the first time. Not with her.

Because Selena had been hurt before. She did too much for the world. And not enough came back to her. I couldn't fuck her like a whore—unless she asked. And even then I'd double check.

Selena was raw. Unfiltered.

Careful.

She's so very real underneath that armor.

I was floored by the amount of pink I saw in her apartment. It was so feminine. I fucking knew the real Selena was buried underneath that other woman she wore as armor.

The pale pink scalloped tufted headboard and all the femininity around the room were nothing that Selena would wear on the outside.

But I'd love to see her in *this* color. Hot pink. Peony petals all over her skin. The scent of pink-pepper and lychee all over her. And me.

And nothing else.

It was my first time getting Selena like this, and I looked back at her. *I was right about you.*

You are hiding.

"Your home is beautiful, honey."

She blushed, and her eyes drifted over my chest.

I came down on her mouth again, making out with her reaching for her nightie. Loving the way she shrugged out of it, helping me, and sliding it down without breaking off our mouths.

My hands went to her panties, tearing at them while she reached for my pants.

This is her. The real Selena.

I helped her or tried to.

I wasn't expecting her to slide down my body. Her lips, trailing kisses, pushed me back to the bed, and I fell back, moving to the center, letting her lips move down my stomach.

What was she—I groaned, throwing my head back as Selena swirled her tongue around the tip of my cock.

Hot, wet heat circled my length and I groaned as she was helping me take off my jeans and my briefs, leaving me in nothing while she did it.

"Fuck." She rose up between my legs like a curious vixen. "Damn honey—"

A growl left me as she gripped me in one elegant hand, her fingers barely wrapping around me as those green eyes met mine while she stroked. I almost came off the bed with that.

Fuck. This woman is determined to destroy me.

"Selena, come here."

An impish grin curled her lips. "Why? I can not enjoy you, too?"

And then she swirled her tongue around the tip of my dick and tried to take me deeper. Those green eyes watching me carefully, her pink pouty lips stretched over the head.

I gripped the sheets and not her hair as she worked her mouth over me slowly taking me inch by inch until she was halfway.

I closed my eyes with a groan, biting down on my lip as she did that thing where she swallowed me as much as she could. She always did this before she took all of me.

Selena always did this to me when I least expected it.

Or she woke me up with this. Every single time she did, it stopped me from breathing properly.

She's going to kill me.

And I'm going to fucking love it.

"Keep going, *Gatita.*"

I didn't even recognize my voice.

She moaned as she did, and I growled in approval.

My hand was unable to stop from reaching for her, fisting her hair in one hand as she moaned, taking me deeper, making a mess out of my cock. I groaned and sighed as she worked.

Damn, I did not want to come in her mouth.

I mean, I *did*—but not *this* time.

"Selena." I tugged on her scalp, groaning as she took me deeper, sinking low until her mouth took all of me. "Damn, honey. *Just like that*...that's my good girl."

I felt her throat work around me as I tugged. Shit...she was going to love the same shit I did.

"No, honey, come up here." At that, she obeyed, letting me go, her lips swollen from taking me and out of breath.

She crawled up to me, straddling me like a lioness about to take her man.

While normally that shit got me hot, I wasn't that type of man right now.

Absolutely not. Not now.

I rolled her over smoothly, pinning her hands to her sides, loving her gasp, her eyes going wide. "I bet you're used to being in charge."

She nodded breathlessly, and my eyes raked down her body, loving the way her tits rose and fell, her stomach dipped, and her legs were spread open for me.

"See, *Gatita*, in bed, I do things a little differently."

I looked at that pretty pink center of hers, glistening from going down on me.

I'd keep that in mind for another rainy day.

The scent of pink pepper and lychees and guava was all around me, in my taste buds as my eyes met hers.

"I'm in charge here," I smiled softly. "You obey me."

I obey you at work.

I sank down onto her, my elbows bracketing her head as I kissed her slowly.

"Do you think you can let me do that, honey?"

166

Her eyes bat several times at that. Her throat worked as I saw her thinking. I bit my cheek to not grin.

Don't freak her out. Don't smile.

"How?"

I bit down harder on my cheeks.

"Should I show you?"

She bit down her lip and I caught a hint of nervousness in those eyes.

She's scared.

And my humor vanished as I realized her thighs were trembling.

In an instant, anything calm or arousing I felt evaporated.

"Are you afraid of me?" I asked softly. "Or afraid of what will happen if you give yourself to me?"

I didn't dare to breathe as I waited her response, my heart constricting at the thought that I might be the cause of her pain. Any of her anxiety.

She was safe with me.

Her tongue darted out to wet her lip. "Both."

"Why?"

I already *knew* why.

But I wanted to hear her say it. She looked like she'd rather do anything but admit it.

I stroked my thumb across her cheekbone in a feather-light caress, trying to infuse the touch with all the tenderness and reassurance I felt, silently willing her to let me past the fear I saw clouding her eyes.

"What if I want you to stop?"

Then I stop.

Unease coiled in my gut as I scanned her face, trying to decipher the emotions playing across her delicate features.

Someone had hurt her before.

I fucking knew it.

That's why she was *terrified*, why she thought I might cause her pain, even in the bed. It's happened before.

The first tendrils of rage blossomed, white-hot and all-consuming. I wanted to give in to it, to hunt down anyone who had dared to lay a hand on her.

But I couldn't, not now, not when Selena needed me to be her rock, her safety.

Don't freak her out.

Swallowing back the fury threatening to choke me.

Closing my eyes, I struggled to steady my voice.

"Do you know what a safe word is?" I barely recognized the sound of my voice.

"Yes." But the words out of her mouth were soft. Uncertain. And I didn't like that.

I brushed her hair back, keeping my eyes on hers.

"Do you want one?"

Someone hurt Selena.

"And you stop?"

Yes. *Always.* "I stop."

"Just like that?"

She doesn't believe me. Because someone didn't stop.

I was trembling with the effort to not lose my shit. I stayed focused on her, closing my eyes as I waited to speak.

"Sex is not a one-way street. It's not about my needs. It's also about yours. I've never hurt you and I'm not going to hurt you. I promise you that. I will be whatever you need me to be."

I still didn't look.

"What safe word, honey?"

"Milkshake." My eyes opened. Green eyes blinked innocently at me. "Is that a good word? I can choose another—"

How is she so fucking adorable and sexy?

I kissed her hot and quickly for a second. "*No*, that's—"

I broke off trying to get myself to calm down from the arousal and rage warring with the current amusement I felt.

"It's *yours*. It's *perfect*."

It could be some random city in Thailand and it would be perfect.

"You say that word, I stop. *Entiendes*?"

"*Understood*." She whispered. I smiled. *She's trying, too.*

I noted Selena hadn't spoken much Spanish to me since I had come into her life. I spoke it, but I could see Selena trying to connect with me too.

In her own ways.

"Good girl, will you let me love you?"

"Yes."

Fucking.

168

Adorable.

I smiled wider, dropping my lips on her, feeling my cock, wet at the tip and ready for her ache to slide into her.

But I needed to know she was ready for me too. She was soaking wet, but I wasn't a small man. In any sense.

"*Kellan,*" she moaned, as the length of my cock ran along her pussy, and I groaned.

"I want to make sure—" I broke off as my cock pressed into her. I couldn't think. "*Honey, I need to—*"

I wanted to eat her out.

Make sure she was ready for me, but I couldn't stop. I couldn't do anything.

"Just go for it," She whispered, desperately grabbing at me, meeting my lips as I sank into her at her words.

I would've laughed at her echoing my own words back to me now. Like this.

But I couldn't summon a single fucking bit of humor.

I pulled back. "I forgot a condom." My brain was all over the place.

Her eyes met mine. "I'm on something. I have to be."

Given our jobs. I didn't need that reminder for her.

Didn't even want to imagine her in a situation like *that*. I was losing focus again. I nodded. I could do that.

Even if I never had sex without a condom. I could—for Selena. She trusts me even though she's been hurt before. And so I trust her to not do me dirty.

"We can stop if you want?" Selena whispered. "Do you need your safe word?"

Ducking my head quickly, I hid my grin on her collar.

She's out here trying to make me feel safe.

This woman is going to try and meet me toe to toe.

All the time. She was going to drive me crazy. And I loved it.

"No, I want you." I gasped at the feel of her around me. "Honey—"

I couldn't think, just pressed my lips into her skin.

"Hold me, just breathe…there you go."

She did as I sank into her, a whimper left her. I smoothed Selena's bangs back, kissing her soundly as I pressed further, groaning into her mouth.

"Fuck," I breathed.

"You're tight, *Gatita*," I licked her throat, kissing her where I knew she'd shiver. And I slid further. "So fucking beautiful."

Selena moaned as I closed my eyes to the stretching sensation of her around my cock, hot, wet heat wrapping around me.

The clenching increased the deeper I went, and it felt like sin, and I swore for a nanosecond I was going to die. That was it. I was dead.

I couldn't catch my breath. I was drunk off the scent of peonies and lychees and hot pink peppers and—*Selena*.

I was shaking with the force of trying to fuck her like a wild man. And resisting. *Later.*

After you warm her up to you.

"Tell me your word."

"Milkshake." *Good girl.*

My arms shook as I breathed. "Just…say when I can move, honey."

She nodded, and I felt her ease, and I was losing my mind. Shaking wildly in her arms because Selena felt like a hot and tight vice around my dick. And I was going to die like this.

"Why are you shaking, Kellan?" Her whisper cut through my thoughts.

Because I'm trying not to lose my mind.

She was so sexy and so adorable at the exact same time.

How was this even possible?

I bit back my response. When I first met Selena I thought she was a sex kitten.

She wasn't.

She was just pretending. Once I took the mask off I just saw a woman who'd been hurt too many fucking times for me to do the same.

Because it didn't matter what I wanted.

And right now, she was clenching down on me, and I had to *breathe*.

"You do not want to hurt me?"

I shook my head.

No. Of course not. She was so much smaller. Even if she was fierce. She was Selena.

She's my honey.

"*Kellan.*" *Yes, honey.* I lifted my eyes to her. "*When.*"

Selena kissed me steadily as I drew myself out. I fucking ate up all the noises she made. All the tiny little mewls.

I groaned a little at the sensations. I was going to die like this. Holy. Shit.

"Better?" She nodded frantically, reaching for me again. I didn't even know what to say at that moment.

So I didn't. I just made out with my girlfriend while moving inside of her, groaning with the sensation of her pussy clamping on me as I stroked deep.

Drunk off *this*.

And when I kissed her, in that moment, nothing else mattered.

I never wanted this to *stop*.

"*Kellan*—" Her eyes were wet as she looked at me. My body moved inside of her like it had all the time in the world.

I cupped her face, holding her close as I moved in a rhythm that felt like I was rediscovering better sex for the first time—with her.

I don't even know where it came from.

"*Puedo amarte?*"

Can I love you?

Emerald eyes widened on me. "Ámame?"

Love me?

I nodded unable to stop myself. "I wanna love you. I do. If you'll let me, if you'll have me. I won't hurt you. I promise." I swallowed around my emotions. Around the pleasure.

"You promise..."

"I promise."

Because initially, even if I wanted to fuck her brains out—I couldn't hurt Selena. I could never hurt her. *Not that girl.*

Not the girl who clawed her way out of Havana. Every man before me had fucked Selena over.

Even I wasn't a monster to do that. Use her like every other man before her? Nah.

It took her a nanosecond before she stamped her lips over mine as her answer. I groaned giving myself into her plunging so deep I could shatter.

But I wouldn't. Not yet.

Not when I intended to do this all night.

CHAPTER 19
SELENA

I DID NOT RECOGNIZE MYSELF. OR HIM.

Not anymore.

I thought I did not deserve love.

I did not deserve nice things like that romantically.

But now I had it.

I felt like Kellan pulled me apart every single time he was in me. And being with him? I felt safer than I had in years.

Every evening, without fail, he would come to my apartment.

I had taken to staying there instead of the Lion's Den, even though we still found ourselves tangled in those sheets from time to time.

His hands skating over my body as he curled into me there at the manor.

Now, he was in my bed in my apartment in the city.

Kellan had all but moved in at my insistence, the transition so seamless and natural, I didn't know what to think.

Now, I couldn't stand the thought of him leaving. At all.

We never talked about the future. But…suddenly, it didn't matter anymore.

He understood me. In a way I had not experienced with a man before. Something new filled me when I was with him, an emotion I had felt a long time ago.

Kellan's love was weightless, lighter than anything I had experienced.

Despite our different upbringings, he made an effort to get to know me, constantly seeking out the things we had in common rather than focusing on our differences.

When I wasn't with him? I waited until I came home to him. I wanted the time between us to last forever and I got that Kellan wanted that too.

From how we took our coffee, how I ate breakfast vs him, and how we worked out. What we did after. How we relaxed. He was interested in *everything*.

Following me to the gym.

And then following me into the shower after. Taking me with a desperation I had always felt in him, but it was another thing feeling it. Feeling him.

Curled up against him at night, he introduced me to things he enjoyed growing up, while I told him stories of my time in Havana.

Before everything happened.

When I was little, Diego and I would run to the ice cream man and fight over the same cone...

He would laugh and share his stories about his sister who he called a little devil. Becca.

"I swear to God, Gatita, if you ever meet her, you'd love her. But she'd team up against me with you..."

I laughed enjoying this side of him. The older brother. More serious than I thought he'd be. Even though he was younger than me, we were more alike than different.

"Do you see her often?"

He shook his head burying it into my neck. "Nah, Reed's got it on paper I can't tell anyone what I do in case he needs me for assignments like you, so I make up excuses all the time. It's fine. I feel like I'd kill Becca if I spent too much time with her."

Because we all had alias's. Some of us more than others.

His eyes landed on me, brushing his lips over my nose.

"Do you ever go see your Mama, honey?"

"No," I whispered feeling oddly small compared to him. Most men did not make me feel like this. Maybe Gabriel sometimes, but I trusted Gabriel. "Ever since I came to America, I've been working with Gabriel. It's hard to tell her what I do too."

He nodded against my throat. "You ever think about taking a break?"

I let out a breath holding him close to me, my fingers in his hair.

He loved it when I did this.

"All the time. Maybe go somewhere warmer...New York City is cold."

He let out a breath. "It's getting colder outside. But after Kuwait I don't mind it too much. I'm guessing it can get worse."

"Sometimes," I murmured rubbing his scalp. "Sometimes it does not. But I don't like it when it does."

He groaned as I rubbed behind his ear and a helpless giggle left me. *This baby.*

"You wanna be on the beach, somewhere warm?"

"Hmm," I mimicked him smiling down at him in my arms. "I do."

His grin was wide and silly. "You ever think about a vacation, honey?"

My smile dipped a little. "I cannot leave Gabriel with all this."

He nodded his eyes narrowed on me. "You're loyal to Gabriel?"

"Si. He is good to me." I told him in Spanish. *"Gabriel was with me from my very first day in Titan. He is my boss but he is also like my brother."*

Kellan absorbed that. He listened attentively, asking questions that made me feel like he was uncovering parts of myself I had yet to discover.

I never told him about what had happened to me. I knew he knew there were things I didn't say.

But he never pressed.

There were still aspects of my past that I wasn't ready to share with him, particularly the things I had done and my history with Nathan. The life I had in Havana.

And because of that?

Every day I spent with Kellan was a day spent in the life I never wanted with Nathan.

I found myself falling deeper for Kellan. It made me feel so guilty because I thought that was what I wanted.

But there was this voice in my head, telling me I was betraying Nathan, betraying myself to be with him.

A woman used by so many people in so many ways, and Kellan was from this good family.

A good man with a baby sister he adored.

He texted her all the time. With Kellan, he made me want a future I never dared to dream of, one where it felt like…everything was my *choice*.

Not based on anything but love.

Love for me had never been a thought I had ever considered until he'd come into my life with his smile lighting it up.

And I knew I'd be stupid to think otherwise.

I thought I wanted life with Nathan.

And now I don't want anything else in the world Kellan. He is the only thing in the world I want.

Part of me wondered if this was too fast. I'd met him.

And yet my soul knew his. I knew his goodness, I saw it in his eyes.

I craved his presence and needed to keep him buried deep inside me for as long as possible. And he did.

Night after night, I found myself with him, our bodies moving as if the world belonged to us alone. Nothing else mattered.

He became someone else in bed with me. Someone I craved. He was something else when he was in me.

That's it, come around me. Say my name, honey. There you go.

You're so pretty when you scream, just like that.

Give it to me, Gatita…let me feel you come again.

The moment he walked through the door, I was in his arms, kissing him with a desperation that suggested years of separation rather than hours. Like I needed him.

I melted around him, surrendering to his every touch and thrust, shivering and quaking until I shattered with his gruff words whispered against my lips.

Just like that, honey. Say my name. Every single time. Good girl.

Every inch of my being felt raw and exposed, as if he had stripped away not just my clothes but the very layers of my soul.

I felt like I had been starving, hungry for years, for something like him, and when I had him, I couldn't let him go.

When I was with him, I felt like Kellan was filling spaces in me with his love. I felt fuller and like I was floating with him. The parts of me that hurt not so much with him.

In bed, Kellan would love me for hours, his praise and encouragement washing over me in waves.

Say my name when I hit that spot. Right there? You're so beautiful, honey. Keep coming for me.

Little by little, my resolve was crumbling.

That was where his energy went after I fed him. *In me.*

This wasn't sex.

Parts of me became aware this was something else.

When I came, sobbing into his mouth the first few times, I cried in his arms after every orgasm, overwhelmed by the intensity of them.

He moved over me, coaxing me more and more until I came even harder the second time, screaming as I did to his groans of pleasure.

I clung to him as he rocked into me, each push inside of me driving me over.

When I finally fell apart, my nails dug into his back as I drowned in him.

His lips moving over my pulse, my face.

He was *everywhere.*

His lips mapped every curve and hollow of my body as he rolled me onto my stomach or side, making love to me with a tenderness that left me shaking.

There you go, my good girl.

That's good, isn't it, honey? Keep going, just like that.

I would break, time and time again, clinging to him like a lifeline, terrified that if I let go, I would drown.

In those moments, I knew with a certainty that defied logic or reason that I couldn't survive without him, that he had become as essential to me. What started out as just lust began to transform into something else where sex with Kellan felt like healing.

Tonight was no different, laying on my side, kissing him, with one leg over his hips, as he thrust into my body with those strokes that drove me insane.

I was shaking at how good that felt as he held me so close to him, I was one with him.

"You're close?" He broke off from my mouth to growl it over my lips.

A whimper left me. I was.

He brought me tight to him, his hand behind my head tucking my head into his shoulder, as he delivered a series of sharp sweet strokes to somewhere that made me come apart.

Sobbing into his neck, he held me as he drove deeply in me.

I felt the pleasure course over me in waves, muffled screams escaping.

I couldn't stop things from leaving my lips in my native tongue, unable to think straight. I told him that.

Don't ever stop. Love me forever. Just you. Just me.

Kellan's eyes shifted as he drew back, not stopping.

"I can feel you coming harder," he growled into my lips. "Should I keep you like this forever?"

I was not even ashamed of my nod, and he sealed his lips over mine with a groan, driving me to insanity with the way he moved.

The orgasms came slow but so sweet it shook through my entire body. I felt the tears running down my cheeks Kellan wiped away as he never stopped moving.

I didn't know how I thought straight *without* him.

This is where his energy goes.

As he groaned against my lips my entire body felt the shivers going through me feeling his heat in me.

Love you.

The thought formed in my head and I wanted to say it but I felt too afraid. It was too much. Too fast. Too soon.

I barely knew him.

But he knew me. I felt like he knew me.

"You are holding back with me?"

I could feel how strong he was sometimes when he moved me around.

He never left me as he held me close to him, his lips on mine.

"I don't want to hurt you."

But those last few motions of his hips felt different. And I wondered.

"You...hold back with me...all this time?"

His eyes went dark and low, like he was...changing again.

Something rushed through me and he groaned low, closing his eyes.

"I felt that." I felt the heat all across my face and lower. "I don't want you to hold back. I want all of you."

I'd love that. For hours.

"I remember that day when you saw me. From dancing. I'm

surprised you are so sweet when I know you are also…not sweet sometimes."

No, sometimes he was a savage.

He stilled, his lips pressing to my shoulder. For a moment, I wondered if I said the wrong things as he throbbed in me.

He pulled back, looking into my eyes. "I don't want to freak you out."

He had already explained to me he did not want to disrespect me.

But maybe I wanted that from him. Because it was not the same thing.

"I wasn't proud of not being sweet to you. Just wanted to bring you peace."

Because he thinks you need it.

But maybe I needed both?

I whispered into his lips. "Amarte es paz."

Loving you is peace. His eyes watched me with soft heat and low-lidded warmth. I continued. "Estar cerca de ti es mi paz."

Being with you is my peace.

He pressed his lips over mine softly, and I said.

"Y te siento en cada parte de mi ser. Quiero sentir eso otra vez."

I feel you in every part of my being. I want to feel that again.

"You want to feel me again be *not sweet, Gatita*?"

As he said the words, he nudged a little, and I gasped against his lips, loving the smile he gave me.

I gasped into his mouth. "¿ahora?" *Now?*

"You remember your word?"

Milkshake.

His smile was slow and small, his eyes banked with heat. "Should I be not sweet?"

I kissed him long and slow as he slowly slid out of me. I could feel him already hardening again. And then he turned me over onto my belly, moving a pillow under my hips, and I gasped.

He'd never done that.

I felt the shivers running down my spine wherever he pressed his lips. When he slid back into me, I groaned with the sensation of him filling me deeper than I could've ever imagined.

His length stretching me open, wider, deeper—fuller than I ever felt. And then some. It was endless.

Pleasure, white-hot in my body went off and whimpers left me.

He echoed the sentiment as he settled over me, his hands reaching for mine, lacing our fingers, and pumping, an animal whimper left my throat as he laughed low in my ear.

"You're going to love this," he growled.

I already do. I did.

I love you.

"I can feel you losing it already around me. Maybe I should be not sweet more often." Yes. All the time.

When he drove inside of me, I came with the second thrust. And he growled in my ear as he began moving inside of me with much more forceful thrusts.

"There you fucking go," his voice was dark as I clenched tighter. "Come around me, honey." I screamed gripping the bedsheets tighter.

I love when he's not sweet.

I cried his name into the pillow as he pounded into me through my orgasm. His hands grabbed a handful of my hair tugged with just enough pressure. His tongue swept across my cheek as he slammed into me.

I screamed.

"Does my girl like it when she turns her man into an animal for her?"

Yes.

My screams turning into sobs as he worked, groaning his approval into me slam after slam into my body. Tears flowed down my cheeks as my body lit up with sensations from the inside out.

Wave after wave of relentless pleasure rushed through me every time he sank in deep, my hips squirming, until he grabbed my throat.

And in turn I felt my pussy clenching around him. It was too much.

"Don't run from it, honey. You can take it."

A noise left my lips. *"Kellan—"*

"Just like that, squeeze down on me...*there* you fucking go."

I screamed holding onto the sheets for dear life. *"Kellan!"*

"Tell me you love it."

I cried out feeling my body spasm. *"I love it."*

"You love me," he growled in my ear as he worked.

It wasn't a question.

I caved in without thinking, a rush of moisture flooding my center at the admission as I came again. I felt it leave my lips.

"I love you."

It made sense. I did. I trusted him. I love him. For a second I thought his thrusts would falter, a noise left him.

And it only made him go harder.

CHAPTER 20
KELLAN

She loves me.

If I had a smaller restraint when it came to fucking Selena everywhere?

That tiny bit of my leash snapped in half when she told me she loved me.

That night I took Selena in a way that cemented me inside of her body. I'd never leave.

And every single time we fucked after that? We were animals.

Everywhere. The shower. The kitchen island.

I was losing my ever-loving mind with this woman. Hearing Selena say those words? I'd lost my shit.

While I considered myself fairly logical and rational. Maybe even reasonable.

With Selena?

I was no better than a man who'd been crawling through the desert and had stumbled upon an oasis.

Like I had been waiting my entire fucking life for someone who matched me at every fucking level. Someone who pushed me.

Encouraged me. Challenged me.

Met *me* eye for eye and watched my back. My partner. A team.

I was completely utterly taken by Selena. Body and soul.

It started from the moment I met her, but lately it had grown into something I felt like was an inferno raging for her.

The hot pink, the vibrant colors, the laughter in my ears as she looked at me with those eyes. Selena was everything I wasn't.

Don't be stupid, savage.

I'm trying, honey.

I blamed it on us being older siblings. Both of us having a deep seated need to be responsible for others and therefore ourselves.

But it was more than that.

Selena accepted me. At every turn. With everything I wanted.

Initially, I saw her as a challenge.

Something to win over.

But the more I got to know her, the more I buried deep inside of her pussy loving the way she cried my name. Held my face.

Whispered she loved me with every thrust?

I fucking loved her.

"That's my girl," I crooned as she came around me again. She was doing this adorable thing she did where she held onto me tighter as she came like she thought I'd leave her or something.

I wasn't fucking going anywhere.

I braced my arms around her head, grinding deeper with every thrust feeling her clamping down wildly. "That's my good girl, is that better?"

She whimpered as I said it.

"Tell me what I wanna hear."

"I love you." It was a sob from her lips as her eyes opened, wet and teary eyed from the intensity of her orgasms.

"And I love you, honey." I smiled against her lips. "Now hold onto me, because I'm not done with you yet."

ANOTHER NIGHT I TOOK HER NEAR HER WINDOWS ON ONE SIDE OF HER living room, overlooking the cityscape.

The dark backdrop with the neon lights glittering over her skin made her look unreal as I fucked into her from behind.

I held her face in one hand, my other arm wrapped around her waist to keep her standing.

My girl loved when I growled the filthiest shit I could in her ear. But within some limits.

Because deep down in the back of my mind—every single time I made love to Selena, I was aware I was her first like this. All hot pink and bright and lush like a blossoming flower under me. I would never ruin her. Not unless she wanted it. Unless she liked it and begged for it.

Then I would.

The first man who hadn't treated her like shit. Not just to go down on her. But the way she reacted around me?

I wasn't an idiot.

I knew there were lines I couldn't cross with Selena. Words, I couldn't use. Things I couldn't say. I would never dream of hurting her like that.

Some women got off on hair pulling and their ass's slapped and I didn't mind any of that long as *she* wanted it.

With Selena?

I was someone else entirely.

I was adapting to her needs. Listening to her come all over me with a few thrusts in the right spot.

And then hauling her back as I pounded one out in her. One after the other.

Afterwards we both laid there in the bathtub soaking in the scent of peony blossom bubble bath I got for her.

"I am turning into a savage like you."

I chuckled feeling heat fuse into my chest with the lust I felt. "Better a savage with me than without me."

She'd turned with those eerily bright eyes of hers then, a little watery and cheeks flushed with steam and heat. "I do not ever want to be without you."

In her voice? Those words were the world.

"You never will be." I promised it to her. "I'm here to stay, *Gatita*."

"You are different from most men," she whispered wiggling her toes a little as she rested against my chest. "Not like everyone else."

"That might be a good thing, hm?"

She nodded. "A little scary."

"Why's that?"

I already knew the answer. But it took her a second to say it.

"We have not known each other for very long. I've worked with people for years and I feel like I know you better than anyone I have ever met."

I felt the same. I didn't know how to explain. Just that when I was with her, my heart settled.

What started out as thinking she was just some hot girl from the airport turned into seeing this softer woman with enough coaxing.

But she didn't answer my question.

"Why does it scare you, honey?"

Her eyes met mine then when she realized she hadn't. I hoped my smile was reassuring then.

With all her curves wet and lush against mine?

My brain was functioning at half capacity.

"Because you are real."

I nodded. "Because I am real." And? The truth. "Because this is real. And you know it too."

Her cheeks tinged with pink was all the answer I needed.

"What do you want from me?"

I felt my lips curving in a wider smile. "Isn't it obvious?"

She stared at me curiously so I leaned in to brush my lips against hers. "Just you, *Gatita*."

And I had her. She was mine.

She chose me.

CHAPTER 21
SELENA

LOVE YOU, GATITA.

I loved every part of him.

Even the things that drove me crazy.

When we cooked in the kitchen late in the evenings, he had become a constant source of...home.

He was my safety, my partner, and in every way, he became a part of me in a short time, because I trusted him from day one to take care of me.

They said in life, you do not know people after ten, twenty, or even thirty years.

I knew people who found out their spouses of fifty years had been cheating on them for forty of them. I knew trust could be shattered in an instant.

In a second.

You could know someone your entire life—and not know them at all.

But my soul knew Kellan.

I recognized him and his presence in my sleep, and my body stayed calm whenever he slid into my bed.

Because I knew him. I knew his heart.

He was sunshine and gold and wonderful.

He was all the brighter things in my life. All the things I *wasn't*.

Just like Gabriel, I was a shadow.

If I had spent a lifetime in darkness, Kellan would have helped me step into a light I had never imagined for myself.

I knew him. And he knew me. Driving me to laughter with everything he did. Kellan liked making me laugh.

He would hover, sampling and taste-testing every dish until I found myself swatting his arm, and then he ate snacks from the jars I had restocked for him, watching me with mischief in his eyes.

He was always ready to steal treats.

Or kisses.

One night, when I caught him in the act with my spatula. "No, you savage man."

He flashed me that golden smile of his, the one that made my heart skip a beat and my resolve crumble. Him with his messy blonde hair and softer blue eyes. So much softer than me.

This baby.

Shaking my head, I turned away, only to feel his arms snake around my waist, his hands wandering teasingly.

I swatted at him, pretending to frown. I had been setting everything out for dinner tonight. But, of course, things were *missing*.

I did not need to be a detective to know *who* was moving them around the kitchen.

"I'm angry with you. I know you put the olive oil on the top shelf."

And all of the seasoning.

He did this on *purpose.*

All. The. Time.

His lips pressed into my pulse, making a shiver run down my body and clench instinctively. "Did I, honey? I must've missed that. Should I get it for you?"

This demon child.

I huffed a breath as he smiled, kissing his way down my neck.

Now, it was hard to think.

"I would get it myself, but I know someone hid my little step ladder too."

I had a tiny one with two steps to get to the cabinets' top shelves.

I could feel that smile against my pulse.

"Honey, I didn't see that little pink thing you use for the top shelf."

He is not even ashamed.

He pressed his lips down my spine, and in my new pink nightie he got me, I felt every single one.

"I'd be happy to grab the olive oil for you in exchange…"

He was not a baby, he was a lion in my kitchen looking for his next meal.

After he ate all the snacks.

I held my breath as he sank to his knees behind me, his lips on my thighs, his tongue swirling patterns.

"W—what's that?" He made that adorable humming sound as he moved his tongue over my panties. Before I had a chance to even start cooking. "*Kellan.*"

"Sit on my face," I felt his tongue against my pussy, and I moaned, reaching for his head. "Come on, honey. Just a little kiss."

How does anyone think straight with him?

Tugging him into the bedroom, I tossed my nightie off, wrapping myself around him as he was all over me.

I would never get used to the way he urged me to sit on his tongue.

My thighs shook from the effort of the position as my hands gripped the headboard.

Unable to stop my hips from grinding down, his growls always made me finish harder.

I threw my head back, rocking my hips as his hands skated up and tugged my nipples.

I shrieked as I came into his mouth. And he kept going.

When his arms banded around my trembling thighs, I tried falling back, and he would follow, not letting me go.

This man is a savage.

I was shaking wildly, unable to keep myself up as he slid out from under me, kissing my thighs and dropping me to all fours.

His tongue was *everywhere.*

Trailing patterns on my skin.

I loved this.

When he slid into me slowly and evenly, I was going crazy, letting him manipulate my body until he settled. Letting me adjust. I loved that even when he was not sweet, he was still kind.

Gathering my hair in one fist, he began long and easy moves, and I began to shake from the first few thrusts. He hit so deep I felt tears in my eyes.

"That's my good girl, you're close already, aren't you?" I *was*.

He groaned, picking up his hips, the sensation of him moving was electrifying and I was grabbing the bed sheets as he moved harder as I cried out.

The tug on my scalp felt delicious as he slammed his hips in, burying himself deeper than before. A wild scream escaped my throat.

"Are you okay, honey?" He gasped, stopping for a moment. "Do you need to use your safe word?"

No, I never even thought about that word. I wanted more of him. Rougher. Harder. I trusted Kellan to not hurt me. Not after the life I had. He made me feel alive.

Like I was someone else, someone new, someone better.

I pushed back on him, feeling his length stretching me wide, hitting somewhere so deep and sweet, my brain stopped working.

"Don't stop." And then I felt bolder as I moved my hips, pressing into him, working myself on him.

His hands coasted over my hips, his voice like velvet and gruff. "Damn, honey, *look* at you…working yourself on me. Bet that feels good, doesn't it?"

I nodded desperately loving this sensation, the image of me fucking back onto Kellan's hard cock was making me even wetter as I cried out. "Don't stop, don't stop."

"I'm not gonna stop, baby."

I screamed into the pillows as the sensations drew closer, wave after wave coasting over me while curling my fingers into the sheets and working my hips for relief.

"Keep going, honey."

Kellan did this thing where he held onto my hips and began pounding into me in time with me moving back, and I screamed louder into the sheets. So close. *Right there.* I was right *there*.

"You can take me so well, can't you, honey?" His hands came up to grip my hair, and something in me snapped as he growled in my ear, bending forward and changing the angle to something delicious. "Be a good girl and stay still for me, *Gatita*. I'm not done yet."

And then he *pulled* it tight as he rammed home.

I screamed as my orgasm coasted over me, making me shake and falter in my movements.

Wave after wave, the knots of pressure inside of my body shattered and snapped while my eyes filled with the image of Kellan moving behind me, inside of me, working his massive cock in me like a savage man possessed with the need to fuck me.

To cement himself into me. To stay there forever is a part of me.

Kellan did not miss *anything*.

A wild scream left me as it intensified the pleasure.

"Kellan! *Don't stop!*" I didn't even know what was happening but I wanted him like this. Just like this.

"I have no intention of ever stopping, honey." And my entire body responded to him. "We both know you take me so fucking well, I would never stop."

He groaned as he pulled back, still driving his cock into me prolonging my orgasm into something more intense.

I was a mess under him as he worked me through the sensations. I felt like a live wire. Every sensation drawn out endlessly.

"That's my girl...right there." His thrusts made me sob as he hit *that spot* over and over and *over* while he held my hair tight.

The pinpricks of pain helped ground me to the moment.

"Don't run from it, *Gatita*. Feel me, feel it."

I was lit up from the inside out.

My body shaking, my fingers gripping the sheets tightly as I trembled. A noise left my lips as I felt another orgasm building, except this time—this one might kill me.

"Make me feel like I'm a fucking savage taking you like this," he snapped his hips into me brutally and I screamed again. I *loved* that. "Such a good girl taking my cock so well, I told you I'd take care of you, you really thought I wouldn't follow through on that?"

I was a mess. A *mess*. And he was going to kill me like this.

And then he was there holding me, baring me down to the bed with his weight. I felt wild as he pinned me down with his heavier body.

"Gonna take care of you and this little pussy," he nipped my ear, letting my hair down, holding down my arms instead over my head as his hips drilled into me. "You gonna come for me again and let me fuck your brains out, *Gatita*?"

A muffled sob left me as his hips shifted, delivering sweet strokes pulling my orgasm from me.

I screamed louder as it felt like this one hit me with the force of a tsunami. I was dying.

There was no other words for it.

Whimpers left me as I felt it drawn out, my hips bucking back, thighs shaking wildly. All the while, Kellan growled savage words against my skin.

"That's my girl, there you fucking go...I know, baby. It's a lot...but you can take it."

My throat was hoarse as I cried out with the pressure.

His fingers laced over mine, gripping tightly, as he moved slower, whispering in my ear, that I should *keep coming* for him.

Oh. *My*.

I lost my mind.

I did. I was shaking so hard as I came down with that dark voice urging me for *more*.

This man is going to kill me.

Long moments later he finished, pulsing in me with quiet groans of my name, my fingers gripping his tightly.

I love you, honey.

I love you, Kellan.

Sex never felt like with anyone else.

I felt at peace with him. In the moments after he laid with me, we pressed kisses into each other's skin and I found myself laying there feeling like, I could do this forever. I said it out loud.

He made a noise into my neck as he kissed me.

"*Love you, Gatita.*"

Eventually, I got the olive oil.

～

WE MADE DINNER ALMOST EVERY NIGHT WITH KELLAN TEASING OVER my shoulder, following me around the kitchen, handing me things, and, at times, keeping things away from me for kisses in exchange.

I liked those the *most*. I liked him the most.

I didn't know relationships were possible like this. In my mind, men had only used me for sex and discarded me.

Kellan was a different kind of first for me.

The kind that made me think of lazy mornings in the sun, soft kisses, and his golden skin.

Days went by, and having him in my space became *our* space.

And it felt easy to have him with me.

He was not as organized as me.

He tossed his shirts on my couch, and I would pick them and wear them to sleep instead of my nighties. He lost all his socks all the time. I had no idea where they went.

My housekeeper loved him because he hated folding clothes.

But he also snuggled me every night like I was his teddy bear, and he woke up with his tongue between my legs.

Not that I would complain when he would reach for me again and again during the night.

Until I was sore. And even then, I couldn't stop kissing him. As attentive as he was, he would ask me where he left his things, and somehow I would know.

He was so different from me and still Kellan focused on the things we had in common. Which was everything else.

We liked the same movies and food, and activities, and we thought the same, coming to conclusions together. He's a fantastic partner for me. In so many ways. He pushed all my buttons.

And I love him for it.

Some nights, in his arms, everything else faded away. Everyone else.

Nathan ceased to exist, becoming nothing more than a distant memory.

I needed to talk to Nathan, to end things between us, no matter how much it terrified me to break the promise I had made.

Tell him about the beach in Capri. Tell him I don't love Nathan. Not like him.

Yet, deep down, I remained silent, my words caught in my throat.

Sometimes, that's how it starts.

But if I lost Nathan and Kellan? What would I be? Who would I be?

And so I kept my secrets.

Tonight, Kellan picked up some things from the manor.

I found out today while he was gone he had asked Liam to switch out my rent payments with his weeks ago.

My budget app did not tell me anything about this month's rent.

Liam, who did not interact with anyone but Evie and Reed, hadn't asked questions. He'd just done it.

When I texted him, Kellan said I could pay for anything I'd like to, but he said he would not be *mooching* off his lady.

It was my first time hearing some of the words he used. I was speaking more English with him, and in turn, he was patient and kind, his love the kind I wanted to lay in forever.

When I texted him, he'd responded with—

I also took care of your groceries and bills because I'll be damned if I eat you out of house and home.

But you can still cook, honey

I sat there, not knowing what to do. *But...I can do it myself.*

I didn't text him back because I knew his reply now. *I know you can, but let me help you.*

And just like another layer of me crumbled. I had to call Nathan. And I was so afraid. I didn't know why I couldn't do it.

That night, Reed asked if someone could take Avani Malhotra, Alisha's baby sister, back to her college?

I saw the name of the school. Astor University.

Diana Martinez goes to Astor.

I picked up Avani and politely greeted Alisha, still a little apprehensive about her.

Reed looked too absorbed in her, kissing her forehead while I motioned to Avani to follow me. She was a sweet-faced brunette who, despite the signs of tears, had a smile filled with awe as she looked at me.

I grinned back, recognizing *that* look.

I loved when younger girls looked at me and thought *I was a girl from the magazines.*

Avani was around my height and had a similar body type, but her curves were much more pronounced. I noticed it the first time I saw her.

I noted her black turtleneck hiding her breasts.

Her jacket, hiding her hips in that black mini skirt, were noticeable, and yet she was *adorable.*

Her smile reminded me of Diego, all *shy.*

Her long hair, lighter in color than mine, triggered a memory of the girls on the corner.

I couldn't quite put my finger on it when I took her down to *Paloma* in the garage.

Her huge brown eyes widened even further. *"This is your car?"*

Her voice carried a distinctive British accent.

"Her name is *Paloma*."

Avani looked at her with her jaw on the floor. "She's beautiful." I grinned. We talked for a bit in *Paloma* as I drove her back to her college.

She told me she was an English major at school. She was seventeen and turning eighteen soon. *A baby.*

She was *sweeter* than Evie.

And then I realized *why* Avani got under my skin.

She looks like Diana and Valeria. She's not Latina.

But she's a woman of color, as Gabriel says.

Avani smiled at me as she left, and I gave her my number in case she ever needed me.

My mind was swirling.

Whenever girls went missing, it was always a cartel, a gang, or a man.

Always a man.

Angry men who hurt women because the world was not good to them.

Beautiful girls going missing?

What kind of man is doing this?

A police car drove by me slowly while I said goodbye to Avani as she left for her dorm, the silver A arches of her college over her head as she went through the door.

That night, when I got home, I knew I had to tell Kellan about the case. I did not stop shaking as I entered my apartment.

He was already there in his pajamas, and at the look on my face, he was holding me.

I sat him down on the island and filled him in where I was so far.

"You think someone is taking these girls who all look the same..."

I told him about Avani's eyes. Her features. She was the type. Kellan had met her with Alisha, and he said the same thing.

Avani was soft because she had been raised by Alisha. Who I knew *now* as a sweet lady.

Even if I felt a little unease since sweet was not Reed's type.

I didn't say it. He didn't say it. "I think all these girls are going missing for the same reason. I've seen it before."

"You think it's a serial killer?"

I nodded, my hands trembling now when I thought about Avani.

"We need to talk to Gabriel." Kellan's eyes changed then as he watched me explain. I bit my lip as I looked at his soft eyes watching me. "When you work for Gabriel, remember to not lose yourself."

"When?"

One day, he will.

Everyone changed hands, but it was always about timing.

I switched to Reed whenever Nathan was doing something stupid, and then we switched back.

Reed was different and laid back as long as you followed his rules.

Good enough gets people killed.

Hesitation bred long term problems.

And any inclination of trouble?

Must. Be. Eliminated.

His eyes went dark at the mention of that.

But he nodded, absorbing it. Taking in me. In information.

"But that's how I know my gut is right," I said. "I've worked with Gabriel long enough to know to trust my gut. The girls are connected by a person."

"We have to talk to Gabriel."

"And then we have to go to Giroux."

I already could feel my headache.

A beat passed between us as his eyes watched me tenderly. A soft expression in them as he held out his hand. "Come here, honey."

I went across the island into them, sighing into his neck as I collapsed into him.

I did not even realize I was shaking as hard as I was until he tightened his arms around me.

I stood there inhaling his clean scent and his heat, wondering where this had been all my life.

Sometimes that's how it starts.

Gabriel was not wrong.

Where had he been?

And what would I do without him?

CHAPTER 22
SELENA

Alisha had started a charity called the Poppy Project, or Poppy for short, to help women in need...like younger me.

Maybe younger Selena could've gone to Alisha for help if Alisha had existed then.

Kellan told me they went to homeless shelters and schools, gave out clean clothes, food, and pads to women, and he said a lot of those teenagers came back to Poppy to volunteer, and now those programs had spread throughout the city.

Reed called Alisha an angel for a reason.

Alisha was so different from anyone else Reed had ever been with.

I knew that Kellan did spend time around Gemma Marchand, but he bumped into Nathan, and I wondered if they were friendly. Kellan never mentioned him.

I did not ask.

It was later one night Kellan asked me. "Do you want to go with me to the event Alisha has to go to tonight?"

Kellan explained to me Reed had a last-minute job to attend, and he needed Kellan.

"A party?"

He considered it. "I think. Not sure what influencers do. Reed mentioned there would be lipstick and makeup, but I don't know how these events work."

I hadn't been a bodyguard to celebrities.

Only ambassadors occasionally.

I didn't know what to pick. I went into my closet and picked out something appropriate that I thought would fit a makeup party?

The silver floor-length dress with heels on was beautiful, but it was the split all up to my thighs that I loved; it made the overall decent outfit gorgeous.

Just the right amount of sexy. I had my gun on the thigh that wasn't exposed, but I wore a chain on the thigh that was. I did my earrings and hair before moving on to my makeup.

"Honey, should I wear—" He stopped talking as he saw me. I was doing my mascara.

"Hmmm." I mimicked the noise he made. I put the wand down and turned to look at him shirtless and in nothing but black slacks. I blinked.

His throat was working as he took me in. "You're wearing that?"

I nodded. "You look good in white. Try that one." I pointed to the options in his hand. He gaped, not moving.

"Do you have any idea how beautiful you look right now?"

I felt the smile appear easily. "We have to go. After, you can have your way." I smiled at the heat in them.

He nodded. "I'll hold you to it." His eyes raked down my body. "I love you, *Gatita*."

"Love you too," I kissed him again.

My heart was beating wildly in my chest as he put on his white button-down. I did his hair, and he adjusted my outfit before we went to his car. We'd take a taxi to the event since parking was horrible.

But he would drive to Alisha's. When we got there, I was really nervous about meeting Alisha. I had avoided meeting her twice now.

Trying to keep a polite distance from her to be professional and not cause conflict. Reed had liked her for three years now. I did not want to be rude.

But when Alisha opened the door, her bright hazel eyes twinkled, her smile so warm in her tiny silk black robe, it was contagious.

I did not have to introduce myself as Kellan grinned that smile I wanted to kiss.

As Alisha went to the room to change, Kellan turned to me. "See, not bad."

I smiled. "No, not bad at all." And he kissed me softly. "What if Reed sees?"

"Trust me, Reed isn't paying attention to us." He kissed me again, pressing me into him. "Just let me, *Gatita*."

He dipped his head. "I know you're not wearing anything under this dress. Spread your legs—"

I gasped as he reached, cupping me with one hand, hot and firm against my center and making me moan. "Reed isn't coming out here."

He whispered in my ear. "Trust me, honey?"

Yes.

I gasped as he crowded me into the wall, and I was drowning in him. I did trust him. I did. And he felt so good. I had been hungry since he'd walked out shirtless and looking like he could eat me. "Right now?"

"Right now." I bit my lip, looking at the closed bedroom door Reed and Alisha were in. "If Reed's getting busy, we might as well."

"How?" The words left my lips before I could stop it. His grin was wicked.

"Spread your legs." Long moments later, his fingers worked deep inside of me while his tongue and teeth worked on my nipples. I was coming and hard as he whispered filth into my skin.

Such a good girl. I'm going to fuck you so sweet when we get home.

Kiss me when you come.

Long moments passed as he went back to my nipples. This man was a savage.

"Not—" I whimpered, feeling my legs nearly giving out as he held me up with a powerful arm. "Not again."

"*Again*," his growl over my skin, tugging on my nipples, felt like bliss as he continued.

But what if we got caught?

A rush of heat flooded me at the thought.

"You know what?" He muttered. "If Reed's getting some, I might as well." I was confused. What was Reed getting?

I came until Kellan was satisfied, and I couldn't stop shaking.

And only then did he carry me into the other bedroom. This one was all pink and pretty like a teenage girls. Avani's.

He took me into the bathroom that had belonged to someone once, Alisha's sister, his eyes roaming over the pink room.

He shook his head in amusement as he cleaned us both up. "Sit, I'll help you with your mascara."

What? And then he withdrew my mascara tube from his pocket.

At my shock, that stupid smile was back. "You don't like when I mess it up. I don't like seeing you upset."

He held up the mascara. "Now make that fishy face you do when you put it on."

I kissed that smile off his face our laughter mingling.

I love him. I love him so much. I don't love Nathan like him.

When Reed finally came out of the room, Kellan was still standing with me in the circle of his arms, showing me photos of his family on his phone to distract me from touching him.

I took one look at Reed's hair and his lips and felt my cheeks heat at what I had heard briefly out of Alisha's room.

But it quickly shifted as I got a load of what he was wearing.

He *never* dressed like that unless something was going down.

"Take care of her. I'll be out late tonight," he said to both of us, grabbing his jacket.

Kellan and I both nodded. Reed didn't care if Kellan was wrapped around me. We just had to do our jobs.

When Reed left, moments later, Alisha stepped out, her long black hair styled to one side and her makeup shimmering in the soft light, making her light hazel eyes brighter.

She looked beautiful in her little black dress, the fabric clinging to her curves in all the right places, and like mine, it sparkled a little.

A warm pink colored Alisha's cheeks as she caught both of us admiring her, and she ducked her head shyly.

Kellan called a taxi, grinning at her with a look. I knew he teased her often about Reed.

I didn't have girlfriends.

Not in my line of work. Evie was not the same, more of a little sister than someone who was my girlfriend.

In the taxi on the way to the event, Kellan sat up front while Alisha and I shared the back seat.

"I love how the side slit looks with your legs," she complimented me with a smile. So did Kellan. I caught his *look* from the front.

"Is it from the new Davina&Co collection?"

I nodded, pleased that she noticed and was making an effort to connect with me.

Nothing like Reed's past.

"I know they've been designing clothes for the last decade, but that last collection…"

Kellan grinned from the front. "Alisha's designing clothes for her brand. She might be looking for a model."

Alisha laughed at me as I blushed. "I'm working on some but I would love it if you wanted to. I need all the models I could get…"

I listened to her talk realizing she was nothing like anyone Reed had ever been with.

She's good for him.

She squirmed in her seat a little, biting her lip, and I wondered if she was comfortable.

The event itself was glamorous and I had been to a few events like this. Influencers had shown up, and Alisha was greeted by tons of people.

But I saw Kellan was looking at everything, scanning, as he said. *Alisha is a girl from the magazines.*

It occurred to me then Alisha was the kind of woman I saw in magazines growing up. Someone I wanted to be. Someone I admired. She was different.

Because she was herself in so many ways.

While I was pretending? *Alisha was real.* And it made me see her differently.

Suddenly, a commotion caught my eye.

A blonde woman launched herself at Alisha, and I instinctively moved to intervene when Kellan gently brushed me back. As the blonde held Alisha, a familiar face appeared behind her.

Nathan.

I did not even think as I went to hug him. It was automatic.

He had been my partner, and I noticed his frown directed at the woman. *Gemma.*

That was Gemma Marchand.

"How are you, *muñeca*?" He greeted me, holding a water bottle and wrapping an arm around my shoulders.

His touch felt familiar, yet foreign for some reason.

Kellan.

"Not too bad, you?" I replied, trying to maintain a casual tone despite knowing I was sleeping with Kellan.

Living with Kellan. And promised myself to Nathan.

"Babysitting," he grumbled, and I bit back a laugh.

Nathan muttered something about princess duty, correcting Gemma that she'd had five drinks instead of four when she wanted to argue. It was good to see someone giving it back to him.

Next to him was a dark-haired woman in a long black dress covering from the neck down, who seemed amused by everyone around her, but she did not participate.

She introduced herself as Sonya. Teasing Alisha and Gemma from afar. She gave me a polite smile when our eyes met, hers a darker green than mine.

I turned to watch Nathan practically lift a drunk Gemma off.

My smile vanished when I caught the look in Kellan's eyes.

Why does he look like that?

I was not even sure if he had met Nathan since he arrived here. His eyes did not even acknowledge me; they were solely focused on Nathan, sizing him up as Nathan argued quietly with Gemma.

The other woman hissed at him about something. *Good for her.*

Maybe she is not the same Gemma anymore.

Nathan paused his argument with Gemma for a moment as though he caught me staring, and looked over at me.

I smirked at my old partner. *"Te lo dije."*

I told you so.

I had not seen Nathan since he left, and I did not want to. I was with Kellan now. I need to end it.

"Really, Lena?" Nate gave me one of his grins. "You wanna do this here, *muñeca?*"

The last person I expected to get involved with was Kellan. *"Don't call her that."*

Everyone froze, turning to him, except for Nathan, who laughed.

Because he loved this stuff. He did not even know I was sleeping with Kellan. He just knew how to get a rise out of people. Kellan's jaw tightened, his eyes hardening.

Why was he...he was mine.

He does not ever have anything to worry about.

But that was a lie. I felt it in my chest.

I need to tell Nathan. I needed to end things with Nathan, and as much as it hurt, I knew I had to. I didn't understand why Kellan would be so upset.

He did not express the same things Nathan had.

I was still making the choices I was. And I couldn't wonder for long when I felt Alisha reach for my hand, Sonya eyeing me with concern.

Both of them reached for me.

"*Selena,*" Alisha said with the other woman trying to diffuse the tension. "Did you know Gemma speaks Spanish?"

I did not. And then suddenly, I got to meet Gemma Marchand in person.

She's like a princess.

Blonde hair swept back, her blue eyes big and warm, and her soft pink smile as she took me in. I couldn't imagine someone like Nathan loving someone like Gemma.

She complimented my eyes, and I felt my cheeks warm, realizing I was meeting her for the first time and that I knew so much about her but only from Nathan.

Who was not the kind of person I wanted to listen to anything about right now...

Nathan enjoyed goading people, but he didn't know about me and Kellan.

And Kellan...*We were together.*

Every night he was together with me.

I don't know how long I stood there talking to Gemma in Spanish while Kellan stood close to Alisha watching me and her. Gemma kept making sure I was involved, and it made me love her a little more.

"*Chicas!*" I heard a voice call out. *Lara Ford.*

Lara was tiny, at maybe five feet tall, with her dark hair in two buns and her black mini dress. She looked like a doll with delicate features and doe eyes.

But I had known Lara for years, and even if her looks hadn't changed much? Her life had.

I knew Gabriel watched over Lara and they were close. And just like Liam Sullivan, Reed took over to protect Lara with the O'Hara brother's. But with the way Lara acted on stage?

You would never have guessed her background. Her history.

I knew enough to know what she had been through. And enough to know Gabriel would kill for her.

Kellan had told me he'd gotten all the sex toys he tried out on me from her which had been ironic. That had been a night. And I hadn't been able to walk the next day.

This version of Lara Ford smiled at me softly, recognizing me, and her eyes sent me a silent look. I shook my head.

I would never tell anyone who Lara Ford really was. I knew *that* look in her eyes. I knew a girl like me when I saw one. Lara pretended in front of everyone else she wasn't close to Titan.

Or Killian O'Hara. Or Gabriel. But with her there, the night slowly transformed into something else, something no client had ever done for me before—Alisha made me feel like I was one of her girlfriends.

Alisha had an energy about her that people gravitated towards. I could see why Reed liked her when I found myself laughing easily, the sound bubbling up from within me.

I felt like a *normal* girl with her *friends*.

It felt different from the girls on the street. These women felt like they were in my league.

I could feel the weight of Kellan's gaze as he stood close. Nathan, maintained a watchful distance, his eyes never straying far from Gemma.

I could see it even from here, the way Nathan watched her.

The way she ignored him.

And I wondered, even if Gemma had changed, what if she did not want Nathan?

What if this was just…lust between me and Kellan.

But it did not feel like that.

How would you know?

Nobody has ever loved you.

No, but men lusted for me.

That's all they ever did.

Men wanted me as an object in their room. Someone to show to their friends. Someone who did not participate in their pleasure. I had been with people before for a long time who simply wanted to use me.

Kellan did not use me. He made me realize I deserved to be loved. I never felt that love with Nathan.

This was not the same. I could feel it.

Trust your gut. Gabriel's voice was in my head.

Gemma leaned in, her voice lowered to a whisper.

She switched to Spanish and asked me how I had ever tolerated Nathan and his motorcycle making so much noise in the mornings.

I laughed harder when she told me she threw her shoe at him the first morning he had shown up with it.

Gemma's neighbors hated both of them because of how loud she'd cursed him out with that bike.

I covered my mouth as she told me Nathan had brought his gray truck the next day.

I had never known that side of either of them.

Nathan would just keep bringing his bike even if we complained.

"Are you sure you're not Latina?" I teased her, and she blushed.

"No, just one angry French woman." She laughed. "Pretty sure, my people invented the word *revolution*."

And then she teased about how if Nathan continued to be stubborn, she would hold a revolution against him.

I laughed so hard with her.

Kellan looked over with a smile at us, overhearing little bits and pieces. More easy laughter talking to Gemma, who was funny with a sharp tongue and throwing her blonde hair back to tease Alisha.

This was not the woman Nathan had described at all.

But Nathan, I could feel him watching.

He could hear us, but he wasn't as close as Kellan. I could feel Kellan's intensity, curiosity, and jealousy emanating from him with Nathan near.

This baby.

I wanted to reach out to him and hold him close to me. That's all he needed sometimes. He got like this outside when he made me sit closer to him in public.

He just needed some kisses, and I could see he wanted to pounce.

Outside, he switched between that lion who played with me and this man. And that man's jaw was granite like he was ready to attack something. When Alisha excused herself to the bathroom, Kellan accompanied her, standing nearby in the hallway.

I could still see him, his silhouette visible through the doorway.

The moment he was gone, Nathan approached me, and I felt a familiar prickle at the back of my neck.

Here it comes...

"You're *with Quarterback*." Nathan's words cut through the air.

I did not like people reducing him to nothing. Not even his name. "His name is Kellan."

Everyone called him that for all all-American good looks. He was handsome. Like a playful sun God who decided to spend time with me and tease me in bed.

I like Kellan.

Lara, who had been talking to Gemma for a bit, saw me and Nathan with a look that told me Lara was distracting Gemma.

She began to motion enthusiastically and overly so to show Gemma something while Gemma laughed. *God bless Lara.*

Sonya, the attentive dark-haired woman with millions of dollars of diamonds on her, stood near me all night. She was on her phone typing something.

I kept my voice down. "Don't look at me like that."

"I kept my half," he said quietly, a hint of desperation in his tone. His eyes were dark and hard as he looked at me. "I just turned—"

"*The deal's off*," I whispered, my words trembling as I looked into his stunned blue eyes.

Guilt and regret twisted in my gut, but I knew I had to be honest. "I cannot do it. I'm so sorry."

I reached for his hands, feeling them grow cold as the color drained from his face. I hurt him. And I didn't want to.

The words tumbled out of me, a confession I could no longer hold back. I admitted to being with Kellan and liking him too much. It wasn't fair to Kellan or to Nathan.

"...I see the way you look at Gemma. She is yours. She has never stopped being yours—"

"She's *with someone else—*"

Tears stung my eyes as the weight of letting him down settled on my shoulders.

"You'd *throw it all away because you're fucking Quarterback-*"

"Don't *talk about him like that.*" Anger surged through me once more, my voice hissing in defense of him. "*Nathan. He has a name—*"

Nathan's expression turned fierce. He drew closer to me, his anger evident, and I felt so bad for hurting him.

"*You call it off because you want to have a fling?*" The accusation in his words struck me, and my own expression crumpled as he let go of my hands. "*Lena, what are you doing?*"

He was so much closer now, and I could see the fear in his eyes.

This is why Nathan was breaking. He has always wanted to be a father.

"He is *not* a fling. I just want to try—*For him.* I will never be yours. I never have been. Not like her."

The truth spilled from my lips, raw and unfiltered.

Gemma. Had. Always. Been. Nathan's.

"You don't love me. You want me because you are afraid—"

"*Afraid?*" He was trying to keep his voice down and thank God for Lara animated and talking to Gemma gesturing like a wild woman, with Gemma's back to us.

He got in my face, and I returned it. Like I always had. I prayed Kellan did not see us.

"Yes! Of being with someone who might love you."

The words were a revelation, both to him and to myself. I was so close I could see his shock in those navy eyes.

He'd been my partner for years. *I know him.*

"Nathan. You don't love me."

"*Of course, I love you,* Lena."

He looked at me in disbelief. He motioned to us with his hands. "You and me, Lena. That's all it's ever been."

That hurt. He wasn't wrong.

It had been me and him.

But I didn't love him the way I loved Kellan.

"Not the way you love *her.* I see your eyes." He still loved Gemma. With everything he had. We were so *close.* "I see you. This is not that love."

Nathan ran a hand down his mouth, his eyes taking me in with a new understanding. He swallowed hard as if seeing me for the first time.

"You love him." Those hard blue eyes so different from Kellan pierced into me.

Too hard. Too much of the edge I did not need. I did not want Nathan. *Never.*

It wasn't a question but a statement of fact.

My hands shook as I nodded, ducking my head, feeling my eyes blur, confirming the truth he had uncovered.

If my mascara ran, I wouldn't be as upset as Kellan because he would know I cried.

"Does he love you?"

He loves me more than I love myself.

"Yes."

With Nathan, the future was a predictable journey lacking anything. But with Kellan?

There is love.

Sonya appeared at my side out of nowhere.

"Selena," she said, her voice a gentle interruption, her accent crisp. "I just found the *perfect* shade of mauve to match your dress. Shall I show you?"

I forced a smile onto my face, my gaze fixed on Nathan's expression as he closed his eyes, a silent acknowledgment of the shift between us.

He extended his hand, and without hesitation, I placed mine in his.

In a gesture that echoed a distant memory, he pressed his lips to the same spot he had kissed years ago.

A nod, a silent understanding passed between us.

Just like that.

Despite our complicated history, Nathan's protective nature towards the women in his life, towards me, remained steadfast.

At that moment, I knew he respected me enough to let go.

Just like that. Because that was Nathan.

"I'm sorry."

"I'm sorry," he echoed, shaking his head.

I *want to cry. I do.*

But it was not fair to Kellan.

I realized it didn't matter what my past was or who I had been. Maybe when I made my promise, I did not want love.

But now?

Now I *wanted* it. Craved it.

Choosing Nathan would be accepting love like an IV drip.

Choosing Kellan would be like being drowned in it.

That's what he felt like. He felt like I was walking into the sun after spending years in shadows. And I couldn't get enough of him.

With Kellan, I wanted something more...something past the girl I was. He made me feel things I thought were a dream.

He was *real.*

My eyes burned, and I knew if I ruined my mascara, Kellan would know and go after Nathan, even if Kellan had a tube of my mascara and lip gloss in his pocket.

He carried my makeup wherever we went because he knew it was important to me. Kellan made me realize love was not just big moments, but all the little moments in between.

Even as I stepped away with Sonya, I felt the hairs on the back of my neck prickle as Sonya rubbed my hand gently.

Looking over my shoulder, I saw Kellan was no longer standing there.

Maybe he did not see that argument.

That was for the best.

CHAPTER 23
KELLAN

I'M GOING TO KILL NATE FUCKING WYATT.

I watched that *entire* conversation as he tried to corner my girl. *Only after I left?*

Alisha had been in the bathroom, and I was standing at the only entrance and exit, keeping an eye on Selena.

It looked like Selena was turning him down, shaking her head several times. *Atta girl.*

It took every single fucking thing I had in me to stand there and not storm over there and grab him, to break his arm the moment he kissed her hand.

Because for Selena I was an absolute monster.

I couldn't think straight.

I knew I was losing my cool around everyone and it didn't even matter.

Because the bone-deep seated need to possess her filled me.

I wanted to fuck Selena right in front of everyone.

Sit her up in a bar-stool and slide that skirt up and pound that pussy until she screamed my name.

Until I was so deep, she did that sexy little whimper and begged for more. I wanted Nate fucking Wyatt to watch me while she came her eyes locked on mine as she cried out.

I was a fucking savage.

I was her savage. And right now, he was entirely too fucking close to my girl.

Why was he so *close* to her?

And then I saw *her* face. *I knew that face.*

She looked ready to cry.

What the fuck did you say to my girl?

And he put his lips on her?

I was going to murder him. In cold blood.

I don't think Selena even knew how much of a fucking demon I was.

Gemma seemed like a nice lady, but he made Selena cry. I saw nothing but red. I didn't even notice Alisha stepping out by my side.

Instead, I let her lead me back to the girls who had decided to ditch this beauty event for a townhouse owned by Sonya.

Who seemed the most level-headed out of everyone in the group despite looking frail and wide-eyed in all black.

While I found Selena, I tucked her into my side trying not to shake as she cuddled into me.

Trying not to kiss her so often that I looked like a hungry, starved man deprived of pussy for years when I knew I'd take her home and work out my frustrations against that tiny little spot in her.

The one that made her sob my name when she came so hard from it.

Her smile was aimed at me, despite the emotion in her eyes and the fact that Nate fucking Wyatt looked upset?

It helped. Just enough.

I kissed her instantly, claiming her mouth knowing full well she was my honey. My girl.

It temporarily calmed me down with her as everyone was figuring out their ride situation.

I didn't miss the way fucking Wyatt stared.

Look all you want, motherfucker. She chose me.

She came home with me.

She came *on me* every single night. And there wasn't a single fucking thing Nate fucking Wyatt could do about it.

"What's gotten into you, savage?" Selena murmured. Little did she know how true that was.

"Nothing, honey. I'm solid." I was lying. I was not okay.

She was the only thing that mattered—*the only one* I cared about.

And I'd be damned if I let anyone, especially Nate fucking Wyatt, come between us.

He made her cry.

As we made our way to Sonya's townhouse, I kept Selena close, my eyes constantly scanning.

But the primal urge to claim what was mine, to make it clear to Nate fucking Wyatt that Selena belonged to me, coursed through my veins like a raging inferno.

We went to Sonya's, where the housekeeper took us all in, and Sonya had the foresight to text her beforehand since she ushered me and Nate into the kitchen with lots of food.

My stomach growled as I ignored him.

For now. I was starving.

Earlier tonight, I wanted to let Selena sit on my lap and grind on my dick while it was inside of her, while I sucked on her pretty tits. But now?

Now, I wanted to take her in the roughest version of me possible. Be not sweet to her. Take her in every part of her and make her scream she was mine as I did.

I hadn't even taken the first bite when Nate's words cut through the silence.

"You're serious about Lena?"

This motherfucker.

His tone was laced with something I couldn't figure out, and my grip tightened on the knife, the metal cool against my palm.

You kissed my girl. I wanted to shove the knife in my hand into his throat.

I chewed slowly, each movement deliberate as I tried to control the rage simmering beneath my skin.

Images flashed through my mind—Selena's tear-stained face, Nate's lips on her hand, the way she trembled in my arms when I held her close.

Or shoot him with the gun at my back. I took a breath, Selena's voice from earlier coasting over me.

Kellan, you will take me home with you?

Yeah honey, I'll take you home with me.

Because Selena was *mine.*

She chose me.

I went home with her tonight. She lives in my arms. I didn't owe Nate fucking Wyatt shit.

Reed would be upset with me if I killed him tonight. *Right now.*

"You made my girl cry," I said, my voice low and controlled. I watched as Nate's eyes widened. "The *only* reason I haven't put this knife through your hand is because Reed would be pissed if I caused a scene in front of Alisha."

"The only reason?"

No, because I loved Selena too much to fuck this up.

I wanted to hear from her, not him why he kissed her.

Why she looked like she was ready to cry. *Not him.*

I didn't want to waste my time with him. *Not Nate fucking Wyatt.*

"You call her anything but her name again, I'll kill you. Plain and simple. You don't look at my girl. You don't talk to her. And if you do? No more Lena. No more Gemma." I watched his eyes change at the mention of his charge.

Yeah, I caught that too.

"That a threat?" He looked like he was mocking me. *I could shove this fork in his neck.* "You show up to Titan and you threaten me?"

I could kill him right now and it wouldn't matter a bit. Not. One. Bit.

"That's a *promise.* You touch my girl again, I will break every single fucking bone in your body for making her cry. I don't give a fuck if you were her previous partner. Or whatever the fuck you were." The red in me was a living thing, constricting around my lungs, tightening around my body. If Nate fucking Wyatt could tell I was serious he considered me then. "She's not yours. She never will be."

She chose me.

And there was a glint in his eyes I didn't recognize as I said it.

Nate studied me, a muscle in his jaw ticking, his expression unreadable. I didn't give a fuck. He made my girl cry. I would break his fucking fingers for touching her.

"She chose you?" his voice was quiet. "Is that what you think?"

"Did I fucking stutter?" My voice was lethal. What the fuck did he mean by that?

Who the fuck cares?

Kill him. Kill him right now. End him.

I barely tasted anything craving Selena instead. Her fingers running through my hair. I waited for her by texting her.

Her response was instant.

We are going home now. X

It soothed whatever storm was brewing in my chest. The urge to fight Nate was there but I focused on Selena. On Alisha.

I couldn't kill Nate. Reed would have my head.

I walked out of the room ignoring Nate and immediately saw my girl giggling with Alisha. Both of them linking arms and Alisha's laughter spilling into the hallway.

Oh, she's been drinking.

A sleepy grin appeared on Selena's face, directed solely at me.

For me.

Instinctively, I pulled both of them into my arms. Alisha snuggled into my chest as Selena leaned up to kiss me.

"Let's get you two home," I said, gently corralling my girls out and calling us a cab back to Alisha's place. In the cab, Selena kept murmuring things to me that Alisha wouldn't understand. But I did.

Take me home, savage. Take me again.

Easy, Gatita. You're tipsy and I'm in a mood.

Why?

I didn't get a chance to explain.

It wasn't until we stepped off the elevator onto Alisha's floor that an unsettling sensation prickled at the back of my neck.

Before I could fully process the feeling, Alisha stumbled backward, letting out a startled noise.

Instantly, I was on high alert, and I felt Selena shift in my arms, responding to the potential threat.

My mind raced as I began scanning our surroundings, with Selena seamlessly following my lead.

The apartment door was open. *Shit.*

"*Gatita*, stay with her," I instructed, drawing my gun as I cautiously entered the apartment.

I methodically cleared each room, finding nothing out of place until I reached Alisha's bedroom.

Double. Shit. I knew it would be on the fucking bed. *It was always the bed.*

A pair of Alisha's underwear lay on the bed, with another fucking note?

I swore, quickly taking photos for Reed when I heard Alisha's scream behind me.

Selena was pulling her back, understanding the gravity of the situation. Someone broke into Alisha's home and we had to get her out of here.

I cursed under my breath, reaching for Alisha. "Honey, call Reed."

And Selena, following my lead, she nodded, tucking her gun into her leg that was covered and any other moment, I would appreciate it, but right now? I had a crying Alisha in my arms.

Deep down I acknowledged the pride I felt at Selena following my lead. As a team.

Selena was on her phone texting him, and since he'd been out, God knows where.

We would stay with Alisha until he got back. It didn't take him long. Selena's eyes met mine.

She shook her head as she took the call from Reed.

Alisha sobbed into my chest, shaking wildly as I rubbed her back.

She'd been out of it too, a little more than Selena since Selena was technically working, but with me around, she'd be fine. I figured Alisha had a little more out with her friends.

And she cried harder as I soothed her.

Selena looked at her with sympathy. "We have to take her to Reed's."

And then effortlessly, Selena and I switched again, where she took the lead, my chest swelling as we alternated smoothly, Selena in front while I had Alisha.

When we got to my car, I saw Selena's expression at the coupe. She could take Alisha in my car.

No way I was going to let my girl go alone.

I handed her my keys. "Take her, I'll take a cab and meet you there."

She didn't bat an eye at me, giving her directions. Reed had given me his address and a key card to the building he lived in, in the event anything ever happened.

It was an imposing tower that had maybe forty apartments, luxury high-rise vibes, and dark in the night, and I met Selena in the underground parking lot. "Reed lives here?"

"This is K2. He stays on the top floor."

Selena knew what she was doing.

She explained what this building was. Reed had named it after a mountain that was impossible to climb. And his place in the tower was impossible to break into.

My girl and I didn't miss a step the entire time. I scanned us into Reed's place at Selena's direction. This place was a locked box.

I entered the code Reed had told me to memorize weeks ago. And then we were off in a private elevator, Alisha between us with my jacket around her shoulders.

Selena explained that the rest of the building was residential space, including the front desk.

Only the lobby was open to the public, with the receptionist manning the desk, but Selena had explained Reed had this private elevator for himself along with the entire top floor.

You needed a keycard, or you needed Reed.

K2 was a fortress with strategic design and state-of-the-art security measures providing safety and seclusion.

By the time we got upstairs, Selena had typed another pin in, letting her in.

The door clicked open to illuminate his apartment in its enormous black and navy detailing, and the lighting on the floor turned on for me to get a glimpse of it.

Reed lives here?

"You have to disable the alarms in the apartment with the key card. They are silent. They do not alert you. But they alert Reed and Gabriel."

She swiped the keycard quickly.

"What happens if you forget to disable the alarm?"

She looked over her shoulder, turning on more lights and speaking quickly.

"It traps you inside the apartment. None of the doors or windows inside this apartment will open or close. Which means—"

"Any room you are in, you're stuck in." I almost felt sorry for whoever decided to break into Reed's apartment. That would be a trip. She nodded, motioning to Alisha, and she took her.

"The only time you do not is if someone with access remembers to disable it for you."

I looked around as Selena took Alisha to the living room.

The penthouse was huge, with high ceilings and sprawling with an open plan layout.

Selena navigated easily, showing her familiarity. I had never seen a screen as big as the one in his living room. Selena sat with Alisha as we both waited for instructions from Reed.

She covered Alisha with a blanket as the other woman cried silently.

And when Reed showed up, I saw it *all* over his face.

I motioned to Selena, who was sitting with Alisha.

He was ready to murder someone.

Selena came to me moments later, taking my hand and moving out of his way, telling me we needed to go back to get prints and see if we could find anything.

We have to get Alisha's things.

She was staying at K2? *Alisha was going to be devastated.*

Which also meant she wouldn't need me anymore unless she left the tower.

Because this place was something else. I realized something. "Someone's fucking with Alisha."

I felt something there because of Selena's expression. "Do you have a clue?"

"No, but I'm going to talk to Gabriel about this." My stomach soured as we drove back to Alisha's.

Selena and I moved together to go in there in full work mode.

She grabbed Alisha's things while I wandered around the place.

Checking for prints, but also? I had seen Avani's window open when I was clearing the apartment.

She had the room with the fire escape, and it was easy to miss with all the books and shelves in there. If they came through a window...then they had to have shown up outside on a camera. Because they took the fire escape.

Motherfucker left the door open to fuck with our heads. I went back to the hallway. "Honey, I'm going to check something out."

"*¡No hagas nada estúpido!*" *Don't do anything stupid.* She called from Alisha's bedroom.

215

I grinned. "I wouldn't dare."

I went back and peered out the window, looking all around on the fire escape. The streets were dark, the lamps lit up, but I couldn't see what I needed.

When I went downstairs, I found a camera about a block away.

I called Selena, asking if she had a way for us to pull images off a security camera. She did.

Moments later, when I came back, Selena had Alisha's items packed, and she'd called a moving company to come with Garrett and pack it all away for Alisha since I'd explained to her on the drive here how important this place had been for the woman.

Selena was grabbing some of the Polaroid photos from Alisha's fridge of her, Avani, and her friends. Into a neat pile before putting them into her bag.

She raised her sister in this place. It's going to gut her to leave it.

We will do what we can. Reed is going to kill whoever did this. I saw his face.

I did, too. I sensed shifts on the horizon, visible in the lines of concern etched on Reed's face.

I wouldn't be surprised if he worked from home and stayed with her for the time being.

As she set down all of Alisha's items that she could find, I was impressed as we'd split tasks easily.

There was no argument—we were just assuming our roles together. Working with Selena felt like something in me slid into place.

We were a team.

"We make a good team," she said softly, her eyes warm, taking me in as though reading my mind. "You are a good partner."

And then my mood dimmed a little at the mention of partners.

I shouldn't bring him up.

I *couldn't* stop it.

"Why did Nate kiss you?"

CHAPTER 24
KELLAN

SELENA'S BEAUTIFUL EMERALD EYES WIDENED SO MUCH I COULD TELL I shocked her. *Good.*

"I saw him kiss you. Why did he touch you?" My voice was deceptively low aware that I didn't want to startle her. No. Not after he almost made her cry.

"It was nothing, he just—" She's nervous. Why?

"*Nothing?*" I cut her off.

"It was just my hand—"

I was on her in a second gripping her neck with a force I didn't know I had. And Selena because she was my girl, she trusted me, her legs immediately parting for me that drew a primal satisfaction to my chest.

It calmed me down only slightly that she loved me as much as she did. My fingers squeezed gently around her throat, her lips parting and emerald eyes batted up at me.

"Did you forget *all of you is mine?* He doesn't get to touch you. *Nobody* does the way I do."

Especially not Nate fucking Wyatt. I didn't like the way he looked at her. Not once.

A small delicate pout formed on her lips as she looked at me. She wanted me to kiss her. I knew it. Selena didn't mind me rough.

The dark chocolate hair she had framing her face made her look radiant and her skin had glowed until Nate got near her. She glowed with me.

Nate only tamped out her light and I fucking hated him for that alone. Only this time, I saw how wet her eyes were right now on me.

On me.

She was staring at me like that.

Fuck. The raw sensations of guilt seeped through me, sinking into my skin somewhere sore and sensitive from Nate's smirk.

Fuck that guy.

Never want to hurt you, honey.

"Kellan—" I stamped my mouth down on hers needing that connection more than anything else.

My tongue thrusting into her mouth because she was mine.

Not his. *Mine.*

She nearly lost her balance clinging to my shoulders, helpless against my wrath. My cock digging into her stomach while she squirmed against me.

I didn't give her a chance to compose herself. Didn't think twice about taking what was mine.

Because Selena was.

From the moment I saw her she was.

My light.

My pink and lush flower. She was my girl. Not his.

Never his.

"I don't think you understand the lengths I would go to for you. I am a jealous man. When it comes to you? You call me your savage. I am fucking savage."

I saw her eyes widen as I said the words.

"I can't think straight when I see another man around you. When I see him touch you like you're his? *You're not. You're mine.*"

I wrapped an arm around her waist and tugged her close until our bodies were flush. I was losing my mind with her scent.

It seemed amplified the longer I was around her, my cock losing its mind if it couldn't get in her.

My voice went dark, as I spoke. Summoned from the depths of my fucking darkness as I growled it into her skin so she'd remember.

"I take you home. I go to sleep inside that pussy. I'm the only person who gets to see you like that. *You're my girl.* You've been mine since the moment I met you—"

"*Kellan—*"

"*Why did Nate kiss you?*" My mind raced. "What did he say to you? Why did he make you cry?"

She shook her head unable to meet my eyes. And I fucking hated that. "It's not like that. I promise. Can we talk about this at home, please?"

"*Why can't you just tell me now?*"

"Kellan," she breathed, her hands coming up to cradle my face. But her eyes, they wouldn't look at me. She was hiding something from me. "I will explain everything, I swear. But not here. Please. Let's go home?"

Home. She was asking me to trust her and to have this conversation about where we lived.

Not in the midst of the shit at Alisha's apartment. It went against everything I wanted. I trusted Selena.

I didn't trust Nate. And right now? I needed her.

A breath escaped me. I didn't even realize how hard I was breathing.

I needed her to calm down. "But I need…" I couldn't voice what I needed. I just…needed it.

Slowly, I dipped my head in agreement, leaning into her soothing touch, her hands on my face holding me.

Her eyes were darker with how close I got. "You need?"

I knew that look. Softer. Subtle. But I knew my girl.

"I need you," she whispered. "I need you too."

"You need me, honey?" I was already reaching for that slit in her dress. Lush, tanned thighs parted for me. I licked her lips feeling her tongue dart out to meet mine.

"*Yes.*"

Wildfire spread through my veins, leaving no part untouched wherever she touched me. Always her. Only her.

"You're my girl."

"I am yours."

She guided me back until I sat on a barstool by the kitchen island, the same spot where she'd agreed to be mine only weeks ago.

Her hands roamed my shoulders and my chest as she murmured for me to breathe in Spanish.

There's nothing to be jealous about.

I am yours.

You are my home. My love.

Remember? I love you. Only you.

Selena was tugging at my pants, hands stroking my cock, her mouth soothing me. I groaned at the sensation of her hands gripping the head of my dick.

Stroking in time to her words like a drug fueled dream. I was panting at her words. Losing my mind because nobody did me the way Selena did.

She was heat all over my skin.

The fire trapped under me.

I wanted to protect and hold Selena close to me because I knew— my entire being knew this woman. I was a good profiler.

I was damn good at my job.

And my entire body recognized her? As a part of me.

Soft, lush, strong, and defined, my girl matched me in every way possible.

She was mine.

She was mine.

She was mine.

And I kept telling myself as she reminded me.

I didn't know her for long.

I didn't have to know her for long, to know *her*. In our line of work, you met families that had been together for twenty-five years to find out the husband had girls locked and dead in his basement.

Or people who had gotten married and switched up on each other last minute.

Husbands who left their entire will to their mistress and the wife finds out at his funeral.

That was a thing in our industry.

Knowing people for a long time?

Meant nothing if you didn't know their heart, their motivations, how they reacted under stress. Under duress. People's priorities told you a lot about them.

Love was nothing without trust.

And I trusted Selena.

I didn't trust Nate fucking Wyatt. Not one bit.

My voice was savage. "I don't want that motherfucker anywhere near you—"

"Because he kissed my hand?" Her eyes searched mine.

"No," I held her face in my hands, my thumbs brushing under her eyes. "Because he made you cry."

My heart was thumping harder against my chest as I uttered the truth. "I tolerate a lot of things, *Gatita*. I obey you at work. I do whatever you ask and I will show up for you every single time. Every. Single. Fucking. Time. But the moment someone hurts you? All of my bets are off."

There was no more nice guy. Not that I even considered myself one to begin with. My mask was on solid. And the moment anyone threatened Selena—I was a fucking beast.

Her eyes took me in and I could feel her resistance crumbling as she looked down at my lips. She whispered the things that calmed me down. Quieted my demons.

I belong to you. No one else.

Just you.

I love you.

Lychee and pink pepper wafting over me, all over me, making me drowsy, realizing how fucking much I adored her. My eyes drifted over her silver clad gown, her lithe body moving closer to me.

All I saw was flashes of silver in my arms, and I threw my head back to watch her gasp, loving the slick heat of her coasting over the tip of my dick, feeling her sink onto me right there.

I adjusted her in my lap, her legs on either side of me.

Warmth rushed through my bloodstream like molten lava.

"There you go, honey." I groaned, taking her lips in mine as she gasped a little. A little whimper left her as she wiggled, and I bit back a laugh. "Too much? Need help?"

I loved how easily she nodded, struggling a little to take me fully, and I dropped my lips to her breasts, sucking hard as she tangled her fingers in my hair, sinking the rest of the way on me.

Both of us moaned at the sensation of wet heat all around us.

"That's my fucking girl," I crooned looking up at her. "You take me so well now."

As she sank onto me fully and adjusted, I closed my eyes, losing myself in sucking peach tipped nipples into my mouth. Selena was clenching wildly around me already.

"You feel fucking incredible. *Mirame, Gatita.*"

Look at me, Kitten.

Those eyes locked with me as I looked up at her, her hair falling around me like a curtain and enclosing into our little bubble. "You're mine."

She whispered into my mouth. "I'm yours."

I let her kiss me all over my face, my smile that she loved, and she began moving her hips. "We cannot stay for hours, Kellan."

No, I couldn't fuck her like I usually did. Taking my time. Endlessly inside of her. I had the energy and stamina.

I just couldn't do it *here*.

Which meant she wanted something from me that I would gladly give her.

My lips curved into a wicked grin. "You want me not sweet, *Gatita.*"

She nodded into my kiss, her body molding to mine, settling as she worked on me, making my vision hazy.

"Fuck, take me a little more…just a little…there you go." I coaxed her deeper, my hands gripping her ass, her hips, anywhere I could. "You just wanted me all night, didn't you?"

She whimpered into my mouth as I felt her yielding to me. Stretching wider with every thrust inside of her.

Her little moans as I went deeper until I rubbed against that spot that made her cry out.

"I don't have hours here, honey," I growled into her mouth. But I could make it count. "Wrap your arms around me."

Obeying with ease, Selena held on as I pumped up into her. Wet, hot heat enveloped my dick and I was losing my shit already.

"*Kellan.*"

"*There* you go…is that better?" Selena nodded, her lips pouty from being kissed, eyes soft—*my* girl. "Every part of you is mine. Tell me who you belong to."

"Y-*you.*" She moaned as I stood up with her, gasping a little at the change in position.

"I don't like anyone's hands on you like that, especially not *anyone* kissing you," I growled slamming her down on my length.

Selena cried out in my arms, emerald eyes fluttering as she clenched over and over.

I did it again and again setting a pace I knew she wouldn't last.

"Nobody gets to touch you like that—nobody gets to see you like this—" I didn't even know what the fuck I was saying. "Look at me when you come for me. Say my fucking name when you do."

"*Kellan.*"

There you fucking go.

"You choose me?"

"I choose you," she cried out into my ear, I drove her down until she creamed all over me.

"Damn straight you do." *Every single time.*

Selena's muffled screams as she came hard were all I heard, and I felt a wicked grin curve my lips as I fucked her even harder.

Burying my head into her neck, I fucked her like an animal, taking me deeper with every thrust thanks to how wet she was.

Her screams grew wilder as she held on.

"*There* you fucking go, honey." Selena coming on my cock was gorgeous. "Come all over me."

Her lips met mine desperately sobbing as she kissed me. "*Dios… Kellan…*"

Reed cared about results.

Not if I fucked Selena seven different ways before dawn.

CHAPTER 25
SELENA

I WANT TO POUNCE ON HIM.

I was sitting next to Kellan as we watched for the man that had broken into Alisha's apartment—Tony Lopez.

I was supposed to be focused on the target. Not Kellan.

But my body had other thoughts.

My body wanted him just as much as he wanted me. It wanted to climb on top of him and ride him until we needed to leave.

The evening sun was setting leaving us in a SUV with tinted windows and it shone over Kellan's sculpted body, his hair gleaming, his eyes bright as he took in the street. Protecting us. Watching out for us.

Nobody could see us. But I could see him, and my heart raced as my eyes drank him in.

Kellan was beautiful. But in a way that I didn't think I would react to. *Maybe a little like a younger Gabriel.* But Kellan's eyes were bright and soft as he turned to me.

"You doing okay, *Gatita*?"

I always blushed as his smile crept up slowly on me. His eyes lighting up. There were two sides to every person. But Kellan's sweeter side made me more crazy sometimes. His smile lit up mine.

"What are you smiling at, savage?" I tried to keep my voice contained and not breathless. I think I failed.

"You look pretty in twilight."

And my cheeks hurt from how wide I was smiling and turning away a little. *Why did he do this to me?*

"But you look pretty all the time, honey."

In my head I heard Evie's squealing and screaming. *Oh my God he just said that about you!*

She knew he was all around me, all the time. Evie peeked every so often curious about us, and Kellan got along with Evie just fine. He got along with *everyone* for this reason—his sweetness.

And right now, those ocean eyes were raking down my dress, my jacket on, my boots, before coming up to me again. "I want you, *Gatita.*"

And then he was not sweet—I loved him like this the *most.*

"This is why you convinced Reed to take a break and go home to Alisha?" I teased feeling my heart began pounding and my nipples hardening. "To get me in this car?"

His teeth were sharp as he playfully reached for me with that eager grin. "Is it working? Should I take my clothes off?"

This baby.

How did he make me laugh and turned on at the same time? I couldn't stop laughing as he tugged me into his arms. His teeth bit my ear, playful and happy.

"Not here, savage. How did you get Reed to listen to you?" I winced as he tugged. "Why are you like this?"

When it came to Alisha, Reed listened to *no one.*

"Mmmm." He shrugged lightly looking so adorable I wanted to kiss him if he wasn't kissing my nose. "Told him Lish needed him more than I did. Besides, I'd rather be making out with you, than sitting next to Reed. He was miserable he wasn't with Alisha."

"That was smart." I agreed as he licked my face. "You are an animal."

"But you think I'm clever, honey?" And he gave me those eyes. Only he made me laugh like this.

"I think you are very clever to do this."

"Ahh." He was nuzzling into my neck like a hungry lion a moment after and I laughed harder.

This baby.

"Rather be here with you than Reed. You're way more cuddly. You smell even better."

Even as I laughed at his actions, my mind was aware we were on an assignment. Alisha's apartment had been broken into. I suspected it was a serial killer after her, and it had pushed Alisha into K2, and into Reed's arms. Kellan and I knew that is what Reed wanted.

But to Alisha? She liked her independence and her home. It was not ideal. And I felt for Reed.

He worked harder than anyone and his happiness was important to me as well.

Reed had taken care of me for years, and he was the best older brother we had. But Alisha's life was changing too fast. And that was life in Titan. For me and Kellan this was normal, but nobody was after me. Kellan was not losing his mind the way Reed was.

Alisha was a civilian. I promised Kellan I would talk to him about my conversation with Nathan, but I did not get the time. I didn't make the time.

Not now with Kellan nuzzling my neck. Or how happy he was to have me with him as he hummed. "I could eat you, honey."

I tangled my fingers in his hair as he bit down on my skin again.

"No biting."

"Sorry, I'm getting carried away."

Instead, when we had finally made it back and dropped off all of Alisha's things, Kellan and I had gone home to pass out. We were both tired, and Reed wanted Kellan to find Lopez the next night.

The suspect.

When their results yielded nothing, Gabriel had gotten Killian O'Hara involved.

Killian had found an address within the day having more of his guys on the ground. And so now?

Kellan and I were waiting for Lopez to show face.

"I cannot show up with a bruise, savage."

Kellan made a noise of regret. *This baby.*

"After," he growled into my skin.

"After." I threaded my fingers through his hair tugging gently, knowing he liked that. He groaned a little.

"I'm gonna die from the head scratches, honey."

I laughed harder when he pretended to 'die' on me. His weight heavier than before since he was putting on more muscle.

"Quick, I think I kisses to bring me back to life."

"Oh?" I kissed him once. Twice. Quickly. And the third time I went in he licked me again. "Stop making me laugh so hard."

His grin was wide. "But it's fun." My heart was going to burst out of my chest with this man.

"You are going to kill me."

"Aw, don't say that, honey. I would never—"

"I know."

"That hurt—" he fake groaned holding his chest. And then he turned hopeful big blue to me. "Another kiss?"

This baby.

"Why not?" I kissed him again laughing into him as he hungrily stamped his mouth over mine.

"This is way more fun than being on a stakeout with Reed—" he muttered in between kisses.

"Why, because he is strict?"

"I was gonna say cuz I can't kiss him."

"Stop smiling, all I get is teeth when you kiss me," I licked his lips biting down a little to his groan. "You drive me crazy."

"You're welcome."

Our laughter mingled as my eyes took in the road.

Having Kellan here was smarter even if he was distracting me. Reed would kill Lopez. We needed a lead. Not a dead man.

"What are you staring at? Is he here?" Kellan broke off and looked around and I smiled at him taking in the sharp lines of his profile, the intensity of his gaze as he scanned the street for any sign of Lopez. Just like that he snapped back into an operative.

He's come really far since I met him from the airport.

Now it felt like years ago but it was some months.

Life at Titan moved differently.

But there was something else there too, a sense of unease that I could not shake. I knew I needed to talk to Kellan about what had happened with Nate, but I wasn't sure how to bring it up.

I did not want to distract him from the mission at hand, but at the same time, I knew that keeping secrets from him wasn't the right thing to do. Besides, how would I know about my future with him someday, one day if I did not?

I should tell Kellan.

"We have to focus," I murmured trying to distract myself from wanting to pounce on him. "Put me back down." I was halfway over the center console and on his lap.

"It's been quiet so far," he said, his eyes fixed on the building where Lopez was holed up in and he didn't let me go. "Lopez is upstairs, we saw him go up. What do we do if he doesn't come down?"

I considered his question for a moment, weighing our options. I knew he had been paying attention.

"Do you want to know what Reed or Gabriel would do?"

"Both," his curiosity written all over his face. I forgot he protected Alisha, he did not work alongside our boss's.

I took a deep breath, preparing myself for his reaction. I explained that Reed would go in there, hold his family back, and go after Lopez directly. He would tie him to a chair and bargain with him until he got the information he wanted.

Reed offered people incentives.

"Reed gives them what they think they want," Kellan murmured his lips finding my temple. "Motivation."

"Exactly, but if Lopez get's violent, Reed will kill him."

"And Gabriel?"

"He would shoot him and dig into the wounds with his hands. I saw him do this to a man before," I said simply, watching Kellan's eyebrows shoot up in surprise. "Gabriel is direct."

"No shit." Kellan swallowed. "Dig into his wounds, huh?"

I told Kellan how far Gabriel went to get what he wanted. Reed and Gabriel were two different people and I kept telling Kellan so he would know what the other wanted. What the others did.

In this world—in the world of Titan—it was important to be able to tell Reed and Gabriel apart since they blended so seamlessly, sometimes I think people forgot about Gabriel.

And as far as I knew, Gabriel had left Kellan alone.

Because of you.

He's giving Kellan a chance.

"Do I want to know how you know this?"

I bit my lower lip, feeling a flush of heat rise to my cheeks.

"I'm a little in between," I admitted, shrugging my shoulders. "It works, si?"

Kellan's eyes widened, and I could see the wheels turning in his head.

"*Gatita*, you are so incredible."

I pressed my lips together looking away, batting his hands away. *"Kellan, we cannot—"*

"We're just waiting—" That smile was back. The one that destroyed my panties all the time.

"Maybe later—"

"Maybe now."

This baby.

And I bit my lip at the way his voice sank deeper into my body as I looked at him watching me, his eyes gleaming as he took in my body. My tank top dress and boots with a jacket.

"Push your seat back."

His eyes went wide, and without hesitation, he did. I was grateful we had tinted windows.

He leaned back, thinking I was going to climb him.

Instead, I leaned into him, kissing him, my hands working his pants as he gasped. "*Gatita, maybe later—*"

"*Maybe now*," I whispered his words back to him, kissing down his throat, loving the sounds he made as I gripped his length, hot and heavy like steel in my hand.

"Should I kiss you better?"

I loved his groan as I took him in my mouth, taking as much as I could. I didn't want to make a mess, but I wanted to pounce on him all day long. I sucked and licked and Kellan groaned, his hands on my neck and hair when I sank even deeper on him.

Oh fuck, honey.

Just like that.

And I *loved* serving this man.

I loved feeling like this with him. From someone who had been used by men, I realized when I was with the right person, everything felt better. Less like a service and more like my body's desires. And my body wanted Kellan.

I sucked harder, using my hands and stroking him. Moaning as he grew louder, and I loved the sounds he made. I don't know how long I stayed playing with him with my tongue or how long he groaned and tugged my hair in his fist.

"Just like that—" he broke off as his hips thrust up into my mouth, and I *loved* that. Hitting the back of my throat, and I swallowed over and over the tip. My mouth stretched wide. It was messy even for me. Kellan was not a small man and I struggled to take him deeper.

But with Kellan, I didn't go somewhere else. I was present. The entire time.

"Honey, let me fuck you—I can't—"

I sucked harder feeling him swell. He was right there. He couldn't hold back. I loved him like this.

Twisting my fist around his length faster made Kellan groan my name as I swallowed him whole, my nose meeting his stomach. Over and over again. My lips stretched wide around his length.

"Holy...fucking...there you fucking go...such a good girl taking me down..."

I was soaking wet with his praise, my eyes watering as I took him so deep, I choked on him. His groans kept me going.

He tastes like mine.

I moaned around the feel of him pulsing, hot spurts of Kellan in my throat, and I swallowed without thinking. His hand tightened on my neck and I felt my body clenching imagining him losing control later.

"Take it all from me, honey. Just like that...you're so fucking gorgeous taking my cock."

When I felt his thighs shaking, I licked him clean, feeling like I could do this all day.

"Going to be not sweet with that pussy tonight." I couldn't *wait*. "I'm going to lose my mind with you."

"I have been like this since I met you," I whispered back like it was a secret.

"Just me?"

There was a look in those blue eyes I didn't know *where* it came from. He had no reason to be jealous. But he was. I didn't think Kellan would be threatened by anything. Not when I loved him so much. But sometimes I saw a hint of something in his eyes.

I wondered...if it came from him feeling like he didn't belong as a Titan. Except he did. He belonged at my side. My partner.

My other half.

Even after what we'd done...did he doubt it still? That there would ever be anyone else? I couldn't stop my smile at the look on his face.

This baby.

"Just you. I am yours."

I held my breath, waiting for his reaction, but before he could say anything, his attention snapped back to the building, eyes burning brighter now with a predatory glint in them.

"Lopez is moving."

CHAPTER 26
SELENA

KELLAN WAS A GOOD PARTNER.

We walked in separately, and he sat in the back of the bar.

With his ball cap over his head and a drink in front of me, Kellan was watching me flirt with Lopez and getting *nothing* out of other man.

Lopez had landed in jail for assaulting his pregnant girlfriend. Even I got the creeps from him. But Kellan had his gun, and I had mine in my purse in case anything happened.

I dropped Valeria's name as my friend that I was meeting later Downtown. And still nothing.

Part of me saw he was nervous, his feet shaking, his eyes watching the bar like he knew Kellan was there. He couldn't. Nobody did.

The car had tinted windows, and Kellan circled around the block before he walked in.

Lopez hadn't seen us. Lopez was touching me then, reaching out, and pulling me closer. I threw some flirt into my voice even if I wanted to vomit.

What are you doing tonight?

I'm meeting up with a friend of mine.

Not me?

His smile made me want to rip his throat out as he told me it was urgent and he would stay if he could. I saw a police car rolling outside, and Lopez looked at his phone.

It was in the evening now, though. I didn't know parole officers worked that late.

I sipped the drink in front of me, tasting the bitter alcohol and fighting the urge to grimace.

I did not drink anymore now that I had my new life.

I could see Kellan's blond hair covered as he sat in the back, pretending to be on his phone with his drink.

Every so often, I felt his eyes on me, watching. I knew this was killing him, but he was professional. He always was despite being green-eyed.

As Lopez looked up, he reached out and stroked my arm kissing my cheek which felt like poison on my skin after Kellan's kisses. I resisted the urge to stiffen.

Lopez said he hoped to see me again in the neighborhood. I smiled politely and went back to my drink, my thoughts buzzing. I could feel Kellan's stare from across the room.

But Lopez didn't ask for my number.

Something's wrong with him. He's scared of someone.

I waited a few moments and I paid for my drink and left, quickly exiting. As I did, I saw Lopez get into the cop car. *I did not know cops handled parole.*

Because where *else* would Lopez be going? I would talk to Gabriel about this later.

I didn't look back as I walked to where Kellan parked the SUV we got from Gabriel, who had a host of cars in his garage alone for this reason.

Walking into the garage where Kellan had parked, I got to the car.

It took maybe a few *seconds* for him to come up behind me, crowding me in, his nose at my throat. "Are you okay?"

This baby.

His scent was all over me as he pressed me to the car, kissing me with a desperation I felt every *single* time he did.

"I'm okay."

"I'm not. *Gatita*, I need you."

"What are you going to do on assignments where I need to do this?" I rushed to open the door.

His eyes were a little wild. "Lose my mind."

This baby.

In another second I was in the backseat, scrambling to yank his pants off. I wrapped my legs around his waist thankful for the dress I wore.

His smile was full of dark promise. "Thank fuck you got a bigger car."

I laughed at the look in them and at how crazy he was sometimes. "It's because you are big, savage."

"Damn, straight I am." He groaned as he rubbed the head of his cock against me, yanking my dress higher. "And you fucking love me."

I do.

"*Kellan*," I moaned as the head of him pressed against me.

"*Shh*," his whisper was dark against my lips. "I got you. I know your body like my own. That little pussy's soaked for me. Were you thinking about this the entire time you had my cock in your mouth?"

A little sob left me as he growled it into my ear, a rush of moisture flooding between my legs as he kept going. "You're so pretty when you're like this. You're going to let me in, aren't you, honey?"

I nodded, gasping as he worked himself into me inch by inch, stretching, filling me up. I made a noise he quieted.

"I wanted to do this to you the first day I met you in *Paloma*. Wanted to fuck you like this forever." As he pressed deeper, he whispered. "*I want to be with you forever.*"

My eyes locked with his as he slid into me all the way, deep enough to make me see stars and stop thinking.

"*Siempre?*" *Forever?* I whispered into his mouth, watching his ocean eyes over me. Before he could respond, I saw the lights.

Red and blue. *Cops?* I gasped and pulled his head down to my neck. "*No te muevas. Cops.*" *Do not move.*

He stilled, pulsing in me, letting out a breath into my neck. Kellan swore softly. "Hell of a date night this is…"

I felt a laugh leave me softly. He nuzzled close. "I could get drunk off you."

Smiling, I held his head to me as the lights got closer, my hands covering his hair. "*Shh.*"

If they come near him, I will sink my claws into them.

I looked at the rearview mirror, which I prayed did not reflect us back. Just his plain black jacket tonight.

"Come down on me more," I whispered holding him tighter to me. I closed my eyes wishing the stupid police away.

How was I supposed to think with him inside of me?

Kellan sank lower with a groan until he felt like he was a part of me from head to toe. I did not know how to focus.

Kellan wasn't a small man. *Anywhere.*

No, he was enormous and he barely fit inside of me to the point where it stretched and burned a little. And right now his cock was stretching me wide open right where I was most sensitive.

Sinking deeper. Making me light-headed just enough to know I couldn't breathe properly.

I felt myself pulsing around him, clamping down tighter and tighter and unable to hold back my own whimpers.

"I feel like a fucking teenager like this."

"Do not move, savage."

And then his tongue darted out and I felt my lips break into a grin as he licked me a little.

I made a noise, squirming a little and Kellan groaned.

"We will get *caught.*"

"We won't get caught, I promise. I know you can take more of me."

"If I take any more of you, you will *live* inside of me."

"Then that's right where I wanna be," he growled hungrily. "Fucking perfect." At his words I felt a rush of heat between my legs.

I moaned as he sank deeper than before.

"Damn, honey."

This baby.

I moved my hand over my mouth, feeling like any noise I made might expose me as my shoulders shook. His did too.

"Stop it, savage." I whispered as I pulsed wildly around his heat. He felt like silk and steel stretching me wider than ever it felt like.

"Stop being irresistible. Your pussy's clenching down on me so hard, honey I'm seeing stars."

"You feel bigger like this," I bit back a laugh, covering my mouth again. *This man is going is to kill me.*

"That's funny you should say that—"

I squeezed his head to mine. "*Shh.*"

The lights were moving past us, and I pressed my hand around his head down to me, holding him closer, my lips pressing to his hair.

And because I was dating the devil who had a sense of humor, I felt something tickling my neck.

"I can feel you smiling."

"You gotta admit it's funny, honey."

"Shh."

Only he could have a sense of humor while deep in me.

"I can feel your tongue—"

"Shh, *Gatita*. You'll get us caught—"

I was going to *die*. "*You* are licking me."

"You taste good." I heard the laughter in his voice.

"I *cannot* believe you right now."

I felt his evil grin against my neck as his shoulders shook.

"Stop massaging my cock like that."

"Stop pushing deeper."

"Stop taking me deeper. I can feel how wet you are. Can't wait this shit cop to leave to fuck that little pussy. Gonna be not sweet with it now."

I all but came right then as my body clenched so tight Kellan groaned.

"You like that, honey?"

Dios. Don't get him excited. He'll just fuck you right in front of the cops and then get arrested with that stupid smile on his face.

I swore a little as he chuckled, his voice dark like sin. "I think you do. I can feel you squeezing my dick like you never want me to leave this body. Want me to stay?"

My heart is going to explode.

A whimper left me as I realized I was clenching so hard I was going to come.

"Shh," he whispered in that voice. "Don't worry, Gatita. When they leave, I'll be so good to this little pussy. There you go...good girl... clench tighter..." he swore as he gripped my shoulders and stayed so tight to me I felt every inch of him and my vision blurred.

How was anyone supposed to think straight like this?

"*You are so beautiful like this,*" he kept going until I felt the pressure crest.

"Kellan," I whispered shaking now even harder. "Please...please..."

He quieted down with a sigh. "I'm accepting my fate, *Gatita*. You can kill me now."

Except now I wanted him to *move*. Just keep moving in me and never stop. Make me come. *Hard.*

236

When the lights were gone, I waited a little longer feeling like I was on the edge of agony. I could still see them. Could still feel Kellan's heat driving me insane. It took more effort to focus with him throbbing inside of me.

"Kellan—"

"I know, I feel you. Don't worry, Gatita. I'm gonna fuck this little spot the moment they're gone."

I wanted to cry.

Dios Mio. Just leave you've already check the stupid parking lot.

What crime is being committed here besides Kellan murdering me?

Why does NYPD check parking garages and not actual crime? Do your jobs.

I held Kellan so tight, I felt his lips at my pulse again, pressing over and over.

"*Breathe, Gatita. You're tensing up.* As much as I appreciate your pussy trying to strangle me, I don't like you scared, baby. I need you to breathe."

I didn't even realize I was holding my breath.

I felt like any sound I made they would know.

"There you go, breathe for me." He sighed as I relaxed a little.

The cops would know if I moved.

They would know I was secretly having sex with my boyfriend in the backseat of an SUV owned by a college professor *that didn't exist on paper.*

I sighed as I saw the lights move past me. Leaving the garage.

"Clear."

It was a squeak. I barely said the words before he drew up.

Madre de Dios.

That took me so much effort I felt ready to pass out. I felt drugged.

He stayed still for moments as I felt him harder than anything inside of me. I felt his grin flashing white, canines out and sharp.

His tongue did that thing again and I gripped his hair.

"*You* are going to get us killed, you savage."

With that silly grin, eyes sparkling, clearly pleased with himself, Kellan looked down at me. My heart sputtered a little.

"Hold on tighter, honey. I think I like the idea of you writhing on my cock longer."

"Don't you dare—"

"I dare."

I blushed harder feeling the heat all over my cheeks, my face, the darker lights of the parking lot thankfully hiding most of us.

A whimper left me.

"That's why you let me sleep buried in you all the time, because you love me."

Why was he so cute and dangerous at the same time?

I did like him like that. I liked him in me all the time. Or when he woke me up like that.

He's beautiful.

"Admit it, I think that got you excited as much as me." His tongue darted out a tiny bit and he looked gleeful.

I felt the heat crest my face as my walls clamped down on him over and over.

His eyes became low-lidded as I did that and he drew out a little, his smile dipping.

"Did you like that, *Gatita*? Did I feel good in you?" His mouth parted over mine as he gasped. "Because you felt unreal the entire time. It took everything in me not to fuck you right through it. You're even tighter now. Breathe for me, *Gatita*. Let me in."

I clung to him as he spread my legs wider and sank deeper. A low noise left my throat.

Every single thrust hit somewhere deep and sensitive. I'd never get used to the size of him.

"Did it get you excited knowing I'd still fuck you?"

Shameless. He was *shameless*.

"I think it did, *Gatita*."

I cried out as he picked up the pace, his head tucked into my neck, teeth tugging at my sensitive earlobe.

"You're so fucking wet, honey. Did my girl like almost getting caught?"

Yes.

"*Harder*," I sobbed meeting his eyes, his forehead pressing into mine. "Te necesito."

I need you.

He growled as he looped one arm under my knee, drawing my leg up closer as he began pounding it out inside of me.

"You need me? Need *this*?"

"Yes."

Kellan relentlessly slammed into me.

"Need me to tear up that little pussy—"

"Yes."

I grabbed his hair as he fucked into me like an animal. "Harder."

"Harder? Any harder and I'll break you."

I was going to come just like that. I *loved* when he turned into a savage.

Kellan never felt like any of the other men in my life.

I held onto him kissing him as I felt the pressure coast closer and closer.

"Harder."

When he started moving this time, his hips took me like a man possessed.

Broken sobs came from my throat as heat rushed down to the center of my body where I clenched tighter and tighter around him.

"I can feel you losing it on me," he whispered into my lips. "You're so fucking close, aren't you?"

His hips ground out on my clit and the sensation was electric.

"Be a good girl and come all over my cock."

I exploded coming apart at the seams of my body from that.

"Shit, honey." Kellan worked harder as I cried out into his mouth. *"Come all over me...there you go..."*

After being worked up for *this* long?

I sounded like an animal with Kellan thrusting deeper with every thrust. Sobbing. Crying. Biting back my screams.

Dios, he's going to kill me.

I was grateful that stupid cop was gone because there was no way someone wouldn't know that I was being destroyed in this car with how hard he was going.

I could feel my orgasm soaked us, between my legs, the seats. I was going to die from this man. Who *never stopped moving*, dragging out every sensation until I was shaking so wildly he had to hold me down.

His entire body pressing down on me and my eyes rolled back, thighs shaking, body heaving.

Every slam made me lose my mind.

"Kellan—"

"I think I could watch you come like this all night, so mindless when

239

you get fucked for being such a good girl," he growled his teeth sinking into my neck, as his strokes changed driving me a little insane. "Should I, honey?"

I couldn't even think.

A squeak left me as he ground down again. His smile was smug as he pressed his forehead to mine.

"I told you. I'd obey you at work. But you, obey me in bed. Now come for me again, honey. Let me feel that pussy get tighter."

My eyes rolled back as my body bowed to him.

He did not stop.

And I did not want him to ever.

CHAPTER 27
KELLAN

As much as I liked Alisha, I was torn between my relationship with her and my boss.

My very ruthless boss, who was not the kind of man you kept shit from.

It was only after I took Alisha to Poppy that she showed me the note the receptionist at K2 had passed her.

My face fell almost immediately. "Did that note get dropped off at K2?" When Alisha nodded, I took it from her scanning it.

You can't run from me.

"*Motherfucker. I need to take you back.*"

"*What?*"

"Alisha, he's going to be angry."

No. Correct. Reed was going to be livid.

She held my arm then, her dark hair swirling around her shoulders. "No, Reed hasn't had a decent night's sleep since I brought this to his door. It's just a note. I live in a fortified tower. It can wait until we return. Whoever it is won't do anything in broad daylight."

She was wrong. Reed wasn't the type to look at it like just a note. He was going to filet my ass if I didn't tell him.

And he didn't need his sleep. He was like a fucking machine.

"*Lish—*"

"It's my choice." Hazel eyes met mine with determination. "It can wait a few hours."

"He's going to be angry."

He wasn't angry. When I did bring her back to K2, he was *volcanic with rage.*

I knew Reed was angry when the entire room was arctic chilly and he was radiating a quiet menace from him as he sat in the kitchen waiting for us. He didn't say a word. And that was the first sign I knew I was *fucked.*

I stood there knowing full well I was guilty as sin.

He didn't even look up from his tablet in his black shirt looking menacing as he didn't look at me but I knew I was as good as fired.

"Kellan," he said quietly. "Did Miss Alisha give you the idea that you couldn't wake me up when her life was being *threatened*?"

Shit.

"No, sir, it was my fault."

Alisha cut in not realizing she was making things worse. "*No, it was my choice.* I told him it could wait."

And then Reed looked at me and I felt the full force of the storm brewing from him.

Shitshitshit. I fucked up.

"You should know Stephanie tells me everything that makes it into my building—*Especially* any packages addressed to my girlfriend."

Shit.

"*Yes, sir.*"

"What will you do from now on?"

I took a step back as he took a step forward. I fucked up big time.

"*Report everything to you.*" I ducked my head not able to look at him. This wasn't the kind of man you pissed off. Not without consequences and I fully expected to face them.

"Head home," his voice was ice. Oh. Shit. He was gonna kill me later. But first he'd go after Lish. Who I felt following behind me. Reed's voice was filled with frost as he said. "*Not. You.*"

I winced as I walked out of K2 aware Reed was about to tear her ass up. I needed to call Selena and tell her everything.

"Honey, you got a second?"

"Claro, que si." *Of course, I do.*

I gave her the rundown as I went to my car.

She swore in Spanish. "I told Gabriel about Lopez and the cops. He is having someone on Killian's team follow him." I didn't know who Killian was but he was important to Titan. "He is taking care of it."

"Yes, but this means Alisha's stalker, knows she moved in with Reed. So those cameras Reed put up in her old apartment are useless."

"Someone is watching her," Selena muttered.

Someone we didn't spot. Someone who knew how to make people look away.

"Lish wanted to wait to tell Reed. Except Reed already knew," I explained. "His receptionist told him."

He expected me to be a better operative and tell him regardless of what Alisha wanted, which was *difficult*.

"Si, they tell him everything. Those girls work for him as his secretary sometimes. They know his schedule. And it does not matter if Alisha leaves K2, he is aware of everything."

Shit. "I fucked up. I wanted to respect Alisha but Reed knew everything the entire time."

That meant I had to tell Alisha that I would respect her wishes while telling Reed everything about her that she had no clue about.

I mean, I could do it.

But I was under the *assumption*, Reed and Alisha talked about everything like me and Selena. I thought Alisha knew…about Lopez, about us working her case.

I told Selena this and she listened to me as I got into my car.

I realized at that moment how *wrong* I was about their relationship when Reed wouldn't even look at her while reviewing surveillance from K2 and how that note had slipped into the pile for his receptionist.

He doesn't tell Alisha everything.

He keeps things from her.

My parents told each other everything. They were equals. Teammates. *Like me and Selena.*

Alisha deserved to know what we knew. *Nobody* had told her. And it didn't feel like my place.

Alisha had no clue the shooting was related to her house being broken into. She had no clue about *anything*, so she kept the note to herself, thinking it wasn't a big deal.

Reed *never* told her.

I understood where she was coming from.

I just didn't know what to do about it.

When he says jump, you better fucking jump. Don't ask how high.

"*Gatita*, I messed up."

"Where are you now?"

"Coming home."

"Preparando la cena, ven a casa."

Selena was making dinner and she wanted me to come home to her.

"I'll be there in a few. Love you, *Gatita*."

When I did get home, Selena was finishing up dinner.

"At least we tell each other everything," I told her going to kiss her. I was in her arms immediately. "I didn't know Reed kept secrets from Alisha. I was under the impression Alisha knew everything about her situation."

I have a home with her. I love this woman.

Her smile warmed me from the inside out.

"Honey, do you think Reed is going to be okay with what I did?"

Selena spoke in Spanish. "*Everyone makes mistakes, and it was not your fault. Not Alisha's, either. Alisha was not wrong. In the future, though, tell Reed everything. Even if you tell Alisha one thing, tell Gabriel and Reed as soon as you know something. She cannot hate you if she is a dead woman.*"

She sounded like an operative, but I also knew this is what she was telling me about the differences in leadership.

She cannot hate you if she is a dead woman.

I processed that. "That's true. But I didn't think Reed kept secrets from her."

"He keeps secrets from everyone," Selena murmured brushing my hair back. "Come clean up, you are hungry, no?"

"Always."

What did it matter if I *respected* Alisha's wishes if she didn't make it because of some creep? She couldn't hate me dead.

Being an operative meant making difficult choices. Sometimes, ones that tore me apart. I liked Alisha, though. *She deserved to know.*

It would tear her apart when she found out. I told Selena this. She paused then. Her eyes met mine with an expression I couldn't figure out.

"Honey, I know Alisha. She can handle the truth. It might suck at first, but she's a good woman at heart."

As I said it, Selena nodded. "We will go to Gabriel. We can explain it to him. It's not my place or your place to decide what Reed cannot tell Alisha."

"Because she isn't a civilian."

"She is Reed's woman, and he is our boss."

"But Gabriel can kick his ass."

Selena smiled. "Hmm."

Selena was closer to Gabriel, and he was Reed's best friend. He could do something about it. Right?

"Any leads from Giroux?"

I didn't know if the Lt from the police station had updated us on anything.

Selena shook her head. "I know Reed asked us back at Titan when he brought Alisha, but I did not find anything else. The girls did not tell me anything, and Giroux is not talking for some reason."

I saw the way she chewed her lip. I had pounced on her in front of everyone, not giving a shit. That was my girl, and I let her toss me around. That shit was fun with her.

"You think Giroux knows something?"

Selena nodded looking at me then. "I know he is not telling me something. I have to go to Gabriel anyway for this so we can go together."

And so I sat down and had dinner with my girl, feeling like I was forgetting something important, but my mind was too absorbed in the last few days.

"Did you have a good day today?" She bit into her salad.

I told her I went to Poppy, but it was just with Alisha. Her eyes shifted a little as I said that, and I caught her tells. But as she did, her hand spilled her drink on her nightie and she quickly went to change in our room.

My attention instantly diverted again, I was following her with single-minded focus, grabbing her present from my coat.

As soon as I saw her naked, I was pouncing.

I tore the nightie from her hands, tracking my hands across her body, loving the way she gasped and laughed low.

"Easy, savage. I am changing."

"You don't have to. You can just be naked. I have something for

245

you," I turned her gloriously tanned body around. "I picked it up in the city earlier today."

Reed had been staying with Alisha the last few days, so I didn't have much to do but explore the city without Selena.

It gave me something to do, and I passed by a jewelry store earlier today. "Lish talks about Davina&Co all the time."

I hoped Selena liked it.

The lady at the store had lost her mind when I wanted it. I took it out of my pocket.

"*Kellan.*"

I loved the teardrop pendant the moment I saw it. Turquoise surrounded by diamonds on a strong enough chain for her to wear all the time. She was my girl, and so money was nothing. I watched her take it from me and look at it. Her. In nothing but that necklace.

That was a fucking dream.

"Do you want to put it on?" *Please say yes.*

And she nodded.

"This is beautiful." She blinked back her emotions. "Your eyes are this color."

"Then it's perfect for you." I slid it on her, showing her it didn't have a clasp. It just went around her neck. And once it did centering itself right between her breasts, I swallowed hard. My chest expanded a little. A lot. I didn't imagine the girl I met weeks ago, would be this important to me.

I didn't ever wanna let her go though. Something about her made sense, it sat right in my soul to be with her. And I wanted to follow that feeling.

"I asked them to remove the chain so it just goes over your head. You can wear it all the time so it won't get caught," but I couldn't really speak properly. It came out gruff. "You look beautiful, baby."

I saw her blinking rapidly as she kissed me, pulling me to her, walking me to the bed, never breaking her lips from mine all the while. I fucking *loved* kissing Selena.

I felt every inch of her naked body, smooth and toned, pressing on me then and I held on as she straddled me.

With nothing but that necklace on.

I sighed with a smile on my face.

That's my girl.

246

CHAPTER 28
KELLAN

GABRIEL WAS IN MIDTOWN.

Scarier than ever and looking meaner than a motherfucker.

He took one look at us, pale icy eyes piercing through the dimly lit room, and asked for the update while sitting at Reed's desk.

Selena took the lead, and I leaned back, letting my girl do her thing.

I took in the black and navy surroundings, the silver trims glinting under the soft lighting. With Evie's touch the manor was brighter, warmer, but this was Reed's for sure.

Titan Midtown wasn't as cold as the manor, but there was something off about this place.

I didn't know if it made Gabriel uncomfortable. Or not.

It was strange seeing him outside of the manor where he lived and breathed his ice. In the shadows of the office, his eyes were pale and brighter, taking in everything with an intensity in them.

I could see his brain working, but there was darkness in them. Something haunted in his expression. I barely got any emotion out of him.

I did get a chance to scan through him when Selena talked. His entire demeanor was that of a lazy predator, coiled, ready to strike at all times. Iced out.

His jacket was off, his tie loosened, his fingers were messing with his gray cufflinks every so often.

His phone blew up every few seconds, but he had it on silent, so I only saw the light of the screen lighting up.

Gabriel ignored everything and he was helping her patiently find the right words when she struggled with some of them.

I had always thought of him as a mean motherfucker, but I realized he tailored his approach depending on what he was dealing with.

He respects her.

"I'll have Killian look into Lopez. I don't know why Giroux is being difficult," he said, his tone sharp. "Unless he's protecting information or he doesn't have it." Gabriel's gaze drifted to the desk next to his—*Liam Sullivan's.*

"What are we missing?" He asked.

"No se." *She didn't know.*

In that moment, I realized Gabriel wasn't the kind of leader who lost his shit when his operatives were working without all the pieces of the puzzle.

"You looked into Senegal?"

Selena nodded at his questions. I didn't know what she was working on the side. "I did, I found a few flags you might want to look at it, the embassy…"

The way she responded, her cadence, the way she seamlessly switched between Spanish and English as Gabriel interjected with questions in English and Spanish adjusting for her—it was something else.

She's in a league of her own, and I can't help but admire the hell out of her.

Her eyes were bright as she spoke, and as words fell out of her lips for a moment, I just took her in.

Gabriel was looking for some people leaving Dakar out of all places, and Cape Verde and he had Selena working on it.

"They gave me flight details and passport information…"

She was working her ass off. All the time.

And I loved that she got her breaks from me. I kept Selena on my schedule and took her to bed every night in my arms.

Tempted to reach out, I held back brushing her wispy bangs out of her eyes.

I could do that later when I got her alone. *Kiss her.* Cuddle her to me. I felt a soft breath leave me as I watched her, blinking slowly so I wouldn't miss a second of her, tipping my head to her. She smiled wide at Gabriel nodding at something else she said, like a little girl getting praise. I knew Selena loved Gabriel differently. Like a mentor. Like a father figure.

Fuck, she's adorable.

I didn't realize I had been smiling like an idiot with her, until I caught Gabriel watching *me*.

Fuckfuckfuck.

I quickly schooled my features, straightening up.

Icy eyes shifted away to Selena, and he listened to her, nodding, not interrupting, and letting her run with her judgments on things.

Gabriel tipped his head, his eyes bright. "That's good shit. I'll text you when Killian has an update."

I had something. "One second."

Both of them looked at me and I felt a tiny bit nervous now.

"It might not be my place to say this, but I work with Alisha every day. She's a fucking saint."

Selena's warm eyes didn't change. And in that moment I realized *she knew* where I was going with this.

I took that as encouragement as I looked at Gabriel. His pale eyes were cold as he took me in. He didn't like me. I knew that much. But then again—Gabriel Monroe hated everyone but Reed. So I wasn't surprised.

"Alisha doesn't know anything." I continued. "That isn't fair to her. I know we are operatives, but..." I told Gabriel everything. His eyes shifted when he knew about the K2 note and how Reed had been upset.

"She wanted to wait until she got to her charity?" Gabriel's eyes were dark as he said it. Maybe he wasn't happy, but I went to bat for Alisha.

"She said, she didn't want to live her life afraid anymore. And I think Ree—Mr. Whittaker is still keeping things from her but now it's compounding."

As much as I liked Reed, I didn't want to see her even more terrified. Or see her break. She was too good of a lady to watch her break. Because when Alisha found out what we knew? She'd be devastated.

Gabriel's eyes looked cool, a sudden gleam in them, and he leaned back listening to me explain my perspective. "That so?"

I told him all about her. Selena didn't interrupt me once, only nodding to most of what I said. And I understood even if she believed she wouldn't have done something, my girl, my partner was my team. And damn if it didn't fill me with pride.

His eyes flickered to Selena, who simply nodded motioning to me. I had complete faith in her.

I respected her more for being open minded enough to change her mind.

She has my back.

"I'll take care of Alisha."

Something went through Gabriel's eyes as he said her name. Maybe he was upset for her as well? I nodded, grateful he took the time out to hear me. As we left Gabriel's office, Selena looked pleased.

"He likes you," she smiled.

How could she tell? He had barely acknowledged me. When I voiced my confusion, her smile only grew wider.

She tapped two fingers to my heart, her eyes gleaming a little. "He knows *you*. He is only tough, when he wants to see what you are. Gabriel also appreciates you defending Alisha. I can see it in his eyes."

She explained to me her belief that Gabriel would die for the women in his life, Evie, herself, and he wouldn't tolerate keeping secrets from Alisha's safety after she kept the note from Reed because she didn't think it was a big deal.

"He doesn't sit here all the time, does he? Sullivan sits here." I asked. "I thought Gabriel worked at the manor and that was his domain."

"I don't know what's going on. You will realize sometimes you will do jobs but you do not know why. You have to trust that he has the bigger picture."

"It's a little like Reed keeping things from Alisha—"

"No," Selena interjected, her hand grasping mine as she pulled me into the lobby downstairs. "Sometimes we make choices. Decisions civilians *cannot* understand. They would not."

She went on to explain that each job was unique and that sometimes our jobs were connected, but we couldn't do our jobs right if we knew everything.

Because that isn't our job.

"Your job is to follow instructions, do your best for your people. When it is time? You will get more information. Right now? Our job is to solve the case. Gabriel will give you the bigger picture later."

"And you trust Gabriel's word implicitly?"

"What?" She didn't understand. I remembered Gabriel walking her through things, simplifying bigger words for her.

"Like you trust Gabriel no matter what?"

"Si. *Always*." Conviction in her eyes. "I trust him with my life."

There was a warmth in her expression and fierce respect when she spoke of Gabriel.

"He was there that day…" I trailed off as she nodded. That day he'd caught me with her up against the wall. Her eyes sparkled a little as she watched me.

Even as the sun hit her hair, I moved her wispy bangs out to see them. Her breathing hitched.

"Kellan," she grabbed my wrist. "No."

I backed off immediately, heeling to her word. "Sorry, you gotta focus."

"We talked about you." She pressed her fingers to her heart. "Gabriel is good here. They both are."

"Why do you trust Reed?" I probed further, curious about her perspective on our other boss.

Since I was a part of the bigger lie, I was keeping from Alisha now. And I didn't get it.

Selena took a moment to consider her answer, her brows knitting together in thought.

Selena considered her answer. "Reed is private, but his secrets are to *protect. Always*. Reed will be very clear with you. He'll say, go do something, and this is what I want. Very *clear* instructions. Your job is to protect Alisha. *That's i*t. You do not talk to Giroux. I do. But I do not guard Alisha. *You do. Entiendes*?"

Reed likes his clear-cut lines where he can see them.

I nodded as she continued. "Reed breaks up his tasks, but everyone on his team is aware. He puts himself in danger all the time. Gabriel does all the things behind the scenes."

"Why didn't you tell me any of this at the beginning?" I asked.

As I said, she shifted again, her eyes drifting out into the distance, as if lost in thought. She peered into an empty room in the building we were in, her brow furrowed with concentration.

I didn't know what this place was.

Maybe an office space people rented?

She pulled me into a room, her grip tight on my arm, and looked around as if ensuring we were alone.

"Gabriel does not like weakness," she said, her voice low and urgent. "He believes weakness is not trainable. He kicked out all of the previous people Reed picked up the last few times. For one reason or another. He moved the *few* he liked to different teams. *Not ours.* Nobody sits on *this* team. You and Garrett are two people that have lasted—"

"And Liam Sullivan," I said, looking at her intently. "Don't forget about him. You think Reed keeps him away because of his disability?"

I knew Liam had a cane which meant he was strictly desk job duty. IT work with Evie.

She nodded, her hair brushing against my cheek. I leaned into her more, nudging her with my nose. I couldn't stop touching her.

"Gabriel would never go after someone who couldn't fight back. Nathan and I were, you say, burnt out?" I nodded, and she continued. "We were both burning out. Nathan's assignment to Gemma is his break. You are mine. We cannot do anything until you, Garett, and Liam settle down. Reed is also hiring more people. But Gabriel, he likes you because you are still here." *It was that simple?*

I hadn't known I was getting a second boss until Reed onboarded us. And I had worked with Reed years ago. I just couldn't find anything about Gabriel Monroe.

"Gabriel does not do taskers like Reed. His jobs are different. You will see."

"Gabriel asked you about me and you?" She nodded, and I saw her left shoulder move, her body squirming a little. Just a little. She was holding back. "Reed doesn't care what we do, so long as we don't impact the mission."

There it was again.

"*Si*, but Gabriel wants to know everything because he believes every piece of the puzzle is important for the bigger picture. Reed does not care."

Because Reed's taskers were different.

Taskers were our job sent out. Tasks that needed to be completed of all types. All of Reed's were legit contract work. Security negotiations. Issues companies had. Things that were documented.

Gabriel's was not.

She looked down, her eyes uneasy for once. "Sometimes Reed will give you a job, like Lopez. And you first thought he was just a shooter. I went to Giroux. Later on, you found out he was the one leaving the notes at Alisha's apartment—"

"The bigger picture."

"Si, but that day when Reed came to Alisha? He already *had* the bigger picture. He wanted me to go to talk to Giroux to slide another piece of the puzzle into place. For him. No para ti." *Not for me.*

"Gabriel cares about you and everyone. And he cares about—"

"I just think we deserve to know though. If that assignment puts any one of us in danger, we should have the full picture."

I nuzzled into her neck a little more, tugging her closer.

"You have to stop cuddling me," she whispered.

"No, you love me cuddling you."

"Sí, pero estamos trabajando." *Yes, but we are working.*

"I can multi-task," I whispered back into her neck. "Keep going."

I felt her breathing hitch.

"If our lives are in danger, Gabriel would pull us out, and Reed would take over fully. Reed throws himself into danger first, *always*."

He always had.

"When Reed handles something himself, like…That night, he left us with Alisha. You saw his clothes?"

I remembered the fatigues and boots along with Reed's full black attire. I nodded.

"Reed was going somewhere that night. To someone. Someone he did *not* tell Alisha. Or us. Pero ella no sabe esto, vi su rostro, sus ojos."

But she does not know this, I saw her face, her eyes.

He said it was work related but he looked ready for a fight.

"Sometimes in our job, we have to tell the people we love things they can never find out about. It may hurt more than the truth."

Which meant Reed was hiding a lot more. Selena and I talked and told each other everything. *We don't have secrets.* Cuddling her close, I inhaled the scent of lychee and pink pepper.

"This is what you wanted me to learn, hm?"

"Gabriel asked me if I liked you, I was honest. I did," she whispered back breathless now. My heart melted at her words as I brushed a stray lock of hair from her face.

"You went to bat for me?"

"What?"

"You defended me, honey?" I asked, as I tilted her chin up to meet my gaze.

Selena watched me with a confused expression like she was surprised I even asked.

"The first time I saw you. Your eyes, your face, are sweet. I thought the moment you showed up, Gabriel would go after you. But he did not. He is watching, but he likes what he sees. Even when you make mistakes, he is looking at the full picture. He leaves you alone. Reed also is your partner so it helps you."

And her. She helped me. Selena was a huge part of why I was where I was at. And why Gabriel left me alone.

"You've been protecting me even now?"

She was. This woman *wasn't* my equal.

She had always been better than me.

Standing in front of me like a shield. My lioness.

I wanted to do the same for her. Be there for her in that sense. Her man. Her shield. We were a team.

"I am your partner," she murmured. "I have to."

True, but she probably does it without even knowing it.

I dipped my head, finding her pulse racing, and pressing a soft kiss there. *Thank you.*

My hands reached for the space between her thigh-high suede boots with those heels and her tiny dress. Nobody fucking wore those shoes like Selena did.

"You have to?" I dropped my voice lower and felt her trembling now.

"Why are you like this, savage?"

"You love me like this." I grinned into her neck. "And I'm your savage, there's a difference."

I felt her light laughter around me.

"You are—"

"Insatiable?"

"*Crazy.*"

"That too."

That strip of flesh that drove me insane as my lips trailed down her dress, tugging the fabric down. Lower. Until I tugged her bra down.

I tugged her nipples with my teeth.

She moaned, holding me, and I worked my fingers under her panties. I groaned at how wet I found her.

"Kellan—"

"Gatita," I murmured, my lips brushing against the soft skin of her neck. "Just a taste."

She clung to me as I made quick work of my pants, her fingers digging into my shoulders as she pressed herself closer to me as if she couldn't bear to be even an inch apart.

"Not hours, here," she whispered, her breath hot against my ear.

I grinned as I lifted her up into my arms. "No, only at home."

Home, with her. My girl. My lioness.

"Hold onto me."

She was *only Gatita* with me.

And it made me feel ten-feet tall as I sank her down on me. I pressed my forehead to hers, our breath mingling together as I began to move inside of her.

She was mine. I had nothing to worry about.

Nobody was going to take her from me.

She chose me.

CHAPTER 29
KELLAN

I was at Poppy with Alisha one afternoon when the entire day took a dark turn.

The weather was chillier. I noticed the draft. Her boots clicked across the floor. I heard her moving around, but she was close to me so I didn't worry too much.

I had been on the phone with Reed, who was asking me if she was okay given everything we knew and didn't tell Alisha.

"Lopez is dead," Reed was saying on the phone. I couldn't tell Alisha. "We found him today…"

When I say jump, you jump.

You don't ask how high.

I turned to see Alisha moving towards an open door, and I immediately went to her.

"Reed, give me sec, Lish, don't go outside, it's freezing—" I broke off as her face fell. And the moment I saw what she was staring at? I scrambled to grab her.

And thank fuck I did.

There was a *dead* girl near the dumpster.

I was scrambling to get her in my arms, swearing, and telling Reed to come to Poppy.

"Gabriel and I are on our way over."

Alisha was in my arms, both of them aware of her screaming and running over.

256

"Get her out of there, Watts."

When they got there, she was in shock.

Reed was on her in an instant, and I handed her over to him while Gabriel's eyes took in Alisha. Who was breathing heavier.

Since I was with her all the time, I didn't think Gabriel had met her, so this might've been his first time interacting with her.

Given the way he looked at her, I could see him taking her in.

Her stockings. Her knit sweater. That hair all over Reed and that little sound she made as Reed soothed her, cuddling her to him.

Imposing in his suit, Gabriel's pale blue eyes turned to me.

"Tell me what happened. *Now.*" As Reed held Alisha to him, she was shaking as she explained her side to him.

I kept my voice low as I told Gabriel everything, the energy around him ice cold, wrapping around me as he listened. Gabriel turned to Alisha with an unreadable expression on his face.

"*Wait*," Gabriel's eyes flashed with rage, his expression becoming wild as he looked at Alisha. Reed watched his friend, his jaw tight.

"We have to tell her. Now."

Reed looked ready to shoot Gabriel. "...I need to get her *home*..."

But Gabriel's pale blue eyes were locked onto Alisha, a hungry look within their icy depths and the way she watched him *back.*

"Tell me what?" Alisha was trembling, and I saw Gabriel reach into his jacket pocket, pulling out a pair of blue gloves.

Did he just carry women's gloves around?

Her hands were shaking so wildly that he pressed the gloves into them hanging on for a second longer, and Reed looked furious at the gesture.

"Not now," Reed said.

This was her *first* time meeting him. I knew because I spent every second of every day with her when Reed wasn't with her.

"*Now*, she needs to hear it. Just rip it off like a bandaid."

"You're on thin fucking ice, Gabriel."

Alisha's eyes looked at Gabriel as if he held the answers to *everything.*

"*Don't you dare* Gabriel—"

I needed to step in for Alisha's sake. "Mr. Monroe—"

Gabriel was intense as he went after her. "You have a serial killer obsessed with making you his next kill."

When he said he would handle Alisha? *Somehow, I did not see it like this.*

It unfolded at a breakneck pace, with Gabriel relentlessly bombarding Alisha with information, her expression growing more and more stunned with each passing second.

She was trembling. "*What?*"

"It's not a stalker. It's a serial killer. You match the profile of the girl outside...you got involved with Reed... It's Reed's fault you're in this mess since he was so distracted with you."

Holy Shit. He just—

"*I'm going to murder you.*" Reed looked ready to kill Gabriel, and then I was floored when Alisha stepped between them.

"*No, you will not.*"

I had never heard Alisha snap at him like *that*.

The delight in Gabriel's eyes was evident, his lips tipping up a fraction in amusement as she snapped on Reed.

Both of my bosses are fighting over Alisha.

It made sense. Given who Alisha was. Alisha was a *stunner*.

She had her own business. She was intelligent and hilarious, always radiating the kind of warmth that would thaw out Gabriel.

Alisha was the kind of beautiful you had to kind of suspend reality for. And *then* she went and fed you, juggled her sister, and her charity?

Plus, Selena and I *had* gone through her social media.

Alisha was a straight keeper.

But if this was her first time meeting Gabriel...why did they look at each other like they knew each other.

When would Alisha have met—Oh. Shit.

Something happened the day Reed brought her to Titan.

It had been her first time there.

Something had gone on between the three of them.

And right now?

Reed looked at Alisha like he didn't recognize her, his usually calm eyes searching her face.

Alisha looked back at Gabriel, even moving closer to him, her eyes searching Gabriel.

I didn't think Reed *or* Gabriel missed *that*.

The latter shifted in obvious pleasure, as Alisha said. "*He is the only person who told me the truth this entire time. Please, go on.*"

I just stood there like an outsider, watching Gabriel's eyes change, softening as he looked at her. I didn't even recognize him.

"I've been looking into your little problem for the last few weeks with Selena and Quarterback here."

Those hazel eyes were directed at me then, filled with a fury that made me want to take a step back.

"You knew?"

Shitshitshit.

Hit with the full force of her hazel eyes and her rage, I shook my head. "No confirmation, Miss Alisha. It was all just suspicion, especially after the shooting."

Reed turned to stone, his eyes on me then wild with rage.

And then Alisha lost her mind. Oh. *Shiiiittt.*

I didn't miss Gabriel's eyes gleaming as he took her in, never leaving her face.

"What about the shooting?" I completely forgot she didn't know.

Alisha's voice rose as she looked at Reed, Gabriel, and me, asking us about it being a random day, a *random* attack.

I closed my eyes, and when I opened them, Gabriel looked like he was proud as he watched Alisha.

He explained to Alisha that they thought Lopez was working with the person doing all this. And then he told her *even more.* I was *stunned.*

The question left my lips without thinking. "Giroux talked?"

Gabriel nodded, never taking his eyes off Alisha, and I felt sick to my stomach for Reed. Because I saw the look in her eyes as she looked absolutely floored.

"Is this some sort of sick joke?" I could see Alisha's chest rising and falling. I didn't miss the way Reed did, too. *But Gabriel?*

I had *never* seen Gabriel like this.

Reed's energy grew more and more volatile as Alisha was maybe a centimeter away from Gabriel now.

Her eyes were huge on her face as Gabriel looked softer down at her. Gabriel told Alisha he found Lopez dead and that she could stay with me or Reed.

And then he said. *"...Unless you'd rather come back to the manor with me."*

With me. I didn't miss the sound of his voice, the way Alisha looked disoriented as he all but told her to *come home to him.*

Everyone knew what he meant.

Reed's eyes went wide as Gabriel said it, and my eyebrows shot up to my hairline.

He was going after Reed's girl *right in front of him.*

Gabriel's voice went low as he took in Alisha. "You don't look so good."

I didn't miss the way his voice changed, and neither did Reed. The only one who looked gone was Alisha.

Reed's reply was savage. *"She's not fucking good. You just dumped months worth of information on a civilian. She is not an operative."*

Out of nowhere, pale blue eyes flashed at me. *"You do not see or hear a thing."*

I composed myself instantly, as Gabriel turned to Alisha, dipping his head a fraction, his voice gruff. "I'm sorry."

For what? What did he do?

"I figured out your problem. I told Reed I just needed some time to think. Aren't you pleased?"

I did not miss the way he said that last bit. Nobody in the room did. *Gabriel is worse than Nate.*

"*Gabriel*—" If Reed could shoot him in that moment, I got the feeling he would.

"Mr. Monroe—" I began.

"You're in shock, but you'll thank me later."

Alisha's breathing quickened as Gabriel looked at her with satisfied expression and longing.

I realized, at that moment, Gabriel Monroe was absolutely *gone* for Alisha.

Because this was nothing compared to what Nate Wyatt had done. Nate had at least waited for me to leave, and he hadn't known I was with Selena. He must've known at some point that night. *But Gabriel?* Gabriel was Reed's shadow. His best friend.

But...Selena had said Gabriel was above Reed in some ways.

For a fraction I saw *something* in Alisha's eyes that made Gabriel stop. I stopped.

And *then* Alisha turned on Reed with a furious expression.

Gabriel tipped his head back, triumph in his eyes, lips tipping up as he took in Reed.

Oh, this motherfucker.

"*We just talked about this.*" I saw Alisha turn on Reed, her chest rapidly moving. She was panicking. I knew her tells too.

"Miss Alisha—" I tried. I did.

"Angel, I think you should sit down. You look ready to…" Reed's voice trailed off as Alisha's mouth fell open, but no sound came out.

She was struggling to breathe, her chest heaving with each labored gasp. It was a lot to take in, I knew that.

We had all gotten the information in small doses over time, but what Gabriel did to her?

It was like dropping a information nuclear bomb on her.

Because Reed never told her.

There was no other way to break it to someone who had a serial killer after them.

And Gabriel looked at her with soft concern, but pride in his eyes, his head nodding as he took her in.

He knew that.

He knew all of this.

And that's why he ripped it off.

He was…testing her. For what?

Alisha isn't a Titan. Unless she's his.

Then she would be.

Because Gabriel was the kind of man who would be with his *equal*. If not *better*.

I saw that look when Gabriel looked at Alisha.

The way I watched Selena. I spent my days with Alisha.

I knew Alisha was out of Reed's league. Selena and I were tickled by the princes in Dubai promising Alisha kingdoms.

I knew the CEO of Roadsters, Matteo DuPont, was good friends with Alisha. They talked all the time. The luxury car designer who drove F1 cars for fun? He was right up her alley.

And she was right up DuPont's.

I had seen photos of them together over the years.

I respected Reed as my boss, but he was dating out of *his* fucking league.

And right now, he was denying *Alisha*. I couldn't be mad at Gabriel for giving her that. Selena was my girl *and* my partner. Selena was better than me, and I respected the shit out of her. I would tell her everything.

261

Sure, Reed wanted to protect her, but you could do that and still treat her as an *equal*.

I did it with Selena every damn day, and she was an operative, just like me.

Gabriel tipped his head to the side watching her carefully, his eyes soft with a wicked gleam in them.

He had her right where he wanted her...

And I knew then *why* he did it.

Selena had warned me Gabriel was a master manipulator. He had given Alisha everything Reed *hadn't*. That wasn't longing in Alisha's eyes.

That was recognition of her worth.

Alisha had just realized Reed never saw her as his equal. Not with the secrets he kept. And Gabriel went after her with *that* alone.

He's the only one who's told me the truth...

Gabriel leveled and made her his *equal*.

Something Reed hadn't done.

Alisha was gone turning on Reed. "I can't believe you right now. How many secrets did you keep from me? *How could you not tell me?*"

And Gabriel's eyes were amused, a gleam in them as he looked at Reed's predicament. If Gabriel, in a bad mood, was scary?

Gabriel in a good mood was frightening.

Alisha started hyperventilating, and I didn't miss the way all three of us got closer to her.

Because she was just terrified finding out someone was after her.

Regardless of whatever *that* was between my boss's, Alisha was *still* my charge. She didn't look happy with Reed.

She was my priority. Over *anything*.

Reed's eyes flashed with panic as he reached for her, and she stepped away from him in horror, backing straight into Gabriel who looked at her like she was his existence.

"Don't baby me!"

She was going into shock. I could see it. I could feel it.

"Panic attacks are good. It usually means she's processing it." Pale blue eyes that were completely gone as Gabriel watched her spiral closer to him. Reed saw it too, his fury cresting over.

Even though I knew what he was doing. There was no way Reed didn't.

"I don't think you should've told her all that, Mr. Monroe—"

"Fuck off, Quarterback. She needs to hear it."

"Don't be mean to Kellan!" She snapped her eyes watering.

And he *yielded.*

Nobody yelled at *him.*

Gabriel's expression shuttered with regret at her panic. And he was not the kind of man who knelt.

Before anyone. Oh shit, he's fucking gone for her.

I saw as Alisha closed her eyes, rubbing at them, her shaking her head, looking devastated. *Processing.*

Both of them reached for her at the same time, Reed's expression ferocious as he looked at Gabriel.

Reed's going to kill him.

Gabriel met him with a challenge in those eyes, eerie and bright as he reached for Alisha.

Reed was faster, hauling her into his arms the moment she passed out, his hand coming to hold her head to his chest, his eyes wild, his entire face looking ready to rip Gabriel to pieces.

Reed held Alisha close as he growled through his teeth. *"Watts, take her—"*

I only hesitated the moment I saw Gabriel tear off his jacket. Were they *serious*? Fuck professionalism, these two were wild.

Alisha just passed out.

I wasn't expecting Reed to hand her over to me, passing a quick glance over her. I took her, knowing full well he was going to lose his mind.

In the next instant? *All hell broke loose.*

Both of them reacted with a fury that had brewed and I watched in utter disbelief as Reed aimed for Gabriel's face who ducked easily.

And then they just went at it.

CHAPTER 30
KELLAN

I didn't even see how Reed got a hold of Gabriel, too busy holding Alisha close to me.

She was out cold. I picked her up in my arms, protecting her from the two idiots fighting over her.

Stepping back I watched as Reed landed on Gabriel, raining blow after blow, his hands wrapped around Gabriel's throat as he slammed him into the wall, cracking the plaster.

"This is what she stopped me from doing to you that day," Reed's growl was savage as he smashed his fist into Gabriel's face. *"She can't stop me now."*

"She didn't say no to me," Gabriel spat with a wicked look in his eyes, shoving Reed back looking ferocious.

I had never seen the other guy look like that.

"I can give her what you can't."

It pissed off Reed so much he tackled Gabriel.

I looked down at Alisha lying in my arms. She wasn't the type to cheat, I knew her.

She's always with me.

She's never without me.

Or she was with Reed.

Except...the day Reed had brought Alisha to the manor.

I'd been too absorbed in Selena to notice. He had stepped away with me, Selena, and Garrett. It was the only time I knew she had been with Evie...who was *never* far away from her brother.

Reed had gone looking for Alisha so she didn't get lost in the house in case she needed something.

I knew, because I got lost in the house without Evie.

And I knew *exactly who* had been in the house besides Evie.

She didn't say no to me...

I can give her what you can't.

This is what she stopped me from doing...

I fucking knew Gabriel looked off that day when I'd seen him briefly.

Reed's reply was to land another one on Gabriel.

I couldn't step in until I heard a female cry out and then Nate Wyatt burst in through the double doors to the space we were in, with Gemma Marchand hot on his heels.

Gemma's opal eyes took me in with Alisha in my arms. She was running to me in another second.

"Go, Kellan!" She took Alisha into her arms from me, sinking to the floor.

Nate and I moved, trying to separate Reed and Gabriel as they continued to go off on each other.

I had never seen either one of them like this.

"*She's out of your league—*" Gabriel's eyes flashed enraged. "*She can handle this!*"

"*She's my fucking girlfriend!*" Reed was *gone,* all that violence unleashed.

Nate's expression was ferocious as he hauled him back with a strength I didn't know he possessed.

"*Now is not the time you two fucking idiots.*" Nate forcefully yanked Reed away from Gabriel. "Get off each other!"

I grabbed Gabriel, shoving him back with all my might as he fixed me with a wild, furious glare. He was heavy as fuck. With three inches on me and at least fifty pounds, the guy wasn't easy to get. Nate on the other hand, wrestled Reed back.

"Sit the fuck down," he barked at him.

"*She* doesn't need you to fight him," I snapped at Gabriel in turn, my voice laced with anger and frustration. We both knew who *she* was. And I knew it would be the only thing that would stop him.

I wasn't wrong about him wanting Alisha, but I knew I was missing pieces.

Like what he did with Alisha that day she came to Titan...*she didn't say no*. Gabriel's eyes flashed dangerously. "I can fight you instead, Quarterback."

"Pick a time and place," I shot back. "Maybe not when there's a fucking body outside."

And Alisha blacked out. Gemma's face drained of color, her eyes widening in shock.

"What body?" she asked, her gaze falling to Alisha's unconscious form cradled in her arms. "What is happening right now? Someone needs to explain it to me."

Reed's stormy eyes, previously blazing with rage towards Gabriel, now filled with a profound sense of regret as they settled on his girlfriend, he looked like he was in pain holding his side.

I'd seen Gabriel land a few blows into his side.

"*Wyatt.*" Gabriel spat Nate's name like a curse, his voice laced with venom, those eerie pale icy eyes flashed on his tanned face. "*Do your job.*"

Nate rolled his eyes as he roughly shoved Reed into a corner.

"I got it," Nate growled, his tone leaving no room for argument. He pushed Reed towards Alisha, his voice firm. "Stay with her. *Duchess, don't move.* Stay with Gabriel while Watts and I take care of the clean up." With a curt nod in my direction, he motioned for me to follow. "Just show me where it is."

And with that, I found myself trailing beside Nate fucking Wyatt, ready to deal with the task of handling a dead girl's body. Like it was another weekday at Titan.

The dead girl was leaning against the dumpster and the street and alley was empty of people. Adrenaline coursed through my veins, my heart pounding against my ribcage.

This was my first time working with Nate since *everything*. But Nate showed no signs of *anything* with me.

He was professional as fuck. Even explaining it to me as he did it so I would know what to do. *When* it happened again.

Nate moved with cool efficiency, contacting someone named Killian O'Hara who promptly dispatched men to handle the lifeless body.

Killian.

That's who Reed and Gabriel had been with. He kept popping up as someone clearly important to Titan.

"What's her name?" I asked, my voice sounding distant and hollow, even to my own ears. "The girl?"

Nate barely acknowledged my presence, his gaze fixed on his phone. "It doesn't matter. I texted Giroux, and he'll be tracking her down now."

I watched in a daze as Nate handled the situation with a detached nonchalance, rolling his eyes as he lit a cigarette while we waited for Killian O'Hara's men to haul the body away.

"This is routine?" I asked.

Nate nodded, not even bothering to spare me a glance. "I've been dealing with this shit for seven years with those two."

But Reed started dating Alisha recently.

I knew Nate had figured out something had happened, but...he didn't even ask. *He didn't give a shit.*

He looks bored.

Up until this point, my interactions with Nate had been limited. But here we were, dealing with the aftermath of a dead body. And Reed and Gabriel fucking fighting.

"Watts." His next words caught me completely off guard. "I hope you take care of Lena."

Why wouldn't I? She chose me. She was mine.

But was she?

After what I just saw with Alisha? I wondered if it was possible after years of working with Nate if Selena harbored anything romantic at all for him.

I *knew* Gabriel had done something to Alisha.

Why else had he apologized? I would never repeat it.

What didn't she say no to?

No, I knew that's why Gabriel said I was supposed to see and hear *nothing.*

I saw the look in Gabriel's eyes as he took in Alisha.

So did Reed. Alisha goes home to Reed...*That doesn't mean she can't want Gabriel.*

But then my brain wondered if Nate gave Selena something I *couldn't?* What was it? Because that was *why* Alisha leaned into Gabriel. That's what Gabriel said to Reed.

Did Nate give Selena things when I wasn't there? The thought made my blood boil.

I studied him then, really taking in the man who had been my girl's partner.

Selena cared deeply, her heart on her sleeve. She felt everything with an intensity that burned into me, that I inhaled when I swallowed her cries into me. Nate was the opposite.

Nate was a rough all around Viking, exuding cool, unflappable calm as he methodically cleaned up the mess.

He had done this thousands of times.

The detached air as if nothing could faze him. Save for Gemma, who he eyed like he *wanted* her.

I didn't miss anything.

I just didn't understand it. I wanted to talk to Alisha because I couldn't tell anyone nor would I mention this clusterfuck she was in with Gabriel and Reed.

And then it dawned on me.

Selena never told you why he kissed her hand.

I knew why Gabriel was attracted to Alisha. I could see it. He was ice. Alisha was warmth personified.

Deep down, I had realized Gabriel craved a woman who kept him stable. Someone to balance out all that...tundra of a heart of his.

Do Selena and I balance each other out?

Her lip gloss was in my left pocket. It was her favorite one and I had it on me because she forgot it at home.

Nate held my gaze for a moment longer, as if searching for something—an odd glint in his eyes. As if he was scanning me.

I had nothing to worry about when it came to Nate.

He was a part of Selena's past.

I was her now. Her future. Her everything.

She chose me. She was my girl.

Not Nathan Wyatt's.

CHAPTER 31
SELENA

W<small>E HAD A FEW CALM DAYS AFTER THE DEAD BODY OF AN UNIDENTIFIED</small> woman, where Kellan just told me that Reed had gone home with Alisha.

He had disposed of the body with Nathan, and that's all he told me.

I could see it in his eyes something was weighing on his mind. We were lying side by side in our pajamas on my bed. With the soft lighting around us, we talked.

"I admire you a lot," Kellan's voice was muffled into my hair.

"Why?" I didn't understand it.

"You don't think you're incredible?" He sounded surprised as he drew back a little.

I shrugged lightly feeling the heat on my cheeks. "It's my job to do this. This is the bare minimum. Gabriel has high expectations."

His eyes changed a little at the mention of Gabriel. "When do you think I'll trade hands?"

I bit my lip, and his thumb brushed over that spot, forcing me to let it go. "When he feels you need it. Not sooner. He will wait."

I explained to Kellan that Gabriel was a patient hunter.

He would wait for the right moment, and when he went in to get what he wanted, nothing would stop him.

As I said that, a look went through Kellan's eyes. He let out a breath.

"Nothing will stop Gabriel from getting what he wants?"

I shook my head, unsure of why he looked like that. *Is he nervous about Gabriel?*

"No, he waits to make his moves, but when he does, he's deliberate."

He looked concerned. "What happens when he doesn't get what he wants?"

"I have never seen that happen." In all the time I knew him? Even if something looked like it wasn't his? He would manipulate it until it was. Until anything was.

He didn't settle for less. I told Kellan this.

"Do you trust him?"

"*Implicitly.*"

He grinned at me a little. "You sound like me now."

"I am practicing."

His grin grew wider if possible as he stuck his tongue out and licked my face. "Why are you like this, savage?"

And my protests dissolved into laughter as he tackled me to the bed. His wild energy was contagious. *This baby.*

I spent days and nights with Kellan since Alisha had gone home with Reed after that, and I just wish Reed would stop being a stupid idiot.

I was telling the truth, everything he did, he did for Gabriel.

His shadow.

It did not surprise me days later after the incident though?

Kellan got a phone call from Reed.

Alisha broke up with Reed because she finally had enough of Reed's lying, and so Kellan didn't come home for days.

I had no idea if he was getting any sleep, when he was eating, or how he was holding up.

But we were *operatives.*

We were supposed to function regardless of sleep. Regardless of our feelings. I was angry at Reed. Worried about Kellan. I knew it was irrational.

I can be switched out for Kellan. We can take turns.

And I turned to Gabriel who told me he'd handle it. I clutched my necklace over my heart in my fist as I texted him all day while working.

His absence in my home felt strange, and the teasing that usually accompanied me as I prepared dinner alone was…painful.

I never realized how much space Kellan took up in my life and how he had taken my quiet little life and filled it with color.

He'd come in with his smiles and playfulness following me around the apartment, throwing me over his shoulder, tickling me for fun.

He was everything I wasn't.

And everything I wanted more than my alone time.

I never thought I would meet a man I liked more than Gabriel. But I loved Kellan. And I missed him like I never missed anyone.

In the time I had known him? He had become a part of me that I needed.

I needed to trust Kellan to do his job.

But in the meantime…

I can do mine. I can solve the case.

Days passed without Kellan.

As Nathan said, *I needed a sounding board.*

Gabriel was busy, and Reed worked all the time after his breakup.

Which left my old partner. So, one evening, I called Nathan who was still guarding Gemma Marchand.

He answered within the first ring, his voice a familiar comfort.

"*Lena*, what's up?"

"You want to be the Watson to my Sherlock?" I tossed his reference back at him since we traded places. Sometimes, I was his Watson.

He chuckled, the sound warm and inviting. "Hit me. But fair warning, Gemma's nosy as fuck—Ow. I was being nice."

I laughed unable to imagine Gemma Marchand bossing Nathan around. But she did.

For a moment, I found myself missing this aspect of our partnership. I began to talk, the words flowing freely as we fell into our old rhythm, bouncing ideas off each other—Gemma listening in the background.

I was pacing back and forth in the pink nightie that Kellan had gifted me.

I detailed everything to Nathan, every piece of information I had gathered since Kellan's absence.

I didn't want to overwhelm Kellan with the details when he finally returned and if I solved the case before he came home?

Maybe Gabriel could catch who Alisha's stalker was.

I was trying to be considerate of Kellan, who was working so hard.

I wanted to hold him when he got home, make him dinner, and tell him everything so all this could be over. So he could come home to me and stay here. Be safe with me. Play with me. I did miss him.

"I never took you for the type to like Quarterback," Nathan said casually. "But I get it, if we find out who the fuck is doing this shit, he comes home."

"Exactly," I smiled.

Nathan chuckled as Gemma said. *"I would feel the same for Nate."*

That surprised me.

"I did not know you were friends again," I said without thinking.

"Don't worry, Lena, I still want to murder Nate in cold blood every Tuesday, but for right now—we are calling truce to help you."

Nathan found that amusing.

He still loves her.

"I would love to help you both solve your case. He says we will work together like a team." She sounded so happy about that, and Nathan laughed low.

"Duchess, if I don't let you, you'll throw your shoes at me again."

Gemma made a noise of embarrassment. "It was *one* time—"

"It was more than once—"

"Well, if you wouldn't *hide* things from me—"

"*Oye*! Both of you!"

They snapped out of it. Gemma made a pfft noise he laughed harder.

But I knew Gemma's shoes being thrown was not the only reason why Nathan was letting her help.

"Gemma, do not listen to Nathan, everyone has wanted to shoot him at one point in time."

"I want to shoot Nate every day," she muttered and I laughed.

Maybe Gemma Marchand and I had more in common than I knew.

"Duchess, you fucking love me—"

"I will stab you in the throat with a fork—" she growled.

"You'd love that too."

Gemma sounded like she wanted to strangle him.

"Baaaack to the case, Lena…"

I laughed as we worked together late into the night, our minds focused on the task at hand and my investigation.

I did not notice my phone going off, and the screen lighting up with a message from Kellan saying he was coming home.

I didn't notice anything but solving the case.

CHAPTER 32
KELLAN

ALISHA BROKE UP WITH REED.

Because Reed lied to her about someone named Lucy Devereaux.

Suddenly, Gabriel's honesty would be great right about now.

I stood in the hallway at the Primrose with Gemma staring at Nate with something on her face other than annoyance.

Nate silently stood with his hands in his pockets leaning on the closed door in his black suit.

He kept his eyes closed as we heard muffled shouting coming from the room.

Even with the space, I could *hear* it, and I saw Gemma's eyes pleading at Nate as though he would let her in to stop it.

Earlier Gemma had been shouting at Reed before I heard Nate's grumbling, before both of them had stepped outside.

Gemma looked ready to fight Nate over it.

After a long minute, Nate blew out a breath, without opening his eyes, held his arm out and Gemma looked upset as she walked into him.

Why is he all over Selena if he wants Gemma so fucking much?

Gemma settled into his chest, her expression defeated as Nate put his hand on the back of her head tucking her closer. I looked away.

They had been there before Reed had gotten me out of bed and away from Selena's arms.

She kissed me steadily until I told her I'd come back and love her right. I had no idea what the fuck Reed had done. But I saw it coming from a mile away.

When I say jump, you jump. You don't ask how high.

I winced listening to her and Reed fight and I saw Nate frown deepened.

Gone was the man who didn't care. He cared now…I saw the way he held Gemma now. *That's Alisha's best friend.*

I couldn't respect Reed right now.

We all heard the yelling stop for a long moment. Nate let out a breath as his eyes opened something in them I didn't recognize.

Gemma opened her eyes, looking up at Nate for her cue to go in there. But he shook his head at her, as he brushed her hair back with softer navy eyes.

"We need to talk when we get home, Duchess." His voice was low as he held her face in his hands. "Stay with Watts."

And she didn't fight him even though it looked like she wanted to.

I stepped in closer to her as Nate turned and before he opened the door he turned to Gemma giving her a look.

Gemma pouted at him and took a few steps back.

I realized he was asking for privacy.

She let out a breath, brushing back wisps of her hair falling out from her updo, and turned away to look at me, her eyes downcast and her mouth turned down even deeper.

Nate walked into the room, sliding in and shutting the door quickly.

She cast those cornflower blues up at me. "Are you going to stay with Lish?"

I nodded. Reed needed to handle his company and something told me Alisha would rather have anyone other than him.

When the door opened it wasn't Nate who walked back out. Reed stepped out, his eyes red rimmed and his mouth turned down.

He fucked up.

He didn't even look at Gemma who took one look at him and went back inside to Nate.

Reed's eyes landed on me. "Take care of my girl, Watts."

His girl. Still? Did they not break up? Or was she just angry?

I saw the look on Reed's face.

Devastation didn't even begin to cover what it was. I had seen Reed nothing but together and even in his fury, he never looked like *that*.

"Yes, sir."

Even though I had no idea what was coming for me. Or how long it would last.

A few days into Alisha's breakup, fucking Gabriel showed up.

I saw *that* shit coming from a mile away.

Alisha had looked up from her phone in her little black robe wiping her eyes as he walked in. Gleaming pale blue had locked in on her.

He didn't even acknowledge me as Alisha stood up and wrung her hands.

I got out of his way.

He was such an opportunist.

I saw Alisha's face take him in with shy wariness and he didn't say a word as he watched her with an indecipherable expression.

It wasn't my business if Alisha decided to sleep with him. Not after Reed.

She ran from Reed. I couldn't imagine Selena or me keeping secrets from each other that ran this deep to make one of us leave.

The only thing I never told Selena was the clusterfuck between Gabriel, Alisha, and Reed. It took me by surprise when Gabriel didn't stay.

He closed the door behind him looking at it for a long moment. Had Alisha turned him down?

Why is he leaving if he doesn't want to go?

His strides long, purposefully cut through the carpeted halls, elegance and flowers all around him.

He didn't look at me.

I walked back in to find Alisha standing in front of the door, her hand trembling as she looked down at it.

Her eyes were wet when she met my gaze, a haunted expression on her face. I recognized *that* look.

Without hesitation, I pulled her into a hug, noticing the way her lip quivered just before I held her.

Whatever *was* going on, Alisha didn't look like she was enjoying it.

"You want to talk about it?" It wasn't the right thing to do.

No matter what her relationships were? Both of them were my boss's.

And I didn't need to know what Gabriel's relationship was with Alisha to do my job.

She slowly asked for my discretion, and I made a pinky promise to never say a word.

"I don't have any romantic interest in Gabriel..."

But somehow I wasn't sure it was a two way street. "He was here to win you back for Reed."

She looked at me, her usually bright eyes dulled from crying so much. "I think some relationships are multi-faceted and complex, but Reed is my entire world. I love him so much."

As she said that her face broke a little. "Reed needs to work through things himself. We all do. Space is good. To cope a bit."

She glanced down at her wrist. *It's not my place to ask. I can't ask her even though it's burning in my throat.*

I spent my days as her guard and friend. I got her flowers and cookies she liked, the same way I did for Becca whenever she went through her breakups growing up.

Not like I could kick Reed's ass for being a fucking idiot who kept secrets from the love of his life.

I didn't sleep well without Selena, but also because I had to keep one eye open for Alisha. All the time.

This was different than being in Alisha's apartment.

It was a public setting where I couldn't control the variables. I was on edge with housekeeping, any male dropping off parcels or room service to her door.

I was barely getting any sleep, and I missed my girl so fucking much. One night Alisha came to me a little red in the face. We'd bumped into Reed earlier that day at some cafe Downtown Avani liked.

"You can go home tonight," she murmured. "Reed's on his way..."

I was surprised to say the least. "Is he?"

She bit her lip and nodded at me looking a little wary.

"I'll wait until he's nearby and then head out—"

"To Selena."

I nodded. To my girl.

Wanting to crawl into her arms and pray that Reed would fucking stay and fix his life—his heart, Alisha.

I didn't blame Alisha for not wanting to live with him. When Reed was close, I slipped out.

I needed to feel Selena's fingers threading through my hair, holding me to her heart, and letting me sleep there. Just for one night.

Because Reed was *thorough*, and he wouldn't leave Alisha all night.

The door shut quietly behind me as I stepped into the apartment, my body aching with exhaustion for no fucking reason other than I couldn't think properly without sleeping next to my girl even if she let me take her perfume with me to the hotel.

It wasn't the same as Selena.

Honey, I'm home.

I just want to lay on you and let you do that thing to my hair.

Need to fill you, feel you, love you. Just hold me.

As I entered the room, Selena was on a phone call, the speaker on, and I made my way in.

Until I recognized *Nate fucking Wyatt's voice.*

I stopped moving.

"...the body of a woman the other day, Valeria. Killian just got me the name, and Watts was there. Lena, Watts knows about everything and he's okay with it?"

Know what?

"It doesn't add up to him."

No. Because I didn't know something?

"I did not tell him," she said, and I felt my heart plummet into the depths of my stomach.

Tell me what?

"I keep meaning to. I haven't had a chance. I will. Once all this blows over. I mean, we have the case—*did you say Valeria?"* What? *She just moved on from...what did she not tell me? Who was Valeria?*

What was Selena talking to Nate about?

"You know Valeria?" Nate's voice came through clear. "Gemma knows about everything we talked about. Took a page out of Reed's book and talked to her finally...*I know, Duchess."*

And *then* I realized something.

Selena had been working the case without me, conducting her own investigations while I was away...

And not just with anyone—with her *former* partner, the man whose very existence seemed to cast a shadow over our relationship the entire fucking time I had been with her.

The bitter sting of something seeped into my blood. Hot fury like nothing I'd ever felt before inside of me.

Nate.

Fucking.

Wyatt.

Who knew what I didn't.

The *exhausted*, jealous part of me felt like I was losing my girl. And it grew like a drum beat in my ears, louder and louder.

Like I was being pushed aside in favor of her former partner.

I had come home, hoping to find peace in Selena's arms.

Not Nate fucking Wyatt in my home.

"Valeria was the girl who told me all those college girls were missing—" Selena cursed. "The *cops*! We've been going to the cops. Valeria told the police, she said they came around all the time. There's a connection between Lopez showing up dead now, the police, and the girls. The notes, everything Giroux said, it's all linked. It's someone on the inside. Every single time I went to the precinct, I felt a chill down my spine. Like someone was watching me. *What if it's a cop?*"

Why did she choose to tell Nate, while leaving me in the dark?

My hands were shaking, my blood ran cold with ice.

She was *my* partner.

My girl.

My team.

I had always believed that we were a team.

And yet, here I was, standing in the shadows, listening to the woman I loved pour her heart out to another man.

To Nate fucking Wyatt.

The emotions swirled within me, a toxic cocktail brewing.

"*Muñeca*, you don't ever have to ask me for anything, I would still move mountains for you even if you weren't my wife."

I stopped breathing.

I heard my heart *shatter*, the pieces scattering across the floor.

Every one cutting into my skin.

What the fuck did he just say?

CHAPTER 33
KELLAN

"I'M ALWAYS GOING TO HAVE LOVE FOR YOU, *MUÑECA*. NOTHING WILL change that."

What did he just say?

"You are going to drive Gemma crazy, but I love you too."

A feminine voice laughed and said something I didn't hear anymore over the buzzing in my ears.

I'm always going to have love for you. Nothing will change that. If you need me again...

Selena, the woman I had given my heart to, the one I had trusted with every fiber of my being, had been keeping *this* from me *all this time.*

She was *married. To Nate fucking Wyatt.*

I felt like I couldn't breathe, as if the walls were closing around me.

But I had been with her. I was with Nate's wife?

The bone-deep exhaustion that had consumed me earlier was now replaced by a searing pain. I couldn't breathe.

Couldn't think. Betrayal sucked.

I saw nothing but red, a blinding, all—consuming anger.

"I bet you drive Watts insane, you little psycho."

Selena's laughter lit up the apartment, the sound piercing through me like a razor-sharp blade.

"Tell me if Watt's breaks your heart. Gabriel bought a chainsaw he wants to test out—"

"No, we will not be talking about this chainsaw business—" Selena cursed him out in Spanish and told him she was hanging up.

"Gemma wants to play detective. We'll get back to you. Just get some rest and fill in Watts on *everything* when he does end up coming home. We both love you, *muñeca*. Be good." Nate chuckled, but it was like salt in an open wound.

"Love you too, *pendejo*."

As she hung up the phone, I stepped into the kitchen, my heart pounding in my chest. My mind was racing. A million questions ran through my mind.

She was Nathan Wyatt's wife? I felt lightheaded as I stood there, sleep-deprived. Confused. Out of my mind.

Selena was sitting on the island in her pink satin slip.

A little yelp of surprise left her when she saw me. A smile spread across her lips, a smile that once would have filled me with warmth and happiness. *"You are back."*

But the smile quickly faded as she rushed over to hug me, her arms outstretched, seeking me.

Normally, I would have grinned, would have pulled her close, and held her tightly. Except she saw the moment, something was wrong. She stood at arm's length.

"What's wrong?" Those green eyes grew wide as she looked at me, confusion etched on her face. "¿Qué pasó? No te escuché entrar."

What happened? I did not hear you come in.

"You're Nate's wife?"

But as I looked into her eyes, as I saw the guilt and shame that appeared across her face, I knew that it was true.

"You're married?"

I can barely breathe right now. She was my girl.

Her green eyes widened as if she were seeing me for the first time.

I had *never* known a pain so intense, so *white-hot*, a pain that threatened to *consume* me entirely.

The exhaustion from my demanding schedule and helping Alisha through her breakup weighed heavily on my shoulders. This entire fucking time I dreamed of Selena.

As I listened to Selena's explanation about Capri and her marriage pact with Nate, my eyes grew wider. Getting shot hurt *less* than the words coming out of Selena's mouth.

"You had a marriage pact with Nate fucking Wyatt," I said, my jaw dropping in disbelief. "You promised him that you'd be his?"

Her voice filled with desperation.

"Hicimos una promesa. ¡Nunca lo hice! ¡Nunca me casé con Nathan! Te quería a ti."

We made a promise. I never did it! I never married Nathan! I wanted you.

"Then why did he call you his wife?" I demanded, my voice rising with each word.

"That's *just how he talks! It's Nathan!"* She shouted back at me. "I know you are tired from helping Alisha—"

"Don't try and turn this on me," I growled, my anger reaching a boiling point. "I come home to…"

I looked at her, my eyes wide with disbelief.

"You made a marriage pact with *Nathan Wyatt? That when you turned thirty, you'd be with him?"*

Her eyes were wide. "¿Qué te pasa? ¿Por qué actúas así?"

What's wrong with you? Why are you acting like this?

Why was I acting like this? Was she insane?

"I was just your fucking placeholder? Do you have any idea how he made me feel? How I fucking felt every single time he was around you?"

Holy. Mother. Fucking. Shit.

"What you just said makes Reed lying to Alisha look like a fucking piece of cake. Reed lied to Alisha to protect her. You lied to me because I was your second choice!"

Oh.

My.

Fucking.

God.

I was her second choice.

I was Selena's second choice.

I had been away from this woman, the woman I thought cared for me, for days. For months I had *loved* her.

This hurts so fucking bad. I couldn't control my anger.

"Did you just use me for the past months as your last fling before you said yes to Nate *fucking* Wyatt! *You just told him you loved him. You were*—" I was seething and I could feel my rage bubble and boil over unable to contain itself inside of me. *"You were working the case with him!"*

"You were with Alisha!" She tried to defend herself, but her words only fueled my anger. *"He was my partner!"*

"I am your fucking partner!" I shouted back, my voice echoing off the walls of the kitchen. "*I. Am. Your. Fucking. Partner!*"

I stalked toward her hating the way she backed away from me.

I loved Selena.

And Selena loves someone else. Her fucking husband.

I never stood a chance.

I never stood a fucking chance. And it cut through me like a hot knife.

"I was your support. I was your man. Your team." I was raising my voice, and I couldn't stop. "You come to me. *No matter what. Not him!"*

I didn't understand my insecurities.

Maybe it came from being new in her life.

Maybe it came from being in love with her?

Or maybe it came from finding the first bit of fulfillment I ever had —and losing it all to a man who I *knew* didn't deserve her.

"And then I come home to you, after days of not seeing you, only to find you on the phone with your fucking husband, telling him you love him! What would you do if it was me? What do you call it? Double standards!"

Her eyes flashed wildly. *"He is not my husband! That is how he speaks! He loves Gemma. She was right there—"*

"I don't give a fuck!" I was in her face. "I don't give a fuck about Gemma!"

What was wrong with me?

"You would destroy me with your sharp tongue if you could. If I had been on the phone with a woman that you knew taunted you about my relationship with you. You would lay into me if it was a woman on the phone."

I was losing my cool. Something was wrong with me. Days of not sleeping properly. Days of heartbreak around me. I wanted Selena. Just Selena.

And she wanted Nate fucking Wyatt.

"But it's not just someone," she pleaded. *"He is my friend!"*

I heard nothing, she said.

"He's in love with you! And he asked you to marry him and you kept it a secret from me!"

Her eyes went wide, her mouth dropping open at that.

Double standards? It was past that.

"Since I met you, I have been nothing but honest with you. I wanted you. I chose you—"

Her eyes were wet, stunned. *"I chose you!"*

"That wasn't choosing me—"

"Yes, it was!" Now she was in my face shouting, and I took it. "Mi corazón es tuyo, ahora y siempre! Nadie me ha tocado el alma como tú. I knew you weren't anything like him—"

Her heart was mine, now and forever.

Nobody had ever touched her soul like me.

And I couldn't hear her.

I heard what Nate *was*, and I wasn't.

"What the fuck did Nate promise you that I couldn't!" What did Nate give her that I couldn't?

"A future!" She shouted back. *"He promised me a life. Children. I didn't think I deserve anything or that anyone could ever see me as more than someone to be used.* Nathan offered me a promise for something when we were afraid. I met you, and I stopped being afraid. I took a chance on you. *Creo en esto con cada fibra de mi ser."*

She believed in us with every fiber of her being?

So did I. I fucking believed in us.

I never wanted to lose you.

I was reeling as the reality of what she said hit me, and I felt my head tip back as the words hit me.

Then why didn't I believe it?

Her voice lowered. "Nathan said if neither one of us settled down, then he would give me that. *And I said yes years ago.* I met you. I knew I could never do it. From the first moment, I knew. And I ended it with him a long time ago. I only never said it because there was no point. It did not matter if you could not give me all those things. I just wanted you."

And in my mind? I heard her. I heard every single thing.

She did choose me. She did.

She chose me time and time again.

"You never promised me a life after this, and I did not want it. I do not think you want children. Loving you was enough for me. I made my choice with you. And every day with you was another day I did not want with Nathan. *Eres mi todo.*"

I was her everything. I heard her. I heard in my soul.

She did choose me.

But I was gone.

I was unraveling, my mind a haze of sleep deprivation and emotions in a blender. Because being hurt by Selena hurt worse than anything else in the world.

I'd rather be shot, stabbed, dragged through the streets in a firefight than have to deal with the love of my life looking at me and telling me there was another man in her life. A man who had made her promise in a few months she would've been his.

A man who wasn't me.

And it hurt more than I could ever admit.

"*Kellan,*" Her face broke, those emerald eyes sparkling with her tears. "*Please, just get some rest, and we can talk about this in the morning—*"

"*Why didn't you tell me?*" I searched her face for answers.

I was running on fumes.

Because the idea of Selena ever belonging to anyone?

Triggered every bit of my jealousy like I couldn't believe.

You're the only thing that keeps me sane during this chaos, and I miss you like crazy.

That's what I should have said.

Why didn't you tell me you were working on the case without me? I thought we shared everything.

That's what I should have said.

What happened between you and Nate? Losing you scares the shit out of me.

That's what I should have said.

Be honest with me before this consumes me.

I didn't say that.

"*You kept this from me the entire time we were dating? Did you wait to see if I was the better option? To be your second fucking choice? Was I being graded on my good behavior the entire time? Or was I just a fucking fling!*"

"*Kellan—*"

But I couldn't let her finish.

"You weren't a fling to me!"

The anger, the hurt, the exhaustion—it all boiled over, my voice rising.

"But you kept me as a second choice until you knew I was your first—"

A backup plan. In case it didn't pan out.

Oh. My. Fucking. God.

"I ended it!" She cried out. But it wasn't enough.

"You kept putting it off! *I was your second fucking choice.*" Oh. That. Shit. Hurt. *"Even though you were my fucking first.* I have always chosen you. Every single day I woke up and I chose you. And you only chose me when it was fucking *convenient?*"

"That's not true—"

"You didn't even tell me that the last few days I've been sleep-deprived and exhausted. You've been working the fucking case without me! With your fucking husband!"

"He is not my husband!" Selena was shouting at me now. "I chose you. *I chose you every single day!"*

The word husband hit me like poison.

A cruel reminder.

Of the person she had made that fucking stupid pact with.

"Then why didn't you tell me sooner? Why did I come home to this?"

"I knew you would react like this. You've never talked about a future with me. What was the point? I took a chance even though I was afraid. I picked you. I was scared the entire time, and I still chose you. And you are...You are this. Nathan promised me a future. I have always wanted that. You did not—and I chose you! I choose you over and over again!"

And there it was—the fucking truth.

I was *me*.

And he was *Nate*.

"Kellan, please...please let's just stop fighting—"

She had kept this from me, had worked the case behind my back, all because she was upset with my reaction?

And you proved her right.

A part of me wanted to reach out to her. To pull her into my arms and promise her we would find our way through this.

"Kellan—" she broke off breaking at the way I looked at her.

A part of me wanted that so badly.

But the other part of me was too faded in exhaustion to say a word.

"I just wanted to come home to you."

Not anyone else. You were…You were supposed to be just mine.

My eyes burned as I walked away from Selena and I couldn't even look at her.

It felt like my entire heart was being ripped at the seams out of me.

A gaping hole in my chest that threatened to swallow me whole.

Taking in deep breath of the cold night air, my lungs ached. My eyes stung. I could hear Selena crying in my ears. All I could inhale was the scent of pink-pepper and lychees in my lungs.

I didn't even have a place to go without Selena. She was my heart.

Selena was my home.

I walked to my fucking car and broke down. I thought I was her first choice. I thought I was her only choice.

For the longest time Nate fucking Wyatt had been a sore spot in my relationship with her and now?

I never even stood a chance.

I'm not her first choice.

CHAPTER 34
SELENA

I chose him.

I couldn't stop crying.

I knew I was searching for answers in the wrong places.

Work had been the only constant source of comfort for me, but even that couldn't ease the ache in my heart.

I was exhausted and emotionally drained. But I couldn't stay in my apartment. Not after…that.

Kellan left, and I couldn't stand to be in there. Confused. Lost. Alone.

I couldn't calm down. Despite it being late, I found myself Downtown. In the Lower East Side.

I needed to clear my head, and the water always helped. The sea. The salt in the air.

I went to the Brooklyn Bridge.

It helped me think, helped me process the whirlwind of emotions.

My heart threatened to explode out of my chest with the pain I felt.

I felt so stupid. I just didn't know how to even explain to Kellan what my past had been like.

The things I had been through as a teenager while he had been playing football in high school, I had been selling my body on the street. There was no pride of what I had been.

In what I was.

And there was something in me that deep down, did not feel worthy of his love.

I realized that being alone, and being lonely were two different things right now.

And right now?

I felt both watching my world fall apart and all I could is watch blankly.

My past didn't feel dead. It didn't feel like my past. It felt like a living breathing thing that haunted me for so long.

I couldn't shake it.

I couldn't return to the apartment, not when the memories of our argument still lingered in every corner.

Is this why Reed had lied to Alisha?

Because the truth was more painful than lying to her?

I wasn't usually rash.

I prided myself on my ability to think straight, to approach problems with a level head. But now? I couldn't.

Not *anymore. Was this what Reed felt?*

The overwhelming sense of helplessness, the feeling that the ground beneath your feet had given way?

What if Kellan came back and…I couldn't even finish the thought. We had just gotten caught up in our lives.

It never occurred to me that it was important, but now, a part of me wondered if I had kept it from him because I feared his reaction.

Kellan was sweet, gentle, and loving. And I had been wrong to wait to tell him. When threatened, he became someone else entirely.

Tonight, I was reminded of all the men in my life before Gabriel who did not care. I needed space to clear my head. My feet carried me forward. Kellan's words echoed in my mind, a painful truth I couldn't ignore. Because he wasn't wrong.

I did wait until he was the right choice. I did wait until I knew I loved him instead of taking a chance on him. Kellan had taken a chance on me—from day one.

I knew I hurt him too by not letting him in.

But I *had* worked with Nathan, I had turned to him when Kellan was away. But it was *for* Kellan.

Nathan was more than just a colleague. Maybe a brother. Sometimes when he took Gabriel's place and held me, he was family. Reed always called Gabriel his work wife. I was Nathan's work wife in many ways.

Kellan would not understand that even as a joke. Kellan had run with his assumptions, his jealousy blinding him to the truth of my feelings.

And I had no break.

I wasn't Gabriel. I was tired, so *tired*. Part of me longed to talk to someone else.

But who did I have? Gabriel?

The thought flashed through my mind.

When he hurts you, call me.

I knew that if I called Gabriel, if I poured out my heart to him, he might very well kill both Nathan and Kellan.

When he hurts you, call me.

Or he would come and pick me up, just like he always did, and take me to the manor. Gabriel would die for a woman in need.

When he hurts you, call me.

I was about to dial Gabriel's number when a movement caught my eye.

Two figures were cutting across the bridge, only their silhouettes visible in the lamp light. I felt the shift in the air almost immediately. It felt like Gabriel's. These were not late-night strollers or tourists.

When he hurts you, call me.

I need to call Gabriel.

When he hurts you, call me.

And I would have, but I saw the man first. Tall as Reed, but leaner.

Entirely in black, his raven hair styled neatly and falling over one eye. But it was his eyes that stopped me, an electric blue, that glowed under the lights that occasionally fell on him.

I knew *those* eyes.

There was only *one* family with those eyes we knew of at Titan.

Matteo DuPont?

No, this man was larger, his frame more imposing, his face sharper. His movements were fluid. The woman at his side had her face covered by a black mask up to her nose.

Pale blue eyes from her gaze as sharp and unforgiving as the arctic wind that suddenly whipped through the air.

Gabriel...*something* is in front of me.

They didn't spare me a glance, her eyes a pale blue glowing more than Gabriel's, her hair a silvery blonde, long and straight as she moved.

He was watching her with a soft look, his face not covered like hers.

He laughed at something, his dimples deep in his cheeks, and her eyes crinkled as she pointed over the bridge. His teeth flashing sharp in the midnight light.

It seemed at odds how happy he was with his appearance. He was a little frightening.

They were...*enjoying* themselves.

They looked like *killers*.

I was about to pass them in a few feet, my footsteps slowing just enough to pretend I was just taking a walk at night, ducking my face under my bangs.

I can't hear them moving.

"...you go up North..." His voice was deep, *strong*. "...take Whittaker."

I stopped breathing then. Whittaker.

Reed...

She didn't speak at all as his eyes flickered over to me a little. Did I know him? I knew those eyes. His entire family had them.

His lips tipped up a little as he looked away, that dimple more prominent. Who was he?

Did he know me?

No. Not possible. *Nobody* really knew me.

But my mind was already working. It was going crazy.

How many *Whittakers* were there?

No, it cannot be Reed.

But what if it was?

Trust your gut. I needed to call Gabriel. My phone screen was lit up with his name.

When he hurts you, call me.

And then the duo *passed* me, an icy sensation spread through my veins like poison.

Ice clawed its way down my body. Down my spine. Down my throat. *Something is wrong with that woman.*

Something about them...

When he hurts you, call me.

My finger hovered over Gabriel's name on my phone as I turned over my shoulder to watch the two figures walking away.

They move like Nathan and I do before we take someone out.

And when they turned the corner, I knew I had to *move.*

What if it was *our* Reed?

Gabriel's house was north.

What if they were going after my family?

There were lots of Whittakers.

But only one that had helped me in my life. Only one was my brother.

I needed to go. Or I would lose them completely. I turned my entire body to follow them.

My heart was pounding out of my chest with the adrenaline coursing through me. I knew what I felt.

I trusted my instincts and my gut.

It had gotten me this far.

Thoughts of Kellan and Gabriel swirling in my mind, not even paying attention to the broad uniformed man walking towards me.

I hadn't been paying attention, my mind consumed with thoughts of Kellan, Gabriel, *Reed*, now those two.

Before I could react, a pain erupted in my head.

Fiery agony that in my scalp. I screamed. Something collided with my skull.

Pain.

All I felt was pain.

And then, there was nothing but black.

CHAPTER 35
KELLAN

Selena wasn't answering my calls.

She hadn't texted Gabriel.

She hadn't called Nate, who had texted me asking why Selena hadn't messaged him after their conversation the night prior.

Because he knew about us being together. Living together. And then there was me, left to pick up the pieces. I didn't think twice.

I don't know why I *knew* who to call.

When he finally picked up, Nate's voice was gruff. He was annoyed with me.

"What the fuck do you mean if I have heard from Lena or not?" he barked. "*You fucking live with her.*"

He knew? I took a deep breath, my voice shaking as I broke it down for him.

I didn't tell him everything, just enough to paint a picture of the nightmare unfolding around us.

Because it wasn't like Selena to be missing.

"*Listen*, Quarterback, I proposed that stupid promise on a vacation where I missed—I was upset over losing *Gemma, who happens to be glued to my fucking side.*"

Gemma Marchand was Nathan Wyatt's girlfriend?

Gemma was right there…

The entire call.

"Duchess, I need my arm for a second, and then you can have it back…"

I waited until he shifted.

"I asked Lena out of my own paranoia. We have never liked each other romantically. *We never wanted to have sex.* Lena was okay with going to a clinic when she wanted kids because we didn't want *that* type of relationship."

I didn't know it was that deep.

I didn't realize any of it.

That's because you're a jealous idiot with communication issues.

You hurt your girl, jumped to conclusions, dismissed her feelings, and yelled at her.

Fucking scumbag.

Nate's voice was hard. "That doesn't mean I won't *love her.* Do you understand? You've never fucking spoken a word to me. *How the fuck would you know?*" He dug into me then, his words cutting *deep.* "I've been with her since the *beginning.* I killed the people who—"

He paused, sighing heavily. And I heard Gemma in the background trying to calm him down.

"*It doesn't matter.* I would kill for Lena. I already have."

W-what? It did matter to me.

"I send her the fucking flowers in her apartment every single week, all her art supplies I bought 'em, and those fucking milkshakes she loves."

What's your safe word?

Milkshake.

"*I'm the one* she comes to whenever *motherfuckers* try to attack her in *Paloma.* I'm the one who fixes everything for her. I'm the one she runs to when she needs anything, motherfucker."

What do you do when this kind of stuff happens to you?

And then Nate lost his mind.

"I fix *Paloma* just to make sure Lena is safe when she's out driving late. She calls me for *whatever* she needs. Always. Besides the one night you heard me talking to her? I have been by her side since the day she showed up for seven fucking years I have been her best friend! *How are you supposed to be with Lena if you can't handle what it means to be with her?*"

I would do the same for Becca.

And I never *once* considered that Selena's relationship with Nate might've been that of something more complicated than what I saw.

Because you let your emotions cloud your judgment and lost it on her.

I could hear Gemma in the background, telling Nate to breathe. Devastation was one word for how I felt right now. The other? Was sheer panic.

Gemma had been there the entire time Selena had been on the phone with Nate.

Gemma who knew *her* man.

Who snapped at me.

"*You got into a fight with Lena over what?* I told my girl that day we got home from Alisha and Reed's fucking *shit show*. Gemma didn't hold it against me because she knows me. Did you know Lena? Did you hear *anything* she said, or *did you just lose your shit like a fucking idiot?*"

He swore violently about needing a chainsaw right about now.

"*Why are you so fucking stupid, Quarterback? I thought Reed hired you to be better, not a fucking idiot.*"

I said the same things to Becca's exes.

I didn't even know what to say to him.

I heard Gemma talking to him in the background, and he swore,

"*Duchess, text Evie for me...*"

I heard him say gibberish about Neptune, which I took as his call sign.

In Alisha's hotel room, she was getting ready to meet her sister while the gnawing fear for Selena's safety consumed my every thought.

"I'll get this figured out with Evie," Nate said, his exhale out of character since I had seen him around dead bodies. "Take care of Alisha, and don't say *anything* until you *check your fucking emotions*."

He hung up, and I felt like I just got bitch-slapped for being an idiot.

And then the night slowly descended from bad to *worse*.

Selena's tracker went silent.

My girl had dropped off the face of the Earth, and I was powerless to find her.

I needed to hear her voice, to know she was safe.

Anything.

Alisha was alone, her sister having left, and the diner we were in had emptied out. I stepped away for a second, my hand shaking as I dialed

Selena's number. She didn't answer. When I got back, my heart stopped. Alisha was *gone*.

Where the fuck did she go? I raced outside to find her only to see nothing.

I was left to call Reed, *scrambling* to get his girl. Because something had happened to Alisha on my watch. And then?

The hours that followed were pure, unrelenting *torture*. Both of them, Alisha and Avani, were kidnapped.

Because of me.

Alisha had stepped out of the diner thinking her sister had left something there. Thinking it would be a *second*.

I had seen the security footage as Reed had come into the place and the look in his eyes was something I had never seen in them.

The manic fear manifested into a savage ferocity.

And then we were *moving*.

"*I need a gridlock.*" Reed was on the phone with Gabriel who had been in Titan Midtown.

For the first time since I met them, I got to see Reed and Gabriel team up, side by side in full on black their movements swift, communicating easily.

Gabriel took over as Reed's shadow.

Reed was unleashed, calling for a total recall of operatives, mobilizing *all* agents in the city.

The response was immediate, the area swarming with women and men in all black, appearing like wraiths in the night.

And for once, I got to see what Titan *was*.

I didn't even know they had this many operatives under them silently moving around me in organized groups understanding their place.

Because we weren't the only team they had placed in the city.

I was just on Reed's team, and I had never met any of them.

Selena had always said this team was different.

Gabriel issued a city lockdown for all other operatives, every exit sealed, every street patrolled in case bodies turned up...

In case...I wanted to vomit at the thought of Selena being hurt. Of anything happening to my girl.

Selena.

Alisha.

Avani. This is my fault.

I had never felt anything like this emotion running through me. Everything was moving too fast, and Reed and Gabriel were working with another team.

I was teamed with Kieran O'Hara, a young man with eyes the color of warm amber, his dark brown hair tucked under a beanie as he remained collected, like he did this all the time.

Next to him was a man who looked similar to Kieran but had black hair and was looking disarrayed.

"Killian, I'm chill," Kieran was saying. "I swear—"

"You are not. Stop being a punk bitch." He growled.

In a black suit that was already a little bloody and had mismatched eyes, one amber, one blue, he was looking at Kieran over several times, saying something in a language I didn't understand as Kieran nodded.

His movements were fluid and precise as he slipped us both into bulletproof vests and checked our weapons with practiced ease.

The only thing a little off about him was a tiny pink bandaid he had on his index finger with a singular heart on it.

Out of place on him.

But he was composed. Strong. Things I didn't feel.

These guys know what their doing.

Ever since Reed had told me what was happening I felt my blood pounding in my ears, but I took in everything.

The man with the mismatched eyes looked me over with a hard glance and then moved on. Annoyance more than anything else on his face. *Killian...O'Hara?*

I didn't have time to process him. Reed was a man on edge.

The mention of *both* Avani and Alisha, being in the clutches of a psychopath had set him off. And it felt like *my* fault.

And my girl? Where was she?

I didn't need to ask.

Had Selena gone after the case without me? *Why*?

Why else would she be Downtown that late?

She'd been working without me?

That wasn't like her. Was it?

Gabriel's usual appearance was replaced by tactical black and a darker expression than before. He looked menacing right about now and I knew that fury was directed at me.

He barked orders, eyes holding a predatory glint.

Reed looked ready to go after anyone who stood in his way. And I understood, both of them were going to kill whoever was in that house.

I pushed my emotions to the back of my mind. Because if Selena was in there? I was going to get her out. And then the sound of shattering glass pierced the air out of nowhere.

A gunshot. Not ours.

The *moment* the shot echoed in the air, Reed's eyes went *wild*.

"*Lish.*"

Gabriel and Reed were *moving* before the echo had faded, sprinting towards the house faster than I thought possible.

Kieran at my side, armed to his teeth, moved with me as my partner.

And then, in the next few moments, *I would never be the same.*

Suspect. Shot. On the floor.

Clean headshot.

A woman's body near him, naked and bleeding from her head, her raven hair streaming, covering part of her face.

Reed was on her, tearing his jacket off, throwing it over her—I was dimly aware of it being *Alisha's body.*

Reed picked her up into his arms a noise leaving his lips at the sight of blood on the wall and the floor. *"Alisha, nononono, look at me baby...baby...wake up."*

Operatives moved around Reed, giving him cover, some swarming White's body. His voice broke, shouting for a medic, his eyes looking down at Alisha.

My eyes moved past him.

"The *basement.*"

I didn't recognize my own voice, but I saw the door open wide. Kieran moved past Gabriel and me, clearing it for us as he stormed down.

I heard a female shrieking. I just acted, not thinking, my old training falling back on me.

"*Alisha!*"

Avani.

I saw Avani first. Chestnut hair. Dark eyes so big on her face it was terrifying.

Kieran rushed to her talking about how he was with Reed and he was here to help. Kieran hauled Avani into his arms, pressing her crying face into his chest.

One hand holding her to him, the other holding a wicked-looking knife, slicing her out of her binds and taking her shaking body in his arms, his eyes only then taking in someone else on the floor...

Kieran's eyes went dark and wide, showing emotion for the first time that night.

I had looked at Avani.

Not the floor.

My eyes followed his...

My training forgotten, my emotions slammed into me. *Honey*. I only knew because of the boots...*Otherwise*...

"*Selena*..." I sank to the floor, not even wanting to touch her as I dimly heard Gabriel roaring for a fucking medic or he would start taking heads off.

I felt my heart bottom out as I took her in, my breath catching in my throat, my chest constricting with a pain I had never known before.

Honey...

And for a moment, I couldn't process what I was seeing.

Selena? Selena...

*Why was there so much blood...*A noise left my lips.

All I saw was blood, *so much blood,* covering her body, staining the floor beneath her. People were moving around me these operatives in white with a cross on their sleeves. *Medics.*

Gabriel was there, his eyes unhinged as he took one look at Selena on the floor, hauling me back from her. His entire expression was granite as he looked down at her.

"Don't touch her, Watts."

I was shaking with the need to hold her, to gather her broken body into my arms and never let go, but I couldn't move her, couldn't risk causing her more pain.

I can't touch my girl because she's broken.

Medics swarmed her, working frantically to save her life, while I stood there standing next to Gabriel.

He grabbed one of them, his eyes searching.

"She has a pulse," They nodded. "She's breathing."

But I wasn't.

DOCTOR WHITTAKER, WE NEED YOU—

I heard nothing as people moved around me.

Kieran O'Hara, the newest addition to Titan, had entered into our team tonight, and had taken Avani. Reed was somewhere with Alisha.

Alisha wasn't waking up either and I had seen the blood on the floor.

This is my fault. I did this to her.

I almost got my girl killed.

All of them. Over what?

I couldn't breathe.

"Watts." Gabriel's voice sliced through the fog, his tone brooking no argument. "Give me your weapons."

I let him take them from me without moving.

The hours ticked by.

I stood there, my body a live wire with the effort of holding myself together.

"Tell me everything that happened. *Now.*"

I stood there watching them take Selena into a room where I couldn't see her after rushing her to the hospital. And I did.

Unblinking. *Waiting.*

The words spilled out in a stream.

She chose me, not the other way around. And I failed her in the worst way.

I didn't choose her. My girl chose me. I didn't give her shit. I let her down.

He didn't say a word while listening to me. He shifted at my side at the part where I got to the marriage pact that suddenly didn't feel like a big deal anymore. Not anymore.

Not since my girl...I almost broke then, but I continued.

I told him everything. I stood there. I left her. I was angry. And she...

I stared at the door. *Selena.*

She cannot be upset if she's dead...

And I felt Selena's old words sink in as I stopped talking.

She cannot be upset. If she died.

"It's my fault. She's my girl. I let her down...I got her. I did this..."

This was my fault. She will be upset with me.

Because she's alive. She has a pulse. She's going to make it.

And when she does I'm going to let her be as angry as she wants to be with me.

My eyes blurred. I felt a noise leave me broken and defeated.

"I did this…"

No more pink-pepper and lychee.

No more hot-pink peonies all over our home.

No more laughter.

No more cuddles.

No more Selena.

I'm not your honey.

But you could be.

I'm not your girlfriend.

But you could be.

I chose you.

You chose me?

"I did this to her."

I grabbed my chest tighter as I shattered.

This is my fault.

Gabriel's hand moved to my shoulder, as I was moved into his shoulder.

I did this to my girl.

I couldn't see anymore.

CHAPTER 36
KELLAN

SHE'S ALIVE. SHE'S DOING A LOT BETTER. NISHA GRAHAM WILL STAY with her...

Gabriel's eyes took in Doctor Perla, a blonde with a stern expression, but a warm voice.

"Anything else?" He asked.

I looked at Perla, my body aware of *what* he was asking.

*Was she—Did he—*I felt ready to throw something.

"No, your analysis with Agent Wyatt's was correct. After he..." Perla broke off her expression dark. "After the initial attack, it seems he went looking for the other two ladies rather than focusing on Agent Tavares. She has extensive defensive wounds..." My heart bottomed out at the image. "But no sexual assault." Something skated down my spine.

Gabriel nodded, listening to her, his jaw tight.

Multiple fractures.

Traumatic brain injury.

Internal bleeding in her abdomen due to blunt force trauma.

I took it all on the chin, wiping my eyes, feeling the words sinking into me.

Gabriel explained it to me calmly despite his shaking hands and tucking them into his pocket earlier.

Detective White was following Alisha. A fucking cop.

He recognized me from the bar with Lopez and Selena from all the times she went to the precinct downtown to talk to the friends of the missing girls.

And once Selena was around Avani?

He had known she was catching on.

White had acted quickly. Taking out Alisha and Avani before taking them back to Selena's broken body with the intent of taking out all three of them.

I saw Gabriel's eyes go hard as Perla told him everything else. Selena needed to be monitored. She'd stay at the hospital for now.

Why would Selena go after him alone?

She had nothing to prove to me or anyone.

"Do what you need," Gabriel took over. Perla nodded, and he thanked her as she left.

His eyes drifted to another dark blonde male I knew as Doctor Whittaker. I didn't know Reed had a brother who worked for Gabriel. He had never mentioned him.

"I need to go to Reed, Alisha hasn't woken up. Kieran can't leave Avani's side, but he needs to be switched out. I need to go talk to Killian about the other bodies."

Because there had been more.

Underneath the three of them.

I nodded dumbly as he motioned for Garrett and another dark-haired operative clad in black, who stood a few feet away, giving us privacy while also switching with Gabriel for Reed's side. "I'll be back."

Time meant shit as I sat by Selena, still wearing the same clothes I had when we found her. People moved around me, and all I heard was Selena's voice in my head telling me she loved me.

She did. Adam Whittaker came over to check up on me.

He and Reed had the same side profile and oddly striking resemblance. But their eyes were different. I saw his eyes, warm brown, take me in with polite concern.

He had saved Selena's life. Perla had helped, but Adam was the doctor over Selena. And Alisha hadn't woken up...

I just stood there against the wall, watching her through the window. Nobody could see her.

I studied her face, my eyes tracing the mottled bruises and angry cuts that marred her delicate features.

If I had stayed that night? None of this would've happened if I had

302

loved her instead and laid with her. Guilt, heavy and suffocating, invaded my lungs.

Nisha came out hours later, letting me go see her.

And I felt my legs made up of lead.

She looks so small like this.

Hot, bitter tears carved paths down my cheeks as I cradled her hand in mine.

And I broke harder than I ever had, not caring Garrett or the other operative stood outside.

I didn't give a shit about anything. I poured my heart out in whispers, begging her to come back to me, to open her eyes. And be angry with me.

Just be angry with me.

Come back to me. Let me love you. I'm sorry I didn't.

I'm such a fucking scumbag. Come back to me. Yell, scream, hit me.

Do whatever you want to me. Just me. Please.

She can't be angry if she's dead. And Selena is alive.

I want you to be angry with me. Say something.

I refused to leave her side.

I ignored everyone. I just wanted her. If I got any shut eye it was on her bed holding her hand. I didn't leave.

This is why Reed comes home to Alisha.

"I'm sorry, honey."

I whispered into her hand as Garrett stood nearby. I didn't move even as he motioned for me to get up. Do something.

His hand coming down on my shoulder. I didn't leave her. I had made the greatest mistake of my life in leaving her.

I didn't turn back.

I failed my girl.

It took Selena days to wake up.

Adam said sleep would be the best for her to heal.

Nisha Graham, the dark haired nurse, introduced herself to me politely, with warm dark eyes and raven hair in waves.

She reminded me a little of Evie with her smile. Inquisitive and sweet as she watched me.

"I'll be watching over her, is she your wife?"

I'm not your wife.

Not your girlfriend.

Not your honey.

But you could be.

I nodded, feeling my eyes water again as I blinked rapidly, staring at her. Alisha had woken up, and Reed hadn't left her for anything.

The same with Kieran who stayed like a magnet to Avani since I hadn't seen him.

And I stayed by Selena.

Until the day she woke up screaming.

I was there with Nisha when it happened, watching as she scrambled to reach for the IV, Nisha's hands steady despite the adrenaline.

I reached for Selena, my heart in my throat, as her eyes stayed closed, her screams piercing the air as the machines around her went haywire.

"Honey, honey, nononono, it's me—" Honey. Breathe. It's me.

Adam came running, his face a mask of concentration. "Get back, Agent Watts." He reached for Selena, calling out to Nisha as he did so. "*Nisha*, help me."

"I have her," Nisha replied, her hands moving with practiced efficiency as she injected something into Selena's IV.

Selena let out a noise, a strangled whimper that tore at my heart, as Nisha urged her to look at her, *just her, that it was okay.*

Nisha was repeating the words over and over until the medication took hold and Selena slowly slipped back into unconsciousness.

I stood back, my heart racing, as Gabriel and Reed appeared behind me.

Gabriel's gaze took in Selena's still form, his expression hard, while Reed's eyes filled with something softer as he looked at me.

Was it his mistakes, his lies, my own burnout, *that* argument with Selena?

I didn't know. I was angry with him, though I didn't fully understand why. I didn't know anything but her. Reed nodded to Garrett to switch with me. He had to go home to his girls.

And so Gabriel moved me out of the room. I couldn't look at Reed, who looked torn between leaving and staying.

Reed's girls—Alisha *and* Avani—were safe, while *my* Selena lay broken and battered before me.

It wasn't fair, and some dark, twisted part of me resented him for it.

I'm drained.

I don't even know how to process what I feel.

I could feel Gabriel's stare.

"Don't. I already know I'm the reason she's like this. *I failed her.*"

I looked down at my feet, unable to see again.

He had seen the truth etched upon my face, the guilt and self-loathing I felt. I hated who I was.

I wasn't thinking clearly; my emotions were a tangled mess of fear, grief, and rage.

"How long?"

I knew *exactly* what he was asking.

"Since the moment I met her." My voice cracked. "She was mine."

She is mine.

I had never wanted like I wanted her.

The words tumbled out. I couldn't stop them.

The airport, the restaurant, her place. Her heart. Her *warmth*. Life with her. *I had a home.* And now I had *nothing*. I didn't just lose Selena.

I lost *everything*. I wiped my face as I spoke.

Gabriel remained a silent sentinel, offering no judgment, only a steady presence as I laid myself bare. I lost her in one night.

One night.

And I was left *obliterated.*

Gabriel nodding, understanding in his eyes, his eyes drifting to Adam checking over something on Selena, with Garrett and Nisha talking quietly.

Reed had taken his leave, going to Killian O'Hara, the man handling all the cleanup for this mess. Gabriel hadn't left in days.

"She's your everything."

And *that* was the moment, the truth resonated within me.

Selena. Te necesito, amor.

Need you, love.

"*Selena is my everything,*" My voice never wavered as I realized the depth of what I felt in that moment. "Not a single thing matters without her."

Gabriel shifted his eyes and darted to me, breaking from Selena, something coming over his face as I said the words. He straightened his eyes, taking on a brighter quality.

The air around us shifted. Becoming colder as I looked at Selena. *I love her.*

What the fuck did Nate promise you that I couldn't?

A future! He promised me a life. Children... I met you...

I took a chance on you.

You never promised me a life after this...

You never...I never...I never promised her babies. Kids. A life. Nate did.

Every day with you was another day I did not want with Nathan

I was a fucking scumbag. I fucked up so bad.

I didn't give her that. I gave her a fling. Someone to fuck.

Someone who didn't commit to her. Someone who didn't know what he wanted from his girl.

Sure, I loved her—but I hadn't known Selena long enough to myself to give her *more*. Right? I thought it would've taken time to love her. But I loved her for so long time meant *nothing*.

She was *everything*.

What I felt for *her*. Everything. Admiration. Respect. Love.

You never promised me...

And I still chose you!

Her strength, her heart, the way she held herself, her grace.

Her compassion despite all her losses.

I had loved her for so fucking long chalking it up to some form of lust—that I hadn't realized I'd met my match in her.

It had *always* been me.

Nate fucking Wyatt hadn't stood a chance.

He promised me a future.

I promised her nothing.

I fucked up so bad.

I wanted to be her protector so badly, and I was the reason why she lay there. *My* home was lying there, bleeding and broken.

Because of me.

"*She is my everything.*" I took a breath as it slammed into me. I looked at Gabriel. "I'm an idiot."

Before I could even process the fact that Gabriel Monroe, of *all* people, was the one by my side, his pale eyes flashed with a mixture of annoyance and resignation as he muttered under his breath.

"*Here we fucking go.*"

CHAPTER 37
KELLAN

"*You.*"

Nate mother fucking Wyatt storming towards me, his usually suit disheveled.

Behind him, Gemma Marchand was racing behind him, her usual elegance replaced by desperation as she clutched at his arm.

"*Nate! Stop!*"

"*You did this to Lena.*"

In one fluid movement, Nate drew his gun. Gemma stopped like she hit a wall.

The cold metal of his gun pressed against my forehead. The world around us erupted in chaos.

Gasps and screams filling the air as people ducked for cover.

In the *fucking* hospital.

Adam was the only one running towards Gemma, yanking her out of harm's way and into his arms, hauling her back behind a desk.

Another operative with dark hair, rising behind him moving them both behind him his gun drawn.

I saw *everything*.

Gabriel, still standing behind me, remained eerily calm. "Really?" he said low. "Now?"

I couldn't see his face.

Just Nate holding the gun to my head.

I'm going to kill him.

Honey, something's happening to me.

"*What did you say to her?*" he demanded, the muzzle of his gun digging painfully into my skin. "*I know her*, she would *never* do something so *stupid. She had nothing to prove.*"

The ice settled into my chest around the soft spots Selena loved.

Memories of me sneaking bites in her kitchen, while sneaking kisses evaporated like smoke.

Her hands all over me, her hair all over my chest, her smiles at me. Her nuzzling my chest.

It was like ice moved over them, the layers covering her, protecting me, protecting *her.*

Somewhere no one could be let in.

I couldn't explain what was happening to me. Ice was creeping over my veins.

Honey, something's happening to me.

I knew I could disarm him easily, but the consequences of that action weighed heavily on my mind. If he pulled the trigger, either Gabriel or I would die. *Or both of us.*

And neither of those outcomes were acceptable.

"*Nate, do not hurt him.*" Gemma's pleas filled the air. "*It's not his fault.*"

"*It is!*" he roared. "It fucking is. *She chose him. I gave her to him. She was my girl.*"

And in that moment, something inside me *shattered.*

The ice that formed solidified.

That was the moment I lost control.

With a speed and precision that even I didn't know I possessed, I *moved.*

I disarmed Nate, the gun now a familiar weight in my hands.

My finger hovered over the trigger the gun now pointed at *him.*

A part of me reveled in the power I now held over him. Everyone else faded away.

"She's *my* girl." The words ripped out of my throat. "She *always* has been. You were her partner for five years. I was her partner for *five minutes*. And she let me in." I saw *everything.* "You wanna know why?"

Nate's eyes searched mine, as he backed away, his back hitting the wall.

"Wanna know why?" The words tore from my throat like jagged shards of glass. "Because I make her *better*. She's safe with me—"

"She wasn't safe days ago—"

I silenced him with a brutal shove of the muzzle against his forehead, the cold metal biting into his skin.

"You don't love her. You like the *idea* of her. *I. Love. Her.*"

I didn't even recognize the guttural sound of my voice. None of it.

I had been so fucking lost. I lost myself.

I didn't love her enough.

But I will.

I will love her.

As I spoke, something shifted in Nate's usual hard eyes, a moment of emotion that vanished as quickly as it had appeared.

"I love her so much, I scare the shit out of her. Because for *fucking* years, she had a partner who kept her at arm's length, too much of a *coward* to admit he trapped her *in a fucking pact that her bleeding heart kept. Until me. She chose me."*

The moment the words left me, the sensation of being a fucking idiot coursed through me.

It was a sensation that was becoming increasingly familiar to me as the days went by.

I recognized it in my soul. I had been so caught up with Selena, I didn't look out for my girl.

She chose me.

I didn't choose her.

"So *now*, I have to come in and fix another man's fuck-ups. I don't give a shit, because I love her. I would do *anything* for her. You think I'm just some punk kid who can't handle her, *but I already have.* She's been mine since the day I met her."

I felt wild.

Savage.

Hers.

"You didn't see me coming when I got here, *did you?"*

I pressed the muzzle of the gun deeper into Nate's forehead.

The click of the gun cocking once more echoed through the tense silence and the ice hardened in me.

"Do you see me now?"

In that moment, as the world around us faded away and the only thing that existed was the gun in my hand and the man at my mercy, I knew that I had won.

I could kill him.

And I wouldn't give a shit.

Flicking my wrist, I turned the safety back on and handed Nate his gun. I moved past Gabriel.

Pushing past the emergency doors, I gulped down deep breaths. Trying to calm down.

But even as the guilt and the fear threatened to consume me, I knew that I would do it all again in a heartbeat.

For Selena, I would burn the world to the ground.

The door opened behind me and I knew *who* it was.

"What now?" I whispered, unable to meet his gaze.

I couldn't do shit. I had just learned that I had almost lost my woman.

Honey, something's happening to me. Come back to me. Pull me back.

"You can fire me."

"Now where's the fun in that?"

I whirled around to face him, taking in his pale, eerie eyes that seemed to see right through me.

Of all the people to be here, Gabriel was the last one I expected.

He has the worst bedside manners.

"*Is this fun for you?* Me, losing my girl. *You don't fucking understand—*"

And that was the thing about Gabriel. I forgot…who he was. How he moved to tear everyone up.

Coiled, like a snake ready to strike, but you never knew *when* he would lash out.

In a blur of motion, he had me shoved up against the door we had just walked through, the impact echoing through the dim stairwell.

His frame pressed against my throat, six-foot-five inches and two hundred fifty pounds bearing down on me.

The only other sound was my pained groan as my back spasmed and my head throbbed.

"*I fucking understand*," His growl was like that of a demon, his eyes wild and feral in a way I had never seen before. "*Watch your mouth.* Or I will *finish* what Nate *started.*"

Gabriel's eyes were frightening.

"Let me make a few things clear, Quarterback. You are no longer Reed's operative. *I own you. And I am not Reed.*"

He wasn't.

Reed would give orders with violence in his eyes, but Gabriel did it with an arm at my windpipe, squeezing the life out of me.

"From this moment on, you will do *exactly* as instructed. *You are no longer allowed to see her.*"

What the fuck? It was like being shot in the chest in one full sweep. I felt my heart bottoming out to my stomach and stay there.

The thought of being separated from Selena, of not being able to be there for her when she needed me most?

Ripped. Through. Me.

"Not unless *she* wants to." Gabriel's words were like a blade, cutting deep into my soul and he kept going digging the damn thing deeper. "We have two new hires. Shane Alves is one of them. *That* is your new project. You're going to make him your carbon copy. *Do I make myself clear?*"

Those bright, cold blue eyes bore into me, searching for any hint of defiance. I swallowed. Hard. My eyes wide as I stared at his.

"You will see her *if* she wants to see you. *Or you can fuck off.*"

I feel like I'm being stabbed when he speaks.

Leave the Titans? Leave Selena?

No. Never.

One day, Gabriel will take you.

When he does, do not lose yourself.

I stood there, my heart pounding in my ears, the stairwell suddenly feeling claustrophobic.

Honey, something's happening to me.

"Why are you doing this?"

Pale blue eyes watched me like a demon, the air around us shifting. Ice invaded my veins as he stayed silent.

One night. All it took was one fucking night.

For my entire world to come crashing down on me.

And it felt like I would never be the same again.

Obliterated.

I was obliterated.

Gabriel tipped his head back watching me. "What is your call sign?"

"Mars."

I didn't even recognize my voice. Because he had his answer. I swallowed again feeling my entire body become ice.

"Cut your hair. Get a suit. *You work for me now.*"

PART II | MARS

THREE WEEKS LATER

CHAPTER 38
SELENA

"You're all good, Selena. You did great today at physical therapy."

As I lay in the hospital bed, Nisha Graham, my dark-haired nurse with soft eyes, smoothed my hair back, her husky voice over me.

She was my height but curvier on her hips in her soft green scrubs, her olive skin under the lights glowing—she had a soothing presence, and I loved her as my nurse.

I felt different. But anybody would after almost dying at the hands of a serial killer. That's what I had been chasing.

A serial killer.

And he'd caught me that night on the bridge. I dimly remember bits and pieces of what had happened.

I freaked out if I remembered too much, and Nisha hugged me tighter. She was strong and quiet, and I could see why Gabriel had picked Nisha to spend time with me.

She batted those eyes at me, dark pools of chocolate, as she smiled.

"You're okay. You're safe," her voice was low. "I'm just a friend, here to help you."

The other person who worked with Nisha was Adam Whittaker, Reed's brother, who I met with Nisha in the room.

Adam was a few inches shorter than Reed, but his features were a lot like Reed's. Adam's eyes were the softest brown like Avani's, kind and calming over me as he helped me.

And sometimes Garrett Fuller was allowed to come to me. With plants. Lots of them.

The newest addition to the team with Kellan had been the calmest.

At six-six Garrett, blonde and still steel-eyed moved in silence as he set down one large plant after another, filling my hospital room with flowers. Sometimes he brought them for Nisha when she got her breaks. The gentle giant and my nurse got along well.

Nobody else was allowed to visit me.

Not even Gabriel. Gabriel's orders for the last few weeks.

I would die on the inside more if anybody saw me like this.

As Nisha spoke, the scent of amber washed over me, and I felt the tension slowly ebbing from my body.

The first few weeks with her were tough, with me breaking down and her holding me.

All the time.

I had panic attacks and nightmares and needed help going to the bathroom, taking showers, and constant care.

She was there for all of it. I had found peace through her. It was good to have a woman by my side.

I didn't have to pretend to be anything. Nisha explained everything to me.

Over and over until it sank in.

Everything that happened after I passed out. I had wanted to know. As she told me, I got to grieve but slowly. Day by day, I healed.

Initially I had survived on protein shakes, losing weight rapidly, until Nisha began feeding me.

Nisha liked to eat *everything*, sampling new things all the time.

Killian O'Hara out of all people dropped off food for us and it took me a few days to realize he was her boyfriend.

At first, I thought he was doing it for me because Gabriel requested it and then I realized how happy Nisha got whenever she saw him. His hand would come up to her hair and play with it, a pink band-aid on his ring finger.

I had no idea Killian was *dating*.

I had never seen Killian look at *anyone* like *that*.

While Nisha and I sat together eating candy and watching cartoon movies, he dropped by with flowers for her and snacks.

She didn't comment on it, and I didn't know how to ask since it didn't make sense to me.

Killian was not the kind of man who...*dated*.

He never had in the years I'd known him.

The angry teenager Gabriel trained had become a lethal weapon for Titan.

But the more I got to know her? It made sense why Killian was with her.

She made me feel safe, like I was a little girl in need of her protecting. Soothing and calming me down.

Adam often let her explain things to me in her soft, soothing voice rather than me.

He rarely talked over her despite being the attending doctor.

Reed's little brother possessed a warmth Reed did not have and in all the years I had known Reed?

I didn't even know he had a brother. Talk about secrets.

Reed had violence underneath his eyes and intensity that terrified people, but Adam was *nothing* like that.

He was soft-spoken and kind to me in every way, healing and he didn't make me nervous.

Adam and Garrett were the only two men I really interacted with.

The door opened with a soft click. Nisha's eyes drifted to the sound curious. "Mr. Monroe?"

Gabriel.

"Everything is fine," Nisha reassured me turning to me, tucking her dark waves behind her ear. "It's just Mr. Monroe. I'm sure he's here to see you."

Nisha's gentle fingers wrapped around my hands, her touch warm and grounding, anchoring me to the present moment. "It's okay."

I was shaking. I couldn't control it I couldn't stop the tremors and Nisha wrapped her arms around me holding me to her.

"It's okay, breathe for me, Selena."

It's your choice. You give consent, Gatita.

His voice had whispered around my mind for the last three weeks. He existed in my soul. In my veins.

Gatita, Come back to me. I will do anything. Just come back to me.

I can't do this without you, honey. You are my one.

You are my everything.

318

Nisha's presence was *comfort*.

As she pulled the covers over me, she asked. "Do you want me to stay with you in the room or shall I step outside?"

I could be alone with Gabriel.

It was Gabriel, after all. I...knew him. Except, the idea of him seeing me like this? I felt panic.

Something turned in my stomach, and I tried not to freak out. "It's okay."

As Nisha opened the door, allowing Gabriel to enter, the atmosphere in the room shifted. Almost immediately. I felt it.

The dip. It happened every single time.

And this time was no different.

And I knew he was not here for any good news.

CHAPTER 39
SELENA

PALE ICY EYES, USUALLY PIERCING AND FOCUSED, AVOIDED ME completely as he walked in.

Gabriel was dressed…differently. Black on black. Scary. More than usual. And he didn't look at me once.

Gone were the crisp suits and polished shoes, replaced by a sleek, all-black ensemble that hugged his broad, lean frame.

Had he been working on a mission prior to this?

Nisha walked around Gabriel, his energy filled the room, and I felt the temperature drop.

Only this time…something was off about him.

I pressed my lips together, my eyes taking in every detail of his appearance, trying to reconcile the man before me with the Gabriel I *thought* I knew.

Nisha stepped outside, closing the curtains to give us privacy, leaving me alone with Gabriel. Completely.

And although I had done it so many times?

Something was different about him. He walked to the room's far end before sitting down and facing the television instead of me.

Gabriel didn't look at me once.

Not.

Once.

His icy fell on all the plants Garrett had brought me, the cactus, the fern, the pothos vines.

Moving to the cartoons Nisha always had playing on mute.

Gabriel had been the reason why I was alone. Processing. To heal.

To get better.

Nisha explained space would be good for me, rather than be bombarded by people.

But I knew one thing.

If he looks at me, I will fall apart.

When Gabriel opened his mouth, his words caught me off guard.

"When I found you years ago, you told me that the team from New York was your escape from Havana. But because they failed their mission so you were trapped there."

Where was he going with this? Was he not angry with me?

I was confused.

His next words hit me like a car coming straight for me.

"They did not fail their mission."

My heart sputtered to a stop. A shiver ran down my spine as the temperature in the room dropped.

What?

"The entire team was wiped out." He crossed his arms over his chest, his gaze fixed on the television's bright lights, and in that moment.

What was happening right now?

I sat up slowly, feeling my heart racing in my chest. "Gabriel—" I didn't know what to say right now. The pain in my body was mostly gone now, but suddenly places began to *ache.*

"It was my team."

Dios.

Fat, hot tears welled up in my eyes, blurring my vision as the weight of his words settled on me.

"Gabriel, I'm sorry—"

"I got them all killed."

I felt the air leave my lungs.

"One of the team members…was my wife."

The ground beneath me shifted, even as I sat up in the bed, my world tilting on its axis.

Who is she?

Your mujer?

I don't talk about my mujer.

321

One of the team members...was my wife.

The memories of our past conversations flooded my mind, and suddenly, everything fell into place.

I was shaking harder now the ice settling like pinpricks into my skin.

The pieces of the puzzle that I had been trying to solve for so long finally clicked together, forming a picture that I wished I could unsee.

I wished so bad I didn't hear those words.

The pain in his voice when I first met him, the haunted look in his eyes—*it all made sense now.*

"I promised her...a normal life," His voice was quiet. "A normal *wife.*"

And it cut *deep*, like a knife slicing through my heart.

A normal wife.

A normal life.

For a moment, he didn't say a word, and I looked down at my lap, my vision blurred by the tears that refused to stop falling. I was shaking harder.

What did you want to be?

A normal wife.

"I failed her."

I heard him from far away.

I had no idea.

He had never told me that he was the leader of the New York team.

We're starting a company called Titan with you.

Why me? Why did you choose me?

I thought you could use some kindness.

After a lifetime of not having any.

Reed, get Selena clothes.

Whatever you want.

You can stay here as long as you want.

What kind of car do you want?

Reed, she needs a license.

I'll bring your Mom to America.

You want a hug?

I'll take care of you.

Always.

Always.

Always.

I couldn't stop crying. My heart felt...shattered.

"I failed you *once*." I saw him watching the cartoons. Not once did he look at me. "I promised myself I would never fail you—I did. I failed *you*."

Just like...he felt he failed his team?

His words were like a final blow, shattering what was left of my already broken heart. The tears were coming faster now, a silent scream lodged in my throat.

He didn't.

He could never fail me, not in my eyes.

But as he spoke those words, I realized that he truly believed he had let me down, just as he believed he had let *her* down.

His wife.

And that realization hurt more.

I found myself paralyzed, my grief and shock burning into me. I couldn't see anymore.

The tears that streamed down my face were hot, burning trails down my cheeks.

As Gabriel's words washed over me, I knew why he picked me up out of Havana.

He led the New York team...

Gabriel had found me, had given me a chance at a better life, as a way to atone for the life he couldn't give his wife.

And my Mama. He did...more.

He reached into his jacket and pulled out a large manila envelope, placing it on the counter beside him.

"You can go through this on your own."

"What are you—" I started, my voice hoarse from crying, but he cut me off with a gentle shake of his head.

"I'm letting you go." He looked at the envelope.

My heartbeat pounded in my ears. I couldn't see his eyes.

Or his face.

"This is what I never gave her." He had lost her. *He almost lost me.* "You're not a Titan anymore."

His words were gentle, but they cut through me like a knife.

"You're...letting me go?" I asked, my heart bottoming out. *"Because I—"*

"You never failed," he said gently, shaking his head. "I *failed*. I am

the team lead. *You* cannot fail." His words caught me completely off guard. "Watts told me *everything*. Reed already went after Nate."

"You know…" I trailed off, and he nodded in response.

"While it was a gesture I would consider noble, it was not the gesture *you* needed. And he didn't know that, but the moment Gemma walked back into his life, he should've let it go. I would've reacted the same way Watts did. I don't blame him."

He let out a low humorless laugh. "I *know* Watts. I'm not mad at him. Nate needed to let you go like you had let him go. That's *why* Reed replaced Nate with Watts. He trusted Watts to do right by *you*."

Gabriel continued, his eyes fixed on the envelope.

"Watts tried to do right by *everyone*. Reed was hard on him, and while he dropped the ball once, it was the *only* time he did. And it was for *you*. I would do the same for *her*. I know if it was Alisha not picking up, Reed would do the same. *Nobody* is angry at Watts."

"I'm not angry with you." He paused. "I just wish you had told me about Nate. You know I would've straightened him out."

I didn't even think about how to tell Gabriel what I wanted. A life. Marriage. Babies. I didn't know *how* to tell him. Because I served him. But I had said yes to Nathan. I had made a choice too.

Gabriel continued. "*Nate knew better. Gemma Marchand is Nate's final assignment with Titan.*"

I looked at Gabriel like he wasn't dropping one bomb after another on me.

"Nate's choice. He'll stay with Gemma until she doesn't need him. He doesn't want this life. And I don't think he's in the right headspace."

Gabriel explained to me quietly that Nathan *had* been my partner. In the past tense. He had made me choose between him or Kellan.

"*That choice was obvious to a monkey looking at you and Watts,*" Gabriel's voice was annoyed.

He continued that Nathan's inability to support me, prioritizing himself over me, and having a harder time letting me go made it difficult for me to prioritize Kellan—and tell Kellan the truth.

Because the moment Nate knew about Kellan?

It should've been the end.

"Nate's inability to talk to Gemma and their issues made *you* vulnerable. Even the best operatives have weaknesses. Gemma was his. Reed will handle that."

Did Gabriel know what Gemma's family did to him?

"Your promise to Nate was *before* you met Watts. Before you even knew what was happening. There's no malicious intent. Nate needed to get his shit together with Gemma. Misguided confusion. Which is normal given the *stupidity*..."

Gabriel went on to tell me he had handled everything for me to go to Miami and be...*normal*. I just had to decide when. I would *heal*. Be me. *Live*.

I didn't want to leave Titan. But I knew I couldn't stay.

"Your mom is in Miami."

My heart ached at the thought of seeing her again after so long. She thought I taught at a college.

A professor.

Not a killer.

He brought Mama to the states. He did so much for me.

Over what? His guilt? His wife? In her memory?

He made me.

And while it broke my heart to think of leaving the Titans, of leaving *him*, I knew it was right. Because it didn't hurt at all. I thought it would.

But I couldn't remember my argument with Kellan. I couldn't remember anything but *this* feeling.

This new feeling is in my chest.

His voice was soft as he said it. "I am setting you free, *Paloma*."

My eyes shot to him. Something bright and huge was forming in my chest. It felt like...something had unlocked inside of me at the words.

It was as if a weight had been lifted from my body. The wings of something hard beat against my chest.

His voice from years ago drifted back...

Why did you name her Paloma?

My father called me Paloma. His dove.

He said I would go places in life.

I will go places with her.

Gabriel looked at me then, a soft smile on his face like he knew me. He did. I couldn't see him through how hard I was crying.

It's like a firework went off in my chest. And it keeps going off.

I am setting you free, Paloma.

He stood up from his seat, his movements slow and controlled.

325

Gabriel got on one knee in front of my bed, making himself even with me, his face inches from mine, and I cried harder.

"Can I hug you?"

Can I hug you?

My heart ached so bad in that moment.

He was my beginning. And now, I was losing him.

I nodded blindly. He blinked several times as he placed gentle hands on the sides of my head, his fingers threading through my hair.

"I will *always* love you. I am still your family and your friend," his voice was thick, his eyes warmer than I had ever seen them.

Sometimes, he was ice.

"You always have my number. Go get some sun."

Sometimes, he was this man underneath it all.

Gabriel pressed his lips against my forehead. I closed my eyes. He stayed still for a long moment. And I cried harder.

My father called me Paloma...

As he pulled away, I opened my eyes to see his own eyes blinking rapidly.

Without another word, he stood slowly. His footsteps echoing in the quietness of the room as he left.

I didn't watch him go, my eyes falling on the envelope he left behind.

Sitting on the counter like a promise.

I'm setting you free, Paloma.

Did you want to do this?

No. I just wanted to be a normal wife...

You are no longer a Titan.

I didn't think of anyone else but me. I didn't have to.

Did you want this life? No.

I'm setting you free, Paloma.

A slow smile spread across my lips. *I can be anything. I can be just Lena.*

Gatita, you are so incredible. My smile dipped a little at his voice.

What happened to him?

Gabriel never said a thing.

Were we even together after that night?

Was he mine? Probably not.

Where did he stay?

I needed to get my *things* from the apartment…my clothes.

What would you take? What do you have that doesn't remind you of Kellan?

Nothing. And I have the resources to buy my new life. Anything I want. I am free.

This time when you leave with the clothes on your back? *You are starting again.*

I'm setting you free, Paloma.

With something *new.*

I am free.

Reed had been a good big brother and invested all my money into his real estate he owned since I did not know anything about making money.

I was not a poor, hungry girl anymore.

I was free.

I'm setting you free, Paloma.

I was *free.*

My laughter filled the room as my shoulders shook with tears of joy.

I am free.

I am no longer a Titan.

CHAPTER 40
KELLAN

I was finally a Titan.

I barely recognize myself anymore.

Do not lose yourself to Gabriel when he takes you.

I'm sorry. I lost myself, Gatita.

The navy suit, tailored to my leaner body, felt like a second skin, but it couldn't hide the ice that seemed to encase my soul.

The muscle I'd packed in over the last few weeks had tapered me out brutally.

I couldn't shake the darkness, no matter how hard I tried.

So, I stopped fighting it and just went with it. My eyes landed on Selena's mascara tube, which was lying there.

I lived at her home. *Our* home.

I couldn't let her go.

Everything in me ached for the last twenty-one fucking days.

Without her?

I was…a shell of who I used to be.

That first-time lust had turned into the most real relationship I had ever had. And I fucked up.

And I had gotten her hurt.

She was with me everywhere.

This was the only time I got to be around her. And I took it all.

And so here I was, living in Selena's place like a goddamn ghost.

Gabriel had made it clear that she wouldn't be coming back, and

Nisha was tasked with picking up her belongings whenever she needed them.

Weeks had passed since I'd been taken under Killian O'Hara's wing.

Killian, the second-in-command of a fucking crime syndicate in New York, still answered to Gabriel.

A fact I hadn't been privy to until I showed up in front of Gabriel himself, orders in hand, ready to report. I didn't understand who the O'Hara's were.

Gabriel wasn't just dipping his toes in blood like Reed.

No, he was covered in it, making Reed look like a goddamn saint in comparison. Everything Gabriel did was classified, off the books, and shrouded in secrecy.

This is the shadows. The other half of Titan.

The past few weeks had been a whirlwind, with Killian scrambling to get something done for Mercury Group, a company owned by the elusive Lucas Devereux, a CEO no one, for some fucking reason, laid eyes on.

The only people privy to the details were those at the manor, while Shane, Garrett, and I were relegated to the city as operatives following orders.

When I wasn't under Killian's command, I found myself mentoring Shane Alves. He was the dark-haired operative who had witnessed my confrontation with Nate Wyatt. When I'd almost killed him over *her*.

I adjusted my tie, trying to push her thoughts out of my mind.

The ice in my veins seemed to thicken.

The layer over my chest harder now with the time that passed.

Just go with it, savage.

I'm trying, honey.

Weeks ago, Gabriel had taken in my tailored suit with approval before dismissing me on my first day.

He had mentioned that Shane would be arriving later in the day.

Gabriel had work for me to do before then.

Shane Alves walked in that afternoon.

As we shook hands, I took in his features—half-Cuban, half-Greek, with neatly styled curling brown hair and deep green eyes.

Shane had been the one to push Gemma and Adam behind him as

their shield. Shane, like Kieran, had been thrown into the fire by Gabriel.

At six feet even, indicating he was an athlete, Shane was muscular and broad-shouldered, the physique of an athlete and a former Special Forces operative.

He was polite as he shook my hand. He had already been around Reed and Kieran for the last few weeks on and off.

Kieran had left Avani's side after serving as her and Alisha's guard.

Alisha, I'd heard, was doing better but still suffered from occasional migraines and memory issues—a normal side effect of a brain injury, according to Shane, who shadowed Reed sometimes. But she'd eventually get better.

I wonder if Selena had the same issues and who was helping her through all of them. If she got better...

Since White had liked to—

I would kill him over and over again. The sniper that had taken him out had been fucking precise since he'd been locked in a struggle with Alisha at the time.

That headshot had saved *everyone's* life.

I couldn't wonder about the worst night of my life for too long.

My mind was on Shane, who I kept seeing push Gemma and Adam behind him. *Over and over again.*

I paused for a moment when he hit me with the full force of his eyes. His greens weren't *her* eyes, no, they were deeper.

His appearance was dressed casually, because he was going to be under Reed eventually.

"Football?"

"No, Sir. Hockey."

"Did you pick a call sign?"

"Yes, sir. Hermes." The messenger. Low-key, but fitting.

Not bad. He's polite as fuck.

As our conversation continued, I noticed that Shane maintained a professional distance, likely sensing that something was off with me.

He was different from the rest of the team, and I had a feeling he would fit in seamlessly.

Gabriel stepped into the room, clad in his grey suit, his icy disposition following him. And I braced myself for what was to come. If he went after Shane.

Shane fucking surprised me by standing up and offering his hand to the man. "Mr. Monroe. Nice to meet you again, sir."

Gabriel paused in the middle of his walk, clearly surprised by the gesture. Nobody fucking greeted Gabriel but Evie.

Even Reed threw something at him. And Reed was juggling a fuck ton right now. I knew that much.

Icy blue eyes narrowed as he assessed Shane. I was already tensing.

Here we fucking go. Fucking Gabriel and his temper.

I went to move Shane out of the way so Gabriel's fangs wouldn't sink into the kid's throat.

And then Gabriel *accepted* Shane's outstretched hand.

Asking him questions about his family in Spanish and asking Shane how fluent he was in Portugese.

I didn't know Gabriel spoke both.

But I was learning I didn't know a lot about Gabriel. Resident ghost and all.

I watched as Shane gave him a polite nod, almost a bow, like Alisha did, before replying back in *both*. Seamlessly.

They conversed briefly, with Shane commenting on Gabriel's fluency.

Gabriel smiled at that, a rare sight, and mentioned that he had worked hard to learn the languages.

"You're good with Spanish and Portuguese," Shane said to Gabriel.

I stood there, *stunned*, as Gabriel looked more at ease than I had ever seen him, speaking with a genuine smile on his face at the kid.

I translated in my head what Gabriel was saying in Spanish to Shane. *I prefer speaking in anything but English, it's less complicated. It's clear where people stand. Less room for confusion.*

Shane agreed.

It was the most I had heard him speak in one conversation, and it was with a new hire, no less. One he didn't want to kill.

I knew Reed had plucked Shane out from somewhere, but Gabriel rarely liked anyone.

Kieran was a given who his family was.

But Shane was a new hire who, on his *first* few days, had pushed innocent civilians behind him. So they wouldn't take a hit.

Shane had passed Gabriel's test with flying colors. *In the moment.*

And I heard her voice in my head again.

Kellan, Gabriel does not like weakness…

He believes weakness is not trainable. Good enough gets people killed.

Gatita, Shane is more than good enough.

You'd like him.

I realized Shane treated everyone with the same polite friendliness, regardless of their position.

He spoke to Gabriel and me in the same manner, adapting quickly to his new environment.

It was then that I realized none of the guys, *not even me*, had ever treated Gabriel like a *person*.

As I continued to work with Shane during the next few weeks, I found that he either already possessed the skills I was teaching him or picked them up with an astonishing speed that reminded me of…*No. Stop.*

Trying to distract myself, I asked Shane if he had family in Cuba.

He shook his head, explaining that he was closer to his father's side of the family, who were fully Greek.

Shane brought a new energy to the team.

His ability to connect with people on a human level, even someone like Gabriel, was a skill that couldn't be taught.

It was innate, a part of who he was.

Gatita, you'd like this man.

Shane was clean-cut, and he got along with Adam Whittaker.

Both of them were new to Titan when the incident happened, and they passed Gabriel's tests.

The two of them were good friends, close in age, and had a lot of the same interests.

Shane took Adam to the gym, and Adam taught Shane medical basics, which made Shane even more valuable to the team.

Even Garrett took the younger man under his wing due to their shared background in special forces and similar assignments when I was working with Killian.

This week, Shane was with Garrett while I completed the tasks Killian assigned.

The manor was on lockdown, with only a select few allowed inside.

Something had gone down.

Killian's orders.

We were not privy to anything, but I suspected it had to do with Lucas Devereaux. And nobody knew shit.

Time passed by in a blur.

~

"UP," KILLIAN BARKED AT ME.

I groaned a little after being tossed to the ground like a rag doll.

My current mentor was Killian O'Hara.

Technically, Killian was second-in-command of the Irish mob. But his side gig was being Gabriel's personal hitman.

When Gabriel had a job to get done that required finesse. He called Killian.

Everyone called him. At six-two, maybe three, he was two hundred plus pounds of lean and mean tatted glory.

Killian's inky hair was matted with sweat right now, eerie mismatched eyes, one aqua, one amber watched me as he looked annoyed.

He always looked annoyed.

Gabriel had given me a fucking shark to train with. One that was meaner than him.

Pushing me to the fucking limits of my physical strength aside, he constantly wiped me out in hand-to-hand combat.

Like now, when he pitched me over his fucking head to the ground.

"Fuck." I groaned as he moved around me.

For a big guy, I didn't know how he moved so smoothly.

My initial rounds of training with him were different.

He made drill instructors look nice. Rarely gave praise. Wore his perpetual scowl and didn't think much of me.

He was the guy with Kieran that night I found Selena. And now, he was out for my blood.

He'd worked with Selena for years.

After combat, he moved onto training me with several different guns. I had shot before, but Killian's sniper training was intense.

The only time Killian walked away from me was to text someone. I caught the wallpaper on his phone, and it was a photo of his girl.

The first time I saw it, I thought I was hallucinating.

Because Killian's girl was Selena's nurse.

Nisha Graham.

I remembered her dark hair and eyes, olive skin, soft voice. Totally not what I pictured him with.

But then I caught him wearing fucking heart print bandaids and shit and with cookies. He always left for lunch to bring her food and came back in a better mood.

When we were working, Killian and I ran through high-stakes scenarios where I was set to target new people. Take them out.

This was what Gabriel did behind the shadows.

This was why Reed had a reputation. Because it was never Reed. It was Gabriel the entire time.

Today, he came by with a slight smile on his face. From the hospital. Where he got to see his girl and I didn't get to see mine.

"Ready, Quarterback?"

"Ready."

Tonight, I found myself on another rooftop, the cold metal of a sniper rifle pressed against my cheek. My target is a few meters out.

Killian had met me here, his presence as unsettling as ever with his mismatched eyes and the dark aura that perpetually surrounded him.

"We have a tasker," he had said. Killian didn't say much. When he did, it was work-related. Tonight, his bandaid was another shade of pink with little bows.

He always had taskers.

Killian worked with dead people more than the living.

I learned quickly under him, and now, I was putting those skills to use.

My current target was a man in a suit and tie—two buildings down.

The wind whipped around my shorter hair, now closer to my scalp. My jaw clenched as I braced. I steadied my breathing as my finger lightly rested on the trigger.

Through the scope, I could see the target clearly.

Pacing back and forth, his hand holding his phone to his ear as he spoke to whoever it was. I had to wait until he was off to shoot him.

Breathe in. Breathe out.

Squeeze when you breathe out.

I felt Killian beside me.

"Focus," Killian said behind me after showing up with blood on his suit and changing in the car. "You have no emotions. Nothing matters but your next target, clear?"

"Crystal."

I felt Killian's presence behind me, his shadow looming over my prone form.

"*Don't be a punk bitch*," he growled. "Kieran was faster, and he was younger than you when he started."

This motherfucker.

I squeezed the trigger, the rifle kicking back against my shoulder as the shot rang out.

Two buildings down, the target crumpled to the ground, red stains spreading across the front of his suit.

I turned over my shoulder to Killian. "And?"

"Not bad."

Kieran, the youngest, had left his family, and Aidan, the *fucking head of the Irish mob* and their oldest brother, had asked Gabriel to keep an eye on Kieran. Call sign *Eros.*

I didn't read too much into it. It wasn't my business.

Killian never flinched when pulling the trigger, and I wanted to make sure I learned from him.

His movements were fluid and precise, like a lazy tiger in the grass who knew exactly when to strike. Coiled. Waiting. Dangerous.

Sometimes, he reminded me of Gabriel.

But Killian's savage energy wasn't hidden, and it changed *me*, transforming me into something I didn't recognize. Which was the whole point.

Trial by fire made Reed look nice in comparison.

Whatever I started out as in Titan?

It was being erased. No more Mr. Letterman. No more Selena.

No more *me.*

The ice factor chilling out in my heart, the shadows welcoming me when I went to work.

I was becoming someone I didn't recognize.

And the scariest part?

I didn't hate it.

CHAPTER 41

KELLAN

"Where now?"

"We have to make a trip tonight."

"Over the Devereaux's?"

"No, somewhere else."

Killian adjusted his cufflinks, a pink bandaid on his index finger, a reminder of who I fucking *knew* he was with.

I'd seen Killian get sliced once with less of a grunt.

We'd been working together, and I'd seen him kill people without a second glance. But he only wore that pink bandaid for someone else.

Killian moved with a predatory grace, his footsteps nearly silent on the concrete. Leaner, moving like a lithe fighter. I followed behind him, my senses on high alert now that I'd killed a man in cold blood.

Maybe Killian would be civil like Kieran if he didn't look like he spent most of his time around...*this. Death. Blood. Decay.*

I picked up the M200 rifle as I stepped out with Killian.

"Hospital?" I asked, raising a brow. He'd been spending an awful lot of time at the hospital.

Killian's jaw clenched. "No."

He went to the hospital *all* the fucking time, and I knew it wasn't because he *enjoyed* getting treated. And only one lady would work with him.

Nisha.

Dark hair, deeper olive skin, and expressive darker doe eyes like

Evie's. I'd met her briefly with Selena when she'd been working with her.

She'd been *sweet*.

Not the kind of girl I imagined with Killian fucking O'Hara.

Killian looked like he'd bite her head off. But he was so fucking loyal to her in the three weeks I'd worked with him? He didn't look at anyone once.

I fucking *knew* I recognized those bandaids on Killian because they were the same ones Nisha gave out at the hospital. Pink hearts and shit on his ring finger.

I'd caught a whiff of her perfume on him several times. Her coffee cup was in his car. Her sweater in the backseat. Her lipgloss in his cup holder. And sometimes her badge.

Killian had a fucking *girlfriend*. She fixed people. He killed them.

Maybe there was balance in the world after all.

Since Nisha was with Selena.

And I wasn't. The thought of Selena sent a pang through my chest.

I had no idea what had happened to my girl, and I wasn't allowed to find out.

Even Garrett, who usually had a soft spot for me, wouldn't say a word.

If I was injured, I was barred from the hospital she was in, relegated to a separate facility on the other side of Titan, one reserved for Gabriel's people who did work he didn't want broadcasted.

The last few weeks of my life had been a blur of lessons and fights.

Chasing down other criminals and suspects. In the shadows of Titan, more shit went on than I would've imagined.

I'd been in knife fights and shot people with Killian. And he was a brutal fighter. All lean lines of strength and muscle that he threw around without a care in the world. Save for one.

He's got a heart bandaid on his finger.

"I need your complete fucking discretion for what we are about to do." He walked down to the underground garage where he parked a blacked out SUV.

A Roadster. Disassembling the M200 rifle, my fingers worked deftly to pack it away into the innocuous-looking cello case Killian kept in the trunk.

Placing the case amid the other nondescript items I remember the first time I'd done this.

I had thought, who the fuck would ever look at Killian O'Hara and think, *this motherfucker right here plays the cello.*

But then again, *what the fuck did I know?*

How the fuck would I ask him? In the world of Titan, appearances were always deceptive. I used to be a college football player according to my appearance.

Now...I was *this*. Not hers anymore. Something else entirely.

As I slid into the passenger seat, I nodded at Killian. "I only asked about—"

"*Not another fucking word,*" his voice a growl, eerie eyes flashing. "We are going to pick up Kieran. Gabriel hasn't heard from him in twenty-four hours. He missed his last mandatory check-in. We need to move. *Not a fucking question. You will do exactly as I say. Is that clear?*"

"Yes, sir."

I learned quick with him.

It was evident he knew where Kieran was since we were moving. But he didn't mention *how* Kieran was.

Or *why* Kieran had mandatory check-ins.

Killian took off, the neon street lights blurring past the window.

Shifting shadows cast on Killian's jaw, set with tension as he focused on the road. The air in the car was heavier with another kind of tension.

"Do not ask any questions. Do not look at anyone. Just move with me," Killian ordered, his voice cutting through the silence like a knife.

Why did Kieran have mandatory check-ins with Gabriel?

Compared to Killian, Kieran, the baby O'Hara, was a breath of fucking fresh air. He was easygoing, calm, and charismatic. He reminded me of Adam Whittaker if Adam had been born into the mob.

Kieran had been guarding Avani and Alisha for the last few weeks, and I knew he was recently off the hook.

"Where is he?" I asked.

"*Maison De Nuit,*" Killian replied, his tone clipped.

Ma. Who?

He maneuvered the car into an upscale garage and brought it to a halt.

As we exited the place, my eyes wandered around, looking at how, even for a garage, this fucking place was polished. Armed guards. Security checks.

Killian waved his hand in a dismissive gesture, and the moment they saw him, they moved back as he stepped forward. Long strides until we both crossed the floor to the elevators.

"What the fuck is this place?"

His mismatched eyes turned to me. "The club members pay for discretion, and Kieran's rules are strict. Unlike *Teo*. Do not speak to anyone. You see nothing. And if you so much as breathe wrong here, *I will put a bullet in you.*"

CHAPTER 42
SELENA

WHEN I WAS EIGHT, MY FATHER GOT ME A SET OF OIL PASTELS AND A coloring book.

I told him I was going to be an artist, and he looked at me with pride, displaying my work all over the house.

That dream had gotten lost in life with the Titans. Along with me.

But now, as I stood in the art studio in Miami, surrounded by the gentle chatter of my classmates, the sound of waves in the background, and the soft guidance of our instructor—I remembered that girl.

I didn't know where to start in my new life.

But…I thought I might start where I had in my old one. I wanted to be an artist.

As I stepped back from the easel, a smile curved my lips. My work was good. Rusty, but good.

Nisha and I talked after Gabriel left, and she gave me a lot of advice. She had told me to pursue my joy. Painting.

The riot of colors filled my canvas in the shape of a butterfly wing. Hues of pink and magenta and petal pink. Pink was my favorite color. Each shade swirled together and three dimensional petals blossomed from the surface popping out at me.

"Are you ladies having a better time?" Marcelo, the twenty-one year old instructor with a muscular build asked a few of the ladies.

Marcelo had an aversion to shirts.

Which *nobody* complained about.

With his dark, curling hair, tanned skin, and white teeth, everyone swooned over him.

But…my mind always drifted back to someone else.

It had been a month since…everything.

But barely a week after I got to Miami, I was healing. Slowly. Thanks to a combination of rest, comfort, and medication—even if I walked a bit slower. The nerve pain lingered. But I was getting better every single day.

I left the hospital following Gabriel's directions.

To a private airfield. As I stepped off the private jet, the warm Miami sun sank into my skin.

Gabriel had access to a private jet, courtesy of Mercury Group staff informed me that it belonged to Lucas Devereaux, a friend to Titan apparently.

The name was unfamiliar to me, but I was grateful for the comfortable journey.

The moment I picked up a brush and felt the smooth glide of paint against canvas, something within me stirred to life.

Nisha had told me to do things that made me happy.

My mind drifted to the plans I made for the rest of the day—going to the beach, getting a smoothie, and just walking slowly for a bit.

Forever, my life had been shaped by the men around me. It wasn't easy anymore becoming my own person. Not at all. But it felt like I was becoming something now. Someone.

Except there were moments when memories would come flooding back when the scars on my body would throb. And my soul would ache with something familiar.

Amarte es paz.

Loving you is peace.

I tried not to think about him.

I really did.

But instead of letting those moments consume me, instead of allowing those moments to overwhelm me, I learned to acknowledge them. And let it go.

Nisha and I practiced this process, and sometimes Adam would join us.

His presence helped me become used to being around a man.

341

I found out Adam had been a new addition to the team, and under Gabriel.

Adam was gentle; his smile and some features were the only resemblance to his older brother. Everything else was the softest parts of Reed.

Garrett was the only one I felt *anyone* was used to.

For a big man, he was always present and steady, watering plants and bringing Nisha and me food. He was six-six, bigger than Gabriel, and somehow the quietest Titan we had. I got the feeling Gabriel liked him for being a gentle giant.

"How are you today, Lena?" He had picked up Evie's nickname for me. "Doing better?"

"Better."

"I got you the pancakes you said you liked the other day." I had seen, and so had Nisha.

It was a slow, steady process. But Nisha had helped me so much.

You can enjoy your quiet time and romance novels. I would also recommend you find something you love.

The beach, art, pottery, something. And use that to ground you.

Be your center. Healing is not linear. But for you, moving on is necessary.

Being here, away from everything, was exactly what I needed.

Lena Paloma Santos.

That was my new identity, crafted by Gabriel himself.

He had chosen a Latina background for me, providing me with a new passport and a set of IDs to match.

Gabriel got me *everything*.

My new life was tucked away neatly into the envelope including the keys to the White Lotus. A new beach condo I had in my name.

My transition from Selena Tavares to Lena Santos was as seamless as possible. And now I was the owner of a cozy space.

Now, I sat with the evening sun, tanning on the beach and relaxing. The place was one of many owned by the real estate company Mercury Group.

My new living room and kitchen had breathtaking views of the sparkling ocean, filling the space with natural light and a sense of openness. I felt free. Lighter. A better version of myself.

My new long bob felt lighter and easier to manage, and the absence of my bangs made me feel more open. My body felt different. None of the anxiety from New York was here.

I was a different woman.

And that woman wasn't ready to see Mama just yet, not until I had taken the time to truly heal, inside and out. She didn't know who I was.

I didn't know either. In my time in Miami, I hadn't spoken to many people. I didn't want to.

Plus, the nightmares that prevented me from sleeping didn't help.

Nisha had told me…people like *me* lost memories of the incident. *Some*. I had some.

I wish I didn't have any.

The things I did…I cried over. A lot.

But even as I embraced this new part of my life, I couldn't shake the whisper of *his* voice in the back of my mind.

Gatita, where did you go?

Come back.

I didn't want to say anything to anyone, didn't want to acknowledge the part of my heart that still—No.

Not him.

No one but me.

Just a second, Gatita.

But I didn't want just a *second* of happiness, of peace. I wanted a lifetime of it, with me, with Lena, a future filled with love.

With me.

I stepped out onto my balcony, the warm Miami breeze caressing my skin.

I just want this.

I chose me.

CHAPTER 43

KELLAN

Teo?

Alisha's voice was in my head. She called Matteo DuPont, *Teo*.

I frowned at the mention of *club* members, but before I could ask, Killian stepped into an elevator that looked deceptively normal. I didn't know where we were, but I obeyed.

Matteo DuPont was here?

With a swift motion, he pulled out a keycard and entered a code, bringing the elevator to life with a soft whir.

"Do not speak. *Do not say a word.* Not a fucking move against my orders, clear?"

"Crystal."

As the doors opened, we stepped into a long, white plush hallway, carpeted floors, colors marked several doors.

The sounds emanating from behind the doors we passed were muffled, but I could've sworn I heard…no, it *couldn't* be. I shook my head, trying to focus on the task at hand.

Killian stopped abruptly in front of a set of elegant double doors marked with the name "Amber Suite."

Instead of knocking, he entered a code on the keypad.

"If it doesn't open, I'm going to shoot it. It'll alert the guards, but if Kieran is dead on the other side, I will kill *everyone* in this bitch. *Starting with Teo.*"

That's why I needed my gun loaded. As the keypad beeped in green,

Killian swore under his breath in relief. He reached for the ornate door handle cracking it open.

"Not a word," he mouthed, his eyes burning with intensity. I tipped my head in agreement.

As Killian pushed the door open and swept inside, I followed close behind, only to be immediately hit with a whiff of—holy fucking shit was that weed? How much weed?

I coughed, my eyes watering as I tried to make sense of the scene before me. The enormous suite was dimly lit, the air heavy with the odor of…what the fuck was that?

Among other things.

Through the haze, my eyes could make out a lean coiled figure lounging in a chair, half-dressed and smoking.

I swore softly.

It took me a moment to recognize him as *Kieran*, the calm and collected man I had met.

What the fuck…

He looked like a shell of his former self, his eyes glazed and unfocused.

Killian and Kieran were pretty much the same height and build, but *now*? I didn't recognize him.

I saw Kieran's tattoo's all over his body, his ribs, as he inhaled shakily.

My gaze darted to Killian, who was standing near the bed, his posture rigid. He didn't react at all.

Like he'd done this hundreds of times to not be phased by it.

A mess of ropes and restraints all over, and I noticed two women lying there passed out, one still bound to one side.

I couldn't reconcile the image with the Kieran I knew, the man who had been with me the night he saved Avani, even as I was shaking with adrenaline.

Who the fuck is Kieran O'Hara?

"Shut the door, Watts," Killian growled. He looked peeved.

I realized I hadn't closed it behind me, when I did the sound of the door beeping shut was unnaturally loud in the quiet room.

Killian moved around the suite with a familiarity as Kieran groaned some curses in a language I didn't understand.

Killian just tossed a wad of bills on the bed, then made his way to

Kieran.

My gaze drifted to the bed where I saw blood on the sheets, on the girls.

Were they dead? Was that for the clean up crew?

Mismatched eyes darted over the table littered with lines of white powder and scattered pills in colors.

The glint of some of the knives, a set of guns with longer barrels, caught my attention, some of it stained with blood.

Killian tried to rouse Kieran from his drug-induced stupor, speaking to him in a language I didn't understand.

Gaelic?

When Kieran didn't respond, Killian switched to English, his voice laced with concern. "How fucked are you right now?"

Kieran slurred his words and I couldn't make out what he was saying, but the desperation in his tone was clear. I saw Killian blocking his brother from my view.

His mismatched gaze flicked to the drugs on the table, and he motioned for me to get rid of them.

Kieran tipped his head up as I reached and I stopped. *"I'm fucked, not dead."*

His eyes slid to me colder than I had ever seen them, amber washed out into black, pupils dilated as he licked his lips, his voice a dark whisper. *"I wasn't finished."*

Killian motioned for me to stop.

"You're finished, little brother," Killian shoved his shoulder under Kieran's arm, motioning for me to take the other side.

I didn't say a word.

As we hauled Kieran to his feet, the stench of smoke, sex, and God knows what else assaulted my senses, and I didn't even want to know what the knives and guns were for.

I just took a lucky guess that shit wasn't my thing.

Killian's voice cut through my thoughts. "We need to get out of here, take him to Adam. He's tracking this already."

I nodded, remembering his earlier warning about not speaking.

As we half-dragged, half-carried Kieran out of the suite, I took in the elegant walls and decor, each room marked with a color, some of them the same, some different.

"That is one of the Amber Suite rooms," Killian explained, his voice low. "This place uses a color code system. You have to know someone to get in. Amber is Kieran's."

He paused, his eyes meeting mine once more. "The colors signify people. One floor above us, the Sapphire on the doors? *DuPont.*"

I did see the Amber mark as I carried Kieran.

There weren't many, the rooms spaced wide enough apart.

I caught a door marked with a Diamond, before we hit the elevator. And I realized in that moment I thought I heard muffled screaming earlier.

This wasn't a high-end *hotel*; it was a sex club.

"Go down this way, we'll get back to the car quicker," Killian motioned to a different elevator, his voice low and urgent. "No guards. Easier."

I nodded, adjusting my grip on Kieran as we made our way towards the elevator. The questions burned in my mind, and before I could stop myself.

"You come here."

Killian was familiar with the place. And I forgot about the whole no-questions for a second.

I expected Killian to snap at me.

Instead, Killian nodded. "I used to."

"Why did you stop?"

A beat passed. He held up his finger with the bandaid.

His girl.

"Nisha—"

His eyes swung to me with an expression that said he would shoot me if I ever said her name again, and I instantly shut my mouth.

We adjusted Kieran as we waited. A noise left Kieran and Killian said something soft in—"Gaelic?"

Killian nodded, looking a lot more relieved now that Kieran was here. I was tempting my luck but I couldn't stop.

Killian helped me maneuver Kieran into the elevator. He entered a code, and the doors slid shut, sealing us off from the rest of the building.

"Once the code is entered, nobody else can use this elevator. If you ever have to pick him up again without me, I'll give you the codes. If he changes it, there's an override code."

He went on. "But the doors to the Suite don't work like this. For privacy." *I bet.*

I nodded, impressed by the level of secrecy, organization, and security surrounding this place.

Kieran moaned between us, and to my surprise, Killian shushed him gently, his hand coming up on his brother's hair.

As the elevator descended I dared to open my mouth.

"Those women..."

Killian's voice was soft as he replied. "They're alive. It's *all* consensual."

He glanced at me across Kieran's groan.

"Women come to Kieran for...*whatever.*" *Whatever?*

His mismatched eyes held a wicked glint at my expression. "Some people are not vanilla, Quarterback."

"I think you skipped seven flavors past vanilla."

Killian laughed low for a rare second, he tipped his head back, his eyes gleaming, and he looked like Kieran right then. "Some people need a vice."

Apparently.

"Why does he come here?"

I would've thought his home would've been discreet.

I'd never seen Killian's eyes gleam with mischief, his canines were out and wicked.

He motioned to the half-conscious heavy man slumped between us. "Who do you think owns the place?"

I blinked, my gaze falling on Kieran dark brown hair in disbelief, to which Killian grinned wider over.

As we settled into the car, Killian handed Kieran an electrolyte drink, which he grimaced at before gulping it down.

In the light of the car, I could see the extent of the bruises and scratches that marred his chest.

Kieran fumbled with the window, desperate for fresh air, and I helped him.

"Didn't Reed just give him his break after Avani?"

"*Avani...*" Kieran murmured over the purr of the engine.

"Avani's safe. Remember?" I said to Kieran softly. I knew thanks to the girl's chat that she was safe back in her apartment on campus.

His reply was so soft I almost didn't hear it. "Not from me..."

*Oh. Fuck...*Kieran had been on the job for *weeks*. No matter *how good* Reed was with the O'Hara's?

Avani was a surefire way for Kieran to die.

And then the fucking lightbulb went off in my brain.

The women on the bed—*brunettes*—Killian looked at the rearview mirror, at his brother, a frown on Killian's face and eyes curious as though he realized something...

Kieran lost his mind over her?

Killian cut through my thoughts. "You need to text Gabriel, now. Tell him, Eros is cleared."

Well, now it made sense.

Everyone has an outlet.

My fingers flew over the phone.

Not a word. Who the fuck are you to judge?

He never killed those girls.

But you almost got yours killed. Punk bitch.

Gabriel just thumbs up the message. I realized he was probably waiting for the clear. Killian had known where to look.

"What's your outlet now that you don't go to *De Nuit?*"

For a long moment, he didn't respond, and I thought he might ignore my question altogether. But then, without a word, he held up his heart print bandaid.

Nisha. I didn't know how long he'd been with her.

Just long enough for me to know he was serious about her, and he despised me because, not only did Killian O'Hara have to *babysit* me—I kept him far away from his girl. My girl.

I fucked up.

I hadn't been with anyone since Selena.

I couldn't.

As I watched Kieran grimace over his drink, I shrugged off my jacket and draped it over him.

When we arrived at the hospital, Killian was allowed out, but I was not.

He lifted Kieran into his arms, holding his brother close, rubbing his hair, as he gave me a look that clearly said. *"Stay put, or I'll put a bullet in your brain."*

Gabriel had given strict orders to keep me banned from the hospital until Selena chose me again.

It was painful as fuck, but I knew that everything Gabriel did was for the bigger picture.

I understood why Gabriel kept me away from her, and Killian had made it explicitly clear.

Just in case you don't understand why the fuck you're here, you're a powder keg of insecurity and miscommunication that's going to get people killed if you don't get your shit together.

You got potential.

But potential is shit if you don't learn how to control yourself.

Killian had ripped into me like a drill sergeant, his words cutting deep.

Gabriel didn't tolerate weakness.

Weakness is not trainable.

So I knew I wasn't weak.

You will learn to control yourself.

You will obey my orders.

And if you so much as step a fucking toe out of line?

I have orders to shoot you.

Are we fucking clear?

Crystal.

CHAPTER 44

KELLAN

KILLIAN WAITED UNTIL HE DROPPED ME OFF AT MY CAR BEFORE HE said it.

He always took his time, returning in better spirits and a new band-aid with pink hearts around it.

For Killian, that was him being *chipper*. A wave of jealousy washed over me that he got to still see his girl every single time he wanted to.

And I had fucked up. I knew it was my fault—it didn't make it any better.

I had been on my phone texting Shane to make sure he was solid.

"Your wife is gone. Nisha was done with her this week," he said softly over the hum of the car's engine.

What the—

I stopped moving. Nisha called Selena, my wife.

"I'm seeing Nisha this weekend, fucking *finally*."

He said it like he hadn't just stunned me as he tipped his head back in relief over *his* girlfriend. Like I wasn't dying on the inside over mine.

I froze, my hand on the door handle, my breath caught in my throat.

Gone?

"What did you just say?" Gabriel said I could see Selena when it was time—when she wanted to—I stopped breathing. *"What do you mean she's gone?"*

She didn't want to see me. She had left New York. Left the Titans. *Left me.*

You screamed at her, and then she almost died because of you. Who the fuck would want to see you?

Oh. Fuck. Me.

It ripped through my fucking chest.

"She's gone. She's no longer a Titan. She left New York. Gabriel, he let her go."

He let her go?

Selena was no longer my *Venus* or a part of my world.

"*Control* yourself. You're not an animal." Killian's eyes filled with annoyance. "What the fuck did I teach you?"

"Sorry—" I was trying. *I can't let my emotions control me.*

"*Breathe*," Killian commanded. "Don't *be a punk bitch.*"

He turned away, shifting in his seat.

"It's not my business who fucks who. I usually don't care as long as it doesn't touch my family. Gabriel gave her an out. She took it. He has an assignment for you in a few days."

Of course, Killian would deliver news like that.

I closed my eyes, focusing on the rise and fall of my chest, the air moving in and out of my lungs.

It was a simple thing, breathing, but at that moment, it felt like the hardest thing in the world.

"I will shoot you if you lose it in this car."

You've got raw power and talent, so I have to mold you into a weapon fit enough for Titan to use.

Even Nate Wyatt has better control over his emotions.

And so I learned.

Killian stared at the bandaid with hearts on his finger, I desperately sought to redirect my thoughts away from the ache gnawing at my chest. An *outlet...*

Refocus. Redirect.

Find a new—

"How long have you been with Nisha?" I asked him. "You taking her somewhere special this weekend?"

Killian's frown deepened, and I bit back a laugh. I didn't even want to know what he thought *dating* was.

"What does she like?"

"Everything," Killian replied. I shook my head in disbelief, and he scowled. "*What?*"

"What does she *like*?" I asked, watching as he blinked, frowning at the dashboard. "Is it a big deal? This dinner of yours?"

He wouldn't have mentioned it if he didn't think it was.

I knew how Killian talked. And he had shit timing when he did.

He was still a little awkward and a little strange.

I figured it came with the territory of being a former mobster's son and currently a king of the underworld.

Judging by the look on his face, I'd say it was a pretty big deal.

Hang on...what did he do when he met her at the hospital?

"She likes everything," Killian muttered. "But she likes to cook at home more." At home. He went back to her.

"What do you do when you see her at the—"

I broke off at the look in Killian's eyes, which had gone hard as he gave me the side-eye.

Got it.

The O'Hara's were *wild*.

One of them *owned* a sex club and the other one—well—he was *this*. And I had never even met Aidan, the oldest.

At this point, I didn't fucking know what to expect.

I just never took Nisha for the whole mafia type.

And for a moment, I remembered that Killian was only two years older than me.

And he'd grown up a lot different than me.

His eyes returned to the dashboard as he frowned, his thumb playing with his bandaid.

I didn't want to shit on him, he might shoot me, but I did want to laugh.

He's just a person...

"She down to Earth?" I asked, watching as he looked at the dashboard. "I don't know her, but she seems down to Earth." Nisha was a sweetheart compared to him.

Because he sure as fuck isn't.

Killian had that whole Prince of Darkness thing going on for him. Nisha also gave him pink bandaids for his paper cuts.

But he didn't know if she was down to Earth?

I grinned, trying not to laugh at his expression. He looked lost as fuck.

Suddenly, I didn't feel *too* horrible.

"There's this place in Queens..." I told him about Patel's, not missing the look of surprise on his face. "She'll like it."

Killian nodded as I told him about the place, taking a deep breath and putting his gun away. I had known him for a few weeks now, but I knew he was the kind of man who got jealous over Nisha.

Hang on.

"What do you do when you get jealous over Nisha?" I dared to ask him.

"It depends. It's all case-by-case." Killian's throat worked as he looked at his bandaid like a lifeline, inky hair falling over his brows. "Depends on how it freaks *her* out. If she's calm, so am I. If she's scared?" He paused, shrugging lightly, looking bored. "I kill them."

Well. Shit.

"That's efficient."

"If *she's* scared, that's merciful," he said it as a matter-of-fact.

It was obvious to me if Nisha was afraid, he would take it out.

"It's not about jealousy. It's about...something happening to her. That's what it's always been about."

What?

"If something happens to her," his eyes shifted then like a predator's. "That's the only time I react. Otherwise, if it's small things—I stay calm."

No, he didn't. "She keeps you calm."

He tipped his head, admitting it. "But the moment I know her life is in danger, and she calls—"

"You eliminate the threat." He didn't say a word. I'd seen him kill. I knew he would. But only if it was...life-threatening. "Has that happened before with her?"

He tipped his head again.

I dared to ask him what I wanted to. "Do you and Nisha ever fight?"

He shook his head, looking annoyed by that question. "I'm not an idiot."

"Why's that?"

"She's always right," he shrugged, saying it like I was the idiot for asking. One side of his lips tipped up as his eyes flattened out, dark and predatory on me. "And I listen to her, before I speak."

That one hurt.

"You gonna dig the knife deeper?"

"Does it hurt enough yet?" He raised an elegant brow. For a handsome motherfucker he was mean. Lethal.

It *never* stopped hurting.

I looked out the window, not saying a word to him. I never fucking imagined getting relationship advice from a mobster.

"I fucked up." I admitted now after meeting him I saw how much worse it could be. Some nights I didn't sleep.

"I don't go home to my girl with my baggage," Killian murmured. "I haven't seen her at home in forever with everything going on."

That's why he was happy about their date.

Case-by-case. *Not every single situation had the same reaction from him.* And he was a solid mentor.

The rage in me diffused out, still processing the hurt in the back of my mind but calming down as I took in the conversation.

I blew out a breath, processing it all.

"What are you going to do about your wife?" he asked, looking angry once we started talking about Nisha. "I've known Tavares for years. She never had a thing for Wyatt."

No. She had a thing for me.

I realized Killian was talking to me normally now, the way he spoke to Kieran on the phone. Sometimes, I forgot he was just another normal man. I forgot Killian had been with Titan from its conception.

For some reason, I saw a lot of Gabriel in him.

I got the feeling he didn't like me because if he had it his way? I would be right next to *my* girl. Who was right next to his. But he had orders from Gabriel to shape me into a better operative, and so he took his job seriously.

And he respected his girl.

He didn't get his girlfriend almost killed.

"How's Kieran?"

Killian's expression shifted as he looked away from his bandaid. He shook his head. *Not good.*

"This doesn't go anywhere."

Because Kieran had a crush on someone he shouldn't have. Kieran had switched hands over to Gabriel while Shane had gone to Reed.

Mismatched eyes turned to me with a lingering question in them. *Right, he had asked me a question.*

I didn't know how to respond. I just knew I had to go to the manor in a day, which meant I needed sleep, a shower, and a new suit.

Gabriel liked his weapons sharp.

This one had blood on it and smelled like…drugs, sex, and alcohol.

No se.

"I don't know."

~

SEVERAL DAYS LATER, I STOOD OUTSIDE REED'S OFFICE DOOR AT THE manor, the heavy oak barrier before me.

I had expected to meet with Gabriel, but Reed's gruff voice told me to come inside.

He was seated at the computer, his jacket off in a long-sleeved shirt, reviewing some files.

Stormy eyes looked up at me when I came in. Something shifted in me as I saw him. I wasn't expecting—

"I thought I was meeting Gabriel…"

"He isn't here," Reed replied, his tone low and measured. "I'm running things from the manor."

Where was Gabriel then?

I would've frowned had Killian's voice not beaten it into me not to react.

Don't be a punk bitch.

Don't ask questions.

I inhaled the scent of his cologne, mixing in with hazelnut coffee and something…what the fuck was that?

Something sweet. Spicy. Something…*not Reed.*

I took it in, calming down as I inhaled.

Evie had moved out of the manor, which was a fucking surprise for me, so it wasn't her. But I had been out…with Killian.

Life happened at Titan, with or without me.

"He has an assignment for you," Reed set out a folder. "You can figure out the details."

Away from Selena.

I didn't say a word. Living in her apartment was my own fucking hell. Surrounded by her, always waiting for her to come home.

Her scent was all over the place. Pink pepper. Fading out by the day.

The fucking flamingo umbrella holder laughed at me on my way out the door right next to her boots.

Every. Single. Day.

And now, knowing she would never come back?

I couldn't *leave* the place. I had been a wreck the last few days, so I was tempted to text her. To call. But she had a new number.

I wore her fucking necklace around my throat, the one I found in her blood that night, just to ground me.

Keep me here.

I just didn't take it on jobs in case something happened to it. But I put it on today since I was leaving for a longer job.

"Yes, sir," I replied, my voice sounding distant to my own ears.

I reached for the folder, the texture of the paper rough against my fingertips. I didn't even look. I focused behind Reed.

What the fuck is that scent? It was invading my senses and calming me down. Roses, honey with a hint of something spicy. *Focus, punk bitch.*

Looking down at the folder, I knew everything I needed would be in there. Gabriel preferred to keep everything off—record, unlike Reed, who emailed us our assignments. It had been weeks since I last saw Reed, and I had been glad for the distance.

Now, face to face with him? I didn't know what to say. I had come to terms with my emotions, realizing that it wasn't Reed's fault I had lashed out at Selena.

Despite Reed's schedule, which often left him sleep-deprived?

Every time I had left the apartment, Reed had come home with a smile on his face for his girl. He'd always picked her up with a grin.

Hey, Angel.

Hello, darling.

Alisha couldn't get enough of him. Even if they fought? Alisha loved him. She hadn't broken up with him—not really—and they'd been stable. And they'd made it this long.

Reed had set an example for me all along, even if he didn't tell her things?

It reminded me of when Selena said as operatives, we had to make difficult calls. Reed who held Alisha like she was his world and made time for her *despite* it all. At the thought of Alisha, I realized *why* the coffee smelled familiar.

That's her coffee. Alisha took her coffee with fucking hazelnut syrup. Behind Reed there was a diffuser shaped like a woman's perfume bottle.

I didn't even catch it since it was so close to him. *I thought it smelled familiar here.* I took naps in Alisha's old apartment. Before she moved to K2.

"How is Alisha?" I found myself asking, the words slipping out before I could stop them.

Instead of answering, he met my gaze steadily. "I don't blame you for what happened. Knowing what I do, I don't blame you at all."

Reed continued, his eyes softening ever so slightly. "I would've done the same for Alisha if she was missing. If not at the diner, it would've happened eventually."

What was he saying?

"I'm not angry with you." He paused as the words shot through me. "I wish you talked to me about Nate. I would've worked that out sooner."

Reed filled me in on Nate having Gemma as his last assignment with the Titan's.

What? Nate was leaving Titan? *For good?* And if Reed didn't shock me enough he went on.

"Killian said you're doing better."

Was I?

The thought echoed in my mind as I considered his words processing all these emotions coursing through me from the last few weeks.

Outwardly, maybe. On the inside? I was a wreck.

Without her. I feel like shit.

"How do you feel?"

"Solid," my answer was gruff though. I felt like roadkill without my girl because I felt like it was my fault she almost died.

He motioned to the file in my hands, and I knew he didn't believe me, but Reed wasn't the type to press for shit he didn't want to know or need to know.

With a nod towards the file, his storm-cloud eyes were bright.

"*If* your new charge tells you anything of value, call me. Those are your orders."

A new charge? A new client.

Away from Selena. And it fucking hurt.

The only person who was to blame for my problems? Was *me*. I could've asked to switch with Nate.

Do not disobey him. And don't be a punk bitch.

I had to forgive Reed. Even Gabriel, who had shown up to talk to Alisha at the Primrose while she was staying there, I realized that day I could have asked Gabriel to switch.

He hadn't wanted to leave Alisha that day.

I had chosen *not* to ask. And then I thought about how much Killian trusted Nisha with *his* brother?

Relationships were not as clean-cut as I wanted them to be. Nate's and Alisha's words coming back to me.... *I didn't want a romantic relationship... don't like him romantically.*

Because these people had different relationships.

I had been so wrong. I couldn't see Selena for who she was. I couldn't see anyone for who they were. For all my scanning? I got it wrong. *Because of my emotions.*

Selena had been good friends with Nate. And she'd chosen me.

I didn't look at Nate like he was just a person. A partner. That day he had disposed of the body of that girl, he had been professional with me. Because I wanted to prove myself or I was blind?

Because I sucked at communication? For *all* my scanning, I couldn't see what was right in front of me. And now? I knew better. *Who the fuck knew?*

Killian did not suck at communication. No, he communicated pretty fucking effectively, he just didn't *like* to talk.

Control yourself. Don't be a punk bitch.

"Do you need anything else?"

Reed shook his head, his eyes closing for a second as he inhaled his girl's perfume. *No. Dismissed.*

As I left the office, the weight of the folder in my hand was heavy.

My mind drifted to the familiar scent of roses, honey, and—*Stop. Focus. Breathe.*

You have no emotions. Nothing matters, but your next target, clear?

"Crystal," I whispered.

Gabriel wanted a trigger to pull. A weapon.

I was that trigger now.

I adjusted my tie as I walked out, the file clutched tightly, my jaw set, my mind focused on the next mission. The next objective. Whatever it was now.

I went to the library downstairs since Selena loved doing her work there.

Her hiding spot was in the back, where I'd find her sometimes in the manor.

Evie told me about it. I found her curled into a ball here.

Where we'd spent some afternoons. Making out. And then some. Memories washed over me—

Breathe. Focus.

I opened the file in Selena's hiding spot and froze.

What the—

I swallowed hard, once, twice, as I read the contents. A headshot of Selena, her dark hair and bangs framing her face, just as she had looked when I first met her.

But Gabriel let her go...

Target: Selena Maria Tavares
Location: Miami, Florida
Objective:

IT WAS BLANK.

Why was it blank? What did he mean she was my...

Why would he—

I hadn't said anything to Gabriel.

How did he...why did he...

My head spun. A breath escaped my lungs. Faster.

At the bottom of the page, in flat, neat handwriting, I read.

One Shot, Quarterback.

CHAPTER 45
SELENA

AFTER DINNER AND MY SHOWER, I NEEDED TO TAKE MY PAIN KILLERS and get some rest.

Nisha had warned me I had to take them with food, but even then, I was out before my head hit the pillow.

I was so tired sometimes.

I didn't know what to do but sleep. Which was good for me.

In my dreams, I drifted in and out.

My dreams were always strange—dreams of the Grim Reaper and the woman who felt like death, and then the things I didn't want to remember after that. Something hitting my head over and over.

Something slamming into my side.

Being thrown down a flight of stairs and fighting off someone.

A man.

The man who attacked me.

Sometimes to escape and run away from those dreams I dreamt of my brother. I dreamed my brother and I were together in Miami, in class with me, only he was older. And alive.

I was teaching him how to paint and he was teasing me about my crush on Kellan who was sitting there watching us.

"Look," I said in my dreams. "You can mix colors like this."

"You need to wake up," Diego said. "Wake up."

What?

But tonight, they got weird.

Wake up, honey.

Please, just wake up.

I dreamed of Kellan.

Sometimes he appeared in my dreams, and I quickly woke up. Other times, his touch ghosted over my skin, my heart pounding in my chest. Dreams of him loving me were the hardest, the toughest.

Because I'd wake up missing him—my body would ache for his warmth, his kisses, knowing there was nothing real there.

And I'd break down harder.

He did not choose me, even though I chose him.

This time, he was in bed with me, just like all the other times, but he felt real. His hands, I memorized the feel of them against my skin and they picked me up into his arms. His lips moving over my face and I sighed in bliss.

"*Selena,*" his voice was dark and guttural over my skin. "Honey, wake up, I'm here. I'm here. I'm not going nowhere, baby come on."

What?

The sound of him begging me to come back echoed in my mind. I didn't know if I dreamed of those. Or if it was real.

Or what happened.

I just knew I *felt* him.

My body felt heavier than wet sand, weighed down by the effects of the painkillers I had taken earlier, the sheets tangled around my legs.

But he still picked me up and held me his hands brushing my hair back.

In the haze of my dream, Kellan's voice broke as he pleaded with me.

Come back to me, baby. Come on. Come on. I need to call an ambulance. I need to call Reed—

What? Where? Was there an emergency?

I wasn't a Titan anymore, so why was he asking me to return to New York?

In my dream, I reached for his hair, but it was shorter.

Those ocean blue eyes locked onto mine as he cradled my head, looking down into my eyes.

I groaned at being moved, and he set me down.

"*What did you take?*" he asked, his voice laced with concern.

"Come on, honey. Selena, come back. Nononono, baby come on. Shit shit shit."

But the pull of the medication was strong, keeping me anchored in this fuzzy, half-awake state between reality and dreams.

I frowned, the sensations too real to be a dream.

It couldn't be real. Kellan wasn't here; he was in New York.

He wouldn't be wearing a suit. I tried to respond, but my words came out as a mumble. My mind a groggy mess.

Kellan took a deep breath as his eyes watered. *"Come on, how many did you take?"*

This baby.

He glanced at the dresser, searching for something, as my eyelids grew heavy once more. His eyes were wild as he searched my face.

I just wanted to sleep.

"Honey, come on, talk to me. Please, Selena. I need to call an ambulance." Why?

"Two." He let out a breath, but I couldn't believe he was really here. My fingers over his lips.

Shhh, Kellan. I want to sleep.

"Honey..." His eyes widened, his words fading into smoke as I drifted off. I was floating as he held me to him.

"Kellan..."

And I was back to dreaming of the dark things that terrified me. Dark whispers of death.

A man walking to me with eerie blue eyes. Rimmed in black.

A weapon in his hand. He was going to kill me and in my nightmares he came back taller than Reed, menacing, ominous, his laughter in the air.

Something in me warned me.

I only saw him before I died.

In my dreams that man only appeared and then it terrified me back to being awake.

A harbinger—Nathan would say.

Where he goes death follows. She followed.

Only this time I woke up to music. I groaned. I was so warm.

I didn't want to get up, ever.

Nisha told me to give myself good things to wake up to.

Avani listened to K-POP music and now I had a popular song as my alarm. I didn't know how to say their name but Avani loved them.

I groaned, reaching for my phone to silence the alarm. But it turned off without me and I curled back in blissfully into the bed.

Slowly, I felt the bed move and my eyes fluttered open.

The scent of clean linen and familiar cologne filled my lungs.

Even with the painkillers putting me in a heavy fog, my mind and body disconnected from reality—I knew that scent. I knew that body.

"What was that?" He groaned rubbing his eyes. "Is that K-POP?"

Years of training meant nothing as my body instinctively recognized *him* before my drugged mind could fully comprehend it. He was here. *Kellan.* Was. Here.

He groaned a little, jostling me as he laid back down. "I got it, honey." Fingers brushed through my hair then, my new hair, massaging into my scalp. "God, your hairs so soft."

And my entire body responded to him.

"Do you need your next dose? It says 'take with food', do you want anything?"

This is not a dream...

Kellan is here, under the covers with you.

And he is wearing a suit.

No, not a *full* suit. But he was wearing a crinkled white dress shirt, holding me against him.

I was so out of it. I pushed weakly against his chest, slowly rising up as I blinked and licked my dry lips, fighting to wake up.

Disoriented and groggy.

I dared to really look at him, taking in his appearance—the shorter, styled hair that made him look older, the piercing blue eyes that had grown darker. Haunted.

He watched me carefully.

He's still so beautiful...but different.

My eyes drifted down to the rumpled sheets, not fully recognizing this new, sharper version of the man I once knew.

There was something else lurking behind those eyes now—something I knew was Gabriel's brutal influence.

He had crossed over.

You made me a second choice.

Another pop melody came through the air as a second alarm went off, at odds with the feeling of Kellan near me.

"That's my backup, if I miss the first one…" I trailed off. What did I say? Kellan let me go to reach over and silence it.

Earlier when I had fallen asleep, I had been naked against the clean sheets after my shower, but now I was wearing a nightshirt, the thin fabric swallowing my frame. But curving. This way and that.

I had gained weight around my hips and thighs mostly.

I didn't know what to say to him, so I didn't say anything silent.

My drugged brain struggled to process things fully.

For a while it'll take you some time to adjust to things.

But healing takes time.

I grabbed the bottle unsure of what time it was, and slowly padded to the kitchen, his presence following behind me.

Everything felt mechanical as I opened the stocked fridge and grabbed a protein shake, shaking it lightly before taking two more pills.

Swallowing them down, I closed my eyes feeling him move around me, as I drank more.

I needed another one.

Nisha had me eating more as I healed.

She had instructed me on the optimal way to take them for a good night's sleep. And I had gained some weight now with no exercise and just laying in bed.

I didn't mind though—a little extra weight looked good on me.

At twenty-nine I was learning to love myself and my body again. I didn't have to *maintain* my body for anything anymore. I ate whatever I wanted.

I felt Kellan lingering behind me. I couldn't look at him while I processed everything.

In our line of work…in *his* line of work, I didn't ask how he had found me. I already knew it came from his line of information we had in Titan.

I could feel the heat radiating from his body, the faint scent of him surrounding me. Something new. Something I didn't recognize.

Maybe I didn't want to.

My last memory of him was him losing his mind on me and I didn't know what to say. Too much had happened.

"Talk to me, honey. Get angry with me," he whispered right behind me, his lips over my ear and I closed my eyes feeling my hands shaking with the effort to keep still.

Or maybe just from his presence. All hot and strong and unyielding. He had always been strength to my skills. Only now...I didn't want to feel that.

"Yell, scream...just do *something*."

I didn't want to. I didn't want to fight *anymore*—I was too drained, emotionally and physically.

My thoughts were swirling like feathers in wind, floating around me, but too fast for me to catch save for one.

"I do not want to fight."

I never wanted to fight him so I never had from day one. I moved around him slowly, feeling dizzy, like I was drifting underwater. He didn't say a word but I felt his energy around me, enveloping me in it.

I slowly walked back but halfway to the bedroom I felt him move close to me as he followed me.

Crawling into the bed, underneath the covers I was feeling sluggish —I just wanted to disappear forever and stay somewhere safe and warm. It didn't matter if he was staring.

It didn't matter to me anymore.

Kellan wasn't dangerous. Not to me.

He was just not...mine. Not anymore.

What was...happening to me? To my head? Why I did I do into that dark place all the time?

I felt my eyes watering at the thought of for once—I didn't have anything to say to Kellan.

I had already said everything I had to say.

It didn't make sense to say *anything* else.

He hadn't heard me at all.

CHAPTER 46
SELENA

THIS TIME I WOKE UP TO THE MORNING SUN BLEEDING THROUGH THE room. I felt the rays hitting me with their warmth.

Gabriel had done Lena Santos justice by giving me the perfect apartment to start over in.

I stirred slowly, checking the time on my phone, not missing the weight of someone—*Kellan*—close to me.

One heavy arm of his thrown over my waist. I felt it like a familiar weight.

He had slept here? And I didn't care?

Blinking against the light, it all came flooding back—*Kellan was here, in Miami. In my apartment. In my bed.*

Shouldn't I have been more shocked by his presence?

Now in the clear morning light, no longer under the influence of medication, I could think more clearly.

I dimly remembered the night before when he thought…did he actually think I had tried to hurt myself? I didn't even know what to say to him anymore.

"Are you okay?" His overwhelming presence pressed in on me from all sides. "*Honey*—"

"Stop," I cut him off. "I don't want to talk to you." My own voice sounded strange to my ears as the words left me. "Why are you here?"

Why did you stay?

I sat up slowly, my blanket pooling around my waist as I turned to face him. Morning light softly filtered through the windows casting a gentle glow over his features.

He has always been beautiful.

In that moment? In my efforts to find peace, Kellan's presence had always had the power to unsettle me. Disarm me. And leave me a little speechless. Because I still deep down knew, if he felt like mine? I felt like his.

"I wanted to find you," he whispered roughly. I saw his eyes were red. "To say I'm sorry…for being such a *stupid* idiot."

I didn't know how to respond to him.

All of the emotions from weeks ago they had evaporated into smoke.

I felt like I had been left with an empty shell of a relationship. I knew I had made a mistake. I just didn't know what to do about it or what to say. How did I start?

I am sorry I did not tell you I broke up with Nathan and promised to get married to him. I am in love with you and Nathan is in love with Gemma and has been for years.

I didn't even know why my body trusted him still to sleep with me time and time again. But then again, my body had always known him. Even if my heart and mind felt like they were at war. My body *knew* him.

"I don't know what to say to you," I admitted quietly. "I don't want to talk to you—"

"*Gatita…*"

"No." I shook my head slowly. "I don't know what to say. There is nothing…"

"*There's everything—*"

"Left here," I finished for him. We always did have this exhausting back-and-forth. "I tried to talk to you."

Tried was the word.

His green-eyed monster never heard me, never really saw me for who I was. And in a way, I had made my own bad choices too.

I didn't believe it was all Nathan's fault anymore.

I was a person with agency. I could have told Kellan. But I also knew why Gabriel had said what he did—Nathan hadn't truly seen me, only the pain he felt from Gemma.

His obsession with Gemma, was leaving everyone destroyed in the process.

I had known that was why Nathan got into trouble with plenty of women. Why he had been getting wilder by the years.

That pact had been the only thing stopping him from slipping. And I had cut him off.

Gemma was the only thing that motivated *who* he was today. I hadn't spoken to Nathan or Gemma in weeks. I didn't know how to.

Kellan whispered roughly. "I know, honey. I'm sorry."

"It's okay. I forgive you." I just didn't forget it all either. "I don't... want this. I need to...I need to live. I am alone, but *not* lonely."

I didn't miss the way his expression crumpled with hurt as my words landed. His blue eyes went wide with silent pain as he really took me in. I could see it all over his features.

"I like where I am," I said softly. "It feels good here."

I didn't feel lonely at all anymore. I felt...good. Healing, but in a good way.

I laid in my apartment, sometimes all day and read books.

Specifically romance, since it had been introduced to me by the most unlikely person.

I may have only had *one* visitor during my hospital stay.

I didn't tell *anyone*.

Little Avani Malhotra had begged Kieran to sneak her in to see me after worrying about me nonstop.

Kieran, baby brother to Aidan and Killian, had been hired by Gabriel as a new Titan and her guard.

He had smuggled in Avani in his coat with Nisha and Killian outside the door. While Avani had hugged me, crying, Kieran had blocked the door with his family.

I caught a quick glimpse of Killian, who had stood so close to Nisha, he looked like he wanted to tuck her into *his* coat. With that same possessive gaze that Kellan used to give me.

Except with Killian, it was *always* there while he played with her hair.

I smiled into Avani's hair, hugging her tightly.

Working with Killian for years, I knew he was a good man, he was Gabriel's favorite of the O'Hara brothers since Gabriel had trained him.

I had found out about my nurse's relationship with the O'Hara by pure coincidence when he dropped by to see her.

"I'm so glad you're all right," Avani whispered and my eyes drifted back to her. "Lish and I know we're banned from seeing you to not upset you, but I couldn't stay away."

Avani's honey scent floated around the room. Her long cinnamon hair hung loose, big doe eyes dark like Nisha's on me.

Meeting her many nights ago, I understood why Reed was so protective, why he wanted to shield her.

But then again, Alisha had raised her.

Even still, I saw more of her sister in her as she held out her pinky.

I won't tell anyone if you won't.

I smiled, linking my finger with hers.

She kept me supplied with romance novel recommendations, admitting she was a secret reader of them too.

I had no idea Avani was into *some* of this stuff, but I *loved* it.

Alisha texted me too, keeping me in the loop of what she could.

Evie didn't reach out at first, but I didn't expect her to.

Alisha filled me in briefly on the events in Evie's life. As much as she said she could tell me.

Which explained the private jet and apartment since Evie was dating the CEO of Mercury Group.

Gabriel's future brother-in-law, something I never thought I'd see.

Evie was his *princessa.*

Which meant Lucas Devereaux was someone special.

I missed her, but I didn't feel completely separated from her either.

I knew that when I finally saw her again, it would feel like no time had passed at all between us.

The most surprising text came from Gemma Marchand herself at my time in the hospital.

Lena,

Nate talked to me about everything. If you ever need a girlfriend, I am here. Always.

Regardless of what you and Nate have had.

He would like to apologize for his actions and well...if you'll let me I'd love to see you when you're better too.

You are still a girlfriend.

And I am here if you need an ear. Always.

Rereading it again and again as the full meaning sank in for me.

Gemma Marchand was a friend.

Not the girl Nate knew years ago.

I just didn't know how to communicate my feelings. I didn't know how to tell her how guilty I felt for even taking his offer. Why was she so understanding when she was in love with Nathan?

Neither does Kellan. Gabriel was right.

We didn't know how to talk to each other about these things. And I was not ready to talk to anyone.

This new life? It was on my terms. *Sometimes that's how it starts.*

"What can I do?" He said softly as I laid there lost deep in thought.

"What happens when you apologize?...I take you back? You stay here—" *Wait.* He could not mean to tell me...

"You'd walk away from your life? At Titan...?"

For me?

He didn't hesitate for a moment. "I'm with you. I don't need anything else."

And I couldn't deny the impact of his words at that moment, as *Kellan Watts* lay beside me in my bed. I was suddenly aware of him in ways I knew were familiar, but unfamiliar at the same time.

"You look really beautiful," he whispered. "It's good to see you again, honey."

His eyes held shadows. The playful lion I once knew was gone, replaced by a stranger I didn't recognize.

That was Gabriel's shadow in there. I recognized it in my heart. And some part of me remembered the girl I was in Titan.

A pang of something strange went through me. I was happy to be out of Titan...right? And at that moment, I didn't recognize myself either.

But I knew one thing for certain—I loved myself more than I *liked* him, despite everything that had happened.

I chose you, even though you didn't promise me a future.

It didn't matter how many times Kellan chose me. I had never chosen myself.

"I am not your honey," I said softly, not missing the way his eyes widened, horror in them evident. "I don't want to be."

CHAPTER 47
KELLAN

GETTING SHOT HURT LESS THAN THE LOVE OF YOUR LIFE LOOKING AT you like you were a stranger. While in bed with her.

I am not your honey.

But you could be.

I am not your honey.

I don't want to be. I'd rather take a knife to the chest as it sank into my bones, the words hitting the glacier my heart had become with the loss of her.

I didn't recognize my girl. It wasn't even just the physical things.

Shorter hair just above her shoulders, cheeks fuller, adorably so, making her look younger than me. Her body had *changed.* Hips rounding out even *more*, her stomach curving, her breasts bigger, and she looked...breathtakingly *beautiful.*

Selena had changed. Like me. But differently.

I had gotten her something to wear realizing I couldn't have her naked...I couldn't stop thinking about her.

Venus incarnate. Soft. *Lush.* She had changed all around.

I loved it.

What do I give this woman to make her see me?

I harbored no illusions that Gabriel had sent me here to win her back.

When Killian deemed me better?

I realized the *entire* situation in the car had been a test—one I passed without even realizing it. Manipulation. *Deception.*

It has always been about her.

Seeing Kieran deteriorate at *De Nuit* had fucked with my head.

He was so fucking put together.

Until he *wasn't.* I couldn't blame him either.

Not with what I knew about the O'Hara's. But Selena was just taking her scheduled doses. And for a moment, my heart had *stopped beating.*

I just held her feeling my eyes blur at the thought of never kissing her again, making love to her, holding her, her body warm and limp in my arms.

I kept seeing Selena, an uncapped bottle of just sleep medication, and I leapt to her. I didn't think. Just held her, kissing her face, smoothing her new hair back.

She looks healthy. Happy. Beautiful.

Her face pale as she'd fallen asleep. She wasn't dying.

Instead, I found myself falling asleep with my girl in my arms after weeks apart. I just laid there, absorbing her presence, wiping my eyes to avoid waking her for hours.

She smelled like...*nothing.* And that fucking hurt so bad.

Just clean. That was it. *No more pink pepper...*

And I'd lain there like the last four and a half weeks hadn't just happened.

No amount of Killian's training could have prepared me for seeing Selena again. I just held her until her next dose. And then again. Now I was gutted.

I'm not your honey.

I don't want to be.

Where was *my* Selena? Where did *she* go?

Somewhere in there? So far away, I couldn't get to her.

I felt like I was seeing her from underneath a frozen lake. I just watched her, those eyes darker, and I laid there for a moment just breathing.

She was taking me in. "Where are you staying?"

Gabriel is a motherfucker. "Next door."

She breathed out, softness in her eyes as she said. "Gabriel?" I nodded. Watching her palm curled like a petal. Her nails were natural. And for some reason my eyes watered again at that.

Where did she go?

Where was my girl?

We remained silent, our eyes locked, studying each other as if we were strangers. Her hands curled into her chest as she looked at me. I was getting fucking emotional and Selena looked so far away.

I was in her fucking bed. And I didn't recognize my girl.

Didn't know her anymore. The ice inside of my chest cracked open at the sight of her. But it ached now once it did. Leaving me vulnerable to her. Every part of me responded to her, but I didn't even know what to do.

My stomach broke the silence, the distinctive *kworrr* that caused me to wince, a small hum escaping my lips in embarrassment.

Some things never changed.

Her smile was instant. Slow and soft. My cheeks heated as she got up slowly.

"Where are you going?"

She turned over her shoulder, those green eyes laughing at me, and I felt something stir in my gut. "To get you food."

Mr. College Football.

The corners of my lips twitched upward as tears welled in my eyes.

She's still in there.

But more distant than when you last saw her.

I followed behind her, rumpled and disheveled, my emotions in turmoil, as she made her way to the kitchen.

Her steps were slower, more measured, and my heart clenched with worry.

Is she in pain?

I bit down on my lip, trailing closely behind her, every fiber of my wanting her. To hold her. That was my fucking girl.

"I can do it," I insisted, my voice firm.

"I can do it—"

"Just let me—"

Some things never changed.

We both froze in our tracks, just before entering the kitchen, as she glanced over her shoulder, her eyes locking with mine, studying me intently.

Her lack of reaction to my presence cut deeper than any angry outburst.

Her voice was softer now. Slow. "I will help you this time?"

"Yes."

∼

WHY DIDN'T I DO THIS MORE OFTEN FOR HER?

Why was I such an idiot?

Selena's movements were slow but graceful as she passed me ingredients, her body still healing. I had unbuttoned my dress shirt leaving me in slacks and my white t-shirt.

But Selena...she looked gorgeous in that nightshirt.

Her figure had changed—the way her shirt hugged her curves? I was dying. I wanted to hold her close.

When did she get fuller?

Was her butt always that sexy?

I shook my head.

Don't be a punk bitch.

The soft padding of her sandals on the tiled floor broke the comfortable silence between us.

We moved in sync—she got utensils, I got drinks.

Selena put on low music, and for a moment, things felt normal. Just for a second.

I thought we'd be on the kitchen island, but Selena wanted to go to the balcony.

Her apartment was beautiful with feminine details, oceanic art and decor, and Selena's touches. The properties along the beach were owned by Mercury Group, and my flight had been handled by them too.

I had no doubt whatever Killian had been handling had played a part in making my life easier and Selena's.

The view took my breath away—the expanse of the beach stretched before us, waves crashing into the shore. And this was...this is where Selena had always wanted to be.

On the beach.

On her break.

Only it wasn't a break.

In the sunlight, she looked almost petite and soft. *Lovely.* The urge to wrap her in my arms grew stronger with each passing moment.

Instead, I sat quietly beside her until the silence became unbearable.

"Do you have plans for today?" I asked, my eyes fixed on her profile as she gazed at the beach.

Mirame, Selena. Look at me.

"I wanted to go to the market."

She didn't bring anything with her when she left.

Left me. The ache in my chest spread. Being next to her without being hers was torture.

I have no idea what I'm doing. But I'm going to go with it. Just go with it...

"Can I come with you?" *Take me back, baby.*

Her night shirt molded against her breasts with the wind and I didn't miss the way her chest rose and fell. I was still attracted to my girl. *She was so fucking beautiful...*

She nodded slowly.

Yes? *Yes.*

It didn't even matter to me why she had said yes.

With new energy, I returned to my room, the apartment that would serve as my home for the coming month. I changed into shorts and a t-shirt, out of my fucking suit.

I shed my suit, opting for the comfort of shorts and a shirt.

The next week I spent every moment I could with Selena.

We explored markets, lounged on beaches, and I fell in love with her all over again.

It was hard not to stare, to want to trace every new curve.

Everything about her called to me—her fuller breasts, her hips. Selena in a bikini top was sweet torture. I wanted to hold her. Love her. Feel her in my arms. Seeing her in tiny bikinis nearly undid me.

Stolen moments of release in the shower were hollow echoes of what it felt like to love her.

I craved her—my girlfriend who wasn't my girlfriend.

Maybe. Kinda. Sorta.

I stayed by her side, a shadow along the shore.

Selena's body had healed, but there was a new slowness to her movements that tore at my heart.

Honey, do you want to go down to the new art supply shop?

Yes, after we get some smoothies.

And so I took her around. I followed her closely at the markets. Colorful stalls, lively atmosphere all seemed to breathe new life into her.

Her eyes were curious, and I took her in while she wandered in front of me. An easy smile on her lips.

Her necklace around my throat was burning into my skin. But I had her back if she stumbled, or she needed to stop.

When someone got too close to her, I was there. Brushing against her skin, bringing her close to me, and tucking her into my side.

I got you, honey.

I was my girl's fucking bodyguard now. Kinda.

Sorta. In turn, if I did get closer to take her hand she let me. I just went with it.

When she let me take her hand sometimes, my heart soared.

Days slipped by in a haze of cooking for her, finding activities she'd enjoy, anything to be near her. I didn't know why she even let me. But I wasn't about to look a gift horse in the mouth.

And then I was back with her before I could think of anything else. My heart was racing to be around her. And I went out with Selena.

I learned she was passionate about art and the Miami art scene appealed to her.

Slowly, our conversations grew easier. I didn't think about anything but her, so close, so far.

"Did you like that new restaurant we went to today?"

"I did," her expression contemplative. "Everything here is so much cleaner than I thought it would be."

"And warmer."

"Hmmm."

At the little hum she made my chest clenched.

That was the thing about being with your partner…you ended up picking up her habits and she picked up yours. Selena had been picking up how I spoke.

I had been picking up how she worked. And my heart clenched all over again with how badly I fucked up.

Please, just take me back.

Another week slipped by in a haze of tentative moments.

Each day, I found myself asking to spend time with her, cooking for her, desperate to be by her side.

I didn't understand why she was letting me in—I was too afraid to question it.

I searched for activities we could do together—art shops, galleries, anything to keep her close.

I almost lost her. I can't fuck this up again.

Each time I made her laugh, my heart soared and shattered simultaneously. Her gradual acceptance was a balm, but it wasn't enough.

"Gabriel let you go for a month?"

"He did, I was surprised to, I didn't expect that."

To win you back, to make things right.

"I guess he wants me to figure some things out."

"To figure yourself out?"

"I think so." *And you.*

I swallowed hard at the sight of her watching me. And then she'd look away a little nervous of me. Afraid.

I closed my eyes at the ache that blossomed.

Does she know? Does she want this too?

Some evenings, Selena would curl up with her e-reader, and I'd watch her from across the room, drinking in every detail.

When she'd fall asleep, I'd carry her to bed, savoring the feel of her in my arms.

It was torture, having her so close yet so far.

When I laid beside her, my fingers instinctively found their way to her hair.

How do I wake her heart to me again?

My month was ticking away, and I still didn't know if I was making progress. It didn't matter if it took years—I only wanted her.

But what did Gabriel expect? Should I quit Titan? *Stay with her forever?*

I'd do it in a heartbeat if she asked.

But a little niggle of something crossed my brain. I liked myself at Titan now. It had honed me into a better being.

I didn't want to leave it all behind.

I didn't want to leave Selena, but I knew I had decisions to make. One night, I was helping her home, she'd swayed a little after taking her meds.

Without thinking, I pulled her into my arms, her new curves pressing against me.

It was the first time in weeks I'd held her like this while she was awake. She didn't pull away, instead relaxing into me. Hope flared more and more, uncurling like petals in my chest.

"Let me." She let me lift her into my arms. I knew she was tired when she didn't argue. My entire body sighed at this as I carried her into her room.

Once I got her in bed, she passed out quickly. I hated seeing her like this.

It felt like eons ago, I met that salsa dancer who stayed up all night and came into work in the morning.

Who gave me lip. Snapped at me. Now?

I didn't know my girl.

Normally I'd sleep next to her, but days of seeing her in tiny bikinis and next to nothing summer dresses around her curves? I was losing my mind.

Her hips, her body—she looked *edible. I need to go to my room.*

I had my hand on the doorknob about to close the door and leave when I heard her whimper.

That fucking noise.

She mentioned she had nightmares sometimes. I was on her in another second. All over her, hauling her into my arms.

My dick would have to shut the fuck up.

Don't be a punk bitch.

"I'm sorry."

Less than two weeks.

Selena was back to a scared cat and *I had no idea*—I stilled, closing my eyes. One realization sank in.

Alisha.

CHAPTER 48

KELLAN

I WAITED UNTIL THE NEXT MORNING TO CALL ALISHA, TAKING advantage of Selena's art class time.

I knew Alisha would answer—probably still curled up in bed. I inhaled the morning air and let the sun hit my legs as I lay there.

After a few rings, her sleepy voice came through. "Kellan?"

"Lish, you got a sec?" I asked. "I didn't know who else to talk to. I kinda needed some big sister advice."

"For you, always," she replied, muffling a yawn. "Take all the time you need, but I'm not alone. Is that okay?"

I heard a deep murmur in the background.

"Yeah, I don't care if Reed listens." Alisha's silence prompted me to continue.

"So I got to Miami to see Selena and…" I slowly began telling Alisha everything—from the beginning to our current situation in Miami.

"This is so *exciting*." Alisha sounded giddy.

"Why's that?"

"Because it's *already* going in the right direction," she said, her voice low and husky. "Don't you see it? Selena's been letting you in since day one. You date her. You sleep in the same bed. Physically, she wants you close, even if she doesn't admit it or know it. Women don't usually sleep with men if you're just a—*erm*—"

Alisha broke off with a little flustered noise.

A deeper voice murmured something indistinct in the background.

"Just what? What just happened?"

Alisha quickly recovered, sounding breathless now. "*Selena* is letting you sleep with her. *That's all that matters.*"

I filled her in on my month-long trip, and she asked about my plans with Titan. I admitted my uncertainty, explaining Gabriel's vague instructions.

Alisha's voice carried a teasing tone as she responded.

"It sounds like *Gabriel* considered all the options, and he is okay with whatever *you* choose. He wouldn't do something without confidence if he didn't know all the pieces in play, the bigger picture, as *he* says."

She knew him too well.

"You've been spending too much time with him."

"Not too much, I hope," she said, her voice softening with a tease. "Just enough, hm?"

A noise of agreement could be heard in the background.

A lot had changed since I left New York.

If Reed wanted his best friend around his girl, who was I to judge?

I was beginning to understand that most relationships were more complicated than they appeared on the surface. Nothing was clean-cut.

Nisha wanted Killian, which was beyond my scope of understanding, considering *who* he was. All prince of darkness and scary.

Nate wanted Gemma, who clearly hated him.

And then there was Kieran, who wanted…*whatever with Avani.*

Meanwhile, I was sleeping with my sort of girlfriend, trying to make her my real girlfriend.

"I've been spending my days with Selena. I don't know how to get through to her," I confessed.

"I think you already are—" Alisha began, but I interjected.

"But I want to kiss her." Among other things. "I just want my girl back. But sometimes she doesn't feel like my girl anymore." I didn't recognize who we were now. Something felt off.

Alisha was quiet for a moment, and she made a soft noise.

"Something Reed did during our time apart that he kept showing up. He was *persistent* but in a way that was endearing. In turn, it made me reach out to him. You are already doing that. But you have to have faith that your love for her is enough to make her come back to you." Her voice grew even softer as she continued. "He only came back because I let him in. Somehow I think she might do the same for you."

She paused before adding. "I say this because the *only* reason Selena is allowing you to be close to her is because she still loves you. As much as you love her. She's just *scared*."

Reed said something too low for me to hear.

Alisha continued softly.

"I am familiar with being too afraid to take the leap. Especially when you've lost so much. But it's only been a few weeks since you've seen her, after nearly a month apart. She'd been injured. You two weren't together very long. It may be scary for her. Good things take time, right? It will take time."

She took a shaky breath.

"Kellan, that night when I sent you home...*I'm sorry.* I didn't realize how tired you were. I feel like it's my fault you didn't get any sleep. If I just went back to Reed—I never once *blamed you.* It was *my* fault—"

What? Did she really blame herself? "*No,* I was your guard—"

"*No, I knew better*—" Alisha sounded out of breath as Reed moved a little around her. "I knew better."

"*It was Avani*—"

I would do the same for Becca.

"It wasn't your fault. I hope Gabriel told you *that.*" There was a small bite to her tone as she said it. Like he was there. Or maybe she was saying it to Reed.

"At the beginning of my relationship, I was terrified. Not just by my own feelings, but sometimes I think it's the intensity of my emotions for the person I am with. You could be a little more...*persuasive.*"

"With words?"

"*Not* with words." Whenever Alisha's voice got all *proper,* I knew she was blushing.

"I still want her—"

"*Don't pounce*—"

Heat crept up my neck as I laughed. "No, I *wouldn't*—"

"I think there's something about letting her decide what she wants. I think most of the time, Selena sounds like a woman who knows what she wants. And I'm not saying you shouldn't convince her...I just think...perhaps a more subtle approach might help you right now."

An embarrassed noise left her at something Reed said.

"I think when she does reach out to you, you'll know."

"I don't know how to *be* anymore," I couldn't process Selena without feeling guilty. "I feel like I'm good at analyzing everything, and when it comes to Selena, my mind goes blank."

"Everyone has a weakness," Alisha's voice was low. "Just let her reach out to you for her wants. I think you know who you are when you're with her. Just go with it. It hasn't let you down so far, has it?"

Reed said something around her too low for me to hear.

His voice was a quiet rumble that sounded deeper than usual.

She murmured it back to him.

"Sometimes that's how things start?"

He made a noise in agreement. She repeated it for me.

Sometimes, that's how things start.

I never would've guessed. "This was not in the group chat."

I thought being a part of the girl's group chat would help me with Selena, too. Alisha's low laughter mingled with his.

I didn't recognize him for a second around her, and I had been around Reed often.

But maybe Alisha brought out a different side to him. Like I did with Selena.

The Selena who teased me in her kitchen. Who let me tease her. I missed her. My brain was only focused on fixing my relationship.

"This gives you both a chance to work out your problems. Your miscommunication. It's very common among couples. Slowly. I think being away from New York, in a space where you can be whoever you choose to be for her, might be necessary to get *yourselves* together."

I never thought about it like that. I was just going through the motions.

"I don't know what that looks like, but if Selena trusts you this much, you are doing a wonderful job." Alisha paused. "I'd say your last argument with her was a sore subject…"

"It's the *only* subject I think about."

One night. That's all it took to ruin my life.

"That's all right. Arguments happen. Apologize. Tackle it head-on. It's good for both of you to be honest and vulnerable with each other. Without misunderstanding."

Alisha told me when listening to Selena, I had to just hear what she was saying, not my assumptions of what she was saying. Just hear her.

In the background, Reed murmured something at her.

Alisha repeated it, saying if I needed to, I could have the entire conversation in Spanish since it would be easier for Selena.

"It's important to acknowledge the progress you've *already* made rather than looking at what you don't have. Time has passed. Both of you have changed."

We both had. And for a moment, I wondered if it was too much.

"I'm trying," I said.

"I know, darling. You're doing a great job so far." She was sympathetic. "But you also have to forgive yourself. Arguments happen between the best of relationships. You cannot blame yourself for what happened. I think both of you just need to apologize and talk to each other."

"Is all that what worked for you?"

"Well, um…I think different approaches are necessary for *different* people. And what works for one person might not necessarily be—" Alisha hesitated, and I could practically see the blush creeping into her cheeks.

When she started talking like a professor, I knew she was embarrassed.

"Reed did more than apologize."

"*Oh, I've heard,*" I teased, grinning wide, unable to resist the opportunity.

Alisha let out an embarrassed gasp, and I heard his laughter with mine, the tension momentarily dissipating.

He sounds different over the phone like this.

"I miss you guys."

Alisha sounded like she was pushing him off her.

"I am casting you *off,*" she said to him breathlessly before returning to me. "*We* miss you too. How is the weather? It's dreadful here…"

I got lost in the conversation with her, my mind drifting to how I was going to approach Selena.

How did I kiss my almost-girlfriend?

CHAPTER 49
SELENA

OVER THE NEXT FEW DAYS HE STAYED WITH ME KELLAN BEGAN TO SHOW up in subtle ways. Subtle things.

Gabriel's words sank into my skin.

Sometime's that's how things start.

And it was starting.

But they began to crumble my resolve. Little by little he was working himself deeper in my heart.

I woke up in pain one night.

I didn't understand it but Nisha had said even if I wasn't actively injured, I had phantom pains.

Discomfort. Fueled by anxiety. Stress.

The six-foot two sleeping giant next to me. He stirred as I rolled out of bed and a second later he was moving. I felt him around me all the time now like a shadow.

"You okay, honey?" He sounded half-asleep, his voice rumbling from his chest. I forgot despite being enormous, Kellan was this baby.

In the past Kellan would fall asleep on me all the time, at some point in the night he would come squeeze over and take up all my space and stay there.

But waking him up was another story. He'd grumble and cuddle me like I was his teddy bear. Now, he cuddled me like that again.

"I think so, my leg is cramping."

"Where?" He was moving instantly and I was surprised as he kneeled in front of me while I sat on the bed.

He took both of my calves into his hands and began squeezing. Leaning his head against my knees. My heart ached a little at the sight.

His hair had grown out more and more and I threaded my fingers through it naturally.

"Are you sleeping on my knees, savage?"

A low laugh left him. "I'm trying not to get caught."

I felt a reluctant smile tip my lips. Both of us woke up tired, but he was trying.

"Are you in pain?" His voice was low, hesitant like if he asked the question it would hurt me more.

"A little, but I don't think it's real not really."

As awkward as it sounded I explained slowly rubbing my eyes, yawning a little.

"Nisha calls them phantom pains, like it hurt really badly before. Now, not so much. But sometimes if I have anxiety it hurts again."

He was quiet leaning his head against my knees still.

"I'm sorry."

I didn't say anything trying to formulate why he even would be. "Not your fault."

His shoulders stiffened as I said the words like he didn't believe me. We sat there for long moments as he did it moving around to my shins, my thighs. Until it eased.

"Better?" He didn't look at me as he said it.

"Better."

ANOTHER TIME WE WERE AT THE BEACH AND I DIDN'T HAVE GOOD balance so much.

I almost slipped in the sand near the water when it got uneven and he caught me and held me tighter until we reached stable ground.

"My parents took us to the beach all the time," he murmured as he carried me.

The sun hit his hair just right as he looked down at me with a twinkle in his eyes.

"My sister was vicious. She'd threaten to bury me in that part of the beach all the time so she could be my parents only child."

I giggled as he told me how insane the two of them had been. His life sounded so different than mine. All the time.

But I liked that it was different. I liked the promise of something else.

When I had met him in New York, his life had sounded like a soft dream. One that I woke up from when I imagined mine.

Was that why I liked Kellan?

He was simply different. Than I was. Than the Titans were.

"Why did you choose to be a Titan?" I asked him as he set me down looking a little reluctant to do so. "You could be…anything else."

He wasn't stupid and I knew how he thought. But it didn't make sense for someone like him to live our lives. Mostly because most of us became Titans when we didn't have a choice. Kellan *chose* to be one.

Kellan stood there looking a little uneasy or nervous, I couldn't tell as he said. "You ever hear the metaphor about water that stands still?"

I shook my head this time not understanding his English metaphors. Ever. Even Nathan had to explain it to me still.

Kellan's grin was small.

"It's the idea that with no movement or variants in the environment. Water that stays where it is forever, becomes a breeding ground for bacteria. It becomes poisoned. By not growing or moving. Whereas water that flows?"

He jerked this thumb at the beach.

"It will go places. It'll become something bigger. I love my parents. I do. But they are the biggest snobs I know." His grin grew wider at my wide eyes.

"They're nice people, but my father goes to a country-club. And my mom is a part of some wives group. They have expectations, they have criteria, and I love them, but Becca hates it too. She's determined to be on her own and do her thing. But me? I wanted to do something that would always push me, force me to grow up, change, and not be stagnant—I didn't want to be cookie-cutter. You know what that means?"

I understood the general idea. He did not want to fit a mold.

He didn't like being held to one place. He liked things that changed him, made him think differently, taught him new things.

It explained why Kellan was wanted as a teammate.

He was always adapting, changing, shifting, becoming whatever we needed as a team. Garrett was like this as well, but differently.

They each had their own strengths. Garrett was just silent about it.

"You became a Titan for a challenge or…"

He shook his head pouting a little and I wanted to kiss him, looking so adorable standing there on the beach with nothing but shorts on. And his abs.

"I think so. I was getting bored of being a contractor. It was annoying. Everyone around me stays for twenty years getting old doing nothing for the government. When Reed offered this? I saw it as a chance to do everything…"

He talked about how Titan had different concentrations he could focus on. Move around. Grow. And every day wasn't boring.

I did not know this about him.

"You like to be…" I searched for the right word as he drew closer almost. "You like new things and even if it's different you do not care?"

"I like different," his voice was lower now. "I like…unique and interesting, and vibrant, colorful. I don't mind challenges. But I think about my parents and how they might be FBI but they don't realize how snobby they are. The more up the ranks they go they become insufferable to deal with sometimes. If you ever met them, don't tell them I said that." He grinned as he said it and my heart thumped a little louder listening to him.

If I ever met them…because he wanted me to meet them.

"I've never heard you talk about them like that."

He smirked then. "I don't like to…ruminate on the things I don't like. Things that…"

"Not pretty."

"Yeah," he said softly watching me with those blues. "I like to focus on what I can control, what I have in common, and the good things in between." He always had.

With us, he never focused on the differences, only what we had in common. I could tell when his eyes stayed he was thinking about that as well. I just knew.

"I like to focus on the good things."

I knew. I blinked back my emotions looking down at my flip-flop covered feet. My heart was racing in a rhythm I didn't understand. I didn't want to figure it out right at this moment.

"Are you hungry?" That is what came out instead.

"Always."

"Do you still salsa dance?" He asked me one night as we walked outside from a local restaurant.

"Not recently." But I hadn't danced in a long time. He motioned to a neon sign I had missed. It was a bunch of couples there, music pouring out from the beach, lights strung up everywhere. I grinned at the sight. "But you do not dance."

"I can try, I can't promise I got rhythm."

Another laugh bubbled up out of me, my stomach full from all the good things I'd been munching on these last few days.

Kellan did spoil me, paying for everything, getting me whatever I wanted, dropping off flowers, little trinkets. Accessories. Painting. When he learned I liked artwork he began getting me unique things he thought I might like.

If he was on a mission to win me back, he was winning.

And the more I hung out with him? The more I thought about my memories from the city. The ones with him. And Titan.

My life there. My accomplishments. All the things I had done to make sure I could be Venus. Some part of me ached for my old apartment, the life I left behind—for some reason, I couldn't put my finger on it.

"How much?" Kellan asked the guy. Who motioned to him in Spanish and said it was free. He looked at me with wide adorable eyes. "Are you still impressed?"

I felt my lips stretching wide. "I'll be more impressed if we can get you on the floor."

He turned a little red as a few women looked him over but he looked away. I wanted to throw myself across the room and scratch their eyes out.

I didn't even understand why I reacted like a savage now with him.

I was turning into him, that had to be the answer.

When we stepped to a part of the sand far enough away from everyone, I held onto his arm as he moved me in front of me. His mouth dropped to my ear. "*Gatita*, I gotta be honest, I can't move like these guys."

My laugh was embarrassingly loud as I looped my arms around his neck. "I don't mind the way you move."

I hadn't meant it to be sexual but all of a sudden as I pressed into him I felt his arousal. Against my stomach. I pressed my lips together and looked away, hiding my laughter at the situation.

"Now we're stuck here."

I felt a laugh bubble up and then another until I was hiding my laughter into his shirt, his breath mingling with mine.

"Why are you like this?"

I felt his smile in my neck. "Because of you."

Only he made me laugh like this.

We were so close for a moment I swore, I thought he would kiss me. The lights twinkling above us, the music playing around us.

"Stand on my feet so I can pretend to be a better dancer."

I did. Tiptoeing on his shoes as he held me.

"I look stupid, *Gatita*," he murmured against my cheek. "I can't dance for shit."

"I think you are doing great, I thought you would look like those blow up toys at the American car shops. You know? The ones that wave in the wind ten-feet tall—" I broke off as Kellan ducked his head his laughter loud against my body, and his face adorably red.

"I'm way worse than a red tube in the auto repair shop," he chuckled. "But that was good."

Our laughter echoed until we moved further away from the crowd of people. Kellan walking further until we were halfway to the beach.

"Better, much better," he sighed into my skin. "I gotta take lessons to keep up with those folks. That guy next to me was at least ninety-two—"

"Probably older," I giggled feeling lighter than before.

"You're right, a fossil. And he moved better."

Only he did this to me. I laughed so hard my side hurt.

I can't believe he's doing this for me.

My heart was racing wildly in my chest a little at being so close to him. Not quite hugging but not quite apart.

Still stepping on his toes and holding onto him for balance, support, like I always had.

"You ever think about the city sometimes?" He asked me looking out at the water, the sun covering him and me in hues of orange, purple, pink until we glowed.

"Sometimes."

He didn't say a word. A beat passed full of unspoken tension and silence between us. Sometimes I missed my old life. There.

That was the truth.

Sometimes I missed being a Titan.

I missed the manor.

I even missed the things I hated.

Being a Titan had become a part of my soul. Etched into the fiber of my being.

"Did you ever think about me?"

His voice was quiet.

Every single day.

All the time.

Every hour of every day.

Until it consumed me whole.

I looked down at his white shirt unsure of my own emotions.

I did love Kellan. I did. But I...I was confused. I didn't understand what was holding me back from saying it. I didn't know how to describe what I felt.

The buzzing sensation was back.

Sometimes that's how it starts.

Gabriel?

I heard his voice. I hadn't spoken to him in forever.

I almost felt embarrassed too.

I felt...Nathan would say shaken up and stirred. I was back to feeling like a margarita in a blender.

And I noticed Kellan had gone quiet. He had asked me if I thought about him. At all. I watched his softer face taking in the ocean. He didn't look at me like he was afraid of my answer.

Did I ever think about him?

I took a deep breath as I said it. "All the time." He closed his eyes almost relived and my chest ached at the thought of him thinking I didn't.

Because now that he was here, he was always around me, and he wasn't in my thoughts all the time—he was a part of me more than he ever had been.

"I think about you all the time."

CHAPTER 50

SELENA

I JUST FINISHED UP IN ART CLASS.

Gentle sea breezes wafted through the open windows facing the beach as I packed my materials up slowly and measured.

My thoughts drifted through things the entire time.

About Kellan. About New York. Titan. My life.

Where I had started. Where I was now.

I love this new life.

You also love Kellan. Just a little still.

I craved him closer to me.

Whenever he reached for me, my body relaxed around him, instinctively recognizing who it *loved.*

Automatically letting him in every single time.

Unable to stay away from him.

Some nights, he slept beside me, and I felt him so close that it took everything I had to not reach out.

Memories of Titan, being in Greenwich, New York, it all flooded through me. And with Kellan?

I wondered if I made the right choice. I wondered—and I doubted just a little.

He reminded me of our *beginning.*

Were we beginning again? I didn't know what to make of it.

"Your work is really good," Marcelo's familiar, husky voice reached my ears, and I smiled over my shoulder at him. "Your color use is fantastic. It's very feminine."

"I'm trying," I replied, hanging up my apron.

As Marcelo approached my easel, he leaned in close, the sculpted muscles of his bare, tanned torso glistening under the bright studio lights.

"What did you want to do with this piece?"

The spacious studio was designed to be open and airy, with entire walls consisting of floor-to-ceiling windows that overlooked the sparkling turquoise waters and white sandy beach just beyond.

Anyone strolling by could easily see inside.

"I was going to hang it up in my bedroom," I said low. "Make it into bigger pieces until it fits the wall..."

As I was talking, I felt him moving closer, but it was just Marcelo.

I told myself he was fine.

I didn't realize the brush I had in my hand had been trembling. I gripped it tightly as my hands shook. I ducked my head as I spoke and finished.

"That sounds wonderful," he said. "You could do this bolder on the edges. It'll be the end of this painting and the beginning of the next one."

I smiled politely and nodded at Marcelo, his presence crowding me despite the open studio.

I took a small step back behind my stool as he leaned over.

While I felt perfectly comfortable around Kellan, the same couldn't be said for all men.

I have never felt comfortable around all men.

An energy shift rippled through the room, the tension thickening around me.

The studio had cleared out with only a few lingering students; nothing seemed overtly amiss as I turned back to Marcelo.

His eyes met mine. "Do you have any plans after class?"

"She does." I knew that voice.

It whispered love into my skin.

I turned over my shoulder, and Kellan stood by one of the entrances, looking devastatingly handsome in his board shorts and t-shirt stretching across his broad chest.

The sunlight gleamed off his hair, and his eyes burned the brightest blue. Focused on me as he stepped into the art studio.

For a second, I forgot I had told him where it was.

I never thought he'd come.

"Honey, I thought I'd come to get you today so we could grab lunch."

His eyes locked on Marcelo as he walked up to me, his head dipping quickly to kiss me behind my ear in a spot that sent shivers through me.

Kellan's hand found the small of my back as he tugged me close to him.

This baby.

Some things never changed.

My hand found his heart, pressing over it as I looked into his eyes, still steel now on Marcelo. I knew that look.

I felt the anxiety in me, though, as Kellan brought me close to him.

I didn't want a fight.

Marcelo straightened up, his flirtatious demeanor shifting to one of friendly professionalism.

He extended his hand, palm angled up in greeting. "I'm Marcelo, the instructor. You must be Lena's—"

Kellan shook his hand firmly. "Kane, I *am hers.*"

Sometimes, I forgot we didn't travel under our real names.

Kellan hadn't mentioned his name. Because to me, he was my Kellan.

"I overheard your conversation."

I held my breath, waiting for the tension to escalate.

But to my surprise, Kellan remained calm, his eyes softening as he turned to me.

"You mentioned last night you wanted to try something new, honey. I thought I'd come pick you up and take you."

I tried to ignore the way my nipples pebbled at the sound of his deep voice saying those words.

Why did that sound so dirty?

Why did I like it?

His eyes raked down my dress and back up to me.

My mouth opened and closed without a word coming out. Heat pulsed through me at that look.

As Kellan kept his eyes on me, Marcelo stepped back, giving us space.

"I'll leave you two to it," he said with a wink. "Lena, keep up the good work. And Kane, it was nice to meet you."

With that, Marcelo moved on, his compliments filling the air again. I turned to Kellan, my heart swelling with unfamiliar emotions.

"What was that?" I asked breathlessly, hardly recognizing my own voice as his golden head dipped until his mouth grazed the sensitive shell of my ear.

I trembled as he hauled me closer with a sigh.

"I haven't held you like this in weeks," he murmured gruffly. "I missed you. Just let me have you for a second."

He dipped his face into the curve of my neck, tugging me flush against the solid wall of his chest, the hard planes of his body hot against the thin cotton sundress.

And I didn't realize how much I had missed him until I got him this close to me.

"It took me everything not to hit him," he admitted after a long moment, the words muffled against my skin. Something fluttered in my heart as he said the words.

"But you didn't. Why?"

He paused, eyes taking in my white sundress that hugged my new curves.

There was an appreciation in his gaze I hadn't seen since we'd reunited weeks ago. He didn't say a word at first as I set down my brush, hands trembling slightly.

"Kellan?" I nudged him a little with my nose, and his smile was light.

"The thought of any man disrespecting you bothers me," he finally said, voice low. "*Anyone* threatening *us*...But I looked at you just now. I could see how uncomfortable the situation was making *you* feel."

He took my trembling hands in his strong grip. "You were scared. I realized most times in the past, the only person more upset than me... was you..."

His jaw clenched as he trailed off.

"You're my heart, *Gatita*. I will always protect you, be your shield. Be your man...but I failed you in the past, honey. I don't ever want to fail you again." His voice cracked a little as he closed his eyes. "I waited so *long* to say that to you."

When he opened them, they were burning bright on me and filled with emotion.

"Don't get me wrong. I would've torn into him if he had put his hands on you. But he didn't cross that line. So, I'm going to handle things case-by-case now. Your well-being is my priority—not *my* ego."

My heart was pounding in my chest. A mixture of so many different emotions swirled through me.

What had happened to him since I'd been gone?

"I'm choosing you. A hundred times over. I will always choose you."

"You choose me."

"*Always*," his eyes leveled with mine, a faint smirk played on his lips, but I could see the longing hidden beneath the surface. "But if he touched you, and you said no, and you told me to kill him, I still would. In a heartbeat."

This baby.

Some things never changed, but...I felt safer with him. I believed him. And I knew he was telling the truth.

If anyone ever laid a hand on him—I'd do the same.

And then he went on, his voice raw. "I'm sorry. There hasn't been a second every single day for the last few weeks where I don't regret not kissing you that night—"

My heart sputtered a little, listening to him, a longing so intense it nearly took my breath away, but I knew we needed to talk.

"Stop."

He did. His eyes held a wealth of hurt. Pain. I know.

I felt the same.

"I don't want to do this here." I looked at him. "Can we talk about it at home? I need to say a few things."

I regret not kissing you. But I know we need to talk first.

"Yes."

CHAPTER 51
KELLAN

She needed to feel safe.

As Selena and I returned to her home, the one place she always felt safe enough to open up to me, I was reminded of the many times she had asked me to take our conversations home, coming back to me.

Because she needed to feel safe.

And her home was her peace.

Something *I* had taken away from her.

Being with you is my peace.

Waves and waves of guilt and regret washed over me, knowing that I had shattered that sense of security. It was my fault.

And I'd carried that shit with me this entire time.

Does it ever get better?

I would do anything to keep her. To make amends for my past mistakes.

We settled on her bed, leaning against the headboard far enough apart for me to feel her heat and crave it, knowing better than to reach for her.

Selena tucked herself under the comforter, her hands trembling as she hid them beneath the covers.

"My father and brother Diego were shot when I was a girl." She continued. "After that, Mama worked, and she was gone all the time. But I saw as a woman, she did not make enough money. We were hungry, and she gave me everything she could, but we were struggling."

Her eyes were focused on the blanket as she spoke softly. "For women, there are not many ways to make good money."

My heart sank as she spoke.

Because I fucking *knew*—I had *guessed* sometimes. But she had never confirmed it.

And I didn't know how to ask her.

I didn't care if she…had done what she had for money.

"I learned to make good money when I was sixteen."

My heart rate escalated rapidly, knowing where she was going.

"The first time was not good. But every time after that, I did *everything, anything* for Mama. She thought I was working a normal job. I was not. When I was twenty-one, I met some people who said I was beautiful and I could learn to do a different job if I wanted to make more money. I took it."

Her eyes never met mine. Which was good since I was wrecked with every word that left her mouth.

I couldn't see clearly, and my heart ached for that little girl. I had hurt *that* girl.

"Gabriel found me when I turned twenty-two." She explained to me the night she had met him and how pivotal it was to her existence.

Gabriel had saved her life because he thought she had been worth saving. Rescuing her from a life of prostitution. From death.

Suffering. My chest clenched.

Someone had told Gabriel she was stuck in Havana, and he'd plucked her up.

In so many ways. Newfound appreciation and respect blossomed for the man I didn't understand, but I knew he'd taken a chance on me too.

For someone who pretended not to have any emotions, he had more than enough heart to give.

She told me everything about Gabriel in her past. Her first night in America. Her boots.

Everything.

I listened, understanding her and Gabriel, their relationship, his father-like influence in her life.

How he taught a young Selena about *consent* while not being much older than her himself.

Any if not all of my previous misconceptions about Gabriel were obliterated at that moment.

Everything just wiped away to reveal someone else underneath that cold demeanor and grey suit of his.

I was under no illusion; Gabriel was the only reason why we were both here. I didn't see anything but someone I respected.

Someone who brought this woman into my life not once, but *twice*.

Deep down, I knew I owed him everything, and I would do anything for him.

I couldn't even speak as Selena told me how much Gabriel had done over the years.

She paused when she got to the day he let her go.

"I wanted to be free," she whispered, her eyes looking far away as she said the words. "He…wanted that for me."

And then she explained to me separately her relationship with Nate. How he killed for her. How he was always there. I saw Nathan Wyatt in a different light.

"When Gabriel saw us that day together, months ago, he asked me if I said yes." I knew she was shaking. "I did."

And every single bit of her words hit me like a punch. Physical blows raking over my body.

The woman I had hurt, the woman I had failed to protect.

"When Nathan asked me to be his wife, I said yes because I didn't think I deserved better. When I met you, I did not tell you because I believed you would not want me the same, if you knew I was dirty—"

"That's not true," I blurted out, choking back tears as my voice cracked, the anguish in my tone palpable. *"I have never seen you that way. I would never care."*

Not once.

"I didn't tell you because…what if you did not want me?"

She told me I was from a good family. Perfect. Cookie-cutter. But my parents worked to be where they are.

And I shattered. Because the idea of seeing Selena as anything other than perfect was baffling of a concept that just didn't exist in my mind.

"…I felt used…"

"You're not used," the words left me in a rush desperate to make her understand. "Honey, I have never given a shit—"

I couldn't fucking fathom how much she'd been afraid. Of questioning my love for her. I couldn't see anymore.

My vision blurred. "Never. Not once. I didn't care."

Selena wiped her eyes as she explained to me that Nate had asked her to cope with his own emotions from losing Gemma.

I had no fucking clue how deep his feelings ran for the other woman. But Selena explained to me how she saw Nate as not just a partner but a good friend who was offering them both something they thought they needed.

"It would never be enough," the words caught in my throat as I said it to her and she nodded wiping her eyes. "Nate doesn't love you like I love you. He never will."

"It was enough for me *then*," she whispered, her wet, soft eyes meeting mine, rimmed in red. "Not enough *after* I met you."

My heart swelled and ached simultaneously a little listening to her, those words echoing in my mind.

She's like a scared cat...

I had hurt *that* girl.

I had been the cause of her pain, the reason she had been hurt.

After she had opened up to me, trusted me with her heart, I had shattered it into a million pieces, leaving her broken and afraid.

Enough to wander outside to somewhere to go looking for a solution to her thoughts.

I wiped my face. Looking back, that conversation with her and Nate had been so fucking innocent.

Gemma had been there the entire time.

Because Gemma was the only woman he'd ever loved.

Selena told me, it sounded like Nathan was fixing things with Gemma and in turn, he'd calmed down.

"You cannot pay any attention to how he speaks. He sees things differently. He speaks differently. Gabriel is overprotective of me. But I said yes to Nathan because I wanted what he was giving me at the time. Nathan is not...he is not the bad guy."

Now it made sense *why* he blew up on me.

I had overreacted, dismissed her, blown up on her, and snapped at her. For what?

This girl, who had spent her entire life fighting, who had endured more than I could ever imagine.

"I'm sorry." It was so fucking stupid to say those words because it paled in comparison to what I had done. Sorry meant nothing compared to almost losing her.

"I wish I had turned back to you…I never should have—"

"For what?" She asked softly. "You were right about some things. I should have trusted you enough to tell you. Gabriel said it was miscommunication. I should have sat you down so many times…"

Alisha said the same.

"It was my fault too. I did not trust you to tell you calmly at home. On a different day. Explain this to you months ago instead of when you came home tired." Her voice was thick with emotion. "That was my fault too."

"Are you kidding? I snapped at you. *I almost lost you—*"

"I didn't let you in. You were right, *if I came home tired like that and you were on the phone with a woman—*"

"I felt like Nate was throwing you in my face after he taunted me with you all the time."

"But Nathan makes fun of everyone," she smiled a little. "That's how he communicates. He was still my brother and friend."

I nodded. I got that now even if I didn't know how to accept it.

That night, it had felt like my worst fears had been proven right.

"I am sorry."

"*I'm* sorry," I whispered, my heart breaking with every word. "I was the one who got angry with you and then you—"

I broke off, unable to meet her gaze. The shame I felt bubbled over to the surface.

At that moment, I realized what we should have done all along.

"*This* is what we should've done instead of fighting. We should've asked for help. I should've hit up Nate instead of holding back."

But my brain had stopped working.

Selena nodded, her voice soft. "And maybe just sleep together for that night and I could switch with you and go to Alisha. Together."

I never even thought about it like that. I had been tired. Alisha wouldn't have cared if Selena had come with me.

There were ninety different ways for us to have handled that night differently. And we had picked the worst one.

"I can't remember ever fighting with you," I said softly, a hint of wonder in my voice. "I feel like that was the first time I lost my shit with you and we never fought—" I broke off. *We never fought.*

"We have never really had a fight until then…"

I spoke first, my voice filled with determination. "We need healthier ways to fight."

Her voice was quiet as she peered up at me all shy now. "Maybe next time you can just kiss me…"

I blinked, my heart skipping a beat at her words. *I could do that.* And then some.

"You want me not sweet with you?"

She blushed as I said it, and I thought about it, Alisha's words echoing in my mind.

Just let her tell you what she wants…

The words escaped my lips before I could stop them, a desperate plea filled with raw emotion. "Can I hug you?"

She sniffled, her eyes watering, and just as she went to open her mouth, she *froze.*

Her head snapped up to meet my gaze as I spoke, and she sat up straighter.

"What is it?"

"Dios. That's why…"

What just happened?

"Gabriel," she said slowly, each word carefully measured, as if trying to make sense of the pieces that had suddenly fallen into place. *"You*…Why he chose you. Why you are *here.* You are *him.* With heart. *That's why he did everything. That's why he sent you."*

Her eyes filled with emotion.

"You are *his* chance…" She covered her mouth, shock etched across her features as fresh tears spilled from her eyes, her body trembling.

Selena moved towards me, her hands reaching for my face, pulling me close to her. *"You were mine."*

"I still am yours."

Tears streamed down her face, her dark pupils fixed on me.

"He never let you fail me. You are his second chance."

And then, Selena kissed me, her lips crashing against mine with a desperation that stole the breath from my lungs.

I poured everything into her, every ounce of love, every shattered piece of my heart even if I didn't know what was happening right now? I didn't care.

Selena was kissing me.

I missed you so fucking much. Let me love you.

Take me back.

"I forgive you. I will *always* love you in every lifetime. I have never stopped loving you." *I love you.*

"I will never stop loving you," I couldn't even breathe with this woman.

Selena stamped her lips over my mouth, her tears mingling with my own. She was grabbing my shirt, her hands clinging to me as if I were her lifeline.

I broke off, looking into her eyes, my voice laced with concern. "You're hurt—"

She kissed me harder her eyes sparkling albeit, a little shy. "You can be sweet?" She nodded.

I felt the smile stretching my lips that felt like it belonged to a stranger without her. I hadn't smiled like that since I met her.

Fuck. Yes. I can be sweet.

"I can do that, honey."

CHAPTER 52
SELENA

ALL THIS TIME, I HAD BEEN WONDERING WHY GABRIEL LEFT HIM ALONE.

But now, as the pieces fell into place, I understood.

The bigger picture...

Reed had taken Kellan under his wing.

Smiling at him with a knowing glint in his eyes like he did with Gabriel.

It was as if he recognized something in Kellan.

Something he saw in his family. And Kellan, with his presence and the way he made me feel so safe, was the missing piece I had been searching for all along.

He was Gabriel's second chance...if I was hers...

For both of us to grow.

And find each other again.

Reed's decision to guide and nurture Kellan was no accident. It was a deliberate choice. Reed had seen the same thing in Kellan. Heart.

Within Gabriel. Just like Gabriel. Maybe once, a long time ago, Gabriel had loved like Kellan had. Loved and lost.

And he saw himself in my love.

And the way Kellan made me feel, the safety and comfort I found in his presence, the way he seemed to be everything I had ever needed...*it all made sense now.*

"No sé hacia dónde vamos, solo sé que quiero ir contigo."

I don't know where we are going; the only thing I know is that I want to go with you.

He kissed me harder.

As our lips moved together, I realized that he was more than just my love, more than just my partner. Kellan had always felt right to me, like a missing piece of my heart that had finally found its way home. He was my peace.

Did you want this life? No.

But this life had led me to Kellan.

I will never let you go again.

"You didn't fail me," I whispered against his lips, my voice filled with emotion. "You never failed me. I love you." I watched as his eyes widened, emotions swirling within their depths.

"Can I love you?" he asked. As if he couldn't quite believe that this was real.

I nodded, my heart swelling with the intensity of my feelings for him.

"Yes," I breathed, and then our hands were all over each other.

"*Baby, let me—*" he laughed low without humor. "No, just let me —" I let him take off my sundress as he took me in, his eyes banked with heat.

His hands ran down my body. "You look…amazing."

I had been a little self-conscious initially. I had gained some weight with no activity and eating whatever I wanted. But I liked this softer version of me, too.

As I watched his eyes lower over my breasts, which were bigger, and my hips, I saw he did, too.

He closed his eyes. As he exhaled. "*Sweet.* I have to be sweet."

I smiled at seeing his expression, reaching for his shirt. "Next time we fight, you can be *not* sweet."

As I said it, his eyes widened, the depths of the heating as it left my lips. Kellan laid me down as he stripped. His body was harder now, much more muscled than before.

"Honey, I haven't had you in forever."

"*Not hours—*"

"Not hours," he clarified with heat in his eyes. "*Days.*"

My body clenched as I saw him aroused and climbing into the bed with me. To my shock, he didn't kiss me.

His lips pressed over my heart as he settled over me. "I'm sorry to you the most. I will never let anything hurt you again."

Uncurling his hand, I saw him holding something in it. *My necklace...*

"You carry this with you all the time?"

"I hoped—" He began. "I hoped you might want—*But I didn't know.*"

I felt my eyes water as I nodded, moving my hair. He reached around me and slipped over my head. It hit right between my breasts.

Kellan pressed his lips over the pendant.

Over my heart. Moving lower.

Taking my nipples into his mouth, taking his time, biting and tugging and, I gasped at the sensation.

Heat flared through me after so long it felt like coming home.

I feel like a savage.

"Your body's changed," he sucked harder, kissing my chest in between, trailing his tongue across my skin. "I loved you before. But I love you so much like this."

My fingers were in his hair, nearly crying at the familiar sensation of his hair threading through my fingers.

"Do you remember your word?"

No, I had no—Wait.

"*Milkshake.*"

Kellan's blue eyes flashed up to me as he rested his chin on my belly. I caught the emotion in them.

He blinked several times as he pressed kisses over my abdomen, kissing everywhere he could reach, whispering his apologies, his praise, I felt his eyes wet against my body.

His lips opened drifting lower over my abdomen.

"I never thought I would get this moment." He breathed over my skin. "I'm going to savor you. Every bit of you."

My heart raced just enough to know it had been a long time since I had him. Or this.

And I almost forgot how intense he was when he was like this.

His lips trailed lower over my thighs.

"You are so much softer." His hands trembled as they moved over me. "I'm sorry, baby."

"I'm sorry, too."

"*Gatita*, I'd like to apologize to you." He just did. I told him that. "*Properly*." And then he sealed his mouth over my clit and sucked.

CHAPTER 53
KELLAN

"I LOVE YOU, KELLAN."

"Love you too, *Gatita*."

I kept Selena at home with me, wrapped in my arms, determined to keep her safe and sound in them. In all the ways I had failed as a man.

We spent our days cuddling everywhere, as if we were trying to make up for all the lost time. Which we were. I couldn't get enough of her pressed against me.

The way her head fit perfectly in the crook of my neck. The way she was comfortable on me now more than ever.

As we watched movies together, I found myself watching her more than the screen. I cooked for her, did everything I could think of to make her comfortable.

If she had nightmares, which was less around me, I was there to hold her, to wipe away her panic. I was there for my girl. Fucking. *Finally.*

She's your everything...She's my everything.

She was my second chance, my redemption, and I was determined never to let her go.

And then that little niggle of doubt came into my head. The growing tension. I couldn't describe it but even though life at the beach was great. It was.

Part of me knew it wouldn't last forever. The shadows sometimes called to me and I found myself wondering what was happening in New York. The life I left behind.

I couldn't bring myself to make love to Selena fully.

Not just because she was on her nerve pain medication, but because I was terrified of taking advantage of her and hurting her. Because that was the last thing I wanted to hear—Selena crying again. Because of me.

No, I had enough of that.

Alisha had told me to take Selena's lead. Take her lead. As determined as I was to follow the advice Alisha gave? I knew I found myself at a cross-roads.

Instead, I apologized to my girl in every way I knew how.

My lips and tongue explored every inch of her skin, tasting, worshipping. *I'm sorry to you.*

It's been forever, I'm taking my time.

My brain working on what the fuck I was going to *do* with her. I wanted her so fucking badly.

My tongue flicked her clit as I slid my fingers into her. Her response was electric.

I was on my *last* week with her.

It was almost over. And I didn't know what to do anymore. Just knew *her.* Her body. Her love. But I was torn between what I wanted, and what I needed.

The life at the beach was great, but it had never been forever for me. And I loved Selena and I would never want to stop her from staying here.

As much as the shadows were dark, they called to me and they wanted me back.

Deep down, I was afraid.

And I buried my tongue deep in her pussy so I couldn't think straight.

"Get inside me," she whimpered, her fingers tugging at my hair. "Please. We have days."

*Let her lead...*I knew that. But damn, I wanted her bad.

I flattened my tongue, rubbing her little bud in a way I knew would make her thighs shake. When they did, I closed my eyes, satisfaction and love surging through me.

I loved the way her hips rocked into my mouth, the way she trusted me with her pleasure.

"Kellan."

There was something in her voice that made my heart stutter. I was attuned to her every breath, every tiny sound. She was my lifeline, my anchor in a world that had been spinning out of control.

I let her go, sliding my fingers out, kissing up her body, savoring every inch of her.

"I don't want to hurt you." The fear of losing her again, of somehow ruining this *chance*, clawed at my insides.

I hadn't known Selena for a long time.

But every single experience I had with Selena trumped anything I ever had in any woman. I knew the moment I met her I wanted her.

But I loved her over the course of weeks turning into months.

I was racking my brain on how to take her without hurting her. I was treading a fine fucking line over here, rolling her over this way and that. Finally, deciding to crunch up and have her sink down on me.

The moment she did, even just an inch, I was lost.

I closed my eyes. Savoring every sensation, every emotion that flooded through me. When she finally, *finally* stopped, I felt whole for the first time in weeks.

"Kellan," she whispered against my lips. "Eres mi mundo, eres mi todo." *You are my world, my everything.*

I adjusted her legs around my waist, fitting her tight to me, her lips parting against mine.

Her eyes closed, a low noise escaping her that made my heart clench. Kissing her had always been—always would be—my favorite thing in the world. But now?

It was inadequate to express my feelings so I took a page out of Alisha's book and switched to Spanish.

I held her face close to me, those eyes of hers shimmering as she cried.

"When you left, I felt like an empty home. Like I was missing my heart. I told myself I'll wait for you. Until you wanted me. Until you healed. I told myself I would've waited forever for you. If not in this life, the next one. I would find you again in every lifetime. Apologize to you for fucking up so bad in each one. Love you in all of them over and over until you knew who I was. Recognized me as yours. I haven't known you long. But I know you so well. And I know what you mean to me. You are my partner. My love. My heart. I meant it when I said I wanted you forever. I do. If you'll have me? I want you for good."

My voice was hoarse as I held her to me, Selena was crying harder.

"I am yours, honey. I've been yours for a long time. And I'm not letting you go ever again."

"Mi amor—"

"I love you." I had to get it out. "I'm *sorry* it took me so fucking long to get to you—" She kissed me. *"I'm sorry, Gatita. From the day I met you, the moment I chased you down. You felt like mine. I should've told you. I'm telling you now. I love you. I love you. I love you so fucking much.* I want to give you everything," I whispered willing her to understand what I was saying. "A future. A life. On your time."

Nate made her promises I couldn't make.

I fucked up.

Selena was crying even harder. *"You are what I want, most in the world."*

I ate at her mouth as I rocked up, loving the little whimpers leaving her. Each sound, each movement was a reminder of what I'd almost lost, what I'd fight to keep.

Looping her arms around my neck, she kissed me until I lost all thought except her.

"Kellan," she moaned, shaking her head. "I need more."

I faltered at what she was saying, my heart racing. "You want me to be not sweet with you?"

"Don't hold back with me."

Having rolled her over onto her back, I sealed my mouth to hers, swallowing every scream as I gave her what she asked for.

I wedged a pillow under her hips, drawing them higher, until her ankles were at my ears and Selena moaned gripping the sheets.

Nothing existed except for her and this moment.

The fear of losing her, the uncertainty of our future—all of it faded away in the face of our connection.

"You love me, honey."

"I love you."

Once I started, I couldn't stop.

$$\sim$$

"That's it, honey, just relax on me."

I felt Selena's pussy fluttering around me, the afternoon sun washing over my legs as it hit the balcony.

There was nothing better than this—Selena, the sun on my skin, her wet heat tightening around my length.

"That's my girl."

Selena wrapped her arms and legs around me, sighing with contentment.

Her sun-warmed body was languid and light against mine.

After spending days making love in her bed, she was straddling me on her balcony. In her little nightie pooling at her waist.

The walls, higher than us, provided an illusion of privacy that I knew didn't really exist.

But it only made her even more wet for me. And drove me crazy.

I couldn't resist pulling her onto my lap, sliding that nightie up, stretching her where I knew she was hot and tight.

"That's all for me, isn't it, honey?"

She moaned as I tugged at her nipples, feeling her pulse wildly around me.

Her little moans were music to my ears.

"I could do this for hours," I murmured, taking one nipple into my mouth and licking it until it pebbled. When she squeezed tighter around me, a low laugh escaped me.

"Should I?" I whispered, loving her frantic nod. "I think I'm going to be sweet with you, *Gatita*."

She squirmed on me then whimpering a little louder when I sucked and played with both of them.

"Shh. You can't be loud," I whispered, feeling her clench faster at my words. "Easy...easy...open for me."

"*Kellan*."

"It's okay," I murmured. "Just stay like this with me, I just want to make it last. Want you like this forever."

Gently, I rocked up into her, loving her little noises. I thought I'd never get to love her like this ever again. And now that I had? I didn't want to stop.

I couldn't smell her anymore. No more pink petals.

I resolved to get her a new perfume. And fast.

"I think I could stay here tasting you forever," I admitted lapping at her skin. "I love how you fill my hands." I tugged. Bit. Sucked.

When she whispered "*No*," my heart clenched, fear spiking through me. *I don't want to hurt her.*

"I hurt you, baby?"

She shook her head looking radiant in the sun like this. "Take me inside, just like this. I don't want you to be sweet."

"What do you want, honey?"

I want you to be my savage.

As I lifted her in my arms, carrying her inside without breaking our connection, I felt a surge of possessiveness, of love so intense it was almost painful.

I laid Selena down on the couch sinking on top of her and filling her until we both moaned into each other's mouths.

"Harder," she whispered. "I need more."

And I'd be damned if I didn't obey her.

Her savage, deep down—I was always hers.

CHAPTER 54
KELLAN

"Do you want to come meet my Mama?"

"I'd love to, *honey*."

We met Selena's mom at a cozy Cuban cafe at the beginning of my final week. In the years that had passed, Gabriel had gotten Selena's mom out of Havana.

The two had texted and called her mother, thinking her daughter was a hard-working immigrant professor in New York.

Selena's mom hadn't known a single thing about her daughter's work with the CIA or Titan.

In turn, Selena told her stories about her being a college professor and how sweet students like Avani were.

Her mother was around Selena's height, with similar features and warm hazel eyes. She reminded me a little of Alisha—that same nurturing presence.

The moment Selena's eyes landed on her mother, she transformed. Tears welled up in her eyes the moment she rushed into her mom's arms.

I watched, my own eyes stinging, as my fierce, capable Selena melted into an even softer version of herself.

This was Lena.

The real her, stripped of the armor she'd built for survival.

I couldn't look away from seeing how happy it made Selena. Her mother's expression was one of love. Joy. It had been years. Her hands were holding onto Selena's, and then she landed on me.

"Tu novio?" She asked Selena. *Your boyfriend?*

My heart clenched when Selena nodded, and her mother took my hand as I introduced myself.

"What do you do here?" I asked her in Spanish. To my surprise, Selena laughed when her Mama told me about her bingo friends.

As I watched them together, my mind drifted to my own family.

How would I ever introduce Selena to my parents?

The whole "Cuban-spy-turned-English-professor" story wouldn't exactly fly.

Hell, they didn't even know what I really did for a living.

But then again, to Selena's mother, we were both just college professors. Maybe I could go with that angle when introducing Selena to my family.

I wondered if Gabriel had planned that all along—our civilian identities neatly aligning.

When Selena's mom finally turned her gaze to me, her bright hazel eyes were warm and welcoming.

"You are Lena's?" she asked, her accent musical.

I felt a rush of warmth and, surprisingly, embarrassment. I looked at Selena, who nodded with a soft smile.

"I am hers," I replied, the words feeling right on my tongue.

We spent the day as a family. Sorta.

Selena and I carefully navigated the minefield of questions, lies, and maybe half-truths that made up Titan.

She spun a story of a tough semester. A much-needed vacation, finally.

And her mother agreed she worked too hard. It was adorable.

I played my part as the supportive colleague and doting boyfriend—all the while marveling at the depth of love and protection Gabriel had woven around Selena and her mother. He had brought her here.

We hadn't told her mother that Selena was living here now. Because...because I didn't know what to do.

That was a conversation for another day—*after* Selena and I had figured out what came next for us.

I only had days left to tell Gabriel.

In turn, I found myself turning to Alisha more and more.

416

She seemed to be the only one who might have answers.

"There are choices, Kellan," she'd reminded me softly. "You could stay with Selena, return to New York, or even try a long-distance arrangement. Maybe she could visit while you take jobs down here."

Selena wanted to stay in Miami.

I didn't know what I wanted. But I wanted her. I wanted to find a way to make it work.

But I also wanted my life at Titan. Being at Titan was my life.

"Being a Titan gave me purpose. It gave me a reason to change..." I couldn't help myself. "It made me who I was. And I love Selena, I do. I just don't want to have one and not the other because sitting on a beach all day won't make me happy. But I know it makes you happy, and I want to find a way to make it work."

"I feel better here, too," Selena said. "For me, this is healing. I do like it here, but I also..." She turned to me. "Sometimes, I still feel like something is missing in my life. I don't know what. I don't know if it's you. But I understand why you have to be...you."

"So we stay long distance? We visit each other all the time?"

"Maybe. We can do that. I can come to see you all the time..."

But even as she said it, something different entered her eyes.

I didn't know if we could make this work, or how.

But God, I wanted to try.

So I guessed we were going long distance?

I didn't know. How the fuck did I even start? When would I see her? I felt...like shit. I didn't know what to do.

Later that night, alone in my temporary apartment, I called Alisha again.

"Do you think people can heal and want different things?"

"Sometimes when people heal...they grow past the person they used to be," Alisha explained. "Sometimes you don't want the same things anymore."

I confessed to her then about the progress Selena and I had made but also about the lingering disconnect I felt.

"Healing is complicated, Kellan," Alisha murmured. "Sometimes it brings people closer, and sometimes...it reveals that you've grown in different directions. You don't want to lose who you love, but forcing something that's not meant to be? That path leads to misery for both of you."

She paused, and I heard the rustle of bedsheets.

"Trust in the love you have now," she continued softly. "The connection you're rebuilding. That's real, Kellan. Whatever you decide, let that guide you."

"Gabriel wants an answer soon," I said, urgency coloring my tone.

"Did he now?"

Was she asking Reed?

"Very well then. Kellan," she said. "You need to tell her how you feel. Be honest. Tell her you never want to leave her. Tell her you love her."

"I'm terrified to tell her what I want."

"Kellan, when a woman loves you, she'll see right through what you're saying. Tell her what you want. Clearly. It'll open up another chapter for you two."

"You think so?"

"I know so."

I let out a breath. "Remind me if I ever make it back to the city to take you out sometime." Alisha's laughter was musical.

In the background, I heard Reed mutter something about as long as it wasn't a *fucking vegan place*, his voice a low rumble.

"Kellan, I would be delighted to see you again..." Alisha's voice was warm, tinged with affection.

As we continued talking, a sound caught my attention.

"Did he fall asleep?"

Alisha's laugh was quiet. "He did. He does this all the time now..."

I got it.

Even after a month, Selena still had nightmares that left her shaking and me feeling helpless. Because I still blamed myself.

It wasn't my fault.

But it didn't matter.

The fear of losing someone you loved—it was constantly there.

"Lish, you're a solid big sister."

As Alisha yawned, her exhaustion was evident even on the phone. "I am trying my best."

Ending the call with Alisha, I walked back to Selena's apartment. She was on the balcony, looking gorgeous. The night sky was behind her, and the breeze was twirling her tiny dress.

"I don't want to leave you." But even as I said it, I felt the pull of

New York, of the life I'd built there. "I wish that night I had never let you go to solve the case alone. I would have gone with you."

"What?" Selena turned to me, confusion etched across her face. "I never went to solve the case."

My entire being froze.

Wait...what?

Turning to face Selena fully I could feel my hands shaking.

This entire time we thought Selena had gone Downtown for the case.

My heart raced, blood rushing in my ears as I tried to process her words.

Why did she—

"Why were you Downtown that night?"

"I was...clearing my head," she said slowly as if trying to grasp at wisps of memory. "My head hurts, but I wasn't...I didn't do that." Her voice trailed off, uncertainty lacing every word.

"You don't remember?"

Trauma. Memory loss.

My mind raced, trying to remember everything I'd learned about the effects of traumatic experiences. It was normal, I reminded myself, to experience fear and memory loss after such an event.

But it wasn't that she couldn't remember. She just needed the right conditions to remember it.

I could do this.

Reed.

If your new charge tells you anything of value, call me. Not Gabriel. Those are your orders.

And as much as I hated seeing Selena as one, I moved her into my arms.

"Do you want to try something with me, honey?"

CHAPTER 55
SELENA

"Do you trust me, honey?"

I did.

I had always trusted Kellan deep down.

Something about his soul brought peace in mine and there was nothing else in the world like him.

In the time I had known him? Every step of the way he proved to be a good man. The kind I dreamt about as a kid.

And now?

Now I had him.

I trusted him.

The words came from my heart but I felt nothing but apprehension and anxiety as Kellan turned off the lights in the bedroom. Plunging it into darkness.

And I became a little terrified.

"Kellan, I don't know how to remember that night." Was that my voice?

"That's all right, honey, I gotcha." He put his arms around me. "I'm gonna make sure you're all right, okay? But I think for both of our sakes you need to remember what happened to you." I let him put his hands on my hips.

He tucked my head against his chest and I felt his heartbeat pounding in my ears. Strong and steady. Grounding.

"I'm going to take you back to that night, okay?"

"No—" I felt the panic at my throat.

"I gotcha. I promise, just trust me. This time you aren't going back alone."

I tensed, but Kellan's arms tightened around me keeping me from moving—strong and stable, Kellan still made me feel safe.

"Shh, I got you. I'm coming with you. You're going to let me come with you." He rubbed circles on my back. "Breathe for me. In and out. Good girl. Now close your eyes and breathe again."

"We are going back together?" I didn't understand his plan. But I would go with it.

"We are. I want us to go back to the exact moment, both of us left the apartment—"

"But we got into a fight—"

"No, we didn't, *Gatita*. I love you. And you and I are going to the bridge. Come on. Let's go."

I nodded. "Okay." This was scary but I knew why he was pushing me. He had done this when we trained. Done this every step of the way. For my growth. For my sanity. I trusted him.

"I'm right next to you, so let's go. After you left the apartment, where do we go from here?"

"Across the street. I got a cab."

"Okay, now let's take the cab to the Bridge." But I was already shaking. His clean scent filled my nostrils. I was terrified and I felt his arms tighten reminding me he was still there.

And as I spoke to him, I was falling, in my mind I was falling down. Into a black hole. Into the darkness.

Of the night that I almost died.

"*Kellan.*"

"I'm still here." His voice was low. "I'm right next to you the entire time, honey."

And suddenly, I was there. The hum of traffic. The cool night air.

"We both decided to go to the Bridge, honey. Now you're taking me with you on this trip. I'm your partner. I'm your team, remember?"

I nodded. I was relaxing slowly.

"Walk me through it."

I did. I was walking, the streets of New York flashing by in the cab.

"We are going to the Brooklyn Bridge." The words came easily, surprising me. "I thought better near water. So I went down to that neighborhood."

"Go on, honey. I'm here walking with you," Kellan murmured, his voice soothing as his nose gently brushed my cheek. "I'm looking out to the water with you. I'm right next to you."

In my mind, I was there again, standing on the Brooklyn Bridge, the cold metal railing pressing against my palms.

The images formed like wisps of smoke.

I squeezed my eyes shut, but a wall of fear in my mind blocked my thoughts.

"Just keep going, honey."

"I'm scared."

His voice was calm. "Why? What's happening?"

I swallowed. "Something's coming."

Someone. Something.

They're coming.

"I won't ever let anything bad happen to you ever again. As long as I live, I promise," Kellan vowed. "But you gotta let me stand by you." His hand pressed the back of my neck as he held me tight to him, his lips at my ear. "Breathe for me."

I did. It was like inhaling smoke. I could smell something in the night when I was falling through space again. Unable to stand on my own feet, I felt Kellan's arms around me.

"Stay with me, Selena."

They're coming.

"The bridge..." The words caught in my throat. "I was calling Gabriel when...when..."

Panic seized me as figures emerged from the chaos, dark shadows. *Everywhere.*

"They're coming," I breathed. "You have to move with me. We have to run." *They were not safe.*

"No one can see us, I promise. Breathe with me, nice and slow...I'll keep you safe."

A violent shudder tore through me.

"Who do you see, honey?" he prompted gently as his grip tightened. "Tell me who she is."

I saw her. Ice blue. Cold. Death.

"*Muerta*," I choked out. "*La Parca.*"

Death. Grim Reaper.

Death was coming for me, and I was *helpless* to stop them. I screamed a little as Kellan gripped me tighter saying something I didn't hear. Not anymore.

I was gone in her eyes.

I was gone, lost in the vision of Death. Kellan's presence faded, leaving me alone in the darkness.

My mind switched to Spanish, unable to process in anything else:

The Reaper, his eyes were electric. Bright blue.

He is smiling at the woman. She is blonde, long hair, shorter, maybe shorter than me. She is Death.

They make no noise when they move.

They're coming to kill us.

They're coming. They're coming, Kellan. Closer. Closer. We have to move.

"*Honey, wake up.*"

Suddenly, I gasped, my eyes flying open to find the room flooded with light.

Kellan hovered over me, his weight on one elbow, his face etched in worry. I was in bed. And I had no memory of how I got there.

"Reed. We have to call Reed." The words spilled out as I explained everything, my body shaking so violently that Kellan had to move himself over me.

"No, wait—" His voice was calm but firm, his hand cupping my face, steadying me. "*Breathe.* Focus. We have to finish the mission first. Remember? You said something about Whittaker being up north. That's all you told me. Is there more?"

The *woman.* The blonde woman.

I focused, pushing through the fog of fear.

"Her eyes were blue. But not a normal color. Her face was covered, but there is something wrong with her."

Kellan nodded, his expression unreadable. "That's enough for now."

Enough? How could that be enough?

"We need to call Reed."

"Right now?" Thick claws of anxiety filled my insides.

"It's been weeks since we left and I saw Reed, what kind of a state is he in now?"

"All developments about New York now go through Reed, not Gabriel." Kellan's words were measured, careful.

"What do you mean?"

Kellan revealed that somethings had been happening at the manor. During my hospital stay, he didn't know what, but I knew when Gabriel and Reed kept secrets? Things were bad.

"Even if they focus on the bigger picture? If they aren't saying something, something bad has happened.This month we have been gone, all this is happening? What else happened when we were here?"

"A lot of things."

"What do you know?" I pressed. Frustration bubbled up inside me, hot and insistent. "I'm your partner."

"Honey," Kellan began slowly, those blue eyes of his uneasy on me. "I work with Shane Alves now. I can't tell you much, but I can't drag you into Titan affairs." His lips brushed over mine. "I'm sorry."

And then it slammed into me.

I was...I was not—

You are no longer a Titan.

He didn't have to say a word.

My mind raced, images flashing before my eyes—Reed's stern but caring face, Alisha's smile, Evie, and *Gabriel.* They were in danger.

Someone was coming after them—after my family.

For so long, I had convinced myself that I didn't want to be a Titan, that I didn't want that life.

But as I stood there, my truth washed over me. Wave after wave of it. Stripping away layers of the denial I built around myself and the summer.

I didn't want to leave it. *I just needed a break.*

I needed to walk away from it to realize that I never really wanted to leave it *at all.*

Being a part of Titan had changed me, molding me into the person I was today. Through Titan, I had discovered my family, a sense of belonging, and a strength I never knew I possessed.

Reed wasn't just my team lead; *he was my brother.* And he might be in danger.

"I can't leave my family," I whispered. "They never left me."

They'd taken me in, a lost girl from Havana, and given me a home, a purpose.

And then there was Kellan. My partner and my love.

In that moment all my choices hit me. All of them. Every single mistake I made sank into me.

I had been so blind to think that Titan was the problem when, in truth, it was the very thing that gave my life meaning.

They were there, fighting, protecting. And I was…in Miami.

You do not have to be the girl you started with. In that moment of perfect clarity, I knew what I had to do.

The girl from Havana, the scared operative, the woman running from her past?

They were all part of me, but they didn't define me anymore.

I didn't even consider that I had been happy being a Titan.

I just needed a break after what I had been through.

Just go with it.

It wasn't about passively accepting what had happened to me as the truth, as my fate.

But this was about actively choosing my path.

I met Kellan's gaze, my voice steady, filled with a conviction I hadn't felt in months. Filled with my truth.

It was who I always was.

"I'm not going to run anymore," I whispered. "I am your partner."

I always have been.

"I am your partner," I repeated, the words ringing with truth. "I am Venus. I used to think I needed to get away from it, but I never did. I just needed to step into it."

"Are you sure?" His eyes searched mine. "Honey, you just found out what happened to you—"

"I am sure."

This wasn't running or escaping.

This was becoming. I was becoming.

"Yes." I shook my head. "This was so stupid. I was running away… when I should have been…going through it."

Because it wasn't about avoiding everything.

It was about going right through the problem until you found out what you needed to become.

Who I was *always* meant to be. That's why I kept thinking about home in the city. Not because of Kellan. But because it was my home too.

Kellan's face was stunned for a second before he broke into a grin. He knew what I was trying to tell him.

"I am your partner." My voice was stronger.

"Yes, you are, honey."

I leaned in, taking his lips with mine. *"I am going back with you to New York."*

CHAPTER 56
KELLAN

I PACKED MY BAGS THE NEXT MORNING WHILE CALLING GABRIEL. HE
answered on the fourth ring, which wasn't like him.

"Quarterback."

Why was he so quiet?

"I'll be back in two days…with Selena." I cut to the chase, knowing
he didn't like small talk. "Thank you."

I heard the sound of something rustling in the background.

Sheets? *Comforter?*

He wasn't in bed, was he? There was a softer creak and a low
murmur in the background—a fucking *woman*—cut through the line.

Almost masked by the sound of Gabriel moving, sitting up.

Oh. *Shit.*

I think I interrupted him—No. I wasn't going there.

Some doors were better left unopened. Besides, he was my boss. It
didn't matter what he did or who he was with.

I was going to do my job regardless.

His voice was curt. "Text Reed when you land." Got it.

Because it went through Reed. And Selena had already done that.

"Yes, sir." I wanted to ask though. I did.

And as I ended the call, my mind fucking raced because Gabriel
wasn't the kind of guy you just hooked up with.

That wasn't a casual thing.

427

Which meant he cared about whoever he was with. And I knew nothing about his personal life, and nobody ever talked about it.

I'd talk to Selena later about it.

And forty-eight hours later, Selena and I landed in the city. Finishing up everything in Miami together.

The familiar skyline and the icy cold breeze greeted us, and Selena sighed.

"I could really go for a bagel," she murmured to me as we walked to the garage.

I drove us back in *Paloma*, Selena's baby. I kept her in solid condition while she was gone.

Selena sat in the passenger seat, her new hair curling a little at the ends, taking in the colder air of the city—with winter approaching, the chill was evident, and people burrowed into their coats, steaming cups of coffee in everyone's hands as they rushed to where they needed to go.

I turned up the music in *Paloma*, letting the bass thrum around us, and the lyrics were suggestive enough to make me look over at Selena.

She just kissed me. "When we get home, I want you to make love to me." Nothing made me prouder than knowing she could ask.

She could ask.

And I would give her whatever she wanted.

"I can do that, honey. Once we're back at your apartment, I'm not letting you leave."

And her smile was all I needed. As we pulled up to a stoplight, the wind whipped around the car.

A car pulled up beside us, and the driver shouted. "*Yo, white boy, whatchu know about reggaeton?*"

I glanced at Selena, watching as her expression shifted from relaxed to steely in an instant.

Without a word, she reached into the glove compartment and pulled out her gun, cocking it with a sharp click.

The guys in the other car paled, a string of surprised curses falling from their lips.

My lips tipped up in a smirk. *That's my girl.*

Selena tucked the gun away as I accelerated, the familiar streets of New York flying by.

My lioness was back.

"Want to grab some food before heading home?" she asked, her voice casual as if she hadn't just silenced a car full of guys with a single look.

My grin widened. "I was thinking we should go home and just order in," I replied. "Reed said we don't have to show up for two days. Let's chill out."

We both knew her apartment was exactly as she'd left it. And the moment she walked in, I felt my throat tighten with emotion. *It's good to have you back, honey.*

I imagined spending the week lost in her—falling asleep on her chest as her fingers threaded through my hair. "I missed you."

"I missed you," I whispered against her lips. "I made sure to hide everything while you were gone."

She laughed into my kisses, and I grinned back. "Missed you, honey."

"Missed you too, Savage."

I grinned wider.

We were home, we were together. And nothing else mattered for the time being.

For the next two days, we slept it off and basked in just having some time to ourselves. Some space.

We had been gone for a month. Selena had already texted Reed in code.

And then, finally, we made it to the manor. I drove around back to park the car, guiding *Paloma* into her spot next to mine.

Selena, catching my expression, kept leaning over to kiss the grin away. Her touch was playful and kind on me as she kissed me over and over.

"Bet you never thought you'd say yes to me," I teased.

"No, I did not," she wrinkled her nose. "But someone was a savage if I didn't say yes—" Selena broke off, giggling as I held her tighter.

I spotted Evie's white AMG Benz and Reed's Maserati parked next to our cars, and for a moment, I wondered if it was a group briefing.

But the fucking minute I got into the damn place, Selena and I had to stop for a bit.

"Are you seeing this?"

"Yes."

Trees. There were whole trees inside the manor.

"Holy—"

"So many trees!"

The space was filled with lemon trees, cherry blossoms, a whole ass cactus-looking thing, and then some. "Jesus, this is a little much for Evie—"

"I don't know if it's all Evie—" Selena broke off as she smelled one of the lemon trees. "It smells good, though." She plucked a lemon, bringing it to her nose with a smile.

"They're real," she confirmed, offering it to me. "I remember when I was in Italy. Those lemons are delicious."

When we reached Reed's office, he stopped me in my tracks, my laughter dying in my throat.

The door was open, and Reed sat inside. Stormy eyes, strong jaw, and messy chocolate hair glanced back at us.

"Good to see you two. Have a seat. I'll fill you in on the last month…"

CHAPTER 57
SELENA

"THE FOLLOWING FILES ARE CLASSIFIED."

Reed's face was grim as he lowered his voice.

"You aren't allowed to talk to anyone about this information I'm bringing forward. Including anyone outside of this office."

As Reed spoke, I felt that something—*someone*—wasn't here.

"Where is Gabriel?" I asked.

"On assignment. I'm handling operations."

The finality in his tone was clear: *No more questions.*

"A black ops group named Talon is targeting me and my family over a classified op." Reed looked annoyed as he said it. "They're not really targeting, more like playing with their food. They had ample shots to kill me. But they're waiting…"

"*Your life is in danger?*" Kellan said. "Why the fuck didn't you tell us sooner? We would've came back for you!"

Reed laid out two photos on the polished surface of his desk.

"Meet Talon."

My breath caught as I recognized the blonde woman from the bridge, her image seeming to radiate something dark, something not entirely…*alive.*

The photos of her were grainy, at odd angles, like she was more shadow and ghost than real. Just enough for me to know she was wearing a mask in all of them. They weren't clear at all.

None of her face. Not even a single angle.

431

She wore a black baseball cap, and the one photo she did have without one? Her mask was pulled up high, her blonde hair in the moonlight glittering.

But even Reed's cameras didn't get a good angle of her face?

"She's good at hiding," I murmured. "Never turns to a camera, always has her head down. *Someone* is helping her."

Gray eyes met mine. "Selena, you're the only person who has seen her up close. As far as I know. As close as you could've gotten to her. Which means she might have known who you were."

"La Muerta." I reached out to pick up the photo. "Does she have a name? Can you ID her?"

"We can't ID any of the members of this group. But we did ID one, thanks to you." Reed set down another photo—a driver's license image of a handsome young man. Jet black hair fell into mischievous eyes, his smile wide and carefree with deep-set dimples.

"Recognize him?"

The Grim Reaper.

"Matteo DuPont's *brother*?" I asked? "Who is he? He looks so young." *Too young to be a killer.*

"His smile's a little evil," Kellan spoke up. "What is he *seventeen* with those dimples?"

"I have no clue. But he's good at lying low. We've got virtually no information on him. That blonde woman is a Talon operative for sure and looks like that is his team-mate," Reed explained. "He was seen in the city a few months ago, and our intelligence places him somewhere in the city right now. We can't find him. Not on Oracle. Not on cameras. It's like everywhere he goes is a legitimate blackout zone."

"How is it so hard to find him?" Kellan asked looking confused. "You can find anyone with Oracle."

"Almost," Reed's jaw clenched, muscles working beneath his skin as his eyes looked uncomfortable. "Not him. Talon seems to have technology that we don't. Something in their system that allows them to move undetected, shutting down areas of the city grid. And it's not just the city. They seem to be activated all over the East Coast recently." Reed paused. "When he said 'take Whittaker,' he wasn't after me."

"*Which Whittaker—*" I started and then it hit me.

Reed's little brother.

"Adam." And both Kellan and my eyes went wide. "He went after

432

Adam. Which brings me back to Lucy Devereaux. Lucy Devereaux is the Titan operative who was a part of the classified op."

Nathan mentioned Reed needed her months ago.

But what did she steal for him?

I couldn't even process the fact that *Adam Whittaker* had been targeted by Talon.

And then Reed dropped the bombshell of the year.

"Lucy and Adam are *together*. They've been together since she got to New York from her op. Adam was targeted because she was his girl-friend. And he was connected to me. He's fine. He is. But he is no longer a part of Titan."

My jaw dropped.

"What!"

"Que?"

Reed's brother is dating...a jewel thief...how did they even meet?

"A few weeks prior to you two leaving, *Lucas* Devereaux's life was being threatened. Lucas is Lucy's older brother, Kellan. Liam found Lucy *with* my brother on surveillance when we went looking for her. We didn't make a move because she was *safe*. Now, Lucas doesn't know any of this. And you guys cannot tell him. There's a lot happening he doesn't know and I don't want to stress Evie and him out."

Evie was with Lucas Devereaux. I swore a little internally.

Kellan swore. "Are you shitting me right now? What the fuck happened to Adam—"

"Over the last month, we've learned Talon operates on the fringes. They infiltrate our lives through people on the outskirts. Adam was close, but not too close..."

Something has happened to Adam.

"Is he—" I began.

"Alive and *fine*. I promise." But Reed looked upset about his family being in danger. I knew a little about Lucy from Nathan.

And now her brother, Lucas Devereaux, was with Evie? How did Gabriel let Evie date a man without killing him? Maybe that's why Kellan and I had his jet?

I miss one month of Titan and all this happens?

"Evie knew on surveillance, you crossed paths with someone in the city, causing anomalies and disturbances to the electrical grid. That's how we knew you bumped into Talon. But we didn't know the DuPont's were involved until you two confirmed it."

"No offense," Kellan said. "Lish talks about Teo and he doesn't seem like the kind to be in league with a black ops unit."

The DuPont's were a prominent family. High end conglomerate. Luxury cars. The eldest Andrei, was a mystery. But the younger one Matteo, had a crush on Reed's girlfriend, Alisha. They'd worked together when Alisha had been a model.

Now, I was learning—there was a third brother and he was a wanted criminal.

"No," Reed agreed looking grim. "But the DuPont's little brother is a different story. I didn't know he existed. Andrei has kept him under the radar for years. Which leads me to believe, he's a half-brother. I'm collecting intelligence with Shane right now. Selena, you haven't met him, but Shane Alves is the new recruit on the team. I wanted to brief you before our next steps. If you see the DuPont's in the city—do not engage. Do you copy?"

Kellan asked, frowning. "You've met him already, haven't you? You talk like you know him. I only knew about Matteo and Andrei."

Reed's eyes were cold as he pointed at the picture of the man in front of me. "I went to pay Matteo DuPont a visit when Alisha was being threatened months ago. *This* DuPont pulled a gun on me."

"The man in the photo?" I asked. "What did you do? Did you try and kill Matteo because of his crush on Alisha?"

Reed was guilty. I knew Reed. He would try that.

"I did threaten his brother," Reed said casually looking unperturbed by the fact that he did kill people. "Kellan, for the time being, you're reassigned to Midtown to protect all assets. Handle Kieran's check-ins as well while you're in the city."

Oh no, he does not get to take the easy way out of this.

Kellan let out a breath as he frowned at Reed. "Hang on, Teo is the closest thing to Talon. Kieran and Teo are friends. Kieran doesn't know anything?"

"Kieran doesn't know too much. I don't think Teo would betray his family and I think the nature of their relationship is different," Reed murmured looking at us pointedly. "As in, they aren't friends outside of *De Nuit*. Kieran doesn't know anything about Teo's baby brother."

Reed pointed to the photo of the young DuPont.

The Grim Reaper...was...a DuPont...

"Look, this team, Talon, their leadership is extremely strategic and sophisticated. They won't sacrifice *anyone* on their team," Reed's eyes locked onto mine. "We think there's a few of them in the city. Titan and Talon are at a standstill. We will not engage in war. All agents are under orders not to strike unless directly attacked."

Reed looked grim shaking his head. "Lucas told me and Gabriel, Teo's baby brother's name is *Thierry*. But I can't even confirm *that*. He has a *dozen* different aliases. I don't know how old he is. I don't know where he came from. I just know he's known around a few parts of the world and he's spent the last few years cultivating a reputation. You called him the Grim Reaper in Spanish. You weren't wrong. Thierry is *dangerous*."

I felt my throat work. "How much?"

Reed shook his head. "We think he's responsible for the kills in New York. In the past few months? We found fifty markers around the city with Talon bullets. If he's the one killing everyone? He's been busy. Under no circumstances should you engage with him if you see him. He's armed and he's got coverage over him to block out all images of him."

Kellan murmured, his brow furrowed. "We can't fight them. He won't fight us."

"Talon is playing with us?" I asked. "Why? Just face us head-on."

Reed didn't look happy. "It's not their style. Mind games. Misdirection. I think that's how this team has been hidden. The hacker's keeping us up at odd hours. I think they have more than one. They appear, then vanish all the time. It's their thing. I have never heard of these guys—they're that good. And we have no fucking clue who their leader is."

"But you suspect someone," Kellan muttered. "You have a suspect."

"It's not Thierry," Reed said easily. "But he's good. He's connected. And I can't find him."

Reed didn't look happy about that.

"Do not tell Lucas anything you are aware of in this briefing. He knows about his sister, and Evie knows about the anomalies Talon caused. But they do not know anything else, and we intend to keep it that way. While Evie is a Titan, this assignment, the information you two just gave me. And everything in between is *classified*. To just you two."

435

Reed was hiding something bigger from everyone.

I knew it.

I caught the subtle tightening of his jaw, the way his eyes didn't quite meet mine.

After years of working together, I knew Reed's lies like the back of my hand. Just like all those months ago when he wouldn't tell me how he knew Alisha was in danger because of him. He was my brother. And right now? My brother was in the middle of something that was wrong. And I wanted to help him.

I just didn't know *how*.

Reed produced a black card with gold claw marks.

"This is the marker of Talon. This put's people on a hit list. Lucas, Titan Midtown, Lucy—all received them." His eyes darkened to slate. "If you get this card, or see this card anywhere? Report to me. ASAP. Pack your things and run. It means they're coming."

My blood ran cold.

Reed's eyes met mine with regret. "You need physical therapy. And when you do return to field work, I'm switching you, I have a slot for you—it's with Sonya Amin. You remember her? Alisha's friend."

I did. I met her at the party when I ended my promise to Nathan that night, she had taken me away and talked about lipstick.

"Sonya's opened up a domestic violence shelter called Haven. She would like you to help with security. It's all women. And I think you can lead the project..." Reed explained both of us a bit more of what he wanted from us now that we were back.

Reed's gaze intensified as he paused on me. "Selena...This is first time Talon has resurfaced in seven years in New York." He paused his eyes holding mine. "Gabriel had a run-in with them. *Remember?*"

And then it hit me. My eyes widened.

Now, it *slammed* into me with little grace like a shockwave.

Seven years ago...every single member died...including...his wife...

Now I understood the secrecy, the tension. The memory of Gabriel visiting me in the hospital flashed through my mind.

"Any more questions?"

Reed knows.

He is Gabriel's best friend. He knows. About Gabriel's wife.

"*No.*" He didn't need to say another word. I had all I needed. I took Kellan's hand. "No questions. You tell us when you need us."

Reed's smile was tight. "I need Kellan on a few things…" Reed would email out the list to Kellan.

Years ago, I'd sworn my loyalty to Gabriel.

I would die for him.

This is revenge. These people killed Gabriel's wife.

That's *why* the mission was classified.

Lucy Devereaux had engaged with Talon because it was under Gabriel's orders.

And that was why Talon was here in the city for Reed—the face of Titan.

Talon was the team that killed Gabriel's old team.

Pay attention to the details.

This was *already* war.

And it had started seven years ago.

Gabriel had lost once, but I knew with every fiber of my being that he would not lose again.

Not this time. *Not ever.*

And I would stand by his side.

For *his* second chance.

CHAPTER 58
KELLAN

As Reed remained in his office to make a call, Selena and I headed towards the kitchen to find Evie.

We were under orders to not say a fucking word.

Lucas Devereaux was here too, but he kept in the dark about certain things for his own safety.

Something was *deeply* wrong at Titan. The weight of everything Reed was facing? Combined with the threats of Talon?

Some black-ops unit terrorizing him? I could see it was pressing down on him. And Adam was gone. I had barely even known Adam.

"I don't know what to do for him," Selena said softly. "Something is happening, something bigger than us."

"We just do what he says, step in when we can."

Because we were back to being operatives now.

Her fingers clenched around the lemon she was still holding.

"Does that help?" I asked, motioning to the fruit.

She nodded and held it up to my nose. "Want to smell it?"

I leaned in, pretending to inhale, but at the last moment, I kissed her instead. Hard. Pushing her slowly against the wall, I kissed her steadily, softly, like I had months ago.

"Are you sure about this?" I murmured against her lips. She nodded, and I let out a breath.

Selena's eyes filled with determination. "There's nowhere else I'd

438

rather be. Just…stay safe in Midtown, okay? Even if they don't attack, something's coming."

I felt it too.

"I think Reed is trying to stop whatever it is," I said, brushing her bottom lip with my thumb as she bit down on it. "But I think he's always taken on too much."

"Something happened to him, Kellan. The last time he was like this, Alisha was in danger. Now Adam? He's not telling us everything."

"I can talk to Garrett," I offered. "He usually sticks close to Gabriel. He might know something."

Selena nodded, but her eyes were dark and haunted. "I saw them, Kellan…there's something wrong with them. With the woman."

Yeah. I knew what she was saying. I felt it too when I looked at Thierry DuPont.

All the DuPont's had alien blue eyes, pupils rimmed in a black that stood out. Eerie and almost supernaturally bright against their skin.

But it was Thierry's smile.

It was downright wicked. Like the kid was used to causing trouble and he liked it.

Selena's voice broke me out of my reverie.

"…Like those things in scary movies—something is wrong with the woman. The blonde…"

"You mean like a ghost?"

The only other person I felt wasn't human was fucking Gabriel.

Selena frowned a little. "Once, I was in Belarus. It was a hard job. I remember seeing a woman and her eyes they were…dead inside. There was something about her. And the two of them together…" Selena trailed off, visibly shaken. "He is dark too. Trained. When he moves he is quiet. Fast. Dangerous."

Definitely dangerous. I didn't have to be a fucking genius to know that.

But Selena was a trained operative.

She knew darkness when she saw it. Danger. Death.

Selena explained that when the woman's eyes had focused on her, even for a moment, they had been terrifying.

"It was like…she was nothing. She has no soul. But black," Selena murmured. "And they're coming after Reed."

Her eyes held nothing but regret, and I cupped her face gently.

"We're back now," I said softly. "We're not going anywhere. Evie's waiting for us. Let's go see her, I'm sure she'll be excited to see you."

"And you, you are still our family now."

Evie was with Lucas Devereaux. And his sister was with Reed's. Talk about worlds colliding.

Welcome to Titan.

My head was spinning a little. And it wasn't even over.

"We'll go over this at home?" she asked. "I want to talk about it."

I smiled, my chest swelling with warmth, expanding with seeing our extended family. "Yeah. We can go over this at home."

I didn't want to dwell on ghosts, not in this manor that already seemed permanently haunted.

Where is the fuck is Gabriel?

Selena and I held hands tightly as we made our way to the kitchen, drawing strength from each other, even after all that we knew--none of this felt right anymore.

As Selena pushed open the large French doors, a blur of white and green squealed from the fridge and barreled towards us.

Auburn hair and her tiny body let me know who it was.

"You guys!" She was squealing.

Evie.

We were tackled by Evie, both of us catching her, her grin wide as she held onto us. Her eyes sparkled a little with a glow all over her face.

"You are here!" Selena beamed down at her, her eyes glistening as she brushed her hair back.

Evie was babbling excitedly, her words tumbling over each other while Selena and I held her tight. "...*sososogood to see you guys! Luke is here too—*"

"You look different," Selena said warmly. She wasn't wrong. Evie looked comfy in her white chunky sweater, hugging her curves. "You are *glowing.*"

Evie turned red, a shy smile curving her lips as her hands fluttered over her stomach.

Her cheeks looked more plump, too.

Overall, she'd gained some weight, and it looked adorable on her.

"Just some new lotion I got." She hugged us both again, and I grinned. "Luke will be right up—*oh, he's back.*"

She cut off abruptly as a taller man entered the kitchen, his navy suit crisp and immaculate hair.

His face looked like it was chiseled from marble with how aristocratic he looked—out of place in the Titan manor.

Selena shifted next to me as he walked in his blue eyes locking on Evie.

My height. Same build. But *polished.*

Lucas fucking Devereaux. In the flesh.

Evie slid out of our arms. "Luke! They're here!"

"I see that, doll." Ocean blue eyes lit up upon seeing us, and he ran a hand through his blonde hair, an embarrassed expression over his face. "I've heard so much about you two, I had to step out real quick…"

He walked over to us, shaking my hand with a firm grip, smiling at Selena who shot a polite one back at him. She looked at me with eyes wide exchanging a look I interpreted as—*this man was Evie's man.*

Gabriel let this guy around his sister?

Lucas gently pulled Evie in his arms smiling down at her, passing her a tiny bottle of what looked like vitamins.

Evie looked embarrassed as he did and I realized this was my first time seeing her with a man. Ever.

Selena's eyebrows looked like they were going to fly off her hairline. "*Es muy guapo y enorme, como Gabriel.*"

He's very handsome and enormous, like Gabriel.

I didn't hide my laughter as Evie turned beet red and Lucas grinned wider. "*Gracias.*"

Selena's jaw dropped as Lucas laughed. "I can speak Spanish too. Just enough."

None of my laughter was held back at Selena and Evie turning beet red. "I just wanna know how you convinced Gabriel to let you date Evie."

At that Evie turned even redder.

"Si," Selena added in Spanish that knowing Gabriel, he must've tried to kill Lucas maybe a solid three times. And she wanted to know how he did it without dying.

Lucas's smile was wider, his canines flashing as he motioned to Evie to take her medicine.

"Sorry, doll, I think I left them in the back of the car," Lucas murmured, dipping down his lips on her forehead. "Need a second?"

"I'll be right back," she told us, her face a little pink, moving back to the fridge.

"I didn't know Evie dated."

Lucas turned to us blocking Evie from our view then, smiling at me, peppering both of us with questions about Miami. Instead of answering our questions he hit us with a different question.

"Did you guys like the White Lotus?"

And *then* I realized Lucas was the guy who owned *all* the apartments around us and the flights we both took. That's how we'd gotten everything so smoothly.

Selena and I thanked him as Evie returned quickly. Lucas drew her into his side, his hand resting protectively on her stomach as she watched us with a shy smile.

I had missed the glint of a ring on her finger earlier, a small diamond band. A touch of emerald.

Lucas wasn't Evie's *boyfriend. Jesus, how fucking long had I been missing from Titan?*

"I'm starving," she whispered to him. "I could some enchiladas."

His grin was wide on her and I knew Selena mentioned the only way Gabriel would ever have allowed Evie to be with a man is if that man loved Evie more than Gabriel ever could.

Hence, the ring.

"I'll grab the ones Reed has in the fridge for you."

"What's with all the trees?" I asked Evie as Lucas looked at us, my eyes darting between the couple. "When did you two become a thing? How much did I miss?"

Evie grinned motioning to Lucas as he turned beet red. "They were a present from Luke…since we got *engaged*!" She held up the ring.

Selena let out a scream running to hug her. Evie's laughter filling the room as Lucas turned beet-red steadying his fiancé as Selena squeezed Evie tighter.

"Congrats," I shook his free hand. "We are surprised you're alive. Lena and I would've thought Gabriel would've tried to kill you for coming around Evie."

Lucas and Evie shared a look as he said. "Funny story about that…"

442

KELLAN

A WEEK LATER

Selena and I found ourselves navigating a new reality as individuals—but partners too.

We put up a murder board in our closet. Together we sat with dinner and put together pieces of the puzzle.

"Let's go over Reed's briefing," I started. "Approximately a few months ago, Reed hired Lucy Devereaux on a mission—"

"He would only hire her to take something that did not belong to him—"

"But what would Reed—"

"Not Reed—" Selena cut me off, eyes sharp. "*Gabriel.*"

"Right, because only one of our bosses is shady as fuck."

Selena's lips quirked. "Reed does not need anything if he has his woman."

And then there was the mystery of we didn't fucking know where Gabriel was.

Reed had tasked Lucy Devereaux, a woman who straddled the line between Titan operative and something else entirely, with an assignment that had placed a target on both her back and Reed's.

An object.

"Something valuable and expensive," Selena said. "She took it. She brought the item to Reed. And now he is being attacked by the DuPont family. Maybe."

"But what the fuck do the DuPont's have in connection to Reed?"

Selena eyed me. "Alisha."

"No, that doesn't make any sense. Even if Teo had a crush on Alisha, he wouldn't ever do that...would he? What if the DuPont's are connected to Talon some other way? Besides Thierry? Like we haven't figured out if Thierry is the only Talon member? What if the blonde is a member of the DuPont's as well."

"You think the DuPont family is in Talon as a whole?"

I nodded. "Because even if Thierry was Talon...he's not doing all of this around the city. He's got a *team*. You saw how young Thierry looks? No fucking way he's running around the city tearing up Titan."

"This is true. Reed also threatened Teo..."

"Over Alisha." Yeah, I guessed as much. "So that means the DuPont family is *connected*."

"Yes, very much. I have to look into how they are connected."

Selena and I had asked around the network of people we knew discreetly and nobody heard of Thierry DuPont. The motherfucker was a ghost. But he was a *kid*.

Something told me we didn't know anything about him.

"Lucy knew she was targeted by Talon, with Adam—" I said to Selena. "So what did she do? Do you think something happened to Adam?" I asked Selena who nodded.

And whatever happened between the two of them—Reed and Adam —hadn't been remotely good. "Like they got into a fight?"

"Maybe Adam was angry with Reed? I do not know why, Reed is a good brother," Selena frowned a little. "Reed is nice. But he keeps secrets. Maybe Adam did not know who Lucy was..."

"And it led to a fight between Adam and Reed, because if Adam found out his girlfriend was in danger because of Reed..."

She made a noise and shook her head.

"It is not like Reed. Even if Talon thinks he has stole something? Reed did not release that information. This is all suspicion. But Reed would not look so worried if it was that simple."

"Because it isn't simple at all," I added.

Selena nodded. "He's keeping something from us. Something big."

There was a missing piece here, something big we weren't seeing-- something that didn't make sense right now.

"Adam would never hurt his brother—" Selena defended Adam.

"I would kill for you," I countered, my eyes locking with hers,

willing her to understand the depth of what I was saying. "If Adam thought Reed put Lucy in danger, knowing Reed was behind her assignment…There's *nothing* I wouldn't do for you if you were in danger."

And on the subject of Reed—we couldn't ignore Gabriel.

"Where do you think he is?" I asked her. "You know Gabriel better than anybody. He doesn't just leave. He likes control too much."

We still hadn't seen Gabriel since our return, though he'd been checking in with Selena via text.

"I think I might know where he is," Selena said, her face etched with concern. "Reed and Gabriel are staying away from *their* families. Evie was with Lucas that day…Reed was there at the manor. Do you remember when I said, Reed and Gabriel switch teams? All the time? Reed would never leave Alisha alone. Which means…"

No.

Absolutely not.

Selena shot me a look that she only gave me when she wanted me to believe her.

"*Gatita*…" *Nobody* had confirmed Gabriel's whereabouts. Not even Reed. "*You don't think*…" No. *Why would he?* "Why would Gabriel be with Alisha? He has enough on his plate."

"*Who was that woman with him that morning?*"

Something nagged at the back of my mind, but I couldn't quite grasp it. I looked at the murder board we made. We had a map of the city on there.

"No fucking way Gabriel was with Alisha. No fucking way. I talked to her on the phone. And he hates Midtown. K2 is in the heart in the city. He hates the city."

"But he likes Alisha…" she whispered. "And he loves Reed. They are brothers."

Alisha's voice was in my head.

I'm not alone. Is that okay?

I don't mind if Reed listens.

Did Gabriel tell you that?

My eyes widened. "Alisha…knew *him*…Alisha *knew* his reply."

A long time ago Selena kept repeating to me…that I needed to be aware of the differences between Reed and Gabriel.

And then it *slammed* into me.

"Oh. Fuck."

445

Alisha never confirmed it was Reed. Not one single time. Every time I said his name she laughed. Because it was never Reed.

I felt my jaw drop.

"She never told me it was Reed…" I was breathing harder. "His voice sounded different every single time," I whispered to Selena. "Holy. Shit. *Gatita.*"

You've been spending too much time with Gabriel.

Not too much, I hope.

Not too much.

And he had agreed.

He. Had. Agreed.

"The entire time I thought I was talking to Reed…" I whispered to her as her eyes widened with mine, alien green bright on her face. "It was *never* Reed."

What if Gabriel had been there the entire time? Every single conversation…I knew she wasn't talking to Reed…

"I thought his voice sounded different. I just thought it was because Reed let Alisha spend time with him."

My heart sputtered a little as I recalled every conversation I had with her to Selena's wider eyes as she processed it with me.

"Reed does not speak on the phone. He only texts," Selena whispered with concern. "Gabriel will say something. Remember, I told you from the beginning—they are two different people."

She told me Gabriel focused on every piece of a puzzle. Reed liked the bigger picture. Months ago Selena talked in Titan Midtown and Selena told me I needed to know who they were.

"Reed would never let you know he was there."

"But Gabriel would fuck with my head." He was a master at it.

It wasn't like Reed. *Because it wasn't Reed.* Even I couldn't comprehend that. Not with how he *wanted* her. Reed would have to trust him.

Implicitly.

I told her about what little I did know.

She frowned over that, her eyes going dark green. "Gabriel would *never* hurt Reed like *that*—"

"But you told me if Gabriel wants something, nothing would stop him from getting what he wanted. What if Gabriel wanted Alisha enough?"

"Gabriel has a life too though, he has women in his life, I know,"

Selena said softly, shrugging, her cheeks turning pink. "Maybe Gabriel is trying to solve this himself...maybe he's with Alisha to protect her..." She shook her head. "I don't know. But Gabriel would never sleep with Alisha. He would *never* hurt Reed."

Except...I got the feeling he did once.

Selena explained how Gabriel wasn't a saint, and he was allowed to be with women as well. And if he was with Alisha—it was to protect her.

I couldn't imagine Gabriel with *anyone*.

"Besides, he is not with Alisha...I think he is still in love with someone..." Selena dropped another bombshell—Gabriel had been married and lost his wife to Talon seven years ago.

I was *floored*.

"*Wait*," I sputtered. "*Gabriel lost his wife? He was married? He told you this in the hospital?*"

Everyone in Titan is determined to give me a heart attack.

Selena's eyes watered, and she calmly explained what she knew. About Gabriel's past—his fucking *wife's* last assignment, and how he'd found Selena after failing his team.

How he felt like he had—

"*He lost everything?*" I whispered. "Holy fucking shit."

I sat back, reeling with what I knew now.

"*You're* the *only* surviving member of his former team. *That's* why he takes care of you."

My head was spinning right now.

Gabriel was...atoning...

She nodded softly, wiping her eyes. "And everyone around me." She motioned to me. Between us. "That's why I knew...you are him...you are his second chance too. To fix things..."

My heart sank as I processed what she said.

"Your delay from Havana saved your life..." Because Gabriel's old team was dead.

His entire team...

That's why he's such a fucking hard-ass.

"*That's why he doesn't let just anyone on his team. That's why he thinks weakness isn't trainable.*"

That's why he was who he was.

No wonder Gabriel was so protective of her.

Selena continued urgently, her eyes pleading with me. "Thierry DuPont said he was going to 'take Whittaker.' That means he won't stop with Adam. Gabriel knows Reed is next. Reed would not trust anyone else to take care of Alisha. Think about it. When was the last time Alisha left K2? Not *once*. When was the last time you saw Gabriel? Why was her perfume in the manor? Why is Reed always there?"

She was right.

And Gabriel would never let history repeat itself.

"The two of them? I told you before? They are partners. Reed will throw himself into danger. But Gabriel? He will die before he lets Reed do it."

And that might be why he was with Alisha.

"Gabriel is the one with Alisha and he has been since Talon showed up because he doesn't want to lose his only family."

Selena nodded emphatically. "Whatever Lucy took must be crucial. Reed doesn't make moves without reasons. And that object was valuable to Talon. To the DuPont's for some reason."

"And Gabriel would die before he let Reed live his hell—"

I stopped abruptly. Selena's eyes widened, sensing my sudden insight.

"Amor, ta bien?" she asked softly. *Love, are you okay?*

Memories from months ago flooded back.

Is this fun for you? Me, losing my girl.

You don't fucking understand—

I fucking understand.

"He did understand." Everything clicked into place. *"That's why he worked so hard to bring us back."*

Holy. Fucking. Shit.

He did understand. He lost his world. And he gave me back mine.

And I was left reeling again with realizing just who Gabriel Monroe was.

And why he was probably guarding his best friend's girl right now.

I swore softly leaning my head back. *"Welcome back to Titan."*

Selena and I processed what we knew and then she dared to tell me one more thing. "Gemma...she messaged me..." Her eyes met mine. "With Nathan..."

I waited for the jealousy or anything to hit me but nothing did. I felt nothing for Nate Wyatt ever since I knew he belonged to Gemma Marchand for the last fucking decade and always would. Selena told me Nate's story too.

"You want to invite her for dinner?"

Selena's eyes widened and her smile was wide as she nodded.

When Selena reached out to Gemma, the response was overwhelming. Flowers, gift baskets, and groceries flooded our apartment—a gesture of reconciliation.

Gemma arrived with more flowers and catering, glaring at Nate until he apologized to both of us—a surprising turn of events. Gemma seemed proud of him.

As Selena and I prepared our favorite guava drink in the kitchen, I left Nate and Gemma on the couch. The duo took approximately three seconds to start making out as soon as I turned my back.

Meanwhile, Selena searched for her pink stepping stool. I suppressed a chuckle.

Some things never changed.

She frowned adorably at the shelves.

"I know you hid the sugar, savage."

I grinned.

I did hide it. I just couldn't remember *where.*

I was so used to helping her reach things. I forgot about it. But now watching Selena frown I grinned ear to ear. I hid my smile in her pink dress. She looked *incredibly* distracting tonight in that material around her hips.

"What makes you think I hid it, *Gatita*?"

"I'm not stupid, I can feel you laughing."

Which only made me laugh harder, but quietly, until my face hurt as I pulled her down off the chair she was on.

"I'll tell you where it is…in exchange…"

"Not in front of them…" she squirmed in my arms adorably. "What if they see?" Her cheeks were a hue of pink that fascinated me now.

"You don't think they know we fuc—"

She covered my mouth her eyes wide and I grinned.

"*Kellan*—"

"*They aren't paying attention,*" I mumbled putting her hand down. "They've been making out this whole time."

I hauled Selena to the side where I could see Nate and Gemma, who were still inhaling each other. Yeah, I could see how Nate had been in love with her for the last seven years.

"Dios Mio," Selena blinked, noticing them, her eyes going wide and a grin on her face. "I do not think she hates him anymore."

"No, she does not." And then I pointed to my lips. "I need some sugar too."

Selena eyed them and then me before pulling me back into the kitchen. "Okay, just a little but I need the sugar after—"

I didn't know how to tell Selena I *forgot* where I hid anything since we'd been gone. I forgot everything. I was sure maybe one day the sugar would turn up. If not I'd buy her more.

I stamped my lips down on hers hauling her against the wall where I thrust my tongue into her mouth to hear her make those tiny little noises.

"Where is my sugar?" she whispered fiercely.

"I don't know, but I don't think they need anymore," I whispered back. "Come here."

"Not now—"

"I'll buy you more sugar—"

"You do not know where you hid it, do you?"

Busted.

"I never said that," I whispered against her lips. "I can always buy you more."

Her laughter was contagious. "Why are you like this?"

"Can I take you out sometime? You look fine as fuck in that dress."

Her laughter mingled with my kisses when we completely forgot about the sugar.

The second week we were back, I took Selena out again to our favorite Cuban restaurant, the same cozy spot where we had our *second*, first date.

I counted Patel's as a date. But Selena would tell me I counted any moment with her as a date.

Selena looked unreal in a soft peach dress that hugged her curves, her hair curled just a little around her shoulders and her eyes sparkling under the light, drawing the appreciative glances of several other men. I stayed chill. I was working on it.

Working on my jealousy realizing I wasn't going to lose my girl. She was mine. I was hers. I could calm down.

I had gotten her a new perfume, stronger than her last one and the scent of hot pink peonies drifted over to me. I inhaled her into my lungs calming down with every breath.

"...I trained Shane after the hospital." I had filled in Selena on a version of the hospital incident.

One where Nate and I *talked*. Not pulling a gun on each other.

Somehow, I didn't think that would go over well.

"He is Hermes?" She mused. "I met him. He reminds me of Diego if he was an adult."

I felt my chest tighten at the mention of that. I thought she might like Shane. She had met him briefly with Reed.

Nobody believed Talon had pulled out.

Sectors of the city went down every so often like they were reminding Reed they were still here, and not finished.

They didn't mess with him anymore, and that made everyone wonder if they were plotting something bigger.

Or something had happened to them to make them change their course.

Selena's question brought me back out of my thoughts of the current state of the Titans.

"What name did you pick?" She mused, popping a fried plantain in her mouth.

I smiled softly at her expression. "Mars."

I explained to her that Mars and Venus were lovers in mythology, but she had been married to Vulcan.

My grin stretched wider as she realized why I had.

My Venus.

"I am not married."

"But you could be."

I said it quietly aware of my heart pounding in my chest. Her teardrop necklace sitting in her cleavage caught the lights off the restaurant.

Those green eyes I fell in love with widened at my words. My throat felt tight as I said it.

"On your time. Whenever, *whatever* you want. I'm yours. Soy tuyo."

I need you.

I love you.

You're my everything.

451

The moment Selena went to respond someone cut her off.

I overheard a man at a nearby table making an off-hand comment in Spanish about a guy like me being with a woman like her. I got it all the time.

Selena and I realized nobody could guess I could understand *everything* so people often spoke Spanish around me none the wiser.

Which was fine by me. I understood it all.

I knew Selena had heard it too.

Her green eyes locked with mine, burning with something in them that I recognized now. She tossed her napkin on the table as she stood and stepped around it.

For a moment I thought she was gonna reach for her gun.

But instead she perched on my lap in front of the entire restaurant and kissed me with *everything* in her.

I groaned into it loving the way she took charge.

Her hands in my hair messed it up and tugged me closer, tongue tangling with mine.

"I fucking love you, woman."

She laughed low against my lips as she kissed me deeper. Harder. Tongue and teeth until someone whistled in the back.

That little noise left her as I cuddled her to me. I was breathless when she pulled back, her eyes glittering.

This is my woman.

She chose me.

"I will never get used to you being my shield."

"You are mine, we are partners. A team."

I breathed it out. "You know I will always choose you. In every lifetime." I felt my racing heart calm down.

Slower as her palm rested on it. Emerald eyes softened on me as she smiled slowly.

"Eres el amor de mi vida. Te quiero con toda mi alma."

I was the love of her life. And she loved me with her entire soul. I loved her too. I blinked back my emotions holding onto her.

"I love you too, *Gatita*. I never thought I'd get to be back here with you."

Selena brushed my hair back after it had grown out longer just the way she liked it. "But we are here now. I still remember our first date."

"Yeah? What do you remember?"

452

And then she dropped her voice to a whisper, her lips grazing my ear and I heard the dark desire in her husky murmur.

"I remember thinking I wish this man could take me home and be *not* sweet with me."

I felt my grin stretch my lips wide as I tipped my head back.

"Be right back, I gotta pay for this."

"I already took care of it when I told you I went to the bathroom," her eyes met mine twinkling with mischief. "Take me home, savage."

"Oh, now you're definitely asking for it."

Her laughter mingled with mine.

This fucking woman was gonna meet me every step of the way.

And I was absolutely gonna punish her ass for that little stunt.

Green eyes widened watching my lips tip up. "Take me home?"

"Whatever you want, I'm yours. You don't gotta ask me twice, *Gatita*."

DEBRIEF PART I

You've successfully completed your
third assignment at Titan Security.

Your next assignment will be your most dangerous one yet.

*With your favorite jewel thief and **her** favorite doctor.*

Details for your next assignment will be disclosed in the
following files…

YOUR NEXT ASSIGNMENT

Stroke of Chance
Titan Security Book 4

He's about to become her biggest heist…

Dr. Adam Whittaker & *The* Luciana Devereaux

<u>Get Adam and Lucy's Book</u>

OTHER WORKS BY LILAH LANCE

Titan Security Series

Stroke of Luck: Book I
Stroke of Fate: Book II
Stroke of Lust: Book III
Stroke of Chance: Book IV
Stroke of Obsession: Book V (Coming Soon)

~

Underworld Kings

Legacy: Book 1 (Coming Soon)

AUTHORS NOTE

Thank you guys so much!
I hope you loved Selena and Kellan as much I do. Leave a review and share your thoughts!
You can also join my Facebook group and newsletter for more updates and info.

Love,
Lilah

ABOUT THE AUTHOR

Lilah Lance writes romance for all the girls who dream of being loved for who they are.

When she's not writing, she spends her downtime at the beach and traveling.

Get exclusive content by signing up for Lilah's newsletter on http://lilahlance.com where you can get sneak peeks and news before anyone else.